The Making of Another Major Motion Picture Masterpiece

Also by Tom Hanks

Uncommon Type

TOM HANKS

The Making of Another Major Motion Picture Masterpiece

a novel

COMIC BOOK ILLUSTRATIONS BY R. SIKORYAK

HUTCHINSON
HEINEMANN

1 3 5 7 9 10 8 6 4 2

Hutchinson Heinemann
20 Vauxhall Bridge Road
London SW1V 2SA

Hutchinson Heinemann is part of the Penguin Random House group of companies
whose addresses can be found at global.penguinrandomhouse.com.

Copyright © Clavius Base, Inc., 2023
Comic Book illustrations © R. Sikoryak, 2023

Tom Hanks has asserted his right to be identified as the author of this
Work in accordance with the Copyright, Designs and Patents Act 1988.

First published in the US by Alfred A. Knopf, a division
of Penguin Random House LLC, New York, in 2023
First published in the UK by Hutchinson Heinemann in 2023

www.penguin.co.uk

A CIP catalogue record for this book is available from the British Library.

ISBN (hardback): 978–1–529–15180–0
ISBN (trade paperback): 978–1–529–15181–7

Printed and bound in Great Britain by Clays Ltd, Elcograf S.p.A.

The authorised representative in the EEA is Penguin Random House Ireland,
Morrison Chambers, 32 Nassau Street, Dublin D02 YH68

Penguin Random House is committed to a sustainable future
for our business, our readers and our planet. This book is made
from Forest Stewardship Council® certified paper.

For all the actors in the cast
and every member of the crew

So shall you hear
Of carnal, bloody, and unnatural acts,
Of accidental judgments, casual slaughters,
. . . .
And, in this upshot, purposes mistook . . .

Horatio,
to the assembled

Let us haste to hear it
And call the noblest to the audience.

Fortinbras,
immediately afterward

—*HAMLET*, ACT 5, SCENE 2

Contents

The Making of Another Major Motion Picture Masterpiece

1 BACKSTORY

A little over five years back, I had a message on my voice mail from one Al Mac-Teer—which I heard as *Almick Tear*—from a number in the 310 area code. This no-nonsense woman asked me to call her back regarding a thin little memoir I had written called *A Stairway Down to Heaven* about my years of tending bar in a small subterranean club that played live music way back in the '80s. At the time, I was also, sort of, a freelance journalist in and around Pittsburgh, PA. And I wrote movie reviews. These days I teach Creative Writing, Common Literature, and Film Studies at Mount Chisholm College of the Arts in the hills of Montana. Bozeman is a gorgeous if stark drive away. I get very few voice mails from Los Angeles, California.

"My boss read your memoir," Ms. Mac-Teer told me. "He says you write like he thinks."

"Your boss is brilliant," I told her, then asked, "Who is your boss?" When she told me she worked for Bill Johnson, that I had reached her on her cell as she was driving from her home in Santa Monica to her office in the Capitol Records Building in Hollywood for a meeting with him, I hollered, "You work for *Bi-Bi-Bi-Bill JOHNSON?* The movie director? Prove it."

Some days later, I was on the phone with Bi-Bi-Bi-Bill Johnson himself, and we were talking about his line of work, one of the subjects I teach. When I told him I'd seen his entire filmography, he accused me of blowing smoke. When I rattled off many salient points from his movies, he told me to shut up, enough already. At that time, he was "noodling" a screenplay about music in the transformative years of the '60s going into the '70s—when bands evolved from matching outfits and three-minute songs for AM radio to LP side-long jams and the Jimi Hendrix Experience. The stories from my book were full of very personal details. Even though my era was twenty years after what he was "noodling"—our club booked unheralded jazz combos and Depeche Mode cover bands—the stuff that happens in live-music venues is timeless, universal. The fights, the drugs, the serious love, the fun sex, the fun love, the serious sex, the laughs and the screaming, the Who-Gets-In and Who-Gets-Bounced—the whole riotous scene of procedures both spoken and intuitive—were the human behaviors that he wanted to nail. He offered me money for my book—the nonexclusive rights to my story, meaning I could still sell the *exclusive* rights, if there should ever be an offer. Fat chance. Still, I made more money selling him the rights to my book than I did selling copies of the thing.

Bill went off to film *Pocket Rockets* but kept up with me through calls and many typewritten letters—missives of wandering topics, his Themes of the Moment. The Inevitability of War. Is jazz like math? Frozen yogurt flavors with what toppings? I wrote him back in fountain pen—typewriters? honestly!—because I can match anyone in idiosyncrasy.

I received a single-page letter from him that had only this typed on it:

What films do you hate—walk out of? Why?

                                                                        Bill

I wrote him right back.

I don't hate any films. Movies are too hard to make to warrant hatred, even when they are turkeys. If a movie is not great, I just

wait it out in my seat. It will be over soon enough. Walking out of a
movie is a sin.

I'm guessing the US Postal Service needed two days to deliver my
response, and a day was spent getting it to Bill's eyeballs, because
three days later Al Mac-Teer called me. Her boss wanted me to
"get down here, pronto" and watch him make a movie. The term
break was coming up, I had never been to Atlanta, and a movie
director was inviting me to see the making of a movie. I teach Film
Studies but had never witnessed one being made. I flew to Salt Lake
City for the connecting flight.

"You said something I have always thought," Bill said to me
when I arrived on the set of *Pocket Rockets,* somewhere in the
endless suburb that is greater Atlanta. "Sure, some movies don't
work. Some fail in their intent. But anyone who says they *hated* a
movie is treating a voluntarily shared human experience like a bad
Red-Eye out of LAX. The departure is delayed for hours, there's
turbulence that scares even the flight attendants, the guy across
from you vomits, they can't serve any food and the booze runs out,
you're seated next to twin babies with the colic, and you land too
late for your meeting in the city. You can hate *that*. But hating a
movie misses the damn point. Would you say you hated the seventh
birthday party of your girlfriend's niece or a ball game that went
eleven innings and ended 1–0? You hate cake and extra baseball for
your money? Hate should be saved for fascism and steamed broc-
coli that's gone cold. The worst anyone—especially we *who take
Fountain**—should ever say about someone else's movie is *Well, it
was not for me, but, actually, I found it quite good.* Damn a film
with faint praise, but never, ever say you *hate* a movie. Anyone who
uses the h-word around me is *done.* Gone. Of course, I wrote and
directed *Albatross.* I may be a bit sensitive."

I lingered on the set of *Pocket Rockets* for ten days and, over the
summer, went to Hollywood for some of the film's tedious Postpro-

---

* "Fountain" refers to Hollywood's Fountain Avenue. Bette Davis was once
asked her advice for actors wanting to make it in Hollywood. She said, "Take
Fountain"—meaning as opposed to Sunset or Santa Monica Boulevard or Franklin Avenue.

duction. Making movies is complicated, maddening, highly technical at times, ephemeral and gossamer at others, slow as molasses
on a Wednesday but with a gun-to-the-head deadline on a Friday.
Imagine a jet plane, the funds for which were held up by Congress,
designed by poets, riveted together by musicians, supervised by
executives fresh out of business school, to be piloted by wannabes
with attention deficiencies. What are the chances that such an aero-
plane is going to soar? There you have the making of a movie, at
least as I saw it at the Skunk Works.

I was not on location for much of the making of A Cellar Full
of Sound*—which is what later became of some of my little book.
My loss. Bill had me paid another bit of coin when the movie
began shooting, more when the film came out—the man is gener-
ous. I saw the first public showing at the Telluride Film Festival,
where he referred to it as "our movie." In January, I rented a tuxedo and sat at a back table at what was then the Golden Globe
Awards (at Merv Griffin's Beverly Hilton Hotel, the very definition of a H'wood party). When my colleagues ask me about my
weekend in Fantasyland, I tell them I didn't get back to my hotel
until five in the morning, very tipsy, dropped off by Al Mac-Teer
and none other than Willa Sax—a.k.a. Cassandra Rampart—in
her chauffeur-driven Cadillac Escalade. There was no other way
I could sum up the experience in terms they'd understand. Willa
Sex? No way! I'd prove it by showing them the Facebook photo
she posted—there I am, with Al Mac-Teer, laughing our heads off
with one of the most beautiful women in the world and her moody
bodyguard.

COVID-19 had been dividing up our country into its Mask/No
Mask politics and turned my job into online classes. Then came
the Vaccine/Anti-Vax dialectic. When Al Mac-Teer called me with
an invitation to join her, Bill, and his merry band to observe the full
duration of his next film, I thought shooting a movie was neither
legal nor possible. But her boss "had a thing" that looked like it
was going to be "green-lit" and shot under "Guild protocols" and

---

* A wicked, surprise hit of the pre-COVID days. Good worldwide numbers—
despite no audience in China. Those nominations and the AMPAS nods were a
salve to the ego. Not a single win, but still . . .

I was invited to "join the Unit" from the start of Cash Flow to the Final Dub.

"You'll have an ID badge," she explained. "You'll be one of the crew and be tested twice a week. We won't pay you anything, but you'll eat for free, and the gratis hotel room will be nice enough." Al added, vividly, "You'd be a very big dope to say no."

I asked Bill Johnson himself why he would allow an interloper like me to observe what is often treated as something akin to a top-secret project, one with badges and flashing red lights and signs warning THIS IS A CLOSED SET. NO VISITORS WITHOUT APPROVAL OF UNIT PRODUCTION MANAGER.

Bill laughed. "That's just to intimidate the civilians."

One night on location, after another long, hard, yet average day of shooting, over YouGo FroYo, Bill told me, "Journalists—the lazy ones anyway—always try to *explain* how movies are made, as though there's a secret formula that we've patented, or procedures that are listed like a flight plan for a voyage to the moon and back. *How did you come up with the girl in the brown polka-dot dress who could whistle so loud? When did you first imagine that last, indelible image of those blackbirds on the TV aerial, and where did you find* trained *blackbirds? Why,* they ask, *did* this *film succeed when* this other *film went flat? Why did you make* Bonkers A-Go-Go *instead of* Moochie Spills the Beans? That's when I look at my watch and say, 'Hot damn! I'm late for that marketing meeting' and bolt the interview. Those people look at the Northern Lights as having been designed. If they saw how we movie-orphans do our job, they'd be bored silly and very disappointed."

I never got bored. Disappointment? While hanging around for the making of a motion picture? *A fig!*[*]

There is always a good conversation to be had on a movie set, around the Production Office, and during the Postproduction process because most of moviemaking is spent *waiting*. The question *How'd you get started in this racket?* prompts hours of very personal, improbable stories, each saga worth a book of its own.

When I said this to Al, the subject came up about writing a book to explain the making of movies through my time on the movie.

---

[*] Shakespeare's *Othello,* act 1, scene 3. Iago to Roderigo.

I was going to bear witness to so much of the creativity, friction, surface tension, and balls-out fun on the project, what if I were to write about it all and, well, publish a book? Would her boss be enraged by that idea? Chuck me off the set?

"Oh, Cowboy," she said. "Why do you think you are here?"

I hope to have taken myself out of the narrative; to write about the making of a movie like *Knightshade: The Lathe of Firefall* from a first-person perspective would be self-serving, like covering the Battle of Okinawa as though it was about the reporter ("I was worried that sand, stained with the blood of dead Marines, would get into my typewriter . . ."). Much is owed to all who talked with me over the many months they worked while I watched. They shared not just what they do but who they are. If their names appear— there are some whose don't—it means they have seen what I have written and either approved of these pages or okayed the changes I made at their request. I went back to many of them again and again to clarify what I thought I had seen, what they had told me of their own journeys along Fountain Avenue.*

Movies last forever. So do characters in books. Blending the two in this volume may be a fool's errand, wasted effort in the mining of fool's gold. Don't hate the final product. Think of it as *quite good*.

Joe Shaw
MCCA
Mount Chisholm, Montana

---

* Two groups on the Unit asked to *not ever* be mentioned in this book: The stand-ins for the actors who hope to be actors themselves and not be pigeon-holed as stand-ins. And the personal assistants, those who tend to the upper echelon of the key players. Their anonymity was sacrosanct, for if their names and job descriptions were made public, their lives would be made a living hell. Let me say, though, I saw how hard and long they all work, and the ton of nonsense they so expertly deal with. They are loved.

The following is based on a true story.
Characters and events have been altered for dramatic purposes.

"What would be wrong with another franchise?" asked Fred Schiller—a.k.a. the Instigator—of the Fred Schiller Agency. He had once again flown into Albuquerque for a dinner with his distinguished client Bill Johnson. As usual, they were at Los Poblanos—one of Albuquerque's better restaurants.

It was July of 2017, and Bill was about to head into the shooting of *A Cellar Full of Sound,* for which he had also written the screenplay. As was their tradition, the client and agent met to talk about what would come after the present picture was done; the deep look into their future that kept a career going with forward momentum. There was no talk of the movie about to be made, just the options for future enterprises.

"Franchises are killers," Bill said, speaking from well-known experience. The pressures to have *Horizon of Eden* match the quality and popular success of *Border of Eden* and then *Darkness of Eden*—all "written and directed by"—had been like holding on to political office. By the final day of shooting on *Horizon,* Bill had lost twenty-five pounds, stopped shaving to save time in the mornings, drank three shots of ZzzQuil every night to sleep, and had survived the last two weeks of Principal Photography running on the fumes of triple espressos. Bill Johnson, who once typed out this one sentence on his 1939 Smith-Corona Sterling—MAKING FILMS IS MORE FUN THAN FUN—had had none whatsoever completing that last chapter of *Eden,* which took nearly two years of his life.

In his three-decade run of films, Bill was firmly—to the envy of many—in the win column, save a couple of so-so performers and the one unmitigated disaster.[*] Bill now developed his own material, turning down big works that would have replenished his coffers, and with his 10 percent made the Instigator happier, too. *A Cellar Full of Sound* had been a relative pleasure to write, a pain in the ass to prep, and could go any way in the shoot.

But since *Pocket Rockets* had brought Bill back from the disaster

---

[*] *Albatross*—aptly named.

that had been *Albatross,* the Instigator saw that the filmmaker was at the top of his game, and he wanted that to remain the case.

"Franchises become cruel masters. I don't want to work for a cruel master," Bill said. "I don't like *being* the cruel master, except in meetings with marketing."

"Audiences have so many options for entertainment," Fred said over grass-fed veal medallions and garden sunchokes. "They need a reason to exchange their money for a ticket to a movie. Bill Johnson is a reason. A superhero franchise is coin of the realm, like westerns were in the '50s and '60s and action movies in the '80s. The Comic-Con fans go to see *everything.*"

"If only to hate it. Just ask Lazlo Shiviski."* Bill leaned back. "I like the antiheroes, the flawed and haunted ones."

"Marvel would give you the next Thor."

"Tell them I'm Thorry, but no."

"D.C. would give you anything on their slate."

"The Batman, the X-Men, Spider-Boy, Green Giant, Lady Kick-Your-Ass . . . You don't see a glut?"

"Dynamo will back up a truckload of cash and drop it on your driveway if you said yes to one of their Ultra movies."

"Superheroes saving the galaxy and kitty cats stuck in trees. Ho-hum." Bill finished his Blue Sky cola in the tall glass of ice, no straw. "I'm not against the genre, just the tropes in them. Evil lords from other galaxies who speak English. Super guys and girls that want to kiss but never do. Whole cities being destroyed, but we never see the corpses." Bill waved to the waiter and pointed to his glass for another Blue Sky. "And Pat is on me to do a boy-meets-girl movie.† A movie for *her.*"

"What's wrong with that idea?"

"A girl-meets-boy story depends on two things. The girl, the boy, and why they need each other. Three things."

---

* Lazlo Shiviski was excoriated by the fanboys for his *Quadrant: The Seeker,* which was the fourth in the *Quadrant* saga. Bill thought the movie was grave and special, but something pissed off those fans, and they beat the living daylights out of Shiviski and the film. Lazlo had been in the trophy run season for awards with *Luna and Sweet,* the same year Bill was for *Barren Land,* but they both lost every time to Lisa Pauline Tate, who was *due* for her fabulous *The Getaround.*

† Dr. Patrice Johnson, Bill's love.

"The world is waiting for another Bill Johnson motion picture," the Instigator said.

"It will be called *A Cellar Full of Sound* and should be in a theater near them in twelve months, give or take."

"The future is not next year. It's three years from now."

"I'll ponder." That had always been Bill's process. He'd land on some source material by accident, which would spark an idea, which he would then turn into another major motion picture masterpiece.

2 SOURCE MATERIAL

Bob Falls

On the morning of the seventh of July, the sun, a full disk in a bald, cloudless sky, was beginning to sear Lone Butte, California— population 5,417, officially—a rural town in the North Valley, not far from the capital of Sacramento, less than a day on the road from the city of Oakland, a bit longer to the Babylon that was San Francisco. In the heat of summer, with temperatures always hovering at the century mark, the place was more akin in pace and temperament to the small towns in Kansas or Nebraska or Ohio, in Iowa or Indiana. Few of its citizenry *chose* to live in Lone Butte; many left and never came back. Granted, the town was the county seat, but by default, because of its location on the Big Iron Bend River, which had been the main route of commerce during the gold rush. In 1947, there wasn't even a train depot in Lone Butte.*

Like most boys his age, Robby Andersen, who would be celebrat-

---

* Trains made stops in nearby Welles, California, but only at a siding. The nearest depot was nearly an hour's drive away, in Chico.

ing his fifth birthday on the eleventh of September, greeted every morning, especially those on another hot summer day, as twenty-four hours of ripe, carefree living. He would start his kindergarten schooling after the Labor Day holiday, but already knew his ABC's, and his father had explained to him the differences between upper-case and lowercase letters. So, he would surely spell *living* with a capital *L*.

He knew to make his bed first thing every morning right after going potty. Then he'd change out of his pj's and into his play-clothes, before coming downstairs. His father would already be off to the shop when his mother set a breakfast down for him—usually toast, milk, and a fruit, often the plums picked off the trees in the backyard. Robby wanted to taste coffee, to find out why grown-ups drank the stuff all the time, but he was told he was too young. His morning tasks were to put his own dishes on the counter, see if the trash pail needed emptying, give a good sweep to the floor of the screened-in porch and, outside, the back steps that led to the gravel driveway and, just beyond it, those four plum trees. His chores done, he would get out his crayons, coloring pencils, color-ing books, and newsprint tablets and, lying on the braided rug in the living room, lose himself in drawing whatever was in his head.

Everyone who had a look at Robby's drawings—*artwork*, even at his age—saw a natural ability, an instinct for dimension, space, and movement. There was abandon in his drawings, too; there was joy. The boy drew for *fun*.

At 10:00 a.m. on most days, he would put his drawings and sup-plies away in a drawer of the living room cabinet—the *chifforobe*—and leave the house through the screened-in porch, having learned to keep the spring-closing door from slamming behind him. Beyond the plum trees was a short hedge with a small gap worn through it, a passageway used by Robby to cross into the Burns family's back-yard, which also had a quartet of plum trees; the property line had split what had been a small orchard. Their daughter, Jill Burns, was already six years old and the best friend Robby Andersen had in his life. The two played together almost every day, with neither kid bothered nor hampered by Jill's slight clubfoot. At lunchtime, Jill would come home with Robby to eat—a routine agreed upon by both sets of parents. Then, they kept themselves busy until the three o'clock snack time when the radio could be turned on for the shows meant for kids. At four Jill passed back through the gap in the hedge for home.

★ ★ ★

Robby's mother, Lulu Andersen, had worked out this routine with Mrs. Burns and loved the arrangement, for it allowed a slow windup to her long day of work work work. Her mornings were calm, unlike those of so many of her gal pals, young women (still) who all had kids and working husbands and the never-ceasing regimen that was homemaking and housekeeping and child-rearing. Work work work and *work*. Some of those women were raising monsters, little hellions, so Lulu thanked God and the rhythm method for Robby, who did his chores and kept himself busy with crayons and, too, for the baby, Nora, who had been a colicky infant but was turning a year old in two days. It seemed that Nora just might be settling into a female version of her contented, easy-natured older brother. Who in Lone Butte had two kids who caused such little hassle?

Lucille Mavis Falls was called Lulu right from the get-go, after her father had first laid eyes on his daughter and hollered, "What a *lulu* of a baby girl!" from the other side of the maternity ward window. Twenty-plus years later, Lulu Falls became Lulu *Andersen* on January 18, 1942, just weeks after the Japanese bombed Pearl Harbor and the Second World War had ruthlessly, finally ensnared America. Every house in California was blacked out at night against the *next* air attack, including those in Lone Butte should enemy bombs be dropped on the rural towns of the North Valley of California.

Lulu's husband, Ernie Andersen, had been one of her half dozen boyfriends in high school despite his going to Saint Philip Neri (she was a Union High *Yankee* and a Presbyterian). He worked at the Flying A filling station at Main and Grant Streets and, over time, Lulu found herself volunteering to drive the family Chevrolet over to have Ernie fill 'er up and check 'er oil. One thing led to another, and, as Lulu said herself, "That was that." Ernie was the most fun of all the boys her age in Lone Butte, though, at times, as serious a young man as the era had created. And, oh, his eyes . . .

When Nazi Germany invaded Poland and war was declared, he talked seriously about going to Canada to learn to fly planes for the Canadian wing of the Royal Air Force, but his father talked him down from going as "there were plenty of Canuck boys to do that." He knew the United States would, when needed, enter the war and "start doing our fair share." But not able to wait to become a part of the history that was raging up on-screen in black-and-white newsreels shown at the State Theater, Ernie enlisted in the United States Army Air Forces in June of 1941 so he could be ready to fly American planes. As Fate or God or Saint Philip Neri would have it, he had a color blindness that washed him out of flight school. Still, Ernie had a sense of all things mechanical, so his enlistment helped keep the planes of the AAF flying, ready for the coming war. He was sent to an aerodrome in Texas—a place he called Camp Desperation in his many, many letters to Lulu.

Pearl Harbor was attacked on December 7, 1941. On the night of January 10, 1942, at 11:17 p.m., the California Limited stopped at a siding near Welles to take on passengers bound for Los Angeles. Lulu was one of them, riding through the night and most of the next day as the Limited made many stops. At Union Station in LA, she almost missed her coach seat on the Texas Special. After what seemed like a million miles over two nights of knotted-body semi-sleep, she transferred to the Katy Special for a half-million miles more. Then a cold, drafty bus dropped her smack at the main gate of Camp Desperation, where Ernie was waiting for her with a bouquet of what he thought were bluebonnets. They weren't, but Lulu didn't care.

For eleven nights, the bed of a dollar-a-day hotel room allowed Lulu and Ernie, when he had a pass, the best sex of their lives, since they were no longer fumbling in the back seat of a car, on a blanket in the Gum Tree Grove, or finding each other at night in the Little Iron Bend River Public Park. They wanted each other with the bursting passion that spills from the hearts of the young when, separated by time and distance and a global upheaval, they are young no more. Ernie had his duties during the day, but at night he and Lulu downed ice-cold beers and danced to a raucous band at a genuine Texas honky-tonk. They enjoyed cheap meals of Mexican-style food and more ice-cold beer. On their fourth night of great passion, lying naked in sheets damp with sweat, enveloped by the dark of the hotel room, and with only an hour remaining before he had to return to the base, marriage was discussed, agreed on, settled. "And that was that." Their wedding was held at the base chapel with an army chaplain and witnesses whom Ernie knew but Lulu didn't. Outside, a Texas hailstorm threw down stones the size of peach pits.

Ernie had taken up smoking Lucky Strikes, so Lulu did, too, giving her something to do as she reversed her journey away from Camp Desperation, returning to Lone Butte a *married woman* with a husband in the service. When Ernie was sent to the B-17 air base on Long Island, New York, a plan was hatched for Lulu to get to the East Coast, but by then train travel was limited for civilians, especially pregnant women who suffered from weeks of morning sickness. Ernie and other Air Corpsmen were flown to England in new weaponless and seatless B-17s by way of Greenland, then Ireland. As passengers, they simply lay in the naked fuselage of the unpressurized, unheated, heavy bomber. Ernie never felt as cold as he did during that days-long flight, despite his fleece-lined clothes and multiple wool blankets. He never claimed to have seen Greenland, though his plane was grounded there by two days of ice storms, wind, and a ceiling of heavy clouds.

When the war ended, his son, Robby, was two years old and worth twelve demobilization points, according to the Department of War, so Ernie was discharged ahead of the childless servicemen. He needed a full week to make his way across postwar America, back to Lone Butte, and the best sex of his civilian life.

★ ★ ★

The Fourth of July 1947 had come and gone—Ernie was in the parade, once again riding up on the Air Corps float with its papier-mâché twin-engine bomber, his old uniform not yet tightening up at his waist, chest, and thighs like many of the other veterans in the procession. Lulu and the kids waved to him from their claimed spot on the sidewalk in front of Clark's Drugs, the storefront done up in the same bunting and forty-eight-star flags that hung all over

America. The celebration of 171 years of independence had gone on all day in the 101-degree heat. The parade, the Junior Chamber of Commerce BBQ with the Cake Festival and band concert, then the hours of waiting for darkness and the fireworks show made the sober adults exhausted, the drinking adults drunken, all the kids overstimulated, and Lulu just plain *pooped*. The baby upchucking a stomach full of macaroni and pureed beets didn't help. Robby fell into the shallows of the Little Iron Bend River Park as he'd done the year before. Three days later, Lulu Falls Andersen was still pooped.

That morning, Ernie had *galumphed* out of the house and off to the shop. Robby was drawing, Nora was in her high chair cracking saltines and eating the pieces. The breakfast dishes were washed and air-drying in the wooden rack by the sink. The screened doors and windows of the house were open and the big trees— ninety-year-old sycamores—shadowed the front lawn, with physics pulling the cool, scented, soft air into the house.*

Lulu took a Blue Willow mug and saucer and poured that most satisfying *next* cup of Maxwell House from the Pyrex percolator on the stovetop. "Come to Mama," she said to the coffee, adding three slaps of condensed milk. With the help of Elsie the Cow, Lulu took her coffee beige, and the teaspoon scoop of sugar made life worth living. Ernie took his coffee black and strong—he'd lived on it through the war, crediting his "joe" with defeating the Axis powers. Given an hour, such stuff would melt a porcelain cup and eat away the spoon.

"Robby," Lulu called. "Bring in the newspaper, would you?" Robby was always so lost in his coloring that she knew she had to call out to him twice. "Robby? The paper, please."

"Of course!" he shouted. "I almost forgot!"

"Pipes like a church organ," Lulu said to herself, then sipped Maxwell House number two. *Ahhhhhh.*

Lulu heard the front door open, then close, then Robby appeared in the kitchen unfolding the paper. "Can I have the comic strips

---

* Air-conditioning was still *years* away for the Andersen home—for the *world*. Ernie eventually installed a rooftop swamp cooler to blast a column of refrigerated air straight down into the central hallway, but that didn't happen until 1954.

again, Mom?" In the last year, he'd gone from *Mommy* to *Mom,* a crossing from baby into boyhood that rendered a tiny rip in Lulu's heart.

"Of course." The comics were on the inside back page of section 3, and with them, Robby skidded back to his crayons and tablets in the living room, where he would copy and color *Blondie, Barney Google,* and *Dick Tracy,* not bothering with the words in the dialogue balloons that he couldn't yet read.

The *Lone Butte Herald* was the morning newspaper, published and printed right there in town, in the former Merchants Bank Building. Lulu preferred the *Valley Daily Press* for its national features, but it came in the afternoon from Redding, up north, and there was no time to sit with the paper late in the day. The baby would be done napping, the house had to be straightened up, and dinner had to be started.*

Lulu had the morning *Herald* all to herself that day, wandering through its pages from back to front—from the comicless section 3 (advice, radio listings, the crossword) into section 2 (local news and obituaries) and finally the front section, starting with the editorials and letters to the editor on page 6. She had gone to Union High with the *Herald*'s coeditor, Tommy Werther (Tommy *Werth-less* when he was a sophomore), who fought the war from a desk in the navy yard in Vallejo. His editorial that morning lamented the behavior of idle veterans who, in times of opportunity afforded by the G.I. Bill of Rights, never went to school, never went to work, never took on the responsibilities of good citizens but opted instead for a life of hooliganism and lawlessness. Lulu lost interest in the column after two and a half paragraphs.

Pages 5, 4, 3, and 2 were mostly advertisements in bold graphics

---

* Ernie read the *Daily Press,* however, lazily, from front page to final, as he was at the *end* of his workday—home from the shop, in his stocking feet, his steel-toed work boots unlaced on the floor beside the La-Z-Boy, savoring two successive cans of Hamm's beer, pondering the state of the Free World. He finished the paper just as Robby had set the forks, knives, napkins, and spoons, right when Lulu put the food on the table. A television would not be in the house for another nine years, by which time a third Andersen child, Stella, at age six, was talkative and bossy and would want to change the channel.

announcing Summer Sale-a-Thons! Hot Deals! ALL MATTRESSES
MUST GO! Beside them were the lesser stories and those that were
continued from page 1. When she finally folded over from section A, page 2, to the paper's leading headlines, Lulu was looking at a grainy wire-service, two-column square photograph of her
brother, Bob Falls.

★   ★   ★

He was not identified in the caption, but Lulu knew her baby
brother, his wide nose, the crooked tooth in his grin, the question-
mark shape of the back of his head—these had been in Lulu's
vision most of her life and all of his. The photo had been snapped
at night, the harsh contrast of the camera's flash capturing Bob
Falls in a flippantly defiant pose, leaning back in the big saddle seat
of a parked motorcycle, wearing cuffed jeans and a white T-shirt,
his boots resting on the handlebars. He had a beer bottle in each
hand. Other bottles and cans, empty dead soldiers, were scattered
around him on the curb and in the gutter.

LAWLESS GANG TAKES OVER TOWN was the headline. The caption: *A drunken thug. A weekend of crime. Photo by AP.*

Bob had grown heavy. He looked older than his absence of a half
decade should have made him look. His eyes were half closed, sleep
lidded. He was jowly and needed a shave.

The story ran for six paragraphs on page 1, continuing on page 4
alongside the ad for Patterson's Appliances offering pay-per-month
purchases. Earlier, Lulu had skipped the story but had studied the
advertisement.* Now she read all about the two-day "riot" caused
when "outlaw gangs" on motorcycles descended upon the small
town of Hobartha, California, causing a day and a night of "mayhem." Hobartha was a 279-mile drive south on Highway 99, then
59 miles inland.

Lulu read and reread the story, flicking between the separated
pages of the paper, looking for *Bob Falls* in print, but none of the

---

* Lulu and Ernie had been talking about putting money down on a new Norge
refrigerator, moving the old Hastings to the screened-in porch for leftovers.

outlaw names were reported. Lulu read about fistfights, smashed windows, wild beer-drunk partying, and the roar of racing engines up Hobartha's main street at four in the morning. There were quotes—horror stories—from the police chief, a barber, a lady who owned a dress shop, the attendant of a filling station, and many terrorized citizens. The rule of law was restored only when a squad of highway patrolmen arrived. Arrests were made; some of the gang members fled the town, roaring away before dawn.

Had the sole brother to Lucille Falls Andersen fled as well? Or was he being held in the Hobartha City Jail? In another half-second click of her mind's eye, Lulu *saw* Bob Falls—in a jail cell, behind bars, on a hard, bare bench with a tin cup of soup in his hands. (Why the tin cup? Why the soup?)

Lulu went to the house telephone in the front hall, carrying the newspaper. She sat at the telephone table and dialed FIreside 6-344 so she could talk to Emmy Kaye Silvers Powell. E-K and Lulu had known each other since they were schoolkids, since the Silverses moved in next door to the Fallses' old place out on Webster Road in 1928. E-K and her older twin brothers, Larry and Wallace, had been constants for both Lulu and Bob despite Mr. and Mrs. Falls never quite getting used to living next door to Jews. The Silverses were never more religious than having one special dinner on a night called Passover (Lulu and Bob were regular guests at the Seder feast), and they put up a Christmas tree (free of any Jesus-in-the-manger images). But still, Lulu's parents afforded E-K and her family little more than neighborly civility, a coolness that thawed when Larry was killed on Guadalcanal and, months later, when Wallace's B-24 Liberator was vaporized into a mist of metal and flesh somewhere over Nazi-occupied Holland. Capping off that horrible stretch of time, Lulu's father, Robert Falls Sr., had a stroke, followed soon by a lethal heart attack. Her mother's frail temperament led her to fold up like a card table and spend her remaining days afraid and confused, expecting her husband to walk in the front door any second. The pneumonia she caught in late '43 took her life in twenty-six days. But as is the case in this world, some good and godly things happened as well: Claude Brainard purchased the Falls Printing Works for a good price, Ernie served in the war out of harm's way, little Robby went through his baby illnesses with no disasters. Still, Lulu's little brother was a Marine somewhere in the Pacific, and she was alone with a kid back in Lone Butte. If black coffee defeated the Axis, Lucky Strikes and the friendship between E-K and Lulu saved two lives on the home front.

Few people in town had more than a single telephone in the house, and that phone was usually near the front door. A call would have to ring a number of times before someone could get to it. But E-K made a point of picking up her jangling receiver quickly, so as not to wake her husband, George, who worked the night shift at the Westinghouse lightbulb plant. His habit was to come home at dawn and read, falling asleep on the davenport in the living room, not far from the phone.

"Hello?" E-K whispered.

"Did you see the paper this morning?" Lulu, too, whispered into the Bakelite handset, although she wasn't going to wake anyone up.

"No, Lu. We take the *Daily Press*. George does the Word Jumble before he heads to the plant."

"Oh, shoot. Then you haven't seen."

"Seen what?"

"The front page of the *Herald*," Lulu whispered. "It's Bob's picture."

"Bob who?"

"My brother."

This was news that couldn't take a whisper. "Your brother? What in heaven for?"

"Oh, E-K." Lulu's voice caught deep in her chest. "It's just terrible . . ."

"Wait, kiddo," Emmy Kaye said with a hush. "I'll go next door. The Sapersteins get the *Herald*. I'll steal a look and call you right back."

Lulu hung up and looked in the directory for Western Union, which had changed its number since moving to an office in the lobby of the new Golden Eagle Hotel. Simon Kowall answered on the second ring with his trademark greeting: "*WES* . . . tern *Union*?"

Simon had learned Morse code as a signalman in the army. On his return to Lone Butte, he walked into the Western Union office, still in his uniform, to ask for a job and had been hired on the spot. He was glad to tap out, at Lulu's request, IF ROBERT FALLS IN CUSTODY PLEASE CONTACT LULU LONE BUTTE down the wire to the Hobartha Police Department. "That'll be thirty cents, Lucille, the next time you're in town," he said.

Lulu did not notice that her son was up from the floor rug, now standing in the opening between the front hall and the living room. "What does that mean, Mom? *Custody*."

The phone rang *BRRRNNGG!* Before picking up, Lulu managed a smile at her good boy. "I bet Jill is waiting for you next door. Why not go play now?"

"It's not ten on the clock yet."

"Almost." *BRRRNNGG!* "Go have fun." Robby was gone like a breeze.

BRRRN . . . E-K was no longer whispering. "Dear heaven, that is Bob as I'm standing here. I've got the paper in my hands. Is he some kind of *crook* now?"

"I don't have a clue." Lulu sat down in the phone chair with its little table, absentmindedly taking up the pencil by the message pad. "I sent a telegram."

"To whom?"

"The police down there." Out of habit, Lulu took to writing long rows of cursive X's that would eventually cover the page; a worried pencil doodle. "Maybe Bob needs a bailout."

"Sit tight, Lu. I'll set a cold plate for George when he wakes up and come over. You and I are going to *smoke*." E-K smoked. A lot. Viceroys.

Lulu had a sudden desire for a lung full of Lucky Strike. Last winter, Ernie had sworn off cigarettes after a long, vicious bout of streptococcus, so Lulu quit, too. But she also kept a hidden pack in her sewing kit. She'd get it out when E-K showed up.

Lulu went to her bedroom. She had already stripped the morning sheets off the bed. Her husband sweated as he slept, so much that his pajamas were always soaked and the bedding needed changing every morning. In her half of the closet, up on the shelf, she pushed around the folded winter sweaters and holdalls full of the small things that never got thrown out, until she found the old hatbox where she kept her letters. Those from Ernie—dozens and dozens of long, smartly composed pages filled with intricate details of the burdens of his duties, the longing for "all this" to be over, going all the way back to Camp Desperation—she kept neatly knotted up in twine. The letters from her old friends—her gal pals who had married and moved away or had just moved away—were in mismatched-sized stacks held together by rubber bands that were losing elasticity. As a record of her youth, Lulu retained form letters from MGM Studios, Hollywood, in response to fan mail she meant for the eyes of Franchot Tone, kept as a reminder of how silly she had been to assume a movie star would open mail from a girl in Lone Butte and then compose a response.

In the five years since he'd joined the service, Robert Falls had written home to Lulu all of eight times, those letters now aging upright against the side of the hatbox, kept separate from the others by a paper clip gone to rust; six were from his time in the service, two had been written since VJ Day.*

She sat on the bed and separated the wartime gospels of Bob Falls. His first, from May of 1942, had been sent from the Marine base in San Diego, scribbled in a smeared-ink scrawl on United States Marine Corps stationery.

Lulu,

I was in a truck crash and got busted up. I was in the back so took less of a beating than some of the other fellows—one of whom almost died. A dozen of us are in the Infirmary. I've got no broken bones beyond a wrist that looks like barb wire in the X-rays. It hurts like h—l to hold a pen. Got a hole in my gut, too, so I'm drinking my meals for a while. I can walk, as long as I take it easy. The USMC says I'll be laid up for a while, but I'm still their property. I guess Uncle Sam Still Wants Me. There is a fellow in here with a case of, no kidding, the mumps. The guy is in agony. He's still a Marine, too. I hope Ernie is well. I should have joined the Air Corps like him. You married a smart cookie.

Love you lots,
Bob

---

* Victory Japan, August 15, 1945. Victory Europe was May 8, 1945.

⋆ ⋆ ⋆

As a boy, Bob Falls was not shy. He was merely busy *listening*. He would linger at the dinner table until the conversations were over. When the plates needed clearing, he would help his mother and Lulu, listening to their chatter during the washing, drying, and putting away. He was no reader of books beyond what his schooling dictated. When he went to the movies, he had few opinions on the picture other than "pretty good" or "nice enough." He let everyone else talk about the Scarlet Pimpernel's heroics or Bette Davis's brittle voice. He nodded politely when Lulu called *Mutiny on the Bounty* a masterpiece.

When his father expanded Falls Printing Works into a going concern, Bob was only nine years old, but he learned the machinery and how to print a precise number of flyers, invitations, church bulletins. By the time he turned twelve he was at the shop most days after school and every Saturday, so it was only fair that his father pay him a salary of two, then four, then five dollars a week, which he rarely spent, collecting the greenbacks in, first, an old cigar box, then two more. Through his years at Union High, Bob had but one girlfriend—Elaine Gamellgaard, a self-confident young woman who, beginning in the second week of their freshman Latin class, had given Bob no option in the relationship. Elaine arranged for Bob to empty his cigar-box vaults in exchange for her brother's very old Ford. ("All that rust?" Lulu had warned him.) He had the oil-leaking bucket-of-bolts running before he had a driver's license. There was a joke going around—which Bob was sure to have heard, with no comment—that it was a good thing the Japs[*] had bombed Pearl Harbor, or else Elaine Gamellgaard was going to be Mrs. Robert Falls the day after graduation and a mother by Christmas, if not Halloween.

As it was, Bob did not attend his high-school graduation with

---

[*] A note on the use of that racial slur to define the enemy. During the war years, "Jap" was in such common usage that newspapers used the slur in headlines. Other racial slurs were common in a vernacular of ignorance, ease, and prejudice. Using such dog-whistle slurs in these pages is meant to communicate that that was Then, this is Now, and we all know better. And back then, the Germans were usually called Nazis. Not, say, Krauts or Luger-Heads.

Elaine Gamellgaard or anybody else. He turned eighteen years old on the first of February, enlisted in the Marines the day after blowing out his birthday candles, gave Elaine a quick kiss with no promises attached, and was gone off to boot camp after Easter. The jilted Miss Gamellgaard rebounded with aplomb, snagging Vernon Cederborg that September and moving to Pocatello, Idaho. Vernon's heart condition made him no good for the service, but he did teach hydraulics to navy machinists and, postwar, had his own plumbing outfit and five daughters.

★   ★   ★

While USMC Private Robert A. Falls—#O-457229—was convalescing from a punctured gut and a fractured wrist, his class of Marines completed boot camp, weapons training, and was shipped off to take on the Japanese forces at Guadalcanal—a place no one had ever heard of.* Bob's injuries took weeks to heal before he was sent back to complete boot camp, assigned the M2-2 flamethrower as his tool of war, and trained in its use and tactics until, finally, he and other Marines were marched aboard ships and sent sailing over the western horizon to an undisclosed place where he was yet another *Fucking New Guy* waiting for his chance to kill the enemy, too.

Every week, for as long as the war lasted, Lulu sent her little brother a letter, a card, a package—*something*—to a military post office in San Francisco. From there, somehow, her mail would get to Bob. Ernie was in England, but Lulu had no idea where her brother was other than somewhere in the PTO—the Pacific Theater of Operations.

Six of the letters in Bob's return correspondence traveled via V-mail—V for Victory—each short note a miracle of imagination, technology, and logistics. From somewhere in the Pacific, Bob Falls and all the other servicemen would take government-issue pens to single pages of government-issue writing tablets and write letters home. Every guy knew not to write about where they were, where they were going, or even the names of their officers,

---

* Some maps named the place Guadalcan-*nar*.

because censors would CENSOR such critical, top-secret information. Bob Falls joined the Marine Corps to fight the war, but other
guys served their country by reading his V-mail just to blacken
out words like *New Caledonia, U.S.S.* Wardell, and *Lieutenant
Colonel Sydney Planke.* Bob didn't mind that the single sheet of
a V-mail didn't hold much of a letter. True, his cursive handwriting was big and slanted and took up a lot of space on the page,
but he wrote down all he had to say—everything that was allowed,
anyway.

The original V-mail letters were photographed, then shrunk
down to a size smaller than a fingernail and connected to long
spools of microfilm, holding as many Victory-mails as possible.
Airplanes then carried thousands of spools of the microscopic letters across the Pacific Ocean, as many as a *million* V-mails, to be
processed in America, enlarged to half their original size.* The dis-
tinctive V-mail, with the addresses of parents, wives, girlfriends, or
Lulu Andersen lined up with the envelope's transparent window,
made the receipt of one an event. Bob's oversize penmanship made
easy reading; small handwriting made some V-letters undecipher-
able gibberish.

Lulu spread Bob's letters in front of her on the bare mattress.
Taking them out of the envelopes took more time than reading
them.

12/26, '42

Sis Lu,

*I was at a place for awhile, now I'm here. Can't say where here is.
Might as well be on Mars. We see movies outside. All this time and
the only Jap I've seen is Charlie Chan. The other fellows saw plenty
before I got here. You know they get ice cream in the Navy? Now
they tell me. I'm doing good, but the Japs might want to change
that. Haha. Happy New Year. Bob*

---

* Imagine having to deliver full-sized letters. The drain on matériel, aircraft, fuel,
and personnel. Whoever came up with V-mail was a genius.

May 17, '43

Sis Lu,

    *Happy Birthday. Can't believe I have a nephew with my name. Bet Ernie is busting. Some days, I'd do anything to be in one of his airplanes and off my feet. **CENSORED CENSORED CENSORED CENSORED**. The nights are beautiful here. No Japs but plenty of stars. Guys are saying the war won't be over til Golden Gate in '48. Some say Not Done til '51. By then, I'll be either too old, or a General. Haha. Bob*

Dec. '43

Sis Lu,

    The papers might write about our unit and the fight the Japs put up. Don't think for a minute they got the best of me. We are sitting pretty right now, free cigarettes and Coca-Cola. An all-girl band came through and put on a show. Half the guys asked the sax player to marry them. I'm holding out for a tromboneist. Ha ha. Bob

Aug 4, '44

Sis Lu,

    *Got your pictures. "Little" Bob looks like a tough cowboy. When did you start smoking? Sometimes, that's all we do around here. Japs had us busy for awhile but now we're back and sleeping a lot. **CENSORED CENSORED CENSORED CENSORED CENSORED** I miss driving. I dream of that Ford of mine. I must be in LOVE. Ha Hah. Bob*

December 1944

Sis Lu,

    I hope you have a great Christmas and New Years. Back in a place I cant say, but its as good as any. A buddy made corn-bread in a mess kit and it tasted like cake to us. Not sure what else to say. Bob.

October 2, 1945

Lulu,

   Made it to Japan, after all.* How did these people make such trouble? Why did they keep at it for so long? Lots of little kids and lots of old women. We took care of most of their men. V-J Day? I'll believe it when I'm home. Bob.

On a day in 1946, Bob Falls trooped down the gangway of the USS *Tressent* with a few hundred other Marines. Setting foot once again on *Terra Americana,* he was soon mustered out of the uniform he had worn for half a decade. The exact dates of these life-altering events he kept to himself. He spent much of his accrued combat pay on the purchase of a 1941 Indian Four Inline Motorcycle. A few other ex-servicemen did the same thing with other makes of motorcycles, either prewar models or war surplus. The lot of them began riding around Southern California, then beyond, living much as they had during the war, as itinerants, waiting for a reason to move on to the next camp, the next town, the next fight.

   Where Bob had gone was unknown to Lulu until she received his most recent letter. No longer sent via V-mail, it came folded in a brown envelope with a teepee printed on the flap. The postmark said Albuquerque, New Mexico. His full-sized penmanship was in full flower in dark green ink.

X-mas 1946

Sis Lulu,

   I hope you and Ernie and Little Bob have a white Christmas.
   I'm in Albequerque N.Mex. We came along Route 66. You know the joke they tell about this place? It's not new and it's not Mexico. I have a job lined up in Texas. Put this in little Bob's piggy bank. Happy New Years, too. Big Bob.

Enclosed were two one-dollar bills.

---

* After the Japanese surrender, Bob's Marine unit was stationed in Nagasaki, which had been atom-bombed on August 9, 1945.

★   ★   ★

His appearance on the front page of that morning's *Herald* was the first sign she'd had of her little brother since those teepee Christmas dollars. Last July, Lulu had sent news of Nora's birth to the only address she had for him—the APO—a pink birth-announcement card, a letter, and a small square photograph of the baby and the mother. He never saw them.

"Yoo-doodly-hoo?" E-K walked into the kitchen and put on a fresh pot of coffee while Lulu collected the baby from her crib in the tiny nook meant for a sewing machine. They went out to the sycamore-shaded front porch and sat at the old table with the new chairs.

"Give me that little bag of muffins," E-K said, taking Nora in her arms, the first of many Lucky Strikes crimped in her lips. Lulu lit up and inhaled like she had during the war, when cigarettes evolved from affectation to medicant; she smoked to relieve her stress, her fear, and her anxiety during the three years of dark nights.

"What got into Bob?" E-K asked, running her fingers through Nora's adorable baby curls. "Some soldiers came back and can't hold jobs, can't sleep through the night. Some are in mental institutions. I read that in the *Saturday Evening Post*."

"Bob wasn't a soldier. He was a Marine." Lulu poured more coffee, adding her dose of sugar and evaporated milk. "Maybe he was shell-shocked . . ."

"Mysterious is what he is. When we were little, he'd have those eyes open, but his mouth shut, like he was keeping a secret from all of us. Did he tell you that he had a motorcycle?"

"You saw all he wrote." Lulu had shared Bob's eight letters. "I didn't know a thing. If I don't hear from him or the police down there, I'll still have nothing but questions."

The ladies had finished almost the full pack of Luckys when Robby and Jill Burns came in after playing next door.

"Good heavens. It's lunchtime!" Lulu rubbed out what was left of her lit cigarette, hoping Robby had failed to see her smoking.

★   ★   ★

Ernie came home from the shop just after 4:00 p.m. to find the *Daily Press* waiting for him on his La-Z-Boy. The afternoon paper carried a story about the motorcycle gang that destroyed the tranquility of Hobartha but ran no picture of Bob Falls or any of the other thugs. By the time Robby and Jill were out back in the mini orchard playing Wag-a-Bump, Ernie had his boots off and was in the La-Z-Boy with Nora in his lap, tickling his daughter and saying silly things like *Who is this little thing? Who is this in my lap?* Nora giggled, in love. When Lulu brought him his first open can of Hamm's, she also carried the front page of the morning's *Herald*.

"You see anything familiar here?" she asked.

Ernie was confused. He wasn't home for half an hour and here was his wife playing twenty questions. But then he saw what Lulu wanted him to see.

"Jesus H!" Nora cackled again at Daddy's funny face.

While Lulu got the meal on the table—calling Robby in to do his usual chore and set the utensils—Ernie read about what had happened down in Hobartha, the riots and the fracas with the highway patrol. During dinner, the parents kept mum on the subject and stayed quiet all around, which Robby noticed. When the meal was done, his mother sat at the table longer than she normally did, the dirty dishes still in front of them all. His father asked about E-K and her husband, saying that no man should have to work all night to raise a family and there was no way he was ever going take a paycheck from Westinghouse Light. Robby sat, listening to both the chitchat of his parents and the quiet lulls of what was not spoken between them, until his mother let out a sigh and started clearing the dishes. Robby did not have to be told to collect all the forks, knives, and spoons.

"At least his name wasn't in the paper," Ernie said in a low tone as he took Nora out of her high chair and back into his lap. "The town might not ever know."

Nora's very first birthday came on July 9, so every friend of the family, who all had kids of their own, came by to watch the little girl make a mess of her single candle and large lemon cake with white icing. Lulu was still waiting for word about her brother, but the phone never rang nor did a telegram come from Simon Kowall down at Western Union.

After another week went by with no response, E-K and Lulu met up at each other's houses a few times, smoked too much, and eventually turned to the many other topics at hand that midsummer of 1947. Another Negro was playing baseball now. The United Nations was moving from San Francisco to New York City. A young Mexican girl had drowned in the Little Iron Bend River. Phyllis Metcalf had dyed her hair peroxide blond and was showing off her new self all over town. Harold Pye Jr. had broken his leg at football practice for Union High and would never be the same again— a story taken as seriously as when his brother, Henry Pye, had lost his right foot to frostbite during the Battle of the Bulge. Both boys had had athletic futures so promising their pictures accompanied their tragic stories on the front pages of both papers.

Then, Bob Falls turned up in Lone Butte.

★   ★   ★

Before lunch, little Robby was playing on the front porch. He had a blue-striped towel knotted around his neck, tied there all by himself, trying to be like Superman, but he was frustrated because the towel was not fluttering as a super-cape should. Robby ran around in circles, trying to fly with the same dynamic style as the Man of Steel. No dice.

He was playing alone because it was Tuesday. Every Tuesday Jill Burns had a doctor's appointment, an exercise session for her foot. She hated going as the sessions *hurt*. But there were nice people there, grown-ups taking the same kind of classes, men from the war who had missing legs and stumps for arms. Those men made jokes and said funny things that made Jill laugh even when she couldn't understand the jokes. Every Tuesday, they treated the little girl like one of them, like a pal, greeting her by calling out, "Here's General Jill!" No one at the clinic ever whispered about her being a "poor little cripple," though many grown-ups in Lone Butte did.

Robby's mother was inside the house, in the living room, pushing and pulling on a new kind of rug sweeper she had bought at Patterson's Appliances. She had the radio tuned to the *Mid-Morning Musical* on KHSL and was singing along to popular hits from Broadway shows. "Superman" dared a leap from the porch's top step all the way to the grass and, finally, his cape billowed as desired, only too much, so it came down and wrapped around Robby's head. No way for a hero to land at a scene of some crime.

That was when an Indian Four Inline rode past the front of the house, the motorcycle's engine filling the air with a low-throated *dug-gah dug-gah*. The rider, looking for a house he had never visited, saw the number, 114 Elm, and Robby's flight off the porch. He slowed down and made a wide U-turn at the corner, coasting to a stop between the twin sycamores that shaded the house.

Bob Falls was wearing heavy work jeans and worn-to-gray boots. He had a short-waisted jacket made of leather, a jacket like Robby had seen in the photographs of his father when he was in England during the war, with men standing and kneeling in front of their airplane bombers like they were on a baseball team. Some of those men wore dark glasses, but the motorcycle rider had a pair of strapped goggles and a short-brimmed cap. He took both off and ran his fingers through his hair, which needed a combing and a wash.

"Hello, Superman," Bob Falls said. "Just dropping in?"

"I'm not really Superman," Robby Andersen told him. "I'm just pretending."

"Oh," Bob said, rising from the motorcycle's leather seat. "I guess Superman is taller. You must be Robby, then."

"My real name is Robert." The difference was important to some grown-ups. "Robby is a nickname."

"I was called Bobby for the longest time, but not Robby," Bob said, settling his motorcycle onto its side kickstand, unzipping his jacket, and taking it off. He draped it on the motorcycle's handle-bars. "I saw a picture or two of you that your mommy sent to me. I'm your uncle."

Robby knew that his mother had a brother who was in the war. He had seen pictures of him. But this motorcycle rider, in cuffed jeans and a white T-shirt, was a stranger to him. "You're my mom's brother?"

"Yep." Bob tapped a Chesterfield cigarette from a pack, then flick-lit it from a lighter he kept in a little belt holster on his hip. With the smoke between the fingers of one hand, he reached up, stretching his arms and shoulders to the treetops, letting loose with a vocal *arrrr-tuhhhh*. Then he took a deep pull on his cigarette. "Aren't you turning five pretty soon?" he said, exhaling smoke on the words.

"Yep." Robby decided at that moment that *yep* was going to be a word he used a lot.

"BOB!" Lulu was coming out of the house on a run, through the screen door that swung wide, slamming behind her. She had heard a man's voice during a pause in the *Mid-Morning Musical,* so had come to investigate. Her son had never seen her weep, but that was what she was doing as she ran into the arms of the motorcycle man, holding on to him tightly, like she needed to be kept from falling.

The rest of the day brought more events never before witnessed by Robby. His father came home from the shop early, bringing the Packard to a sliding stop in the gravel driveway at the back of the house, then racing through the screened-in porch calling, "Where is he?," letting the door slam behind him. He shook Uncle Bob's hand firmly, pumping hard and long. The two men clapped each other on the back, talking at the same time. Then the three grown-ups sat at the wooden bench table in the backyard, in the mini orchard of plum trees, and drank cans of Hamm's beer. Robby's mom, drinking a Hamm's, before dinner. What a day!

When the newsboy tossed the *Daily Press* onto the front porch, Robby ran and got it for his father, but the paper remained folded, unread, as Dad and Uncle Bob continued talking and downing their Hamm's. Mom was in the kitchen by then, with Nora on her hip, readying a dinner of corn on the cob and hamburger steaks. Robby took his colors and pads out to the orchard and sat at the table, drawing a motorcycle from memory, listening to the grown-up men talk.

"Oh, they tossed some of us in the brig for a few days," Uncle Bob said. "We sobered up and paid a fine and said, 'Gosh, we're sorry.' The papers made more of a mess of it than we did."

"Scared the daylights out of them folks, raising all that hell, though," Dad said. Robby wondered if he should tell Mom that Dad had used a cussword.

"Someone broke a window or two. Not me. And one of the locals threw a couple of fists, and that didn't end well."

"How'd you end up in a gang like that, anyway?"

"We ain't a *gang*." Uncle Bob laughed. "We just break a few rules here and there. Most of them are good guys, the ex-Marines, anyway."

Robby went inside for some of his coloring pencils, sharpening them on the hand-crank sharpener his dad had screwed into the wall on the screened-in porch, just three feet high so Robby didn't need a chair to reach it. His dad had put it in special, just for him. He returned to the mini orchard to make drawings and listen to more of the grown-up talk—words like *settle down, horsepowers, Nagasaki, G.I. Bill, railroad strike*. Both men opened more beers and, when Mom announced "Chow time!" with a laugh, the men brought their Hamm's in to dinner.

Uncle Bob talked and laughed while eating. He took his hamburger steak with extra Heinz 57 sauce and kept drinking beer. He sat sideways in his chair at the end of the table opposite Ernie, repeating stories of growing up in Lone Butte and asking questions about people Robby never heard of. When Lulu insisted her brother hold Nora in his lap for a while, he did so, but not with any ease. The baby girl made him unsure of his every move.

"You can't break her, Bob," Lulu told him. "Think of her as a puppy."

With that, Bob scratched his niece behind her ears. Nora, in the lap of a man she had never seen nor smelled before, wore an expression of blank expectation. "Can I give her a biscuit?" He could. He did. Nora held it in her hand.

The talk turned to how Ernie was running things down at the shop, and he quickly offered Bob a job, since they always needed good men there. Bob turned him down flat. He didn't need money and he was no shop man; the job in Texas had taught him that he and bosses didn't get along. He joked that he'd rather punch a cop than punch a clock. Lulu made coffee to go with the dessert of salt-sprinkled watermelon, so Bob nursed a cup along with his Chesterfields. He let his nephew hold his Zippo lighter, which had the USMC eagle, globe, and anchor on it along with a word Robby could not read.* The boy liked the way the lighter clicked open and

---

* *Tarawa.*

snapped shut. No one got up from the table for what seemed to Robby like a long, long time, so very long that he left the silverware on the table and went into the living room, back to lying on the rug and drawing. The men kept talking and Uncle Bob kept smoking, tilting his head back on the exhale so the smoke wouldn't go in the baby's eyes.

Well after dark, Bob quietly said, "Look at her, she's out cold." He gestured with his chin down at Nora, who had fallen asleep with her cheek on her uncle's chest, her mouth slightly open, leaving a little wet stain on his white, buttonless short-sleeve shirt. "I've bored her into slumber."

Ernie chuckled. Lulu took her sleeping daughter carefully into her arms and called for little Robby to come along for his bath. The men volunteered for kitchen patrol and started clearing the dishes.

After his bath and before bedtime, Uncle Bob showed Robby how to turn the sofa in the living room into a "rack" with sheets and a blanket. Uncle Bob was awfully giggly: he picked up Robby and carried him like a plank in his arms and "flew" him around the living room, almost knocking over a lamp, almost tripping on Ernie's reading chair, before ending the roughhousing with something called a three-point landing. After Robby went upstairs for bed, he secretly sat out of sight on the top step and listened to the grown-ups talk in the living room. When Lulu went to bed at 10:30 she found her son sleeping there. She rousted him gently to his room. The men stayed up until almost 1:00 a.m., when Ernie called it a night.

★ ★ ★

At 7:02 a.m. on the dial of the clock in the radio, Robby expected his uncle would be awake—grown-ups always got up early—but the sofa rack still held Big Bob's sleeping hulk. There were three empty, dented cans of Hamm's beer on the coffee table.

Ernie would normally have been on his way to the shop, but the sudden, surprise arrival of his brother-in-law had made a chaos of his morning routine. He was still at the kitchen table on his fourth cup of black coffee with most of his sunny-side-up eggs untouched, saying to Lulu, ". . . our crews had the sky almost all to themselves when he landed on Saipan . . ." When Robby came into the kitchen, his mother gave his father a shake of her head, and their conversation stopped.

"Uncle Bob is still asleep," Robby said. "Is he going to live with us?"

"Oh, jeez," Ernie said, getting up as he tipped the last of his coffee to his lips. "Let's stay quiet so your uncle can sleep it off, okay?" With a swirl of his son's hair, Ernie was out the back porch door and starting up the Packard. Lulu had a piece of cold toast and a small glass of milk in front of Robby by the time Ernie backed the car out of the gravel driveway and drove off to the shop.

With his uncle asleep in the living room, Robby quietly got out his art supplies and drew at the kitchen table. His mom did the dishes slowly, careful not to make noise. At ten on the clock, Robby crossed through the hedge to play next door with Jill. They filled up pails with water from a garden spigot and flung the water around like they were putting out fires. They loved being wet and cool on a hot August morning.

When they finally came in for lunch, there was Uncle Bob at the breakfast table, wearing one of Ernie's bathrobes, just out of a shower with coffee in a Blue Willow cup and a lit Chesterfield in his hand, the *Herald* spread out on the tabletop in front of him.

Looking up to find someone new, he asked, "Who are you?"

"I live next door," the little girl said.

"That's the answer to a different question," Bob Falls replied.

"Her name is Jill," Robby told him.

Bob's eyes could not help but drift down to the little girl's misshapen foot, but they did not linger there. "Well, Jill who lives next door, can you excuse my appearance for a few moments while I finish this cup of joe? I'll go get dressed as soon as my head calms down to the point where I can taste it in my mouth."

"My dad drinks coffee, too," Jill said. "He calls it java."

Lulu, with Nora on her hip, was making each child a sandwich of butter and jam. "Would you guys like to have lunch in front of the radio?"

"Can we?" Robby was never allowed to eat his meals anywhere but at either the kitchen table or the dinner table! He and Jill ate in the living room using napkins as place mats on the rug, listening to a quiz show on KHSL. Robby's mom made them lemonade and gave them little squares of coffee cake that they ate with their fingers. Nora was put on her tummy on her baby blanket near them and given a pair of wooden spoons to play with, and the three kids kept each other occupied for the better part of an hour.

When Bob had finally tasted enough of his coffee and came through the living room on the way to changing into his clothes, the radio was playing a show with women talking about homemaking. Lulu was hanging Bob's freshly washed clothes on the line to dry in the backyard as Robby and Jill began drawing and coloring. Jill was satisfied creating stick-figure people and houses that consisted of rectangles for walls, doors, and windows and a triangle for the roof. She was coloring everything with vivid if mismatched crayons.

Robby's drawings were professional quality in comparison—pages and pages of Dick Tracy's wrist radio, airplanes flying in the sky alongside, yes, Superman, and fire engines putting out flames in a tall building.

Uncle Bob stood over them for a moment, his hands in the pockets of Ernie's bathrobe.

"You kids got a thing I call talent," Uncle Bob said. Nodding at the flames in Robby's five-alarm fire, he added, "Those look real," then he went into the hall bathroom to get dressed.

While Nora was being put down for her nap, Jill went home, walking herself through the back hedge. Robby then took the comics from the morning paper and, over two radio programs, sat with Uncle Bob and showed him how to re-create famous comic strips in his own hand. Bob kept drinking fresh coffee-joe-java, smoking Chesterfields, looking at crayon faces and penciled scenes. Lulu set an ashtray on the low table in front of the sofa for Bob to use rather than the Blue Willow saucer of his coffee cup. She sat down in the seldom-used reading chair, the one with the scallop-shaped back and armrests. The three of them talked about drawings and cartoons and the cost of comic books at the newsstands.

"You remember Lowell Strueller?" Lulu asked. Lowell had gone to high school with Bob, a class ahead of him. He'd enlisted in the navy the Monday after Pearl Harbor was attacked. "He runs the newsstand in Clark's Drugstore."

"Yeah?" Bob said. "He always did dream big." A commercial was on the radio for Palmolive dishwashing soap. "What time does Ernie come home?"

"Oh, not for another two hours," Lulu said, picking up her empty coffee cup and her brother's cup and ashy saucer.

"I think I'll get out of your hair for a bit. Robby, wanna take a ride?"

"On your motorcycle?" Robby immediately imagined himself on the bike, holding on to the handlebars with a forty-mile-per-hour wind in his face. "Sure!"

Lulu was aghast. "Bob! No!"

"I'll keep it under fifteen, just to tool around town some."

"Absolutely not!"

"Oh, come on," Bob said, getting up. "It'll be safer than when we rode the gutters." On rainy days when they were kids, Lulu, Bob, and everyone brave and reckless enough rode the slick gutters down the Webster Road incline on their bottoms and, some of them, standing upright, as if on ice skates. There had been plenty of tumbles, bruises, and tingling funny bones, but no one ever actually broke any part of themselves.

"I said absolutely not!"

Uncle Bob looked at his nephew. "Your ma says 'absolutely not,' kid. What should we do?"

* * *

Robby's arms were too short to reach the handlebars, so, sitting in his uncle Bob's lap on the wide leather seat, he kept his palms on the gas tank to keep his balance. True to his word—and to Robby's disappointment—Uncle Bob did not go fast at all, though he did rev the loud motor so the boy could hear the *growl* of the engine and feel the vibrant rhythm of the pistons, the chain, and the sprocket of the big machine under him. Making a gliding, balanced turn was like a ride at the county fair.

"Let's see the town," Bob called into his nephew's ear. They cruised around Lone Butte, passing Wentley's Grocery, Robby's school, the public library, Saint Philip Neri's, Saint Paul's, and the Assembly of God churches. As they rode across the trestle bridge over the Big Iron Bend River, Bob said, "I used to jump off this, right into the water!"

Robby could not imagine being brave enough to jump off a bridge so high into a river so cold. "How old were you when you did that?" Robby yelled in the wind.

"About your age. Made me feel like Superman!" Uncle Bob then added, "Don't tell your mom I said that!"

They avoided the city hall and county courthouse with the police station that adjoined the public square. Passing the State Theater— a movie palace worthy of the moniker—Uncle Bob slowed to take in the massive marquee and impressive façade.

"That's new," Uncle Bob said.

"There was a big fire, so they built a new State," Robby told him. The State was over a year old now, having opened with a movie young Robby was not allowed to see.*

"A fire, huh?" The original State Theater was built in 1908. "Your mom and I saw a lot of movies in that place. *Gone with the Wind. Mutiny on the Bounty.*" Currently playing on that day in August was Van Johnson in *Romance of Rosy Ridge,* a Daffy Duck cartoon, a travelogue about the glories of Canada, and a newsreel. It would not be too great a stretch to say that everyone in Lone Butte went to the State once a week, seeing every movie exhibited in its opulent hall. When television came to Lone Butte, Saturday night ticket sales took a hit because of Sid Caesar.

The temperature on Main Street had reached 102 degrees, so most folks were indoors and the traffic was as light as on a Sunday. Bob turned right off Pierce Street onto the north end of Main, where the Chicken Shack Dinner House was still dark, waiting for its 5:00 p.m. opening. The straightaway heart of Lone Butte lay in front of them, a bit more than four miles from one end to the other. The traffic light that was going to be at Buchannan and Main was three years away, but there was a stop sign, which Bob ignored, as he was going so slowly.

"We just pulled a Hollywood," he said into his nephew's ear.

They passed the Golden Eagle Hotel on one side of the street and the Almond Growers Association on the other. Then the bus

---

* *The Blue Dahlia* with Alan Ladd.

station opposite Burton's Department Store. Patterson's Appliances and Butte Auto Sales rolled by. On the block after Madison was Red Hen Shoes, Ordt's Hardware, Lone Butte Music, and a ladies' finery shop. On the other side of the street was the Flying A filling station, the old Western Union office that was now vacant, and a "tavern" called the Shed.

Calling the Shed a tavern was a bit of puffery; the place was a bar. A neon sign of a stemmed martini glass hung perpendicular to the street traffic; colorful illuminated advertisements for Hamm's beer and Blue Label lager were in windows that were too narrow and set too high to allow a view to the inside. The Shed's wide wooden door was open, hinting at the bar's shadowed, dark confines.

At the curb in front of the Shed were four motorcycles leaning into their side kickstands. Robby knew they were not policeman motorcycles. These machines were much more like Uncle Bob's, each with a different kind of handlebar, a variety of chrome parts, and a different-colored gas tank. One was still the color of war-surplus olive drab.

Bob recognized each of the machines as they rolled past. Those motorcycles belonged to three former Marines—Hal, Doggit, and Butch—and a veteran Navy Corpsman, Kirkland. All of them had been in Hobartha for the wild party. Butch and Kirkland had been in the Hobartha jail with Bob.

He veered to the curb in front of Clark's Drugs, shut off the Indian Four's inline motor, and lifted Robby to the sidewalk. The sudden quiet actually rang in the boy's ears. Because his uncle had promised him a Coca-Cola and the comic book of his choice, Robby scampered into the store, but Bob didn't follow. He looked back up the street at the quartet of motorcycles leaning in front of the Shed. Only after a long beat did he follow his nephew inside.

"Is this Bob Falls?" From his perch on a stool by the cash register, Lowell Strueller made the connection immediately. "Because you sure look like Bob Falls." The manager of Clark's newsstand came around the counter to shake Bob's hand and clap him on the shoulder with such familiarity little Robby thought they must have once been the best of friends.

"Heard you were running the place," Bob said. "You know my nephew?"

"Of course, I do," Lowell said, squatting down close to Robby and shaking his small hand. "How you doing, slugger? Your mom and dad doing fine?" Robby nodded as Lowell sprang back up and turned to Bob. "Where the heck you been, Bob? It's good to see you."

Lowell Strueller was twenty-five, a year older than Bob Falls. Prior to the war, neither boy had been very far from Lone Butte. Since their final days at Union High, Lowell had been to San Francisco, then across the Pacific Ocean. On board a task force destroyer, he had witnessed, from a distance, the bombardments, then the invasions, of some of the Japanese-held islands, tiny spots on the big maps. In the late months of the war, his ship had been singled out for destruction by a kamikaze suicide bomber. The Japanese pilot crashed midship, just above the waterline, exploding with such force as to blow a hole from starboard to portside. It was a miracle Lowell hadn't been killed—like the seventeen sailors who had been incinerated by the kamikaze's blast. It was a miracle the ship did not snap in two and disappear with all hands. It was a miracle when red-hot, razor-jagged bits of the ship's steel bulkhead—none larger than a thumbtack—impacted into Lowell's buttocks and thighs rather than his spine or heart or eyes; he wasn't hit by the hunks of shrapnel that were as big as horseshoes. Lowell was the type of guy who spoke often of his good fortune, his cheating of death. He perfected his survival story as he hitchhiked from the navy base in San Diego back to Lone Butte in January of 1946—repeating his miraculous tale to every driver who stopped to give him a lift.

Bob Falls, too, had seen the horizon line of the Pacific Ocean and some of the map-specks of islands. Some seemed like paradise, even with all the rain. Others were coral-ringed hell spots with atavistic jungles of vivid shades of green growth blocking out the blue sky and sea, with red smears of fresh blood, black stains of blood exposed to the air too long, and the smell of spent cordite melding with the stench of bile, offal, and decaying human flesh. Those specks on the horizon grew larger as he and the other Marines drew closer and closer until their wooden landing craft ran aground and they waded ashore as fast as the weight of their gear and weapons allowed, their instincts and fears spurring them on: Tarawa in

November of 1943, Saipan in June of 1944, then, later in the year, Tinian. Bob did not go ashore onto Okinawa until other Marines had been charged with the invasion's first weeks of fighting. There were plenty of fighting Japanese soldiers on Okinawa in the late spring of 1945, but by the time Bob's Floating Reserve Force was ashore, the odds of being killed in action were more in his favor than against.

Little Robby didn't hear much of what the men were saying. He was drawn to the comic books on display, the racks and shelves full of them. The colorful covers showed superheroes, worried women looking over their shoulders, and talking ducks. They were lined up, ready for sale, some for only a nickel, a dime for the thicker and better-printed books. There were cowboys and crooks, a clique of laughing teenagers crammed into a jalopy, streaking fighter planes, and a goofy soldier in a sloppy uniform who was dancing with a mop.

One war comic book cover was an image of a helmeted Marine coming out of the water on a palm-lined beach amid glamorous explosions. Ships were in the distance and landing crafts filled with men were approaching. The Marine was gritting his teeth in determination, a rifle in one strong hand, the other waving to other Marines charging out of the waves behind him. Robby could not yet read the printed words inked in too many large bold letters.[*]

Robby picked the comic book off the shelf and turned to the first page. There were words neatly printed in boxes, along with a small drawing of a Marine's head and face, a rough-shaven man who seemed to be telling the story of a battle. There were Marines crouched in holes, firing machine guns and rifles. One small figure was throwing a grenade, stretched out like a baseball pitcher about to hurl a strike. In the background was a Marine with a large apparatus on his back that looked like the welding equipment down at Robby's father's shop. A hose attached the Marine's mounted tanks to a gun that looked like no other. The Marine was leaning forward as a line of dripping flame—red, orange, and yellow—shot out from the gun in a widening arc, turning a palm tree into an inferno.

***

[*] "Come on, you lugs! We've got a job to do!"

"Hey, look." Uncle Bob was over Robby's shoulder. He pointed to the Marine, the one shooting the stream of fire. "That's me."

With the better part of four-bits (fifty cents) Bob let his nephew pick out whatever comic books he wanted. Lowell Strueller rang up *The Phantom, Little Dot, Tales of the Triple Q Ranch, Professor MacQuack,* and *HEROES UNDER FIRE.* Bob and little Robby took up a pair of stools at the lunch counter—this late in the day they were two of the three customers; an old man was reading a book and having a bowl of clam chowder down at the far end of the counter. Robby's feet could not yet reach the floor but swung idly as he spread the comics in front of him. Lowell presented him with the most amazing drink he had ever been allowed—a Coca-Cola with vanilla syrup, which tasted as sweet and thick as liquid pudding. Would his mother *ever* allow him this when he came to Clark's with *her*?

"Coffee, Bob?" Lowell asked. As the cup was poured, Bob Falls picked out one of the comic books—*HEROES UNDER FIRE*—studying the cover, then flipping to the first page.

The drawings in the book did not explicitly show any of the Marines being killed in action, shot through, blown to bits, or losing limbs as little bits of lead sawed through them—such graphic horror was not allowed in children's comic books—but Bob saw it all before him, nonetheless. He heard the fury and the chaos of the jungle battle. He smelled the liquid fuel of the flamethrower, just as he could smell the burning trees and human flesh. Bob's heart began to race and he felt a streak of sweat dampen his shirt in the middle of his back. Before he made it to the last page, he stopped reading. He didn't see the finale of the battle, the conclusion of *HEROES UNDER FIRE.* He just closed the comic book and slid it back to his nephew.

He clamped his eyes shut for a moment, then lit a cigarette, sucking down the smoke hard and fast. He looked out the front of Clark's store window, at his Indian Four leaning on its kickstand, at Main Street, at a patch of sky over the buildings across the street. The day was beginning to make the turn toward dusk, from midday light to the afternoon's darker shade of amber. For a few seconds, he'd been very, very far away, even forgetting that little Robby was on the stool beside him.

What the fuck am I doing here in fucking Lone Butte and Clark's fucking drugstore?

He turned to his nephew. "You okay with your homework, Robby?"

"Homework?" Robby didn't know what that meant, watching his uncle get up from the counter and go to the drugstore's front door.

"Lowell, keep an eye on this slugger for me?"

"He's good with me," Lowell said. "Okey doke, little man?"

Robby nodded, with the straw of his drink in his mouth, working perfectly in its delivery of ice-cream-flavored cola.

"Thanks." Bob left Clark's Drugs, passed his motorcycle static on its kickstand, and walked out of sight in the direction of the Shed.

★ ★ ★

Robby Andersen would forever recall certain moments of that long August afternoon when his uncle Bob left him sitting at the counter of Clark's Drugstore. He flipped through all the comic books in front of him many times, studying the drawings and coloring, lingering on the advertisements aimed at the kid readers, the funny faces made by Professor MacQuack and his pond-school pupils, the horses and animals of the Triple Q Ranch, and the simplicity of the drawings in *Little Dot*. He wondered how soon he would learn to read in kindergarten. Maybe then he would understand the Phantom.

He spent the most time going over the panels of *HEROES UNDER FIRE* awed by the renderings of real-world events, almost like the photographs in magazines. He wanted to draw with the same fidelity, with equal authenticity: tilting, roaring tanks and jeeps, the trunks of splintered palm trees, the muzzle flashes of machine guns and the movement of slashing bayonets, the helmets and eyes of fighting Marines, the thin slot openings of the small forts where the Japanese enemy was hiding.

Despite his age-appropriate illiteracy, he could make sense of the story like it was an old-fashioned silent movie: The Marines had fought bravely from the beach and into the jungle. Bombs fell on them. Many were killed and wounded. The Japanese soldiers were shooting machine guns from a cement fort, trapping the Americans in holes and behind fallen logs. The Americans threw little bombs at the openings of the concrete fort, but the Japanese soldiers kept firing, unhurt. The Marine with the welding tanks on his back, the one who shot fire—"That's me," Uncle Bob had said—crawled through sand and jungle, almost getting shot time and time again until he was closer to the cement fort than any of the other Marines. One panel of the book showed the Marine, Robby's uncle, crouched down with the tank on his back and a spark of a flame igniting on his special weapon-gun. *Click-click-click* went the spark. The next panel showed Uncle Bob gritting his teeth with a cigarette clamped there, unlit. In the next panel, which took up half the comic book's page, Uncle Bob had sprung out of his cover, firing a massive stream of orange, yellow, and crimson-red flame, a *comet* that splashed and burned into the slotted opening of the enemy bunker. The drawing looked so real Robby sensed the heat of the flames.

The almost-five-year-old boy lost track of the time he sat at the soda fountain counter. Uncle Bob's motorcycle was still parked out front. Customers came and went. A waitress named Marnie took up the tending of the counter just before 5:00 p.m., which was when Lowell Strueller was set to get off work. Lowell had stepped out onto the sidewalk repeatedly, looking up and down Main Street, hoping to see Bob on his way back to collect his nephew. After a whispered exchange with Marnie, Lowell told Robby to sit tight, that he would be right back, that he thought he knew where his uncle had gone off to.

Lowell was not a drinking man. He'd not been into the Shed Tavern but once, for a promised free beer the day after he came back from the service. That was almost two years ago.

The motorcycles, lined up in front of the Shed, were similar to the one Bob Falls had ridden up on, with the Andersen boy on his lap. Jukebox music was coming from inside the bar, and a few bits of conversation. As he stepped into the darkness of the place, his eyes needed time to adjust from sunlight to beer-hall shadow. For a moment, he couldn't see anything.

"Bob Falls? You in here?" Lowell could make out a few figures at the bar, others at the pool table.

"Who wants to know?" The voice was unfamiliar and challenging.

"I'm looking for Bob Falls," Lowell said. "He come in here?" By now Lowell made out the four men, dressed in worn work clothes, wearing heavy leather boots; the motorcycle riders were the Shed's only patrons. Two were playing eight-ball, circling the pool table, holding their cue sticks like weapons. Two were at the bar, one sitting, one standing, the bartender across from them, arms folded, leaning back against the display shelves with the long line of liquor bottles.

"Yeah, Lowell, I'm in here." He was sitting on a stool in a dark corner by the pool table. A tall glass of draft beer, half gone, was beside him on a matching high table. Bob, too, had a pool cue in his hand, the heel of the stick on the floor, like it was a cane. Three players at the pool table meant the game wasn't eight-ball. It was cutthroat. "What can I do for you?"

"You coming back for your boy?" Lowell asked.

The challenging voice croaked up. "Your boy? You been a daddy all this time?" There was a guffaw among the men in the heavy boots. The barkeep laughed out loud.

Bob laughed, too. He finishing the lower half of his pilsner before saying to Lowell "Whip him up another soda, would you, boss? I'll be there in a bit of the by-and-by."

The four men, and the bartender, started singing a poorly performed chorus of "In the Sweet By-and-By." Lowell heard them laughing as he walked back out into the waning sunshine of Main Street.

Rather than ply Robby with more flavored pop, Marnie had given the boy a glass of milk with Ovaltine, which was fine with Robby, but honestly, he wanted to be home and not at Clark's Drugstore anymore. He wanted his uncle to "fetch" him, to sit him back on the big saddle of his roaring motorcycle and ride him again through the streets of Lone Butte, maybe passing by the old, ruined house that was said to be a haunted orphanage (it was neither) and the construction site where tractor-trailers had been delivering huge steel girders.

When Lowell came through the front door, he walked straight past the counter to the rear of the store, behind the pharmacy counter, to the telephone. He dialed Commonwealth 0-121 for the police station by the county courthouse. He reported that some bad elements were currently drinking at the Shed, and what with some of the things that had gone on downstate, someone might want to stop in there and, you know, suggest that leaving town would be a good idea. Asked for a few more details, Lowell mentioned the motorcycles. That seemed to give the policeman who took the call all he needed to hear.

"One of them is Bob Falls," Lowell told the cop on the line. "He's from here." Lowell hung up the phone, satisfied that he'd been a good citizen, and came around from behind the pharmacy counter.

"Robby, do you know where you live?" he asked.

"*Uh-hmm.*" Robby finished the last of the Ovaltine through the straw. "One fourteen Elm Street."

"Let me run you home."

"What happened to the uncle?" Marnie asked.

Lowell rolled his eyes and shook his head—*not in front of the boy*. "Let's go, slugger," he told Robby.

"Thank you, Miss Marnie," Robby said, climbing down from his perch on the stool.

"You are quite welcome. Don't forget your reading." She squared up the five comic books for the polite Andersen boy.

Lowell led him to the back of the store, through the stockroom filled with boxes and shelves of goods, past a closet where cleaning mops and buckets were standing. Parked outside the heavy metal exit door that said DELIVERY was Lowell's prewar Chrysler.

Robby sat, leaning forward in what Lowell called the shotgun seat. He listened with no comments other than "Yes" and "Uh-uh" to a steady stream of questions from Lowell about liking baseball and looking forward to going back to school.

Ernie was home, in his stocking feet, reading the *Daily Press* in his La-Z-Boy, when Lowell walked Robby to the front door and explained the how and the why of what the afternoon had wrought. Ernie thanked Lowell for bringing Robby home, but he did not like any of it, not one bit.

A few minutes later the telephone rang. E-K was calling for Lulu. Word had quickly spread about an incident at the Shed— some hoodlums were asked to leave town sooner rather than later.

One of them, who said he was a local boy back in town to visit his family, took a swing at one of the "fucking badged fuckers." The five toughs—one had parked his motorcycle in front of Clark's Drugs—were escorted to the city limits north of town. Official calls were made to police departments all the way to Redding to keep an eye out for a motorcycle gang that might show up and bring trouble.

For the rest of his life, Robby would remember Lulu crying into the phone and the look on his mother's face as she finished preparing the dinner of pork chops, sweet potatoes, macaroni salad, and an apricot cobbler, a feast she meant to share with her little brother. He'd recall his father's angry scowl at the dinner table. "Everyone in town will hear about it," Ernie said, again and again through dinner.

Before his bath, Robby saw his mother take the folded sheets, blanket, and the pillow—the makings of Uncle Bob's "rack" on the sofa—and put them in the hamper to wash in the morning.

★   ★   ★

Robby started learning how to read that autumn—he began kindergarten just after Labor Day. His unofficial primer was the story of his uncle Bob as rendered in *HEROES UNDER FIRE*. He couldn't figure out all the words at first, but over time (by second grade) he knew them all, knew the entire saga of "I was a flamethrower." He kept the comic book, and all the others he began to buy, storing them first on his bedroom shelves, later in cheap footlockers, and, eventually, in cardboard boxes, so many that he moved them up into the narrow attic at 114 Elm Street, sharing space with his father's wartime Army Air Corps footlocker. During a rainstorm so heavy the river overflowed and the schools were closed, leaks in the roof brought water into the attic, much of it absorbed by the paper comic books in the cardboard boxes. Robby himself threw away the water-damaged boxes and their contents with no remorse. They were just cheap comic books after all.[*]

---

[*] Kept in perfect condition, the collection would be worth between thirty and fifty thousand dollars on today's market.

For the rest of his youth, and well beyond, Robby drew. He was the most gifted student in every art class at Adams Junior High, then Union High. He entered pieces in the county fair and won blue ribbons every summer. In 1957 his watercolor painting of children jumping off the trestle bridge into the Big Iron Bend River was chosen as Lone Butte's official entry at the state fair in Sacramento—for which he won the Governor's Award. Both local papers put Robby's picture on the front page, and for a few weeks he was famous around town as YOUNG MAN IS LONE BUTTE'S CELEBRATED ARTIST.

After Uncle Bob's visit, odd feelings came to color the remaining days of little Robby's summer. He seemed to have a new pair of eyes that noticed worldly details he'd never seen before. Only five years old, he became aware of the sun coming down earlier, causing light that streamed through the front sycamores to become softer, *warmer* if that was the word for it; less white, more orange-yellow, a color called amber. He noticed that the plum trees in the mini orchard out back were losing their fruit and flowers, their branches becoming naked sticks with each passing week. He caught his mother's long, silent looks out the kitchen window and baby Nora's habit of singing songs to herself with no prompting.

He kept to his artwork, now not so much for the fun of it, but because, well, he needed to capture the thought in his head, to get a drawing *right,* to have the shapes, figures, and colors tell a story he had yet to learn.

He expected his uncle to return to Lone Butte—first for his birthday in September, then for the Fall Back-to-School Night, his father's birthday on the twenty-sixth of October, and for Thanksgiving dinner. But Bob Falls never showed up.

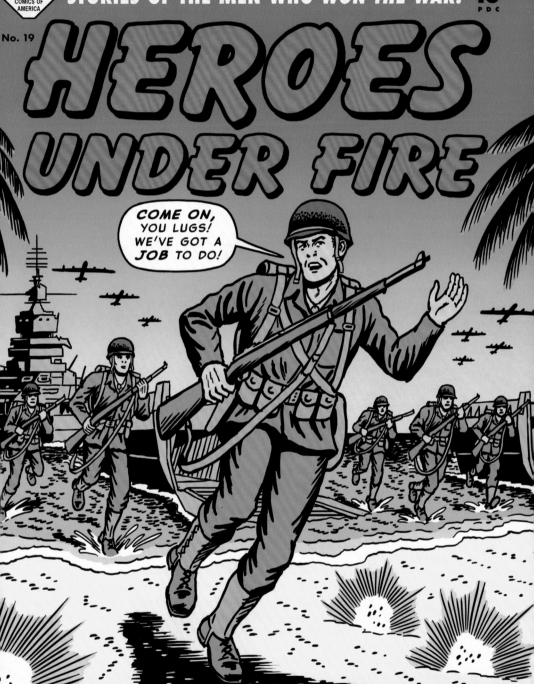

KIDS! SELL THE WEEKLY WIRE!

The newspaper just for Kids like YOU!
ALL the important news of the week
FROM AROUND THE WORLD! Sports! Culture! Fun!
A full page of SPECIAL GAMES in every Issue!

WRITE NOW FOR HOW YOU
can collect subscriptions and
deliver *THE WEEKLY WIRE*
in your neighborhood and
town so you can earn these
valuable prizes:

Dolls

Toy Cars, Planes, Trains

Tea Set

Make-Your-Self Radio Set

Leather Kit

Bike For Boys

Bike For Girls

Tiny Sewing Machine

Footlocker Full Of Toy Soldiers

Pen & Pencil Set

Army Set – Trucks, Jeeps, Tanks, Cannons

Air Force Set – Fighters, Bombers, Rockets

Navy Set – Battleships, Destroyers, Submarines

Telescope

Nurses Set – Toy Stethoscope, Hypodermic Needle, Magnifying Glass

Microscope

Small Typewriter

Wood-Burning Set

Chemistry Set

Magic-Kit

Aquarium

Chess/Checkers Set

Harmonica

Banjo

Guitar

"Learn The Piano!"

Small Accordion

Knitting Needles

Small Phonograph

Costume Jewelry

AND LOTS MORE!

Send now for our FREE Application:

THE WEEKLY WIRE
114 Elm Street, Omaha, Nebraska

Name...
Address...
City..
State...

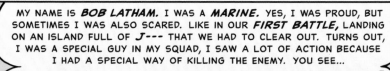

MY NAME IS **BOB LATHAM.** I WAS A **MARINE.** YES, I WAS PROUD, BUT SOMETIMES I WAS ALSO SCARED. LIKE IN OUR **FIRST BATTLE,** LANDING ON AN ISLAND FULL OF **J---** THAT WE HAD TO CLEAR OUT. TURNS OUT, I WAS A SPECIAL GUY IN MY SQUAD, I SAW A LOT OF ACTION BECAUSE I HAD A SPECIAL WAY OF KILLING THE ENEMY. YOU SEE...

I WAS A FLAME THROWER!

"NONE OF US HAD **SLEPT,** KNOWING WHAT WAS AHEAD FOR US..."

"THEY COULDN'T KEEP US FROM **TAKING THE BEACH...**"

1

"THE *FRONT LINE* WAS JUST UP AHEAD BEYOND THE TREE LINE..."

"I WAS NERVOUS, AND *LIT UP* SOME OF THE JUNGLE JUST TO LET THE BAD GUYS KNOW I WAS THERE..."

LATHAM! MAKE A HOLE AND BE READY! WE'LL NEED YOU SOON!

"I WAITED BEHIND A TREE TRUNK AS THE BATTLE *RAGED* AROUND ME..."

"ALL I COULD DO WAS FLICK MY *IGNITER*..."

CLICK-CLICK-CLICK...

"WHEN THE *WOUNDED* BEGAN COMING BACK, I KNEW THE SQUAD HAD GOTTEN BOGGED DOWN..."

2

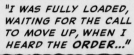

"I WAS FULLY LOADED, WAITING FOR THE CALL TO MOVE UP, WHEN I HEARD THE ORDER..."

WE NEED A *FLAMETHROWER* UP HERE, *NOW!*

PING!

"THE SQUAD HAD RUN INTO AN *ENEMY BUNKER*..."

"THEY WERE SAFE BEHIND A *WALL* OF *CONCRETE*, ABLE TO FIRE ON US AT WILL..."

RAT-A-TAT!
RAT-A-TAT!

WE'RE *PINNED DOWN*, LATHAM. GET AS CLOSE AS YOU CAN AND *LIGHT 'EM UP!*

OKAY, SARGE...

3

"THOSE #@%S HAD *DIED* FOR THEIR EMPEROR..."

"I WAS CALLED ON *MANY TIMES* IN THE WEEKS TO COME..."

"THE ENEMY WAS HIDING *ALL OVER* THAT ISLAND."

"BUT I FOUND THEM WITH MY *FLAME*..."

"THAT WAS MY *JOB. I WAS A FLAME-THROWER*..."

PFC *ROBERT LATHAM,* U.S.M.C., WAS AWARDED THE *BRONZE STAR* FOR HIS BRAVERY.

AND NOW, OUR NEXT STORY OF... *HEROES UNDER FIRE...*

TREV-VORR

Robby Andersen could rightly claim to have attended the cultural horror show that was the free rock concert held at the Altamont Motor Speedway, but without hearing Santana, the Flying Burrito Brothers, or the headlining act, the Rolling Stones, to name just some on the bill. He and thousands of other fans had expected to be a part of the next Woodstock, another day and night of Peace, Love, and Music. What Robby and his carload of stoned pals actually experienced was miles and miles of stilled autos, a daylong slog on foot, and hours and hours of misery, aggravation, and public urination. When they finally made it within eyesight of the stage, there was nothing going on save an escalating tension in the air. And they were hungry. So, back to Robby's Fiat they hiked, and drove home by way of a Denny's in Castro Valley. Yes, they missed Crosby, Stills, Nash & Young, but they also avoided the beatings and deaths, which they read about in the newspapers the next morning. Such things happen when a motorcycle gang is hired as event security.*

Whatever had been in the air, water, or drugs in San Francisco had gone bye-bye by January of 1971. The so-called Summer of Love had been vaporized by many, many social ills, primarily the war in Vietnam, a nation roughly the size of California on the other side of the Pacific Ocean. Again and again, more and more, the news stories of the day were of riots, of protests (and counterprotests to Love America or Leave It), of rocks being thrown more often than flowers, of offing the pigs and reserving the right to refuse service to anyone, of still more dead in Vietnam, and of new corpses—four college kids who were shot in Ohio. One of the

---

* Three and a half years earlier Robby had lucked into the last public performance of the Beatles by walking up to the gate and buying a seat in half-filled Candlestick Park.

few positives one could say about the start of the new decade: at least there'd been no more assassinations. Nineteen seventy was 365 days of volatility and anger and division; some families had not sat down at the same table for Thanksgiving dinner or opened presents on Christmas morning in the same home since Nixon won the White House.

Not so for the surviving Andersens. On both holidays, Nora flew up from Los Angeles to Oakland, where Robby picked her up in that Fiat, then together they made the drive to Lone Butte, laughing all the way, over the bridges and through the traffic to stay with their mother and little sister, Stella, in the new development of cheap but tidy "town houses" called Franzel Meadows. Robby missed the old house in town, they all did, but with Dad dead and gone for ten years and Mom not being the Lulu of a girl she once was, the house at 114 Elm was a waste of space and a lot of work. All this spoke to the purgatory that Lone Butte had become; the Westinghouse Light factory was down to a single working shift, and there was but one place in town to buy shoes. Clark's Drugs served a limited menu for breakfast and lunch. Folks drove to Chico to shop for Christmas. The State Theater played "adult films" on Friday midnights, some in a primitive 3D process that required cardboard glasses with one red, one blue, lens. The trains no longer stopped in Welles, but the interstate, seventeen miles to the west, had two gas stations and a cluster of new fast-food outlets—McDonald's, Arctic Circle, Kreme Palace, and Lord Butley's Fish & Chips Shoppe. Lone Butte was not so much a hometown for two of the Andersen children but an arrow on an exit sign.

Robby had long ago moved to the Bay Area, a three-and-a-half-hour trek by Fiat.

He'd gone to Cal Arts and taught drawing, painting, and ceramics for the public schools in Berkeley and the Parks Department in Oakland. He freelanced for production houses and theater companies, lived with one woman in the Haight in San Francisco, another woman in the Noe Valley during the fun years, smoked a ton of dope at Giants and Oakland A's baseball games. Baseball and being stoned went wonderfully well together. Anything went wonderfully well when Robby was stoned. As his peers moved on to other, harder drugs—hallucinogenics, narcotics, and addictive stimulants—Robby wondered why. Pot was just so *great*!

He'd planned to do his military service before Kennedy was shot—John Fitzgerald not Robert Francis—but the Coast Guard DQ'd him due to a congenital heart condition he didn't even know he had. In early 1971, the draft and Vietnam were no worry, and at twenty-eight he'd landed the most perfect job on the planet after painting the refrigerator of a girl he was seeing in San Mateo. He took her white Kenmore and re-created it, appliance-wise, as a TV playing *The Wizard of Oz* with the flying monkeys coming out of the screen and SURRENDER, DOROTHY written on the sky that was the freezer door. His inventiveness was a hit, and from it a fellow artist named Zelko said he should come and draw for Kool Katz Komix.

★   ★   ★

The headquarters for the Katz was a former vacuum cleaner store in Oakland on Telegraph Avenue, and the place was a great hang. Black Panthers used the mimeograph machines and offset printers—free of charge. Famous fans dropped in to drop out for a few hours, including a wide receiver for the Oakland Raiders, musicians from bands like the Loading Zone and Traffic, and the millionaire who started a UHF-TV channel in San Jose so he could host the weekend monster movie. Robby took on a pen name— *TREV-VORR*—to become a full-time artist in pencil, pen, and ink.* Anyone looking for either person was out of luck, for the staff always knew to say that Robby Andersen was gone for the day, and *TREV-VORR* hadn't shown up—whichever was necessary. Many of the Kool Katz were avoiding someone in their lives, certain unfortunate circumstances, uncomfortable facts of their pasts, or threats to their futures. Oddballs wandered in off Telegraph all the time, some very funny, many very political and argu-

---

* *TREV-VORR* came from the name of a little white terrier owned by the landlord of the Kool Katz HQ. Poor thing got run over by a car on Telegraph, and the shop went into mourning.

mentative, some very *tweaked* or very stoned, depending on their drugs of choice, some narcs and undercover cops who were hilariously inept at blending in. There was a wall switch that turned on a blue lightbulb over the front door whenever the police were making the scene, so anyone holding or just wanting to avoid Oakland's Finest was duly warned. None of the John-Laws ever figured that one out. None of the Kool Katz ever got busted, not on premises, anyway.

Most everyone in the office was usually stoned or looking to get stoned. Music from KSAN-FM played all day as the staff and the visitors laughed and ate and smoked. Robby/*TREV-VORR* would sit at his slanted table and draw. Others wrote the komix with stick figures and descriptions of the panels, which Robby would turn into graphic short stories with pen, ink, and *fucking genius.* Some of the titles were popular, all were subversive, some hardly distinguishable from pornography. *TREV-VORR* drew them, and Kool Katz paid in checks that cleared into kold hard kash.

Many of the women who drifted into the office found themselves lingering because of *TREV-VORR,* beguiled by his quiet demeanor, deep-set eyes, and those liquid hands that could turn pencil on paper into something as small as the eye of an ant or as vast as the entire cosmos.

"You are the only true artist I've ever known," said a girl named Beth, who had grown up in Hayward and had been a sophomore at Cal before discovering pot. Beth made *TREV-VORR* her live-with soul mate, his happiness her life's work, dedicating herself to pleasing him in every way. She fixed up an apartment in the hills, which had a back-porch view of the three bridges that spanned the bay.* For almost five months Beth had never felt so whole, so in love with a place, with a spirit, as she did with the man called *TREV-VORR.* Then one weekend she changed her name to Pandora and moved to the woods near the Russian River with a guy who made his own LSD. Robby lost Pandora but kept her box—the apartment, the back porch, the triple-bridge view.

* The San Mateo, the San Francisco–Oakland, and, in clear skies, the Golden Gate.

On a weekday in January, Robby smoked a joint as he drove to work—the windows of his Fiat cracked to suck out excess haze—then parked in an empty space on Telegraph without bothering to lock the doors. With no radio and nothing of value in the car there was no reason to break into the boxy sedan; there was nothing in it to rip off. If the car got stolen, Robby would claim the insurance and feel sorry for the idiot who stole a Fiat with close to eighty thousand miles.

It was after three in the afternoon, with no blue lightbulb on over the entry door, when Robby found a thick letter on his drawing table addressed to both his actual self and his Katz persona.

> *Robby Andersen*
> *c/o Trev-vorr the Great*
> *1447 Telegraph Ave*
> *Oakland Calif.*

"Trev-vorr the Great" was how Stella Andersen ragged on her big brother with his fancy nom-de-pencil. The postmark, over three six-cent, first-class-mail stamps, said LONE BUTTE, CALIF. A single page of Stella's swoopy handwriting explained an enclosed second letter—a sealed, unopened envelope.

> *Robby,*
> *Look what arrived at the old house. The Post Office knew to bring it out to our place. Mom's brother Bob wrote her and you—out of the blue. I read his letter to Mom but I'm not sure it registered with her. For a while she thought I was reading a letter from you. The guy has been through a lot and is, kind of, apologizing to her.*
> *Did I ever meet our Uncle Bob? Was I a baby? Did he come to Dad's funeral?*
> *Next month, I am going to bring Mom down to the City so I can get out of Lonely BUTTOCK. Can you meet us for a long lunch? Maybe in Chinatown? Only if Mom feels good enough to make the trip. Nora said she would try to fly up on PSA for the day. NO PRESSURE.*
>
> *Love you,*
> *Stella-by-Starlight*

The letter from Uncle Bob had been mailed from Rio Rancho, New Mexico, using twelve cents of stamps. In the return-address corner was a small, narrow sticker, the kind ordered from a send-away bargain catalog, *Mr. & Mrs. R. Falls,* and a tiny American flag. The midsize envelope had the address typewritten on an adhesive label:

ROBBY ANDERSEN
114 ELM STREET
LONE BUTTE, CALIFORNIA
PLEASE FORWARD IF NECESSARY

Robby/*TREV-VORR* weighed the thickness of the letter in his hand as an image of his uncle Bob shimmered into his brain. Being stoned helped: his father and Uncle Bob, sitting in the backyard of the old house on Elm under the plum trees, drinking beer from cans, the kind little Robby would slice open for them with a church key. His father—ridiculously fit and young, leaning on his elbows with his eyes locked on his brother-in-law. Bob Falls—in jeans and boots and a white T-shirt, swayed back in his chair, smoking a cigarette, a wandering god visiting from Valhalla. At his drawing table, Robby's mind turned to details of those boots—his father's steel-toed for the shop floor, his uncle's with straps and buckles for riding motorcycles—and the sumptuous plum trees reaching into the cloudless sky, the cans of beer held in strong fists. *TREV-VORR* took up a soft-lead pencil, drawing twin silhouettes of the two men, laughing, lighting cigarettes with a Zippo lighter.

After re-creating the sight and manner of his uncle in five pages of rough sketches, Robby remembered the letter and opened it up with a penknife he kept on his table to sharpen drawing points.

The folded pages had been typed on some old manual machine— the words pounded into the paper, with extra care and with what must have been a brand-new ribbon and rigorous purpose. The typeface had protracted irregularities—the capital *T*s were slightly cantered, all the *S*s were a hair low on the line, and the *M*s were rectangular boxes of solid-black ink. Each page was single spaced and crammed from the left edge to the right. The letter carried weight.

Christmas 1970

Dear Robby,
    I have owed you this letter for a very long time . . .

*   *   *

By 1959, Bob Falls was on his own.

Years earlier some of the guys had joined back up for Korea, to be Marines once more, to sail back across the Pacific Ocean and kill different Asian people. In the summer of 1950, Bob considered returning to war, if only to help train the Marines who would do the killing. The pay would be steady and a bit better than what he'd been scrounging up as a civilian. Then Kirkland got stabbed pretty bad in a fight up in Eugene and didn't get out of the hospital until a lung specialist had operated on him four times. Doggit fell for a girl in Susanville and wouldn't leave. Bob didn't like that at all—the woman was married to a fellow in the air force, a guy in Korea. But Doggit was in love, so Bob, Butch, and Hal left him, riding on to Reno, the Biggest Little City of transients, i.e., many men and plenty of women waiting out the six-week residency laws to qualify for easy divorces. Wouldn't you know it, in the coffee shop at the Mapes Hotel and Casino, Hal met a waitress just a month short of being an ex-wife, keeping her company until and after her no-fault papers were official.

Bob took a job washing dishes to plant some bank in his wallet, then he and Butch rode south. They stopped anywhere they damn well pleased. By '53 they'd met up with some other guys like them, rode for a while, had some great days, got in trouble here and there, and moved on. In '54 Bob had a scrape with the law that took him off the road: six months in a work camp cutting fire lanes in the Angeles Crest National Forest, the state paying twenty cents an hour, so he got out with close to $250.

In '56 there was a pretty big set-to in Needles—some of the organized gangs were staking their claims by then, so it was not unusual to read headlines like TURF WARS BETWEEN RIVAL BIKER GANGS. When those power plays progressed from busted-bone fights into lethal shoot-outs, Bob wanted no part of them and moved along, pronto. Good thing, as two highway patrolmen were shot dead by some idiot on a Harley-Davidson in Baker, and ever since anyone on any motorcycle was a possible suspect.

By 1958, Bob Falls had been riding solo and drinking more than was good for him—beer all day and whatever at night, often just more beer. Drunk tanks all over Southern California had been his weekend sleeping quarters. He did three months in a county jail for low-grade aggravated assault; he not only took a swing at a sheriff, but he also cracked the kid's jaw!* Oh, he'd wrecked his motorcycle in Indio, fracturing his hip in the accident. So, in 1959, Bob Falls was walking slower than ever, riding a former Police Model Harley-Davidson Panhead that he got cheap at an auction because its front fork had been damaged.

The beer in Flagstaff, Arizona, was just as cold, smooth, and satisfying as beer anywhere else, so he'd stayed around longer than he thought he would, into the second week of August. There was a job in Gallup he knew of, something to do with a roofing company; steady bank would not be a bad thing, and he'd always liked New Mexico, so he decided to head that way. But, as though a force of gravity was keeping him there, he never got around to leaving the confines of Flagstaff. He laid out his bedroll in a field behind a Seventh-day Adventist church, making sure he wasn't around when they worshipped. He took up with some guys at a place called the Fireside, mostly other veterans, who had regular jobs and would spring for the constant pitchers of Black Label, Hamm's, or Falstaff, so the dwindling bank of folding money in Bob's jeans (and the wad he kept in his boot) was rarely touched. But one night, some cops walked into the Fireside because a cabdriver complained that one of the patrons had stiffed him on a fare. Bob Falls, who had long ago become adept at avoiding fucking badged fuckers, found a way to drift out of the place, unnoticed. He slept one last night as an unseen guest of the Seventh-day faithful, and now was just a few coffee cups away from finishing a meal and finally riding east on the 66, hoping to make Gallup with stops only for a tank of gas, a piss, a beer, and a night under the stars.

---

* That sheriff was only twenty-three years old.

★ ★ ★

The coffee shop was a modern place, with red vinyl booths, each with a small, cookie-jar-sized jukebox. The breakfast rush was in midswing as Bob, at the counter, sat alone, carrying the kind of countenance that made other customers naturally leave an empty seat on either side of him. His waitress was old enough to be his mother—a woman doing her job, serving this red-eyed biker type in the hope that, maybe, he'd leave a tip the size of a dime. If she served him enough coffee, maybe he'd stop smelling of beer.

He ordered a big breakfast of steak and three eggs sunny-side up, home fries, and four slices of toasted white bread to soak up the yolks. He wanted something sweet as well, choosing a waffle over a short stack of pancakes, filling the little squares with a lion's share of butter and a wash of syrup. He drank two large glasses of orange juice from concentrate and never let his coffee cup go empty. He ate slowly, listening to the jukebox selections on unseen, tinny speakers—"Running Bear" by Johnny Preston played twice. He let his eyes wander over the customers in the booths—the families on the road with the little kids and mothers-in-law, the Johnny Square salesmen or business owners, a trio of ranch hands who ate with their hats on. Bob pondered the lives of such folks and, for a flicker of a moment, envied the regularity of their days, their routine, the expectations that, at the end of any day, could be judged as met. They all had order in their lives. Structure.

With his breakfast done and plates empty, the waitress removed all but the coffee cup. Bob lit a Chesterfield from his dwindling supply with his eagle-globe-and-anchor USMC Zippo. With refills of coffee that he neither needed nor particularly enjoyed, he lingered and smoked. He'd wait until his breakfast was digested, use the restroom, and then be on his way with nothing ahead of him but the long solo ride east on 66.

He eyed a family in a booth—three kids, a granny, a hangdog father with a wife who looked a bit like Ingrid Bergman. Before digging into their food, they all bowed their heads and clasped their hands in picture-perfect positions of prayer as the dad said something under the din of the rattle and chatter of the restaurant. Even the little kids mouthed "amen" on cue at the end of grace. Ingrid Bergman cut up pancakes for the children and they all began to eat.

"Amen," Bob said to himself, ready to be on his way. He left a fifty-cent tip, remembering the many waitresses he'd slept with who lived more on gratuities than on salaries.

At the cashier, he found he was down to twenty-four dollars and change. And he was out of cigarettes.

He put twenty-five cents into the cigarette vending machine in the entryway to the restaurant, pulled the knob, and fished a pack of Chesterfields from the tray at the bottom of the machine. As he stood up, at eye level, he noticed a bulletin board, covered with business cards, lost-and-found notices, postcards with funny sayings, personal messages, and for-sale offerings. A LOST PUPPY notice was a month old. Either the pooch had been found by now or was living on a heavenly farm up in the mountains. Beside it was pinned a newly posted tract asking DO YOU KNOW GOD LOVES YOU? WOULD YOU LIKE TO KNOW HIS PLAN FOR YOUR LIFE? READ THIS AND LEARN THE GOOD NEWS!

Above the Bible tract was a small tacked-on note card.

Dishwasher Wanted
Good $
Call *ANGEL* MEsa 2-1414

Bob had been a dishwasher at the Mapes in Reno and other places since. He didn't mind the hot, wet work and this fact: the only people who talk to dishwashers are the other dishwashers.

Everyone else tells them what needs to be done, then leaves them be. Bob liked being left alone, ignored along with the Negroes and Mexicans who washed dishes on a permanent basis. The meals were free, so Bob's pearl-diver wages went for beer, gas, a room somewhere, and the women who needed to be with a guy like him for a while. Washing dishes could fill a man's pockets with bank— and quitting the job and the women was as easy as leaving whenever you pleased. Bob thought of the roofing job waiting in Gallup, where he'd be working outdoors, banging nails, lifting shingles or tiles, and hot-mopping tar. There was something in his head saying an *indoor* job might be a nice thing for a while.

Phone calls cost a nickel in the phone booth that had a collaps-
ing door that turned on a light when you closed it for privacy. A little metal plate of a table made a spot to write down notes. Bob slid
an Indian head five-cent piece into the slot, heard it drop and the
phone *cleeng-cleeng*. The line rang and rang, so long Bob almost
gave up to collect his nickel from the coin return, and ride off to the
roofs of Gallup.

"Yeah?" A woman had picked up. She had a slight accent—like
a Mexican or someone of the Indian tribes.

"You still looking for a dishwasher?" Bob asked.

"What?" the lady asked. "We open at four."

"I'm reading a note says you need a dishwasher."

"Oh." The woman on the phone said nothing more.

"Do you?" Bob thought he heard the woman take a drink of
something, a sip. "Can I talk to Angel?"

"I need a dishwasher, yes. Can you start today?"

"I can start now."

"We're closed until four. Come at three. I pay a dollar an hour,
but you get some tips, too."

"Are there meals?"

"Yes. But drinks no. Pepsi you pay for. See you at three. Not
before."

"Three. Okay. But where do I go?"

"You come here."

"Where is here?"

"You don't know our place?"

"I only know your phone number from this card. Mesa 2-1414."

"Are you a hobo? If you're a hobo, never mind."

"Hobo?"

"You're passing through? Never mind. Go away."

"Wait," Bob said, not sure why he was not already off the phone
and on his Panhead, five cents lighter. "Can I talk to Angel?"

"You are," the woman, Angel, said.

Bob Falls wanted to be clear about himself to a person on the
phone he didn't know from Eve. "I'm not a hobo. I'm a dishwasher.
It's pretty simple."

"I don't hire hobos."

"I'm not a hobo."

"What are you then?"

"Angel, I'm a professional washer of dishes, pots and pans, skillets and bowls."

"You have to mop up at closing, too. You stay on for a month or don't come in."

"Okay." Why Bob Falls agreed to the job then and there would forever be a mystery to him. Yet, he sensed a settling of his equilibrium, that his commitment to staying a full month in one place—Flagstaff—was the most instinctive move he'd made in a long, long time.

"A month. Dollar an hour," Angel told him again. "Come at three to the Dough Bun Guy."

"Where is that?"

"On 66 across from the giant man holding a big tire." Angel hung up.

★   ★   ★

Bob spent a few hours finding a place to live—a small motel with no pool—a place no families driving through would consider, because if you had kids, you needed a pool. Fifteen dollars for a week left Bob very, very short—just two one-dollar bills and some change—but sometimes caution belonged in the wind. He took a hot shower and washed some clothes in the bathroom sink. He changed into his cleanest pants and wiped off his boots with a wet towel.

At 2:30 he rode up Route 66, easily finding a giant man holding a giant tire—Paul Bunyan waving a Re-cap—but damn if he could see a doughnut place or bakery or hot-dog stand called the Dough Bun Guy. There was a restaurant across from the Tire Giant, one with a sign that looked like it was written in Japanese. Oh, wait . . . DUPON GAI—CHOP SUEY CHOW MEIN. *Dough Bun Guy*. Bob laughed at himself, at the trick an ear hears. He was going to wash dishes at a Chinese-food joint. Fine.

He parked his motorcycle in the shade of the giant, then skiphopped across the highway when there was a break in the traffic. He didn't want to roar up to Dupon Gai—CHOP SUEY CHOW MEIN like one of those thug gang members he was too often thought to be. At 3:00 p.m., according to Bob's estimate (he wore no watch), he knocked on the restaurant window after rattling the locked door. The afternoon light reflected off the big windows, so all he saw was himself holding up his hand to shield his eyes. Then he could make out the form of a body crossing the floor inside, heard an inner door open and keys turning in the lock of the door he'd just tried.

When the door opened, he was face-to-face with a Chinese woman who was looking him up and down like she was being sold a ten-dollar horse.

"Are you the dishwasher?" *That was the accent,* Bob thought. *Not Mexican or Navajo. Chinese.*

"Yep. I'm here to see Angel."

She let Bob into her restaurant.

The place was done up in a lot of red and gold. There were three Chinese calendars on the walls with colorful renderings of seascapes and mountains and dragons along with the months of the year. On one wall there were two large, wide photos, one of the Golden Gate Bridge, the other of a street in Chinatown—GRANT STREET, the street sign said.

An old Chinese man in cook's whites sat in a booth smoking a filterless Camel between sips of tea from a very small cup with no handle. Two busboys in red jackets were neither Chinese nor boys. One was surely Mexican, the other some Tribesman of the Southwest; both were stacking dishes and bowls.

"Am I the only white guy working here?" Bob asked.

Angel stopped with a spin of her heel. "Oh, shit. I need you like I want a hole in my head." She strode back to the front door and pushed it open. "Out. Go away." She stood to the side to let Bob pass, to get out.

"But you need a dishwasher," Bob said.

"Not you. Go away."

"Hey, come on." Bob could sense a pleading in his voice, which was new for him. "I didn't mean anything." And, really, he hadn't.

"The position has been filled." Angel shot looks at the Mexican guys, like she was going to call on them in a second to toss this hobo out. They looked like they had done that very thing before.

"I'm sorry." Bob felt a flush of embarrassment. He was apologizing but wasn't sure why. This Angel woman made him feel like he was standing in the wrong line, or that he hadn't filled out the forms correctly.

Angel stood in the doorway, looking Bob up and down again. She cocked her head at the sight of his motorcycle boots, recently wiped clean with a wet rag. "You going to do the job or cause me problems? I have enough problems."

"I'll be no problem. I'll solve them." Bob felt himself smiling, something else that was new for him.

Angel looked like she was not so sure. "No drinking here. After we close, I don't care. But not here." Angel let the entry door swing shut and walked past Bob, heading for the kitchen door to the left of the big picture of Grant Street in Chinatown. The old cook watched Bob pass and took a sip of tea. The busboys were now sorting forks from spoons.

The kitchen was very small—there was the oven and stove, wide, round skillets hanging from hooks, a deep stainless-steel sink, a carving table. A restaurant kitchen. The dishwashing area was behind a draining trough with twin sinks of its own.

"What's your name?"

"Bob Falls. Are you Angel Dough-Bun Guy?"

"Dupon Gai is Grant Street in San Francisco. I'm Angel Lum. You saw my father out front. Call him Mr. Lum. Eddie and Luis work the tables. They'll show you how to keep the stations stocked. Clean dishes and setups. Sheila and Maria are the waitresses. They better show up soon. They share tips with the guys and you. A few bucks apiece on good nights. We'll eat before we open." Angel Lum stopped before leaving the kitchen. "You better learn something quick here, Bob Falls. You *are* the only white working here. Eddie is not a chief. Luis is not a spic. Use a word other than 'Sheila' and we'll all watch what happens. Maria, you best steer clear of until she decides about you. She's not fast chums with Anglos. I'm the boss here. I'm tough. I'm fair. But if you call me or my father anything other than Angel or Mr. Lum, I will chop your white dick off and toss it out onto Route 66." With that, Angel let the door swing behind her.

"Jesus," Bob said to himself, not meaning the Lord or any plan for his life.

*   *   *

Back at the Mapes, one of the short-order cooks who had started as a dishwasher—a Negro fellow by the name of Lucky Bill Johnson*—told Bob the important thing in the profession of washing dishes was water as hot as a man could stand. Scalding water made the job easier, as less scrubbing was needed, but tougher because a man had to take it, and some guys couldn't. The Mapes had machines you could run the dishes through, commercial-grade Hobarts. But the pans and skillets were done by hand with steel-wool burrs. Water as hot as Vulcan was called for and did much of the work. Bob discovered he could take the heat.

The Dupon Gai had no Hobart machine, so all of Angel Lum's dishes, bowls, cutlery, and ironmonger supply were washed by Bob's hands in hot, hot water. Bob kept one sink full of steaming, soapy broth, the other clear and hot as a sulfur spring. He rotated a steady load of plates, platters, and bowls from the drying rack to the stations out front, for Eddie and Luis. He kept a metal bucket for the cutlery with the same brutally professional hot water, letting each fork, knife, and spoon, and the funny-looking porcelain ladles for the soups, sit in a near-boiling soak before moving the bucket into the soapy sink, where he would go at them individually with a rough rag, one by one.

There were slow times when not a single dirty *anything* waited in Bob's dishwashing zone. Some guys always kept a few used dishes in the trough, grabbing them up when the boss came through the kitchen, so they'd look busy and working. But Bob was from the same school as Lucky Bill Johnson—when everything is clean go grab a smoke.

Mr. Lum spoke almost no English—born in China, he spoke Cantonese. The man was a damn good cook, even though Bob's idea of Chinese food was chop suey. Mr. Lum did things with chicken that Bob came to crave and had ways with pork that cold-cocked basic chops and were better even than spareribs. Chop suey was not allowed at the 3:00 p.m. staff meal. Chop suey wasn't even a real Chinese food, evidently. Bob didn't know that. Lo mein (the

* No relation to the filmmaker.

noodles) came in varied sauces. The truth was Mr. Lum made bet-ter food for the waitresses, busboys, and the dishwasher than was ordered by the white patrons.

Another thing Bob learned at the Dupon Gai: he'd been putting ketchup on his rice, so the Dupon Gai had to carry ketchup—until Angel couldn't take the sight of it any longer. She suggested Bob flavor his rice with what was in the little glass bottles on each table.

"I don't like beetle juice." Bob had tried soy sauce in Nagasaki after the war; it tasted like turpentine.

Angel leaned back in her chair at the table to give Bob the eye, then said something to her father, something in Cantonese. Bob didn't like that.

"It's soy sauce, Bob," Angel said. "Don't be so *ban cat*.* You probably used too much. Americans always do. And this is Chinese soy sauce."

"Is it different?"

"Of course, it is," Angel said, grabbing up the little bottle, let-ting a quick stream of the black liquid color a fresh bowl of the white rice. "Eat this. Ketchup on rice is just crazy."

"I like ketchup," Bob said. But when he tried the rice with the Chinese beetle juice, the saltiness and the flavor was okay. "That's pretty good," he admitted. "How is this different from the sauce I had in Japan?"

Instead of answering him, Angel laughed out loud for the first time since Bob took the job. She translated for her father in Can-tonese. Mr. Lum laughed, too. Bob had no idea why.

Thursday night was unofficially Chinese People Night at the Dupon Gai, when Flagstaff's small Asian community came to eat—along with the locals who knew authentic food when they ate it—to talk loudly with Angel and laugh even louder among them-selves. Bob had no idea any Chinese people lived in Flagstaff, Arizona—but the place was full, with patrons ordering dishes made special by Mr. Lum, food not on the menu. On Thursday nights Bob washed more chopsticks than forks.

One Chinese People Night, just before opening, Mr. Lum was in the kitchen, waving a knife and speaking Cantonese to Bob, point-

* Stupid dick. Cantonese.

ing to a half dozen whole chickens on the butcher-block cutting table. Bob dried his hands and took the knife from Mr. Lum, handle first. With another knife, Mr. Lum took a chicken and made a show of how he wanted Bob to cut it up. Bob's knife was as razor-sharp as he'd kept his Ka-Bar when he was in the service, and he followed the old man slice by slice. In a few minutes all the chickens were in pieces or diced or deboned, ready for whatever dish Mr. Lum had in mind. The old man seemed pleased, letting Bob know by going out front and coming back with bottles of Pepsi-Cola from the drink cooler, for the two of them. The next Thursday night, Mr. Lum showed Bob how to cut vegetables with a huge cleaver. There was a trick that, once learned, made chopping lightning quick. After that, even on nights that were not Thursdays, Mr. Lum had Bob chopping or deboning or cleaving something.

One Wednesday Angel came into the kitchen, saw Bob at the butcher's block, dicing pork, and laughed out loud. "Look at you, Bob." She was shaking her head. "Just look at you."

Of the waitresses, Sheila was the nice one, maybe because she had a lot of kids and work at the Dupon Gai was a reprieve for her. Maria never came to *like* Bob, but she didn't stiff him on his portion of her tips. Eddie and Luis would go out with Bob after closing, for beers at a place that stayed open late for kitchen workers from all around Flagstaff, the Buena Vista, which drew the only truly diverse crowd Bob had ever drunk with. His motorcycle pals had all been white. The Marines had all been white. Only in the big kitchen jobs and in jail had he eaten, worked, slept, dealt cards, and, occasionally, fist-fought with people of color.

Bob drank at the Buena Vista every night after work. He'd get back to his motel room around three in the morning with a six-pack of cold Falstaff, drinking them down as they warmed up in the absence of an icebox. There were plenty of mornings when Bob greeted the sunrise with a warm beer.

He'd get to the Dupon Gai at three in the afternoon, park his motorcycle in the back, then get himself a coffee. By opening time, all the stations were stocked, Mr. Lum had clean pots and woks, Angel had rechecked everything from the little bottles of soy sauce to the bin of fortune cookies, and Bob would have sweated out most of his beer from the night before.

"You drink too much beer," Angel Lum said to him on a particularly busy Friday night. She had come into the kitchen to singsong something in Cantonese to her father, who did not seem pleased at whatever she had told him. "I can smell your body odor from here."

"Am I fired?" Bob asked, not in a particularly good mood himself.

"No. But you stink."

Angel paid Bob in cash on Sunday nights, when they closed early, before ten, after the families, all dressed up for Sunday Night Out, had read their fortune cookies and gone home. Cash meant no taxes, no checks or banks.

By October his finances were better than they had ever been. Bob was legitimately *flush*. He'd taken up with a woman he'd met at the Buena Vista who called herself Kitty-Bee. Kitty-Bee was a little nutty—the kind of gal attracted to the motorcycle type. She, like Bob, enjoyed her share of cold Falstaff. She went at him in bed with a rough, pleasing need, then slept—out cold—until after he left for work. Kitty-Bee had a husband she was avoiding—either an ex or the real thing—in Fort Worth, Texas, so she was hiding in Flagstaff. Bob never asked if she had kids or not, but she seemed the type.

No one in Flagstaff ate chop suey on Mondays, so those were days off. Bob and Kitty-Bee would motorcycle around that corner of the Arizona territory—she, loving the speed and the feeling she got from holding on to a man, sometimes singing Patsy Cline songs into Bob's ear at fifty miles per hour.

When Bob came in one Tuesday, he wasn't feeling particularly great—the number of beers he'd shared with Kitty-Bee the day before had been more than usual. The staff was eating at a table with a lazy Susan in the middle. Bob lingered over his coffee, not saying much, when Angel sat beside him with a pot of tea and two of those tiny cups. Mr. Lum sat opposite, looking at his daughter and the dishwasher.

"I saw you with a lady, Bob," Angel said, pouring herself a tea.

"When?"

"Yesterday. She was holding on to you on the back of your motorcycle. I honked at you, but you didn't look. She did, though."

"Where?"

"Across town. I honked."

"Didn't hear you."

"She did. Who is she?"

"Her name is Charlotte. She's the head librarian at the main library across town. And the governor's daughter."

Angel laughed out loud and spoke Cantonese to her father. He laughed, too, in his way, and said something to Angel that made her laugh again.

"What did Pop-Pop say?" Bob had been calling Mr. Lum "Pop-Pop" for a week now.

"You wouldn't understand." Angel sipped her tea. "She like beer same as you?"

"No. Her father is against drinking, so I do it for her."

"Why do you drink so much beer, Bob?"

"Why do you sell chop suey in Flagstaff?"

"My father read about Hoover Dam, so we came to see it. The Grand Canyon, too. My mother and sisters said, 'Okay, we saw them,' and went back to San Francisco. Chinatown is a small place. We liked how big the sky is here. Flagstaff and the desert are good for our bones. Here, try this." Angel poured some tea into one of the small cups. Rather than bother to argue with her, Bob sipped the stuff. It was bitter. With some sugar, it might be okay. "Where are you from, Bob? Where did you grow up like you did?"

"You know Lone Butte?" Bob lit a Chesterfield. Angel didn't smoke, but he offered Pop-Pop a cigarette and a light.

"Where is that?"

"Throw a rock from Frisco a few hundred miles and you'd hit my hometown."

"In California?"

"Yep. Up the valley a ways."

"You know the city? San Francisco?"

"Been through a couple of times to see some friends and avoid some not-so-friendlies."

"You didn't go through the city in the war?"

"No. I came and went through San Diego."

"In the war when ships came in and the sailors got off, my sisters and I would go down to the docks to look at them in all those thirteen-button pants with the tight fronts. We could see they all had erections!" Angel laughed at the memory, covering her mouth. "Hard-ons! Those boys were so *faat haau*."*

"I was a Marine." Bob was a bit embarrassed to hear Angel using such language in front of Pop-Pop.

"My brother was in the navy. A steward, but later they made him a signalman. He was killed." Angel left the story of her brother in the navy at that. She sipped her tea. She refilled Bob's cup as well. It tasted less bitter. Sugar would have ruined it.

Mr. Lum said something in Cantonese. Angel said nothing in response. Then she asked, "When are you going to give me a ride on your motorcycle, Bob?"

"Really? You want a ride?"

"Why not? I'll hang on to you," Angel said, getting up, collecting the teapot, cups, and bowls. "Riding on your motorcycle looks fun."

"You're my boss. Say when," Bob Falls said.

"Monday. Next day off," said Angel Lum.

★　★　★

Christmas 1970

Dear Robby,

I have owed you this letter for a very long time.

I know your dad died and I should have written you then. The same goes for your mom. Your sisters I never knew very much, but the two of you should have heard from me a long time ago. You were a little boy when I last saw you and now I'm sure you're all grown up. If you are married, I hope she's a great girl. If not, I hope you know a lot of great girls. Ha ha.

I've been married for over ten years now. My wife is from San Francisco and grew up in Chinatown. I met her at a restaurant she owned in Arizona. She taught me a few things and now we have a restaurant in Albuquerque called the Gold Dragon. We make pretty good bank. It's one of Albuquerque's better restaurants and one of a

---

* Cantonese for "horny" or "libidinous."

very few places for good Chinese food. She runs the place. I work in the kitchen. So, yes, I married the boss.

When I saw you last it was not long after the war. I was a kind of mess. I was drinking then, which is something I was good at and kept at for a long time. I have not had a drink since May 17, 1962. I go to meetings once a week with other guys like me. Many of us guys were messed up by the war, but we weren't always like that. We grew up normal kids but were changed like blocks of wood that get lathed poorly. But that is no excuse for you not hearing from me. You were a little kid and I was supposed to be an adult, but I didn't know how to be one, or how to be an uncle, or how to stay in one place or how to stay out of trouble. As you were growing up, I was getting into a lot of jams and scrapes. Angel said that when she met me for the first time the only place she didn't see trouble was on my clean boots. Angel is my wife, which makes her your aunt by marriage. I never even told her about you until we'd been married.

I don't remember very much about the last time I saw you there in Lone Butte. I think you and I went for a ride around the town and we got some milkshakes down at Clark's Drugstore. Your sister was a little baby and I bounced her on my knee some and you were coloring and drawing a lot and showed me some of your drawings and pictures. I remember your mom telling me I should quit my wandering around and choose a place to stay—if not in the hometown, somewhere. But that just wasn't going to happen.

I hope you haven't had to go to Vietnam—that is how little I have kept up with the family. I don't know if you have been drafted or not. I don't watch the news because of Vietnam. I know what happens in a war. Even if we win in Vietnam, it's not worth how it shapes a man. Some of the guys I meet with tell me I'm not a patriot for saying so, but that's them and Vietnam is no Pearl Harbor. If you did get drafted, I hope you were in charge of showing movies on the base instead of fighting in the jungle. I think of you as a little boy, and the idea of you in Vietnam is just a terrible thought. I saw just a bit of the news one day of a Marine unit burning up a village. When I was a Marine I burned up a lot of villages. Seeing that on TV ruined my sleep for a week. If I ever had a time when I wanted to drink again, that was it. Angel, my wife, asked me why I was so bothered by it but I could not explain—only that it reminded me of too many things I saw when I was a Marine and too many things I did.

I still have bad dreams like most of the guys, but I know where those dreams come from. They are hauntings that come and go and will for the rest of my life. But I don't want you to think I'm some ruined old man. I'm not. Now I'm the luckiest guy in the world. I don't have kids but Angel has about a million nieces and nephews and one of her brothers moved to Albuquerque so we see them a lot. If you remember, I had a motorcycle when I came to Lone Butte and I still do. I love to ride with my wife holding on to me in back. I like my job and have turned into a pretty good cook and I'd love it if you came to our place someday. If you do, the Gold Dragon is very easy to find. It's on Central Avenue right downtown on Route 66 and everyone knows about our place. We'll feed you well.

But I do want you to know that I am sorry for abandoning you and the others. I have made many mistakes in my life but none of them are bigger than not being around for you a lot more than I have been. I can't make up for that lost time with any magic or an explanation that you would even care to hear. There are no excuses for why I disappeared, only the fact that I did. I've got no plans to go to Lone Butte or show up on your door so don't worry about some strange old man seeking you out. I hope that you can somehow understand that I know what I did and didn't do. That you can accept the mystery of how both of us can end up wherever we are and still get on with things.

Come and see us—if you want.

Still Your Uncle,

Bob

Robby/*TREV-VORR* remembered a news story he had seen on TV, a report on a company of Marines out on patrol in the Vietnamese jungle. Stoned when he'd seen it and stoned now, he recalled the stark and grainy footage: a black-and-white village with art-directed thatched huts and barnyards, the Marines looking like giants among the primitive Vietnamese. The huge, lumbering Americans in their helmets and weapons and that guy with the radio backpack talking on a handset were all just boys, trying to look tough, smoking to hide the boredom, misery, and the barely capped terror in their eyes and in the way they stood. Robby—at twenty-nine—was older than all of them, even the Marine officer who was barking and ordering. They all looked exhausted. One of the Marines took his Zippo lighter to the low hanging eaves of a hut to light the leaves on fire. Other Marines did the same with their Zippos. They had been ordered to burn down the village huts.

The Zippos could not do the job fast enough, so one Marine, a fellow with a flamethrowing unit on his back, sprayed a wave of jellied fire across the entire thatched roof of one hut, then another. Clumps of fireballs dripped from the nozzle of his weapon, burning on the ground, self-fueled, sputtering. The nonchalance of the act made the flamethrower look like he was a reluctant kid doing a Saturday-morning chore, raking up lawn clippings from the mower while his pals were off flirting with the girls at the city pool. Within seconds, the Marines had created a riot of fire. They were surrounded by black smoke, inside a cloud of burning chemicals, while the Vietnamese women, old folks, and little kids wept and screamed. The industrial output of the flamethrower, that tank of pressurized napalm, turned that rain-soaked village into Hell on Earth.

★   ★   ★

Bob Falls—Uncle Bob—had been a flamethrower in his war, when he was all of nineteen years old. Robby remembered the "That's me" that Uncle Bob had said about a comic book from World War II, a story about pinned-down Marines saved by one of their own, their flamethrower. Robby remembered the comic book because Uncle Bob had bought it for him and Robby had drawn pictures of what he imagined his uncle had done with his fire maker, a weapon so much cooler and more glamorous than a machine gun's *ratta-ratta-ratta* or a bazooka's *ka-blam*. The *roooaar* of Uncle Bob's M2-2 portable flamethrower turned him into a grimly determined superhero in a fight for justice. Uncle Bob had never been a bored yet terrified teenager in a helmet, tasked with obliterating a farm with spitting balls of gelled flame. Bob Falls had been the Marine who saved the day.

TREV-VORR started drawing the story right then, an epic he could see in his head, one in three distinct sections. He roughed out an outline for a few pages, threw them away, started again, then took time to ponder and shape the images. When he'd roughed enough pages of the whole story, he showed them to one of the staff—a fellow named Barbour—and asked what he thought.

"I don't know, man," Barbour said, scratching his beard. Barbour was sort of the lead writer on some of the titles. He'd come up with the character of S'poo, a rip-off of *Star Trek*'s Mr. Spock who had penises for ears instead of Spock's pointy ones. S'poo was a brisk seller, one of the more popular Kool Katz Komix. "Try to make it funnier."

By the next morning Robby had completed every panel of *TREV-VORR*'s next underground comic, *The Legend of Firefall*.

"Why are you celebrating baby killers?" asked Sky, one of the women in the office who then stopped talking to him. Everyone in the place read what *TREV-VORR* had done, with the prevailing opinion that *The Legend of Firefall* wasn't funny enough, wasn't provocative enough, didn't expose the immorality of war enough, had too little to do with Vietnam, and with final panels that were despicable! It was no Kool Katz Komic! He should sell it to an establishment place as an old-school Superman and Green Lantern kind of title and cash the check. Better yet? Throw the fucker away. Burn it.

"Like America needs *this*," said Avery, one of the artists.

"I don't know," Barbour said again.

"Where did you come up with such *cruel shit*?" asked Zelko. *TREV-VORR* didn't know if that was a compliment or a criticism.

The only vocal fan of *The Legend of Firefall* was Annie Peeke, who inked the lettering for many of the artists. Her brother had been drafted in 1968, in one of the buildups of troops after the Tet Offensive, and was killed in February of 1969. She said it would have made her brother laugh.

And yet, Kool Katz printed *TREV-VORR*'s *The Legend of Firefall* and the thing sold. Mail orders came in from around America, a flurry of them for a couple of weeks. Some came back ripped to shreds, others with swastikas drawn in red marker on every page. *TREV-VORR* received some hate mail from fans who couldn't believe that the creator of *Big Belly the Kop* and *The Trasshhee Family* would one day churn out a G.I. Joe tribute. One fan wrote "Why not just go full Gomer Pyle?!" Some letters came in asking, in so many words, the same question as Zelko: "Where did you come up with such cruel shit?"

THE LEGEND OF FIREFALL

COLONEL THUNDERBUTT

SKIPPER

THE V.C.

DOWN THROUGH AMERICAN HISTORY, MANY A BOY HAS BEEN SHAPED BY THE FUN AND EXCITEMENT OF... **WAR!** READ ALL ABOUT IT, RIGHT HERE IN OUR OWN K.K.KOMIX'S **THE LEGEND OF FIREFALL!**

FOOSH!

HEY! THEIR ARTILLERY JUST WENT AWAY!

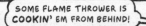

SOME FLAME THROWER IS COOKIN' EM FROM BEHIND!

INTO THE CHOPPERS, BOYS!

THOSE G%$#S ARE GETTING COOKED! WHO DO WE HAVE DOWN THERE?

NOBODY WE KNOW OF, SIR!

AHHH!

AHHHHHHH!

I CAN'T BELIEVE WE MADE IT!

WHO THE HELL IS THAT?

GREETINGS, READER. I AM LT. COLONEL ED "KICKASS" THUNDERBUTT. WHAT YOU JUST SAW ACTUALLY HAPPENED IN VIETNAM.

NO ONE KNOWS WHERE THIS FLAME-THROWER CAME FROM, BUT WE IN THE TOP-SECRET CORPS HAVE GIVEN HIM A NAME: FIREFALL!

WE CHOSE THIS MONICKER BECAUSE, WELL, IT SOUNDS DAMN COOL, AND SERGEANT HOT-STICK OR MAJOR BUN-BURNER WERE ALREADY TAKEN.

I CAN NOW TELL YOU THAT THIS WAS NOT THE FIRST TIME FIREFALL SHOWED UP AND SAVED THE LIVES OF AMERICAN TROOPS WHO WERE TRAPPED BY THE ENEMY-- BY KILLING ASIAN MEN.

WHY CAN I TELL YOU THIS NOW? BECAUSE I AM IN CHARGE HERE!

MANY OF YOU MAY NOT REMEMBER THE POLICE ACTION THAT WAS THE KOREAN WAR...

SOMEONE **LIT UP** ALL THESE CHI-COMS! IT'S A **MIRACLE**, SIR!

LOOK SIR! THE ENEMY IS BEING **ATTACKED** FROM BEHIND THEIR OWN LINES!

THEY'RE GETTING THEIR RICES FRIED!

ONE GI HAD A CAMERA, HE SNAPPED A PHOTO!

YES, IT'S TRUE. PHOTO EVIDENCE SHOWED THAT WHEN OUR BOYS WERE TRAPPED BY OUR LEMON-COLORED ENEMIES, THE MYSTERIOUS FIREFALL APPEARED TO ALLOW ESCAPE AND SURVIVAL.

WHERE DID THIS HERO COME FROM? AND HOW? THANKS TO OUR **INTELLIGENT DETAIL: INFANTRY ORDNANCE TEAM -- I.D.I.O.T --** WE THINK WE NOW KNOW...

THE GOOD WAR! YOU KNOW THE ONE -- MOM AND DAD TALK ABOUT IT ALL THE TIME. WORLD WAR DUECE!

WE BELIEVE FIREFALL WAS **CPL. LATHAM ROBERT FALLSGOOD** -- A MARINE FLAMETHROWER WHO WENT MISSING IN ACTION IN THE BATTLE OF **NO-BIKINI-ATOLL** LATE IN THE WAR.

HE HAD SERVED WITH DISTINCTION IN THE EXTINCTION OF J%$# SOLDIERS IN BATTLES OF

ICHI-BOTTOM

SCRATCH-A-TOWA

KUKU-BONGO

AND VILLA-BOUQUET.

BUT IT WAS ON NO-BIKINI-ATOLL THAT HE DISAPPEARED.

SEE THAT DARK SLIT UP AHEAD?

I DO SIR.

THE JAPANESE CITY OF **NAGASAKI** MET THE SAME FATE AS **HIROSHIMA** JUST A FEW DAYS BEFORE.

FOOM

WOW! LOOK AT THAT MUSHROOM CLOUD! WE JUST KILLED A LOT OF J%$#5!

WE ARE NOT SURE WHERE FIREFALL WILL APPEAR NEXT-- MAYBE IN BERLIN, OR MOSCOW, OR A **COLLEGE CAMPUS** NEAR YOU... BUT WHEN FATE HAS OUR BOYS TRAPPED AND ALL SEEMS LOST -- HAVE FAITH... IN FIREFALL!

3 DEVELOPMENT HELL

2020

BILL JOHNSON

DING!! DING! Ding . . . d-ing . . . d'i . . .

The kitchen-timer bell sounded. Twenty-five minutes had passed.

Bill Johnson had the next five minutes to himself, so he pushed away from his typing table, the special piece of furniture that was a bit lower than a desk or dining table, making it the functionally friendlier height for proper typing on an old-school, operational typewriter. He'd bought the writing machine decades before, the table a few years later. He left the house to get outside, to take in the wide dome of sky, the cool morning air of the New Mexico desert; it wasn't yet 7:00 a.m. Across the street on the golf course, a foursome was getting in an early round. He recognized them—everyone knew everyone in the college town of Socorro, NM—and gave them a whistle and a wave. The foursome waved back.

Bill Johnson is not an insurance salesman or a VP of telemarketing. Nor is he Bill Johnson, the city councilman, manager of the Applebee's, or the valedictorian of Skyline High School class of '19. He is not BJ the IT Guy from the fourth floor—and *nobody* gets away with calling him BJ. He is not the orthodontist in the East Valley Wellness Corporation or the family man next door who, as a Mormon, stockpiles his garage with canned goods, bottled water, powdered soups, and cases of Sprite. All those Bill Johnsons are good men, most likely, who live within the cozy confines of their vanilla, all-American names.

This Bill Johnson, the man with the vintage Smith-Corona Sterling typewriter on a table to match, is the Bill Johnson who writes and directs motion pictures. He has been labeled a genius by some. Those who know him well would agree that the word *odd* should come before *genius*. Currently, Bill Johnson the moviemaker was between projects, creatively adrift.

Out in front of the house, Bill saw the orange tabby cat that belonged to the Pinedos, a couple of houses over. That the cat was still alive was amazing, having survived the heat, the hawks, the coyotes, and the feral dogs that wandered the town. Bill was no keeper of pets but seeing that orange cat sauntering along the fence rim gave him a sense of calm, a reassurance that the latest COVID variant was not killing all of God's creatures.

"Here, puss-puss," Bill called, softly snapping his fingers. The cat ignored him. So, rather than caress the tabby, Bill s t r e t c h e d his hands and arms straight up from his shoulders, imagining his neck was elongating, like he was a rubber giraffe. He breathed deeply, checked his watch to confirm the passing of five minutes, then went back into the house.

After making himself another perfectly pressed double espresso— with a sprinkling of Ovaltine stirred in—he sat back down at the typing table and his Sterling . . .

If I could find some source material, a character or two, in the midst of his/her crisis, then just run with that. Oh, hell ... If making movies wasn't more-fun-than-fun I'd be happy hitting those little white pills called golf balls. But too much of that game and I'd feel condemned. When I get to work, I hear Dylan's Chimes of Freedom and know

Rereading what he had typed, he realized he'd spent twenty-five minutes complaining on paper; his stream of consciousness was that of a wuss. Who cared about his problems?

So that was that for the day at the Smith-Corona. Bill *brr-zipped* the page out of the typewriter carriage and chucked it into the drawer of his table, along with all the other timed missives he banged out at the start of his days. Once the drawer filled to bursting, he'd put his musings into a wooden chest on a shelf in the garage where years of his typing sat ready for either his archives or a fireplace.

He went to the front closet, grabbed his golf clubs, and left the house. He walked to the course to hit around a little white pill before it got too hot.

★ ★ ★

Bill's former work habit was to sit at his typing table and write and write and write like he was Jack Kerouac on Dexedrine, keeping at the keyboard for hours at a time until he either came up with some fever-dream of a story or threw his typewriter out the window in frustration. Too often, his ramblings lost track of both time and logic, resulting in pages and pages of blank-verse nonsense. Alternatively, there were days when he just sat at his typewriter for hours with nothing to show for the time, his thoughts blank, his imagination seized up, a wordless page in the carriage of his writing machine in a state of cosmic stasis. But his self-prescribed discipline commanded that he *stay at the typewriter* no . . . matter . . . what. Type anything. MAKING MOVIES IS MORE FUN THAN FUN. The phone book, the pledge of allegiance, Springsteen lyrics: Spanish Johnny drove in from the underworld last night with bruised arms and broken rhythm and a beat-up old Buick but dressed just like dynamite...

Out of such truculent labor, somehow, his screenplays came to be.

But he was not the same foolish young man he'd been. Since Stay-in-Place Pandemic-Style, nothing of thematic value had been translated from his normally zest-filled brain, through his QWERTY word hammers, onto onionskin. No sluglines or cut tos. No dialogue came about in the timed, twenty-five-minute blocks; no script pages, no theme, no story. As a diarist of late, Bill avoided the fog and slog of staying at the typewriter no matter what. As a screenwriter? He sucked. So, he'd carry his golf bag across the street to the golf course to hit around for a while, to work on his short game, his chipping and putting, for three or four holes, golfing in between the official foursomes who kept score.

He hadn't always Spanked the Spalding, not taking the game up until he'd met Dr. Pat Johnson (no relation) and moved to Socorro. He'd settled in Albuquerque a few years ago, after making a movie* on location and falling for the dry heat, infinite landscape, and fifteen-thousand-year-old tribal history. With his move to Socorro, he'd given up his hillside house overlooking the city but returned whenever the spirit moved him—to eat at the finer restaurants, visit with his poet/artist/plumber/backhoe-operator friends, to sit in the sports rooms of the tribal casinos (to watch the people, not the sports), and to dig around in the flea markets and antiques malls that dot Central Avenue, historic Route 66.

Long ago, Bill vowed he would never again give any gift that was not pre-owned, as in used, and therefore environmentally altruistic. The more olden things he bought and gave, the less landfill there would be to scar the earth. This made gifts from Bill Johnson special, often unique, but way off base on occasion. Not everyone found a forty-seven-year-old AM radio in working condition to be a thoughtful gift.

He'd poke around for old root beer mugs, for appliances, like still-working coffee percolators and a perfectly fine Ricoh mini-cassette Dictaphone, for LPs in various states of play-a-bility, for old penny-a-word pulps, vintage magazines like *Mad* and *Hot Rod Cartoons* and even comic books from long ago. Old magazines made decent gifts for any occasion. Bill had two bankers boxes filled with some actual treasures.[†]

A vast flea market on the main drag in ABQ was Roots 66, owned by Frank and Diedre McHale, which is where Bill found his first set of golfing gear. Preowned golf clubs are a staple of flea markets and junk stores—Roots 66 had bins full of them and old

---

* *Imperion.* 2002. Grossed $637M worldwide. And *Albatross*—a disaster. Both now Streaming on Visonbox.

[†] The Instigator had been sending him materials from the studios making superhero movies, hoping Bill would spark to one title, one super-saga. Comic books and graphic novels—old and new. Bill had only so much interest in them. Into the bankers boxes they'd go.

bags to carry them in, too. Bill settled on some Pings that had been costly when they were new but now were $50 for the set.

"You ever play golf in your life?" Frank McHale asked.

"No. But I've seen it on TV."

"These clubs are not your size."

"Clubs have sizes, do they?"

"Just like pants do. You are too tall for these. Come with me."

Bill followed Frank around the market, to different collections of clubs and bags and gear in various stalls, measuring the shafts against his lanky frame. Frank played the sport, so he showed Bill the proper grip and stance right there in the aisles of Roots 66, being careful on the backswing not to hit any of the display cases. A set of Wilson clubs was a near-perfect fit for Bill.

"Every time I come in here it's the same old story," Bill said as Frank was ringing up the amount and noting the item numbers for the vendor. "You never have anything new."

Bill left Roots 66 with the right-fitting clubs, in a bag of hilariously ugly orange faux leather, and a one-gallon ziplock bag stuffed with used balls. He'd have to buy his own tees, take a lesson or two, and when he was ready to move his game up with a set of made-to-order, custom-measured clubs, Frank would set him up with the pro he knew at the Sandia Resort & Casino. Unless he someday went totally insane there was no way that Bill Johnson was ever going to pay for custom-made golf clubs. Funny, then, that he was so excited when Dr. Pat Johnson gave him that very gift for their first Christmas together as Johnson & Johnson.

*   *   *

Bill had ever had only one agent—the Instigator, a.k.a. Fred Schiller of the Fred Schiller Agency.

Long ago, Fred was sitting in his crappy little office, representing all of three clients, two of whom were seeking work, the third was writing on the staff for a sitcom that lasted thirty-nine episodes on ABC. The agent was barely a part of showbiz. One midday in his office on Wilshire near La Brea, he had no phone calls to answer or to dial, so he reached into the mail basket marked UNSOLICITED, in which a stuffed manila envelope was sitting, and took it down to the coffee shop in the lobby. With a Coke on the table, he opened the envelope to find a typed screenplay written by some guy named Bill Johnson. Fred Schiller had just pulled out the winning ticket at a pancake breakfast raffle.

The script was way too long, but it was a fun page-turner of a read.* Fred spent the rest of that afternoon and the next two days repeatedly dialing the telephone number on the script's title page, hoping to reach this guy named Bill Johnson, but getting no answer. Bill had a night job, so he'd been turning down his ringer as he slept through the day, without realizing that, oops, his answering machine had been unplugged since he'd last vacuumed his place. When the two of them eventually talked for the first time, Fred's opening line was "Is this Bill Johnson, the screenwriter? This is Fred Schiller of the Fred Schiller Agency."

"Well, hello, Fred Schiller," said Bill, just out of a shower and butt naked. "'Tis I. Bill Johnson."

"I've read your submission." Fred paused. "There is no way to fake talent on a screenplay."

"I'm not so sure, but okay," Bill said.

"I want to be your agent. You don't already have an agent, do you?"

"I do not. You can be my agent if you want."

"Great. This is a lucky day for both of us. But I am going to be straight with you. No one will buy *Chase the Calm*."

"Then I am confused. Why are you now my agent? How is this a lucky day for me and you?"

"You wrote too many scenes, too many characters, too many pages, and not enough conflict. Your structure is counterintuitive and what should happen on page thirty is on page forty-two."

"That is by design," Bill said. "I want to break the rules."

"You can't break the rules until you follow the rules. The first draft of your next screenplay will follow the rules. The second draft will, too. The third draft is going to be fabulous, and I'll see that it instigates a ton of interest. Is that agreeable to you?"

"Fred," Bill said, now air-dried from head to toe. "Instigate away."

---

* Titled *Chase the Calm*—179 pages!

Bill had to complete seven drafts of his next screenplay—*Stenographers Can Be Heroes Too*—before Fred Schiller would get to his promised instigating, seven drafts until the page 30 event happened on page 30.

None of the major studios were interested in Bill Johnson's writing. More than one development executive called his work "typing." Few of them actually took the phone calls from Fred Schiller, much less read the screenplay. Still, Schiller proved himself true to his word.

First, he romanced a guy who was rich by way of making wire hangers, a millionaire who wanted to get into Pictures. Fastest way to do that, Fred advised, was to buy up the rights to good material, and Fred happened to have a copy of the seventh draft of a screenplay by Bill Johnson. Wire Hanger Man optioned it then and there.[*]

Second, Fred convinced the hanger magnate that the next sure-fire way of getting in the Motion Picture Industry was to be a Financier. So, guess who put up his own money?

Third, there was the question of direction: Bill Johnson's screenplay was audacious, but the budget was going to be low, low, low. Few directors with any track record wanted to be handcuffed by limited finances, so none signed on.

A young Clyde Van Atta—fresh out of the two-year producing track at the American Film Institute—worked out a schedule to shoot the movie in only seventeen days. Clyde had an AFI pal who'd just completed the cinematography track, a cameraman named Stanley Arthur Ming, who shot fast, on the fly.

The Instigator got the screenplay into the hands of Maria Cross—who was on the cusp of becoming *Magic* Maria Cross—an actor who knew a fabulous starring role when she read it. She jumped onto that seventh draft but had a conflict—she had signed on for a big-budget movie that was to shoot in Canada. Those seventeen days of shooting would have to go ASAP.

With such a narrow window and no director, the Instigator suggested to Mr. Wire Hanger, maybe Bill himself could be the filmmaker. "If I'm getting a rookie, I'm paying rookie wages," said the Financier.

---

[*] For $5K. A lot of money for any first-time writer. A lot of money for anyone.

"Don't pay him anything," the Instigator said. If Bill took no fee, swapping a paycheck for a percentage of the profits on the back end, wouldn't everybody win?

Everybody did.

That first movie, renamed *The Typist*, was damn good, did great box office, and made the wire hanger manufacturer a small fortune (which vanished on his next, and final, adventure in Pictures). Bill earned the first true money of his life, got into the DGA,* and manifest destiny took him westbound on Fountain Avenue.

Bill wrote and directed another film *(Charlie Who)*, then another *(The Nova Bosses)* and another (the first of his *Eden* trilogy). Despite attempted poachings by the major agencies, Fred Schiller remained Bill's Instigator. The alliance was envied all over town.

The Instigator handled Bill's career at the same time he held his hand through the changes in his personal life—the first marriage (a fucking disaster), divorce (no kids so no child support, but more than half his bank), the interim days of wanton carousal marred by substance abuse, a hushed-up DUI, and the second marriage to a lady with two kids—Bill liked those kids—which was lovely for a while until it wasn't. The second divorce cost him even more bank. He'd have been in private-jet territory had it not been for that lack of a prenup. Bill fled the coast (and its women and substances) for the arid, enchanting land that is New Mexico. Bill could still afford his three-bedroom latchkey condominium in the Wilshire Corridor, but he avoided Los Angeles unless he was working on a project. The Instigator would fly commercially into ABQ to meet his client for a monthly long-afternoon-and-into-dinner bull session to plot and plan the continuing career of Bill Johnson.

From the office of Optional Enterprises in Hollywood, the US Postal Service and FedEx supplied Bill with a wide sampling of comic books, graphic novels, and synopses of sci-fi and fantasy properties that were floating around, all of which took less time to read than screenplays and writing samples. Bill read enough of each to sense what was what but never landed on any particular one, save a soft-selling, lesser-known Dynamo title called *Agents of Change* about a group of *very* conflicted super-oddballs, each

---

* The Directors Guild of America.

an Ultra, each a troubled soul. The Rook scared everyone with his looks. The Winter Prince was icy. BoltStone could not communicate his feelings. Bill checked the males off as also-rans, but the women—Ursa Major, who was never able to smile, and Eve Knight a.k.a. Knightshade, who was never able to sleep—they were cool. Not that he knew what to do with them.

After the awards season, which Bill endured without winning a thing,[*] COVID-19 blew up. Showbiz as it had been went away for a long time. America and the world took multiple blows, as did the very small college town of Socorro, New Mexico, where Bill now lived because of his arrangement with Dr. Johnson. If you're thinking having a doctor in the house was a boon, what with the novel coronavirus at loose, you've got the wrong kind of doctor.

★ ★ ★

Bill Johnson first laid eyes on Dr. Patrice Johnson (no relation) on a morning flight from ABQ to LAX—he had meetings at Optional Enterprises, she was to sit in on a symposium at UCLA. They did not know each other, but no way the two did not clock each other. The flight was only half full. Bill was a lanky fellow, with a carriage of confidence and a western-style wardrobe better than that of a forklift driver, closer to that of an actual ranch hand; his pants were weathered western-wear jeans, his boots weren't too fancy, and he wore a belt without any turquoise in the buckle. And he was on the tall side. Patrice resembled the iconic French movie star Catherine Deneuve in modest braided hair, but who was stretched a bit taller and spent a lot of time in the New Mexican sun. She never dated men who were not lanky, taller than her. Bill liked women with braided hair and sun-kissed necks.

At LAX both were catching Ubers at the curb, but nothing was said between them, and both were driven off into the City of Angels (or *Angles,* as Bill called the place) for their appointments. Two days later, on the evening flight back to ABQ, Bill was in his seat when

[*] Writer-director of *A Cellar Full of Sound,* which also lost for Best Sound Mixing, Best Sound Effects Editing, Best Costumes, Best Art Direction, and Best Song. Goose eggs across the board.

a flummoxed Patrice barely made the closing of the plane's hatch, dragging her wheeled carry-on and looking for her place, which happened to be on the aisle, one middle seat distant from Bill at the window. Patrice was still wearing an ID tag, magnetically attached to her lapel, which read DR. PATRICK JOHNSON—NMIMT and was having a slight hassle getting her bag into the overhead bin.

"I'd offer to help you, Doctor," Bill said. "But I'm not sure of the protocol."

"I'm good," Patrice said, plopping down on the aisle. She adjusted herself in her seat, kicked off her shoes, and buckled up. "Hey. I saw you on the plane two days ago."

"I saw you, too," Bill said. He pointed to her ID tag. "I have a brother named Patrick Johnson, but he's not a doctor."

"Yeah," Patrice said. "Someone didn't proofread the name tags."

"Bill Johnson." He offered his hand and she shook it.

"Patrice," she said, unmagnetizing her ID badge to slip it into her pocket.

"Are you in medicine?" he asked.

"Earth science."

"So . . . if the pilot asks, *Is there a doctor on board?*"

"Let's hope there is one," Patrice said.

"What the heck is *Nim-imt* on that badge, Patrick-I-mean-Patrice?"

"New Mexico Institute of Mining and Technology. Where I teach."

"The mining, the technology, or both?"

"I teach everything important to know. And I research. You aren't the director Bill Johnson, by any chance, are you?"

Gonngg!

This was the sound inside Bill Johnson's head. "Why in the world would you say that?"

"Your name happens to be the same as the movie director. You're flying to and from Hollywood. I heard somewhere that Bill Johnson the director lives in Santa Fe. I took a shot. If you're not that Bill Johnson, that's okay."

"You're the first person to ask me that question on an airplane," Bill said. "I don't live in Santa Fe—that town is too slow for me. I prefer Albuquerque. And yes, I am that Bill Johnson."

"Really?" Had he been a presence inside Patrice's head, Bill would have heard a sound much like his own *gonngg!!* "I've seen some of your films."

"I certainly hope so."

"I rent them from the Redbox outside Walmart. I binged those *Eden* movies of yours when I had strep throat."

"Rented. From a Redbox. For what, a dollar a night?"

"*Three* dollars. The trilogy. You must have had fun making those movies."

"Fun? Making those movies almost *killed* me. What kind of research do you do?"

"Without a background in earth science, my papers would be Sanskrit to you."

"How many papers have you written?"

"Not enough. I'm in academia, so it's publish or perish."

"Hell, that's the same as my racket."

She bought him a beer from the drink cart once the plane was in the air. She had a red wine in a plastic glass. They chatted from wheels-up to their arrival in ABQ—ninety minutes that seemed like much less—and rode the shuttle bus to the airport parking lot, sitting together, in no hurry for their conversation to end despite the late hour and the darkness of the night. The bus let them out at the drop point in the lot—she with her wheeled case, he with his worn leather messenger bag.

Bill was no dope. He knew that if he didn't float some kind of request for a bit more time with this woman she very well might slip away off into the regolith; he might not hear that *gonngg!* again. To ask for her number was a college kid's move. Wondering if she wanted to join him for a drink in town was a sleazy businessman's line. Bill wasn't looking to redefine his life, which was one of singularity, nonattachment, of having no needs to fulfill or explain, of hanging around, writing story beats and screenplays, then going off to make movies in places like Malta or Orange, California, and getting good money for his labors. He could drift or not, his choice. He wasn't searching for a partner in all of that. Dr. Patrice Johnson was a fascinating woman who blew up rocks to help the environment and grow better foods. She hadn't asked any questions about movies beyond the name of the one he'd made in Albuquerque.* She knew nothing about his nominations or audi-ence prizes because show business was a thing she rented from a Redbox when she was ill. Earth science was a class Bill never took, but the two of them had talked without ceasing for the last two hours—how often did *that* happen with such a tall drink of water as Dr. Johnson? And hey, that *gonngg!*

"So . . . how do I find you?" Bill put the question to her like he was asking if she knew the time.

Patrice was no dope. She didn't need a man in her life. The last time she stuck her neck out for a (married) man the whole snafu tagged her with a scarlet letter. She was not against having the chance to talk again with this interesting and lanky Bill Johnson, who wore boots that were not too fancy. Without him sitting at the window, the flight home would have been one quick glass of air-line wine and a sit-straight-up snooze. With him, the ninety-minute flight seemed too short. If she responded with any trace of possi-bility, it would be a de facto agreement for this guy to *come around and see me sometime.* Goddammit—*gonngg!*

Patrice pulled out her phone and swiped to her Photos app, scrolling through her pictures of igneous carbonates until she found a snapshot of her leaning in the doorway of her one-axle Jayco trailer. The photo was taken by a student when she was out in the field taking core samples of gypsum to record moisture levels. She was wearing cutoff jeans, hiking boots, and a zip-up NMIMT sweatshirt, a beer in her hand at the end of a long, hot day of labored research. Patrice Johnson knew those cutoffs showed some damn fine legs.

"I live just off campus in in the middle of Socorro. Make a few lefts until you're on the south edge of the golf course. You can't get lost." She showed him the photo of the Jayco trailer. "My house is the only one with a Jayco in the driveway. I work during the day, but I'll be home in a whistle."

Bill had clocked her legs. Her instructions sounded intuitive enough. "What if the Jayco isn't in the driveway?"

"Then I'm out in the field."

"I won't know which house is yours."

---

* *Imperion,* he told her about. *Albatross* he omitted.

"Come back when it's obvious."

Gonngg! Goddammit.

Driving in the late hour to his place up on the hillside, with its epic view of ABQ at night, Bill was amused. His personal Real Life was imitating his professional Reel Life; meet cutes occur in accidents of airline seating and misgendered name tags.

Driving down the dark highway, back to Socorro, more alert than she'd *ever* been after a late flight into ABQ, Patrice thought how handy it was that, should she get married to this Bill Johnson, she would not have to change her name.

★   ★   ★

The town of Socorro, New Mexico, is a bit less than eighty miles from Albuquerque, south on the 25. Bill had never been there; his Google map told him to enjoy the view of the Sevilleta National Wildlife Refuge and to slow down around the towns of Polvadera, Lemitar, and Escondida. He was inside the city limits in just over an hour due to the horsepower of his hot-rod red Dodge Charger, his cruise control set at seventy-four, and the rumbling thrill of seeing Dr. Patrice Johnson on her home turf. Bill cruised the town's main avenue of commerce, California Street, to size up the territory, locate the Walmart and its cheap-ass Redbox, and to scout a local coffee place should this solo expedition of his go south on him. He'd need a boost for a quick exit back to ABQ. For all he knew, Patrice Johnson might call the cops on him, like he was a deranged stalker.

After seeing Socorro end to end, he followed the signs to the New Mexico Institute of Mining & Technology, which was easy to find without any guidance. The campus was in the middle of the town, and in the middle of it was a golf course, green and manicured, surrounded by the New Mexican desert. After a few turns, keeping the fairways of the golf course on his left, he saw her Jayco trailer in a driveway. The neighborhood was a nice one, no doubt housing some of the institute's impressive lineup of science teachers—its vaunted faculty, all professors of rocks and tech.

A ring of the doorbell went unanswered. Dr. Johnson was not at home—so . . .

Bill went back to his Dodge for an old buck slip from *Horizon of*

Eden with his name on it—he'd brought it along for just this need. When Dr. Johnson came home—if this was indeed her house, her Jayco, and not, say, part of an elaborate avoidance of some idiot she met on a plane who hit on her for an hour and a half, she would find this tucked into her front door.

Horizon of Eden
Bill Johnson

That was it. No written message.

To blow time, Bill drove back out onto California Street and found some excellent New Mexican food (he took his chilies green) and constant refills of Arnold Palmers, even though it was a bit early for lunch. He lingered at the place as the locals came in to eat, transcribing recorded notes from his Ricoh Dictaphone, scribbling thoughts into a notebook, pondering ideas for his next movie.[*]

A little after 2:30, Bill returned to the Jayco house, discovering that Dr. Johnson drove an unfortunate choice of car—an O. J. Simpson white Ford Bronco. His buck slip was no longer tucked into the door, so she must be home, Bill told himself. If this was her home.

After ringing the bell, he heard footsteps, the door opened, and it was her. Her hair had been loosened from the braids and was now brushed out, full and down past her sun-kissed shoulders, held in place by a blue bandanna knotted on the top.

"You found me," Dr. Johnson said.

How they both kept on their feet through that first kiss is a mystery—it was a *whammer.*

A few hours later she was in a very sheer sky-blue robe and nothing else. He had tucked himself back into his pants. They were both barefoot, in her kitchen. She showed him how to make the greatest coffee in the world on her German-made ECM Synchronika. If, say, he was to get out of bed in the mornings before her, he'd need to grind the beans, fill the water, set all the gauges, levers, and pipes—this was no one-step coffee maker. By the third morning

---

[*] He was beating out a story with the working title *Down in a Dump,* which luckily was changed to *Barren Land.*

he'd mastered the process, making a perfect double espresso for her, which she took with a half teaspoon of Ovaltine. She liked the chocolate malt.[*]

★ ★ ★

The two never bothered getting married. They were, of course, Bill and Pat Johnson—people assumed they were husband and wife. Bill sold his house in ABQ. Their life in Socorro was serene, yet chock-full. He had films in his head to ponder and write. The Goofy Game That's Fun to Play was always right across the street, sometimes twice a day, in the early morning before the heat or the late afternoon with the sun low in the west. Pat did her teaching and her research and came home for lunch and sex.

When Pat went out in the field, she'd hitch the Jayco to her OJ-Mobile and be gone for days at a time. When Bill made a movie, he'd be away for the long-haul shoots, but the separations did their union more good than harm. They talked all the time on their phones if there was a signal out in her field or on his set. They wrote cryptic texts and lengthy emails that flew back and forth through the Wi-Fi ether. Photos were exchanged all day. Bill kept a letter in process in his Sterling, going on for pages and pages when the feeling stirred him, then he'd send it through the US Postal Service to DR. P. JOHNSON—JAYCO TRAILER IN DRIVEWAY—SOCORRO, NM 87801. No letter ever failed to reach her. If he was doing Post-production in Los Angeles, Pat would fly in and he would fly back. And after every separation, the synchronous expressions of affection were as superb as the Synchronika espressos.

One morning, Dr. Johnson set out to inspect sediments uncovered by a flash flood in an arroyo near Pie Town. Bill saw her off with a Synchronika then assembled a very messy green-chili-breakfast-burrito mash, eating it right out of the skillet. He worked a twenty-five-minute block on his Sterling, nothing more than random notes:

---

[*] When Patrice was growing up in Gallup, to be on time for the school bus, her parents put tiny amounts of instant coffee into her morning Ovaltine. Each year older, they added more. By junior high she was adding Ovaltine to her morning coffee.

CHOCK-TICK, CHOCK-TICK, CHOCK-TICK, CHOCK-TICK . . .

Optional Enterprises

Capitol Records Building 1750 Vine Hollywood

Bill Johnson

Ideal shoot?

As much fun as was ACFOS. (Why is one film a pleasant cruise yet others are cage-matches?)

No rain. No nights past 1 AM. Ok. 2.

Small cast.

Small location (USA)

Warm—no long-johns.

Franchise.

Super hero.

No space. No Time travel. No evil tyrant.

No capes.

No dumb names. Real names.

Well, code names, maybe.

DC. Marvel. Dynamo. ???

Make one up? (lotta work, that.)

After the **DING!! DING!** *Ding . . . d-ing . . . d'i . . .* Bill grabbed his gorgeous, custom-made set of Pings to Spank the Spalding for a few holes. As always, tucked into a pocket of that same orange, ugly golf bag, he took his Ricoh Dictaphone.

On a par 4, he shanked all his shots and took nine strokes for the hole—had he ever kept score, he would have given up right then. With the sun climbing, he paused for water in the shade of a covered bench, had a thought, reached for his Dictaphone, and pressed RECORD.

"A movie with a lot of day exteriors. Shoot practical. On location. Wide vistas. Big sky. Any interior has big windows showing the world outside."

STOP

RECORD

"Most of the story is outdoors. Bright sun. Hot days."

STOP

RECORD

"Maybe that Ultra. The one who could never sleep? Has those visions."

STOP

RECORD

"Ask office for name of that one Dynamo character. Night-what?"

STOP

RECORD

"Totally new chapter from an established saga. All new and improved. Yeah . . ."

STOP

RECORD

(There is an empty gap on the tape of Bill thinking.)

STOP

Bill set his Titleist 4 on a tee, let loose a few practice swings, then took his stance to address the ball. With a jerky backswing and his open hips, he gave the pill a mighty *tap!* The shot corkscrewed some but rabbited along the fairway's edge. Putting his driver back into the orange bag, he had another thought.

RECORD

"Girl needs boy needs girl. But they hate each other."

STOP

Okay, that was it for golf as the morning was turning hot. Bill tucked the Ricoh back into his bag, retrieved his Titleist 4 from the fairway, and walked across the course, across the street, and back into the house.

On his phone, he punched the number for Al Mac-Teer in Los Angeles.

"Yeah?" she answered, pronto. Sounded like she was in the car, headed to the office at the Capitol Records Building, on hands-free.

"There is a super-gal at Dynamo. An Ultra. What's her name?"

"You mean one of the Agents of Change?"

"I don't know. Night-something. The girl who can't sleep."

"Oh. Eve Knight. She's the one Dynamo can't figure out. They've been trying."

"Okay. Thanks." He hung up without saying anything more. They both did that.

He worked the pipes and valves of the Johnsons' Synchronika

for another cup of stimulant, then sliced an apple into a bowl. There was a copy of Dynamo's *Agents of Change* on his work shelf, somewhere, under some of the other offerings sent along by Al from the office. He flipped through the action-packed graphics one more time as he ate and sipped. He was not wild about Eve Knight (Knight with a *K*) as she was portrayed in those pages. He had forgotten that Eve's origins as an Ultra had her as an astronaut who got zapped by some kind of space ray when she was exploring the moon. In the comics, her never sleeping was played like a good thing, as were her new strengths—powers of levitation and her *visions* and ultrafine sense of hearing.

"Well, hell," Bill said to no one. "Anyone can do *that*."

CHOCK-TICK CHOCK-TICK CHOCK-TICK

This Eve Knight character...

What is her mental/spiritual state? Like everyone—CONFUSED.

What is she lacking? CERTAINTY. SIGNIFICANCE. SERENITY.

What is she seeking? What everyone seeks—LOVE. REST. SAFETY.

What is she fleeing? What everyone flees—LONELINESS.
RESPONSIBILITY!

What is her most present need?—A GOOD NIGHT'S SLEEP.

If she can find those things, WE CAN TOO.

So...

LOSE—Moon/Astronaut/Zapped by Ray...

Visitors from other galaxies or realms of fantasy...

Boy Friend...

The other ULTRAS and AGENTS OF CHANGE. Save for later if franchise works—as FLASHBACKS for her origin story?

Eve's Back Story

She was BORN THIS WAY. As a baby, her parents could not get her to sleep—she would be <u>hovering</u> in her crib, but smiling and happy, so Mom and Dad were not frightened by these powers of hers. She was a peaceful kid. The closest she got to sleep was when her eyes rolled back in her head for a few short seconds—that's when she was <u>seeing</u> her <u>visions</u>.

Extended family—a Grandpa around?

As a kid, she had <u>speed</u>. On the monkey bars, she has the <u>strength and agility</u> of a silverback gorilla.

Her <u>Visions</u> are her Powers of <u>Empathy</u>. They are not fantasy or memories. She can hear people in trouble, feel their pain from miles away. She can read minds, like when her mom is looking for bay leaves in the kitchen. Eve is a toddler, can't read yet, doesn't know what a bay leaf is, yet <u>sensing</u> her mother's need, Eve finds the jar that says "Bay Leaves" for her.

There are others like her. Somewhere.

Not a full-time superhero, nor a secret-identity, on-call-when-needed Rescuer. Just a young woman with this unique & heavy burden.

Grand Pa in wheelchair?

She can sense the presence of EVIL. Which is frightening...

Cinematic reveal of her "Powers"–Empathic Tingle leads to her taking action with her speed/strength–saves someone in terrible danger (being kidnapped?). Horrified by the EVIL...

Any attention could lead to discovery, ostracism–she hides away. Mom and Dad keep her SAFE. Are they Ultra? Were they Ultra?

When LOVE comes, it starts as a fight.

Wears her hair in braids

<u>Setting</u>

DING!! DING! Ding . . . d-ing . . . d'i . . .

"There's the girl," Bill said to his typewriter. "Need the boy."

Bill stood up from the typing table and stretched. He made himself another espresso. He had five minutes away from the tide of ideas that were now flowing and rushing inside his head. He was the commander of a clipper ship at sea with a high wind at his back, full sails, propelled onward across unmeasured longitude. He knew what he would type next.

The town is her haven, her "Eden," she is safe there...

Or is she?

But that was five minutes away. He had five minutes.

If the kitchen timer was a treasure for the money, that box of very old comics and magazines was a waste of five bucks. He'd paid for many scattered pages gone loose. Bill had flipped through some of them if only for the nostalgia of the advertisements for send-away toys and the opportunity to earn prizes by selling "The Weekly Wire, America's Family Newspaper!" He'd already thrown away much of what was in the box, the incomplete stuff, the water-damaged pages, the torn-up dog-ears. He had worked part of the way from the front of the box to its rear but had given up a few weeks ago. To make it through this timer-induced break, he took the box down off his work shelf and fingered through the remaining contents, ready to chuck the rest in the trash.

There were more stray pages, a ripped-up cover of a Casper the Friendly Ghost, a reissue of an Archie and Jughead, and, folded in half lengthwise, a very old half dozen pages still held together by a single rusted staple.

There was no cover to this comic book, so he did not know the title or the publishing house. The paper was brittle with age. The artwork and the panels were uniformly simple, so the thing wasn't from any modern era of comic books, but a World War II story of GIs fighting the Japanese on some unnamed island with a narrator—his face was in the upper-left corner of most of the panels. That face looked haunted. And exhausted.

"None of us had slept, knowing what was ahead for us . . ."

Landing craft were surging through the waves.

"They couldn't keep us from taking the beach . . ."

GIs were dying left and right, explosions all around them.

The narrator was hunkered down in a foxhole on a beach. He was not an ordinary soldier with a machine gun or a bazooka. This soldier carried a rig of hoses and tanks on his back. Around him a battle was raging. Soldiers were firing weapons and taking hits.

"I was fully loaded, waiting for the call to move up when I heard the order . . ."

"WE NEED A FLAMETHROWER UP HERE, NOW!"

The narrator was that flamethrower. His eyes registered the commands, he pulled himself up, fighting his fear, his exhaustion, the burden of his weapon. A spark of flame alighted on the nozzle of his flamethrower.

The remaining pages were damn exciting and very adult, really. There was none of the gee-whiz of superheroes nor "Now I have you in my clutches" of standard villains. Instead, there was the horror of close combat, of violence, the roar of the flamethrower delivering a hideous, inhuman death, and the hardened, weighted spirit of the narrator who is ordered:

"Do it, Latham! Let your fire fall!"

Bill wished he owned the remaining pages of this particular comic book. Ah well.

He riffled through the rest of the magazines in the five-dollar box. One old *Mad* had Alfred E. Neuman on the cover in a space suit. Bill set that aside to read later. Under it was another rat-chewed comic, missing no pages but a torn cover that once sold secondhand for twenty-five cents. As a preteen Bill had seen what were called underground comix. Most of them were amusing. Some were immaturely subversive. Some were true art. This one came out of Kool Katz Komix.

The Legend of Firefall. On the cover were these words: "Down through American history, many a boy has been shaped by the fun and excitement of . . . war!"

The idea of boys being *shaped* . . . like blocks of pine . . . on a lathe . . . as Bill had been taught in Woodshop 1 back in junior high school.

Five minutes up, Bill went back inside, grabbing the dictionary he kept close at hand, flipping to words that started with the letter *L,* then *La,* then *Lathe.* He sat back down at his typing table, at the Sterling, rolled in a sheet of his foolscap, and set the timer for twenty-five minutes.

CHOCK-TICK CHOCK-TICK CHOCK-TICK

"Lathe: To cut or shape on a machine with a sharp tool."

FADE IN . . .

He wrote in furious passion until he heard . . .

DING!! DING! Ding . . . d-ing . . . d'i . . .

Bill stood up. He left the house through the front door, stepping out onto the driveway, standing in the spot where the Jayco usually rested. He looked up at the light blue sky. There were some tall, high clouds drifting to the east. He paced back and forth, then walked around in a circle. The Pinedos' orange cat padded around from the side of the house, keeping to the thin strip of shade provided by the walls.

"Well, look at you, puss-puss," Bill said to the cat. The cat said nothing back.

Bill went back inside. He found his phone and punched in Al's speed-dial.

"Yeah?" She was at the office.

"Got a thing," Bill said.

"Oh, boy. What thing?"

"That Ultra Knightshade thing. What's Dynamo doing with it?"

"Copy that."

The call ended with no other remarks.

She waited for the call to go through its Wi-Fi struggles, knowing that if she was shunted to voice mail, he was midswing on that desert golf course across his street, roasting in the midmorning sun. How did they keep the greens green?

Al had waited for showbiz office hours to kick in, but only to be polite. Anyone who was truly working on Fountain Avenue had been up since 6:15 or 5:15—some at 4:15—if only to greet their Pilates instructor. At 9:02 she put in her first of two calls regarding the matter Bill Johnson had laid on her mental index card, leaving word with different assistants. Both her calls were returned, pronto. She had sent a single text on the matter, which had been returned even quicker. At 10:17 Bill Johnson Time, Al gave him his answer.

"Yeah?" No rattle of clubs came through the phone, so he was not whacking his Wilson.

"Dynamo sold it to the Hawkeye," Al said.

"Copy that." Bill hung up.

Nine words in three seconds, an exchange that would seal their twin fates for the next twenty months.

Bill Johnson, her Benevolent Overlord, had changed her life as completely as she now made his doable. Years before, he'd suggested, rightly, that she forgo her Christian name, Allicia—pronounced *Al-i-SEE-a*—and use the terse, masculine Al. Sight unseen, the citizenry assumed she was a man, and she soon proved herself so competent, so proactively assumptive, so badass, she forever-after-and-amen had her calls returned, pronto. Getting one's calls returned, pronto, is the standard by which power is measured on Fountain Avenue. A good number of executive/agent/lawyer folks had had their heads handed to them and their parking spaces moved to the farthest dark corner of the garage by mistakenly thinking the name Al Mac-Teer on a call list could wait. Those foolish enough to log a callback in the end-of-the-day phone dump, when 99.2 percent of calls went directly to voice mail, or were answered by the late-working trainees, were soon crushed ice.

"This is Al," she would say, picking up a call anywhere between 6:12 p.m. and 7:29 p.m.

"Oh, hello Ms. Mac-Teer," some surprised junior desk jockey would say. "I have ENTER NAME OF DOPE HERE returning your call."

"During the phone dump? Really? Put ENTER NAME OF DOPE HERE on for me." Whatever happened next was a hard lesson learned for ENTER NAME OF DOPE HERE. The phone-dump strategy was never practiced again.

She and her boss never said *Hello* or even *It's me* when answering each other's calls. Hellos wasted time. The tenor and tempo of the word *yeah* established all that Al or her boss needed. Pleasantries—*How are you? What's going on? Where are you? Was that restaurant a decent place? Did you have the family for the weekend?*—were saved for personal relationships and business investments, for collaborations beneficial to one's rise up the entertainment food chain. For those in their younger days, they were for getting laid. If you had any friends—or, more precisely, the time for friendships—a phone chat could be nothing but pleasantries. Between Al and Bill, though, time wasn't blown like gambling money.

"Yeah?" Bill had said.

"Dynamo sold it to the Hawkeye."

If you are not in the Business of Show, those words are incomprehensible, like a coded message from outer space during wartime: *"Yeah?"* . . . *"Delta Boxer Shoehorn Mountain of Root Beer."*

"Copy that."

What the hell?

But if you're a member of the Academy, a card-carrying dues payer of one of the guilds or unions, an assistant/associate, a gofer, a writer, a craftsperson, SPFX[*] programmer, a storyboard artist, a content creator just starting out, or a retired veteran residing at the motion picture home in Woodland Hills after a decades-spanning career—those nine cryptic words carry the weight and value of high-grade intel.

Dynamo sold it to the Hawkeye.

Let's break that down.

---

[*] Special effects.

Dynamo is Dynamo, a film studio, creators of the Dynamo Nation of interlinked films; the world of *Ultra Heroes* and the *Agents of Change* franchise.

The Hawkeye is a streaming service, which is either wildly successful or a house of paper that makes no real money. For $7.99 a month, subscribers can watch its selection of certain movies and shows, commercial free. "See what you want, when you want, with the *Hawkeye!*" The service is in direct competition with, oh, just a handful of other streaming platforms like Apple TV+, Netflix, Amazon, Hulu, Disney+, HBO Max, Peacock, VisionBox, Enter-Works, Bee, KosMos, Oprah Winfrey's WinCast, and, from out of Canada, MUCH. The word is that all these subscription models have tons of money but are blowing through cash like buckets of milk in a barn fire.

Sold means that a property—a possible motion picture that had been in development at Dynamo—was now the purchased possession of the Hawkeye.

It—the property—was *Knightshade,* a character in a film with a troubled developmental history. Many screenplays for *Knight-shade* had been attempted by many writers and teams of writers, all of whom were paid big bucks to flesh out the character of Eve Knight and develop a movie for her, yet none of the attempts had clicked; none carried the right magic sauce that moved the film out of Development Hell to the flash of the Green Light. *Knightshade* had been on the Dynamo slate for three years, but now, like so many projects on Fountain Avenue, the movie had become a victim of circumstances vis-à-vis COVID-19 and the glut of expensive blockbusters. *Knightshade* had already cost a ton of money in development fees but still was no tent pole, no opening chapter of a three-film Ultra saga or a new entry for *The Agents of Change.*[*] Rather than laying out the mega-dollars to make and market *Knightshade* in the high-risk/hard-luck dice-roll of cinematic exhibition, Dynamo Nation took the price offered by the Hawkeye. Should the movie ever be made, *Knightshade* would *not* be exhib-

---

[*] Agents of Change had started as the super-trio of Ultras—the Rhino, Sea Lion, and Ursa Major. Since that first hit movie, other Ultras had come and gone. Constellation and the Rook were welcomed as worthy AOC, but don't ask about Multi-Man or the Herald.

ited in local movie theaters; there would be no find-a-parking-place-buy-a-ticket-purchase-a-ValuePack-of-popcorn-soda-and–Red Vines (or Twizzlers on the East Coast)–and-sit-in-a-theater-beside-a-few-hundred-other-patrons experience. No. *Knightshade* would be streamed into subscribers' homes where they could view the film wearing only their underwear in a seat as comfortable as a beanbag chair.

★ ★ ★

Frozen yogurt is why Allicia Mac-Teer was in Bill Johnson's employ. In 2006, she was wearing a name tag and on duty at the front desk of the Garden Suites Inn at the airport of Richmond, Virginia. The airport was situated almost an hour away, but a shuttle service was available on call—this being before the advent of transportation options like Uber, Lyft, or PONY. Back then, cell phones were mere *phones*, with primitive texting that only Gen Xers used with any accuracy or ease. No cameras were on phones yet (except in Asia), no web browsers, no IMDb credits on-demand because no one knew enough to look on the Web for IMDb yet.

Bill Johnson was the guest in suite 4114—overlooking the same "garden" as every other suite—and seemed to be a very busy, distracted fellow. Allicia had no idea he was in Virginia at the start of a three-month-long Preproduction of a movie called *Ask No Questions (Hear No Lies)*. She didn't know he was the man behind the films *The Typist, Charlie Who?*, and *Border of Eden*. Allicia had no idea this Bill Johnson had won the Audience Prize at Cannes for *The Nova Bosses;* Bill Johnson was just another busy man who needed a haircut and, if he wanted a successful future in the Richmond area, some nicer Republican clothes. He had other people with him who did his talking for him. If he smiled a little more often, would that hurt?

Allicia Mac-Teer was trained to smile and she was good at it. She had joined the Garden Suites Diversity in Management Program because there was no way she was going to remain in a Chick-&-Tender uniform—even though she, and most of America, loved that Chick-&-Tender. After nearly seven months at the drive-thru window, she quit, joined the program, and had sallied forth to a position on the front desk, dressed in her smart Garden Suites green tunic, skirt, blouse, heels, and scarf. To some of the lesser minds at the hotel, she was the "new Black girl"—as opposed to the "other Black girls." She forced herself to become indispensable, volunteering to fill in for anyone, anytime, for any reason. At this Garden Suites Inn Allicia Mac-Teer was the answer to the questions *Who can solve this problem? And who will be the Front-Desk Head if she sticks around for three more years?*

In charge of Night Check-Ins, she was instructed, trained, and hell-bent on seeing to the comfort, quality, and enjoyment of all the Guests (with a capital G) of the Garden Suites. Her apparent ease doing those things came from a course she had taken during her five semesters of community college—Business 147—Time Management: The *L.I.S.T.eN.* System.

L.I.S.T.eN.—Let It Settle, Then eNact.

To free herself from the overtaking of written reminders, she learned to imagine five mental note cards, one for each finger of her hand, each labeled with a single task—but never more than five cards. Five mental note cards could be easily remembered and envisioned. As soon as one task was completed, that card was mentally *crumpled up*, gone forever, and only four remained. New tasks came up and got a new note card, but with the *L.I.S.T.eN.* System there would never be more than five tasks at hand or in the mind. If at the end of the workday any cards remained undone, you wrote those down in a composition book labeled TOMORROW, to be completed the next day.

L.I.S.T.eN.—Let It Settle, Then eNact.

If she overheard a guest's disappointment that there was no Special K cereal at the DayBreak Station in the lobby, Allicia made sure a few single-serve boxes of the Kellogg's product were available the next morning, as well as the options of Grape-Nuts, All-Bran, and Rice, Wheat, or Corn Chex. If a sports fan was hoping to watch a soccer match from England on the television in the Garden Lounge, Allicia would check that the proper channel was programmed into the Garden Suites video options menu. By the time Aston Villa took on Manchester City in the Premier League, there it would be on channel 556.

Bill Johnson had returned to the Garden Suites after 9:00 p.m., again. His entourage, the others on the same floor as he—Ms. Candace Mills, Mr. Clyde Van Atta, and, on a lower floor in an Executive Studio, Mr. John Madrid—looked like they had been through a long day riding around Richmond in an uncomfortable van, the Ford that had just dropped them off.* Each carried some kind of backpack or messenger bag. Mr. Van Atta was on his StarTac flip phone, Ms. Mills—with a big purse and a tote with knitting needles protruding from a skein of yarn—was on her Nokia, Mr. Madrid looked like he didn't have a friend in the world. As they all stepped into the elevator, Bill Johnson said to no one in particular, "I'd kill for frozen yogurt with rainbow sprinkles." Then the door closed.

Allicia had heard that—a guest had a need, a desire for frozen yogurt. She Let It Settle, Then eNacted.

The lobby's Evening Station, which had replaced the Noon-Day Station, which had replaced the DayBreak Station, provided guests with a selection of drinks, snacks, and "Lite Good-Nite" treats but no frozen yogurt. The closest spot for frozen yogurt was in the Four-Square Mini-Mall by the on-ramp to the 64, called Ye Olde Ice-Cream Shoppe, which, Allicia knew, had a machine that spit out two flavors of frozen yogurt, chocolate, vanilla, a swirl of both, and offered an assortment of toppings that included rainbow sprinkles. She hit the place up after work on occasion for a cup of raspberry sherbet and knew the name of the girl who would be on duty at this time—T'naiah.

In three minutes, she had T'naiah on the phone with the promise of ten bucks to whoever delivered half-pints of vanilla, chocolate, and a swirled mix of both FroYos, with a cup of rainbow sprinkles on the side before the stuff reverted to its original state of room temp *goo*. T'naiah herself delivered the treats, kept cold in take-me-home Styrofoam tubs, with the colored candy specks in a separate container. Plastic spoons and paper napkins emblazoned with the flowery logo of Ye Olde Ice-Cream Shoppe were tucked inside.

---

* In fact, they had been scouting locations and production spaces in Chicka-hominy Shores, Colonial Williamsburg, Mechanicsville, and Bon Air. It had been a very long day.

T'naiah didn't charge Allicia for the dessert—she was allowed room for "spillage and loss during maintenance"—but did pocket the ten dollars, which was then added to the bill of Bill Johnson in room 4114.

"Duke?" Allicia called to the lobby associate, the fellow who kept the lobby clean, moved cars around as needed, drove the shuttle van to the airport, and had a thing for Allicia.

"Uh-huh?"

"Run this up to Mr. Johnson in 4114." Allicia handed him the bag of Ye Olde Ice-Cream Shoppe products. Duke grabbed it and took the stairs for the exercise.

Allicia picked up the front-desk phone and punched in 7-4114.

"Yeah?" Bill Johnson answered the cordless handset on the nightstand.

"Mr. Johnson, good evening, this is Allicia at the front desk. I hope you're having a pleasant evening," she said by rote.

"No complaints."

"I took the liberty of sending a bit of refreshment to your room just now, I hope it is not too late. Duke should be arriving with it any moment."

"I hear a knock right now. That the Duke?"

"I'm sure it is. Enjoy your evening, Mr. Johnson." Getting off the phone with a guest as quickly as possible was not taught in the Diversity in Management Program but was how Allicia did things. "Alacrity is efficiency" says the *L.I.S.T.eN.* System. Allicia was handwriting a note to Bill Johnson on Garden Suites Inn paper— the address of Ye Olde Ice-Cream Shoppe for his future needs— when the Front Desk phone rang from room 4114.

"Yes, Mr. Johnson, how can I help you?" Allicia answered.

"Are you a clairvoyant?" Bill Johnson asked.

"No, Mr. Johnson. I was raised Baptist."

"Why is it that you sent this frozen yogurt up to me?"

"I heard you mention a craving."

"You did? I don't remember saying that. I remember only *thinking* it."

"You were stepping into the elevator with Mr. Van Atta, Mr. Madrid, and Ms. Mills."

"The sprinkles? You heard me say rainbow sprinkles?"

"Without question. I hope they're okay with you."

"I've no problems with rainbow sprinkles." Bill Johnson laughed. "What's your name?"

"Allicia."

"Okay, Alice. Score one for you. I'm going to enjoy substantial portions of this cold dairy product and candy nuggets like I'm on death row and tomorrow I'll meet my maker with a smile on my face."

"Oh, I hope that's not the case. We value you as our guest."

"You certainly know your lines. For future reference, just the vanilla is my preference. Good night." Bill Johnson hung up. Allicia mentally wrote *Vanilla* on the note card in her head, then imagined it being crumpled up, discarded.

The next day Allicia happened to be working a shift and a half, filling in for Sheila Potts, who was having oral surgery. At noon, she found a sealed envelope waiting for her. Inside was a note scribbled on a long, stiff bookmark—a buck slip—for Optional Enterprises with DACE MILLS printed at the bottom.

Alice,

   You with the dessert and toppings. Can you call me on my cell? Anytime.

Dace

"Dace" was Ms. Candace Mills: suite 4111. There was a number with a 310 area code. From her station on the desk Allicia dialed, got voice mail, and left this message: "Ms. Mills, this is *Allicia* from the Garden Suites Inn returning your call. I will try again later or you can reach me at your convenience. Thank you so very much."

Five hours passed before the 310 number showed up on the front-desk telephone.

"This is Allicia, Ms. Mills. How can I be of service to you?"

"You could arrange for some decent cell reception in this state of yours," Ms. Mills said.

"Ah, yes," Allicia said in the most professional of tones. "We do suffer from some spotty areas."

"I'm still on the Recce,* so if I drop out can I talk to you tonight when I'm back at the Sweet Garden of Allah?"

"Certainly, if that is what you prefer."

"My preference has nothing to do with . . . can you hear me? Can you hear me? Can you hear me? Oh, sh . . ."

★　★　★

Dace Mills sat on a stool at one of the high tables in the Evening Station, digging into a medium-sized tub of mint chocolate chip ice cream from Ye Olde Shoppe. Her knitting tote was on the opposite stool, along with her leather oat-sack of a purse. Minutes earlier she, Bill Johnson, Clyde Van Atta, and the unpopular John Madrid had come into the lobby looking like they'd spent the day on a too-small sailboat in too-heavy seas, all windblown and oversunned. They had stopped at Ye Olde Ice-Cream Shoppe, the men taking their *Good-Nites* with them into the elevators and up to their suites. Bill Johnson waved his pint of vanilla and rainbow sprinkles at Allicia as he passed the front desk, a spoonful of it in his mouth.

When Allicia had a moment free, she walked over to the Evening Station and made a cup of hot herbal tea in a Garden Suites HOT DRINK! container using one of the bags from the plexiglass dispenser.

"Would now be a good time to chat, Ms. Mills?" she asked.

"*Cah oo sitt?*" Dace had a mouthful of green cream in her mouth, so she gave that question another shot. "Can you sit?"

"I can," Allicia told her. "But we've an arrival due in a bit and it looks bad if I have to get up to check them in."

"*Bah ahp-tix.*" Dace let another spoonful of the mint chocolate chip melt in her mouth and came back with "Bad optics."

"How can I be of service, Ms. Mills?"

"Dace. Short for Candace." She jammed her spoon into her leftover ice cream and set the tub down on the thin wooden tabletop, shoving the thing away from her. "If that's a medium serving, they should call it all-you-can-eat."

* Reconnaissance, per the language on Fountain Avenue.

Allicia smiled and sipped her hot herb broth.

"Allicia, I've been in this hotel only about seventy-two hours and you have already made my life easier."

"I'm pleased to hear that." Allicia was not lying.

"My boss can be a demanding little punk sometimes. A request for frozen yogurt at ten p.m. has often landed in my lap just as I'm heading into the shower after a long day."

"I was happy to be of service, really."

"Once, in the South of France—*the Côte d'Azur*—we'd been partying the night before with champagne and *moules-frites* and bottles of wine and did I mention champagne?"

"Sounds like fun."

"Oh, Alice, you have no idea. I took a French guy back to my room! Our driver! His name was *Guy*. I was bold that night." She didn't know it, but her hands found her tub of ice cream and she was spooning another taste into her mouth, letting it melt slowly, then chewing on a few chips of chocolate. "Anyway, *Guy* and I were getting to know each other in a *va-va-va-voom* way when that phone bleated and it's my boss saying, 'Find me a place to pick out some pocketknives.' It's four in the morning. And do you know what I said to him, after catching my breath, since, you know, *Guy* and I had been *vooming*?"

"I can only imagine," Allicia said. She liked this Dace Mills.

"I said 'Sure, boss. When do you want to go?' He said after breakfast. Six hours later I've got him standing in a French cutlery shop, flicking open Buck knives and testing the cutting edges. He picked out six switchblades. Christmas presents, he said. He told me to take care of the bill, the VAT papers, and getting the weapons giftwrapped and shipped back to the USA." Dace spooned a bit more ice cream. "'*Udd ooo yoo 'ake a dis tory?*'"

Allicia had no idea what to make of the saga of French knives. She darted an eye to the front entrance in case those arrivals showed up. "What happened after," she said. "With *Guy*."

Dace laughed as she swallowed. "Oh, I took care of him. For a good long while. And never saw him again, which was *perfect*. Who needs a Frenchman in their life? *Enough*, already," she said, pushing her ice cream away for a second time. "So . . ."

Allicia snapped into her Garden Suites executive management mode, her mental note card at the ready.

"Say I need pocketknives, pronto. What do I do?"

"Tonight?"

"First thing tomorrow."

Let It Settle, Then eNact: "Campers Supply Hunting and Fishing Depot. Rebel Square Mall. Not in the mall proper, but it takes up the corner. If you give me a few hints, I could have samples of knives brought over so you can avoid a trip. Say, a dozen or so?"

"Wow." Dace Mills leaned back in her high stool and, with one eye closed, took in the measure of Allicia of the Garden Suites Inn. "Off the top of your head and straight from your shoulder. I mean it. *Wow.*"

"Are you looking for penknives or full-on blades or Leatherman, Swiss Army kind of knives?"

"Alice whatever-your-last-name-is . . . ," Dace said.

"Mac-Teer. *Allicia* Mac-Teer."

"Ally Mac-T . . ." Dace cocked her head and looked Allicia in the eye. "Are you happy in your work in the hospitality industry?"

"Very much so. The corporation has good opportunities for advancement. I could move on to other Garden Suites in Florida, even the Bahamas. They're opening sites in Europe. Frankfurt. It beats the stuffing out of the other career path I was on." The memory of her uniform at the Chick-&-Tender sent a shudder through Allicia's Garden Suites green tunic. "Oh, my. I must get back on the desk. I enjoyed our talk, Dace."

Dace got up from her place at the high table, reaching for her tub of melting mint ice cream, but Allicia grabbed it for her—it and the empty teacup went into the RECYCLABLES bin. Dace picked up her purse and tote and walked with Allicia to the front desk.

"You know we're going to be leaving you ASAP?" Dace said.

"I hope when you return to Richmond you'll stay with us, it's been our pleasure serving you."

"Oh, we're not leaving Richmond. We'll be in Richmond for months." Dace was not heading to the elevators. "And I want you to work for me."

Allicia heard that. She Let It Settle but could not Then eNact . . . anything.

"Pardon me?"

"People like you are worth your weight in gem-encrusted gold bullion: You. Solve. Problems. Fast and clean. With alacrity. No pauses, no shunting off with 'I'll connect you with our someone other than me.' From rainbow sprinkles to Swiss Army knives in the wink of an eye. You kick ass."

Allicia cracked a smile and shook her head, as though she was not about to believe anything more that came out of the mouth of Dace Mills of suite 4111. The woman was pouring it on a little too thick. All this chatter could be a prelude to *How about we get a drink and talk about your* future? *I have some single malt up in my room.* That sad line of bullshit came Allicia's way all the time and made her cold. Any man who tried this on Allicia became a blank-faced predator, a nemesis. Any woman, too.

"How about it?"

"Ms. Mills. Not to be rude, but how about *what*?" Allicia meant *Stop screwing with me I have to get back to work.*

"You don't know what we do?"

Ms. Mills and those with her were booked under the company name of Optional Enterprises. Whatever Optional Enterprises did was of no concern to Allicia. Make aluminum cans? Develop real estate? Search out small ice-cream shoppes to franchise?

"I do not," Allicia said.

"We make motion pictures," Dace told her.

Let It Settle. Then eNact . . .

★ ★ ★

The next morning, at the Waffle Time restaurant a short steamy walk from the Garden Suites Inn, an off-site meeting occurred between Allicia Mac-Teer and Dace Mills.

"I think I've sweated off five pounds," Dace said, downing the huge glass of orange juice Allicia had ordered, waiting for her—not fresh squeezed but very cold and very orange. "Lord, this humidity, I'm soaked. Should have brought a change of clothes."

Allicia, having arrived early, was at the two-top table with immovable seats. Juice had been had, coffee was coming, and the standard-menu breakfast would be up next. And she was proactively all ears. With a possible tidal wave of information to come, a limit of five mental note cards would not do, so she had a fresh composition book and a 1-800 Garden Suites ballpoint pen at the ready.

Never in her life had Allicia been *offered* employment. Her jobs had come only after applications. Her salary had always been *This is what we pay*—never as much money as she hoped for, barely what she needed. But this meeting with this Dace woman? At Waffle Time? This was an unexpected nod from fate, like something out of a movie. No, a *motion picture.*

Making a motion picture? Allicia had been sounding those words since the night before. *Here in Richmond? That happens? Aren't movies made in Hollywood or Tunisia? At sea or in Hawaii, certainly, but not here; in New York City and places that look like New York City. Richmond does not look like New York City. And what job could I possibly do in the making of a motion picture? I know nothing about . . .*

"Put the pad and pen away," Dace said as a uniformed waitress, name-tagged JUNELLE, came to pour coffee. Dace added two mini-cartons of portion-controlled half-and-half and, grudgingly, a pack of Sweet 'N Low. Sipping, she made a face. "Okay. This is ghastly. But it is caffeine, so . . ." She sipped more.

"I ordered waffles with sides of eggs, bacon, and cottage cheese," Allicia said. "The fare here is pretty basic."

"A waffle for breakfast is like starting your morning with birthday cake," Dace said.

"As a kid, Waffle Time was for Sundays after church," Allicia said. "In high school, we'd come in late, and hang until we'd get too loud and be asked to leave."

"Tell me about school," Candace said. "By the way, this is the chitchat portion of my meeting with you. It's not a test. Once the food arrives, we'll *get it on*. Were you a truant at all? Cut classes and such?"

Allicia took a nanosecond of a pause, weighing how to talk about her school days. Her fifth-grade year, when she was only ten years old, was a horror show. She was growing up in Baltimore when older boys in the neighborhood taught her how to inhale smoke and got her stoned. They then did terrible things to that little girl and left her wandering the streets miles from her home. She was hospitalized and very, very hurt. She was so afraid and so confused. She was talked to by a constant lineup of policewomen, Child Protective Services officers, and doctors. Then her brother was arrested for severely beating one of the predators, seriously wounding another; distant members of her family were involved. Drugs were found and weapons and, oh, the world fell apart. She did not go to school for the rest of that year and lived in a foster home until her aunt and uncle came and took her to their house in Richmond, where Allicia knew no one other than her two grown cousins, Darrell and Micha. She repeated fifth grade in silence. She did not speak except at home. She was silent in church on Sundays. She was sent to a special school and spent many hours with a woman named Dr. Faith—her first name—who loved to read books and talk about the stories in them. For a long time, Allicia did not talk with Dr. Faith. They would go into a kitchen and make pizza for themselves in silence. Allicia liked making those pizzas, the following of instructions to a T. She was thirteen when her uncle died of diabetes. Darrell left for the Marine Corps. Micha moved to Florida, leaving Allicia in high school, living alone with her aunt, often tormented by the most horrible nightmares a girl could have. There were boys in the high school (and some men in the neighborhood) who proved themselves to be blank-faced predators. Her first job was for Maids-of-America cleaning houses, but she quit when a husband would not leave when she showed up to do her work. The guy followed her around the house, asked too many personal questions, and suggested she join him for a drink when she was finished with the bathrooms. She applied at Burger Circus (no openings) and Chick-&-Tender (started part-time), went to community college, looked after her aunt until her aunt moved to Florida to be with Micha. Allicia avoided having boyfriends (none made her feel safe) and checked in with Dr. Faith occasionally. College and Chick-&-Tender filled her life; she was quiet in both worlds.

"I was quiet in school" was how Allicia explained all that to Dace.

"I went to high school like a hen goes to a henhouse. It was a building and I was supposed to be in it," Dace said. Then the food arrived. "That was almost *too* fast."

"Enjoy," Junelle said, as though everybody did at Waffle Time.

"Look at this mixture of batter, butter, and sweet syrup a quarter inch thick. Blood sugars, prepare. I make this vow to you, Alice: this is my last waffle breakfast in the state of Virginia."

After folding one strip of bacon into her mouth, Dace began a monologue that lasted the better part of an hour, according to the Waffle Time clock above the counter. There was no reason to take notes, she explained to Allicia, because there would be no to-do list coming, no agenda, no dos and don'ts. What Allicia heard from Dace was more like a sermon on life than a job interview, a philosophical rap filled with musings and rhetorical questions on human nature. Candace talked about baseball players in the field and astronomers pondering the cosmos in ways that, somehow, had something to do with the making of motion pictures. She talked of muses and airline schedules, the mysteries of creation, and the accidents of genius. She mentioned equipoise, hexes, obliviousness, and something called hang fire. She told stories about "flameouts," "falls from grace," and "the hubris of medium talent." She said movies always started shooting on Wednesdays so that everyone had three days to prove themselves. The incompetents would be fired on Friday night and replaced by Monday. She said that no matter how much you spent on building a bridge, you never owned the river. That Jacques Cousteau helped invent scuba diving.

There was a quality to Dace that made Allicia think of Dr. Faith. She enjoyed the listening.

"I see the confusion in your eyes, Alice," Dace said. "Don't concentrate too much on any of this." She shared an anecdote about how once, on a movie, she'd spent an entire workday learning how to knit, a skill that she credited with saving her sanity in the kookoo work she did. A character actress hired as a Day Player was in a triple banger* for hours and hours because her role was, as yet, still OC.† Dace had knocked on her thin trailer door, just to smooth

---

* A trailer with three separate dressing rooms.

† Off camera.

over any potential problem a too-early Call Time[*] might cause. The actress, in her seventies, was perfectly content and could not have been sweeter, sitting there in the clean, spartan, antiseptic-scented holding cell. She was knitting a scarf out of navy-blue yarn.

"Can I get you anything?" Dace had asked her.

"An iced tea would be super," the lady said.

"I agree!" Dace radioed for two teas on ice for Cast Number 37. Minutes later, an AD showed up with cans of peach-flavored iced tea and red Solo cups of ice. Dace sat on the steps of the triple-room trailer with the door open, sharing her drink with Number 37, talking about anything under the sun other than the fact that the woman had been there all day, but had yet to work a lick.

"Oh, they pay me to wait, honey. I act for free," the woman said.[†]

"What'cha working on there?" Dace asked about the knitting, which led to a description of the scarf being made for a granddaughter in Boston and a treatise on the therapeutic, calming qualities of making clothes by hand, of always having something to do, of being occupied with something other than the job. Dace had never, ever thought it was possible to have an activity in addition to her insane workload. There was no time for doing more; there were only so many hours in her day. How could balls of yarn and a pair of knitting needles *add* to the quality of her day? But damn if old Number 37 did not exude the very essence of *serenity*.

Cast Number 37's name was Sage Kingsolver. She'd been a working actor (though she preferred "actress") since she had one line in *The Alamo,* directed by none other than John Wayne in 1960. Over the next three days, Sage showed Dace how to knit, for which Dace made sure the actress was on the Call Sheet for the entire week. Sage made better money than expected for her three lines in two short scenes and was not Picture Wrapped until 9:58 p.m. that Friday night, when she presented Dace a gift of needles, yarn, and a tote to carry them. Dace spent that weekend knitting her first-ever handmade scarf. The movie was *Charlie Who?* Sage Kingsolver

* The hour on the clock when everyone is to report for work. The official start of the day, time- and pay-wise.

† This is a very old adage used on movie sets, credited to the likes of Orson Welles, Jason Robards, Olivia de Havilland, and Julie "Catwoman" Newmar.

passed away in her sleep four years ago, her photo appearing in the In Memoriam tribute at the SAG Awards.

"You learn as you walk along Fountain Avenue," Dace told Allicia. "Like they say in the Canadian navy, 'There's no life like it.'" Her waffle was gone, eaten in bites between her stories, in the pauses of her anecdotal bullet points. "I ate that whole thing. I predict I will sleep like a baby in about half an hour. So . . ." Dace wiped her mouth and finished her cup of caffeine. "Ally Baba. What do you make of everything I just said?"

Allicia had hung on every word. Instinctively, she knew whatever came out of her mouth could be neither flippant nor hesitant. She and Dace were not two girls out on a gossip fest, new friends who found they had more in common than their ovaries. Over waffles, Dace had scattered flowers upon the waters of what was, really, a turbulent line of work: a stressful job done by vulnerable human beings—all cracked vessels, all fraught with insecurities, all in high-pressure careers of continuous, make-or-break moments. Allicia wondered why everyone in the motion picture business didn't knit for sanity. She took a moment, not to invent some equitable answer that would merely sound smart, but to frame her vocabulary, to capture the gestalt of all she had heard Dace say.

Dace's eyes were locked onto her, her head tilted, expectantly awaiting Allicia's response, one that might be perfect, or could mean the woman had not only just burdened her digestive system but, a thousand times worse, wasted her time. "Give me a bullet point or two," she ordered.

Allicia thought two seconds more. *Bang.* "Making movies is about solving more problems than you cause." Allicia noted the hope-filled, upticked arch of Dace's right eyebrow. *Pow.* "It's not for pussies."

Dace nodded. "Very, very well put."

★　★　★

Allicia gave the Garden Suites Inn a week's notice, during which she trained her replacement, T'naiah, who qualified for the Diversity in Management Program. She sent notes to all her superiors and to the home office, thanking them for their trust in her, for all that she had learned while working for the Garden Suites Inn Corporation of America.

On a Monday morning, Allicia was introduced to Clyde Van Atta who, as a First Assistant Director of the motion picture, was Dace's equal, her cohort and coconspirator. Dace's official title was Producer. "You think you have what this job takes, do you?" Clyde asked her, with a low-budget smile. "Right now, there are people in Los Angeles sleeping in their cars, hoping to get the shot you've been given. You know that, don't you?" Allicia was *gobsmacked* into silence, rescued by Dace, who hollered, "Leave that woman alone! Get in the van, Clyde!" Before they left for a Recce, Dace handed Allicia a Nokia mobile phone with a pair of prestored numbers, those of Dace Mills and Clyde Van Atta. In time, her ear brick would hold twenty-eight speed-dial numbers—each one also written in the composition book Allicia carried in her ever-shouldered messenger bag.

"Time to *get it on*, Alice. Bang! Pow!" Dace said, stepping into the minibus, leaving Allicia to *get it on*.

The immediate problem to land in Allicia's lap was moving Dace, Bill Johnson, and Clyde Van Atta out of the shithole that was the Garden Suites Inn.[*]

★   ★   ★

The title of the movie they were making was *Ask No Questions (Hear No Lies)*. Not that the name mattered at all to Allicia. The movie could have been called *Monkeys Make Bad Pets* or *The Goblins of Tumble Town*. She did not read the screenplay, or even hold a copy of it, until weeks later, by which time she had a supply of buck slips with OPTIONAL ENTERPRISES printed at the top and her name displayed at the bottom (ALLICE MCTEER), her own desk outside the office of Dace Mills, and the task of making coffee just how Dace liked it. The Production Office was on a cul-de-sac in Mechanicsville called Ten Pin Alley, in what had once been the

---

[*] What about John Madrid? He returned to Los Angeles, to his duties as the studio executive assigned to the movie. It was true that he was not liked, because . . . he was the studio executive assigned to the movie. Whenever he showed up again in his duties as the studio executive, he stayed at the Garden Suites Inn.

head offices and manufacturing plant of a bowling equipment company. Allicia Mac-Teer (not *Allice McTeer,* for crying out loud) had helped secure the place and equip it with office furniture, supplies, phone lines, pens and paper and colored highlighters, computer printers and paper, extension cords and surge protectors, corkboards and pins, whiteboards with markers and erasers, envelopes of every size, staplers and staples, folding chairs and tables, coffee makers, espresso makers, coffee and espresso supplies, a refrigerator and microwave, disposable spoons and knives and forks and plates and cups, a cutting board and serrated knife, posted lists of the nearest hospital, police station, dental clinic, grocery store, drugstore, veterinarian, movie theater, delicatessen, and auto shop, as well as the number for the Suicide Prevention Hotline.

Her first day on the job, which coincided with the official start of the film's Preproduction, a.k.a. Prep, had Allicia talking with real estate agents, apartment managers, and absentee landlords to schedule viewings of places to lease. She was to find, approve, and hold housing for some of the department heads coming in from all over America to make the motion picture. Allicia discovered a renovated townhouse for Bill Johnson—a place that would wear better and better over the months of Prep, Principal Photography, and Postproduction—as it was but a short drive from the PO—but Dace took one look at it and claimed it for herself. "This joint screams *me*!" Dace said, throwing her knitting bag onto an overstuffed paisley-printed sofa. "Put *el jefe* in the cigarette factory."

She meant the retrofitted loft that had once been a tobacco warehouse. The owner had installed a hard-wire state-of-the-art stereo system in 1979, and wall upon wall of cataloged vintage vinyl LPs. Bill Johnson loved the place, bragging that, during his off moments on *Ask No Questions (Hear No Lies),* he never once turned on the television but spun discs instead, hearing records he never knew existed, including *Learn the Cha-Cha at Home with Sal Diego!*

Allicia was surprised that some of the departments had been up and running well before she was hired. Locations, for example, had been in Richmond for a month. Transportation had booked local Teamsters. In rapid order, the other departments took over offices and cubicles on Ten Pin Alley: Assistant directors. Casting. Camera. Sound. Art direction. SPFX. Construction. Travel.

Accounting. When Housing was up and running, headed by one Mary Beech, Allicia was no longer enmeshed in the search for living spaces—that was MB's turf. Allicia earned the eternal fandom of MB by arranging a great crew rate at the Garden Suites Inn with just a single call. This was a big win for *ANQ(HNL)*—money was saved and a problem was taken off MB's desk! After but one crumpled mental note card, Allicia was *golden*, but no less on the clock 24/7.

For the next eleven months, Allicia solved riddles, eased pressures, ironed out bumps, and made problems fade away like passing rain squalls. She made sure bottled water was plentiful—cold if needed, room temp if preferred. She made reservations of all kinds—restaurants, helicopter tours, movie tickets. As a Virginian herself, she heard the complaints and settled the qualms of locals who squawked that "that movie crew" was making too much of a damn nuisance! With twenty dollars from her own pocket, she bribed a kid to knock off the noise with his power mower for a morning shoot, then brought him a Popsicle from Craft Service that afternoon. Dace called her twenty times a day with questions and orders: How fast can I get a window AC unit installed? Can you drive a stick shift? *Sal Diego* (Bill Johnson) was not wild about that pizza last night. The crust was too thick, and the toppings were too tomatoey. Find a Neapolitan-style place. Allicia's duties were not unlike those she had performed when she had been dressed in her Garden Suites green tunic, but they were constant, never ceasing, and needed to be done *stat*; she was solving problems that were all like equations needing to be proofed—pocketknives x frozen yogurt + rainbow sprinkles to the 3rd power. There were some lifestyle advantages, like always wearing comfortable shoes and Transpo leasing her a new Jeep to replace that ugly, shitbox Tercel of hers, which meant she could stop logging her gas and mileage. When she was working out of the PO on Ten Pin Alley, a Teamster would take the Jeep out for a wash and fill-up.

From that first Monday of her first week in Prep, Allicia began to understand the demands a movie made of its crew, starting with the Recces. Recces were exhausting daylong road trips in a van with every seat taken by the departments to a site where everyone piled out like from a clown car, talking all at once, splitting off in different directions, pointing fingers at the perimeters, the buildings, the trees, the liquor store across the street, the power lines on the horizon, until, with the site fully inspected and judged, they'd all pile back into the van, immediately get on their mobile phones, talking loudly to be heard over all the people talking at once, as the Teamster would drive to the next stop to be recced. As many as twelve sites were visited on some days, with a fifty-minute meal of Chinese food or barbecue or chicken-fried steaks—at restaurants Allicia had to arrange. When a Recce finally came to an end and they were back at Ten Pin Alley, the departments, with no more pause than a visit to the lavatory or the snack room, would set to work instigating all that had been learned and decided in the last ten hours and 127 miles. It was on Recce days when Allicia had an ever-so-slight tinge of longing for her old, air-conditioned lobby job and her Garden Suites green tunic.

This changed when—weeks into the job—late on a Friday night, in Dace's townhouse, the two women were drinking margaritas with their shoes off and going over the schedule for the weekend—there would be a dog-and-pony show with the Virginia Film Office, show-and-tells with SPFX and the Hair/Makeup Departments, a safety meeting with the ADs, and, that night, for anyone interested, a screening of De Sica's *Miracle in Milan,* the precursor to the classic *The Bicycle Thief,* at the suggestion of Bill Johnson. On Sunday, there was some football game on a big screen at one of the crew hotels. (Guess which one. Allicia asked T'naiah to arrange the buffalo wings.) Rehitting MIX on her blender, Dace asked Allicia what she thought of the screenplay for *Ask No Questions (Hear No Lies).*

"I don't know," Allicia said.

"Not the answer I was looking for, Alley-Oxen Free," Dace poured out more of the boozy slush, refilling both glasses to their brims. "Outside of our inner sanctum, you tell anyone who asks that our script is fabulous, surprising, filled with wonders and *oohs* and *ahhs.* But between us—particularly over alcohol in a glass—you speak straight from your shoulders. Is this script lame? Dumb? Standard? A programmer? Been done already? Or . . ." Dace downed some margarita so quickly she had a brain freeze. She took to tapping herself on the forehead. "Do you think we are making another major motion picture masterpiece?"

"Move your tongue to the back of your throat to warm the sinus passageway," Allicia suggested.

Dace tried it. "*Goh-gay,*" she said. "Hey, that sort of worked. So . . . out with it. The script. Thumbs-up or thumbs-down?"

"No idea." Allicia sipped on her second margarita.

"Why are you recalcitrant in your opinion of our script?"

"I haven't read it."

"Why the hell not?"

"Am I allowed to?"

"You're on the picture!"

"No one's given me a copy. The ones I've seen have assigned numbers on them. I've had peeks at a few pages, in the van on Recces and around the PO. Each page has the crew member's name in highlights printed across the text. Looks like an Eyes-Only Top-Secret document to me."

"Oh, criminy. That's in case a script is lost by some cluck or stolen by some agency spy. Or a copy is snuck to the Hollywood Foreign Press Association before we officially give them an edited version." Dace put her half-empty margarita glass down on the coffee table—she'd be having a third one, certainly—and went into what was a second bedroom that had been teched out into an office. Allicia heard the computer printer power up and in seconds there was the *sha-plop—sha-plop—sha-plop* of pages spitting into the collector.

Dace came back into the living area after a swing by the kitchen island for the remainder of the green elixir. "You'll have a copy in a couple of minutes. You'll read it tonight. We'll talk about it first thing. And we will kill this off," she said, topping off Allicia's margarita first, then her own. There was half an inch of the drink still in the pitcher, so Dace raised it to her lips and drank straight from the spout. Killed: margaritas.

When she had to tap her forehead again, Allicia reminded her—move the tongue to the back of the throat.

* * *

Once you learn the format and nomenclature of a screenplay, reading one is like seeing a foreign-language movie with English subtitles—you forget the translation and comprehend the film as written on the page. The script for *Ask No Questions (Hear No Lies)* was like the movie on the screen but with enough differences that made it more interesting. This is because Bill Johnson wrote his screenplays as rough templates, guidelines for scenes that began in his head, became physically detailed through the months of production meetings and jawboning with his department heads, allowed for spurts of improvisation On the Day,[*] all resulting in whatever was captured in the camera and altered in the edit. Big moments, like the three-semitruck crash, were in the script: if it's not on the page, it's not on the stage. But Bill added new elements to the movie all the time, on the fly, via whims that came to him the night before shooting or in the car on his way to the set. And if an actor had a worthy idea that made the scene fly a bit higher, it might make it into the Locked Print.

The screenplay that Allicia read—all in one sitting, despite the wooze caused by all that lime, tequila, and triple sec—said nothing about TREASURY AGENT ABBOTT THORPE (played by Ross McCoy) teaching himself the cha-cha in his lousy apartment by listening to an old 33⅓ LP. When the president of the United States calls Thorpe at midnight, the record needle is lifted off the phonograph, and Thorpe takes the call, mid-cha-cha. Bill added the cha-cha bit On the Day, pitching the idea to McCoy that morning over coffee and muffins in the Hair/Makeup trailer. McCoy was very sleepy when Bill came in to talk about the idea and had trouble imagining what the director was talking about. But then bought it.[†]

"So, here's what I think of the script," Allicia said. She and Dace were in the snack room. Dace was slicing whatever was sold as a

---

[*] On the Day: when shooting the scene in question.

[†] Ross McCoy, then, was on the ascent of his bounce on Fountain Avenue. Allicia found him to be, yes, gorgeous, but also a *dog*. He came at Allicia hell-bent on bagging her. She did not like that at all. Which only made Ross desire her more. In today's world, he'd be brought up on sexual harassment charges. The same would have happened for three members of the crew who subjected Al to discomforting comments and contact.

bagel in Richmond, Virginia. Allicia was frothing some half-and-half with the primitive Viva! cappuccino maker.

"Not here, Loose Lips," Dace told her. "My office, door closed." At this point in Prep, staff was working early on Saturdays.

Dace's office overlooked the parking lot on Ten Pin Alley, her window partially blocked by three sad palm trees that needed tending.

"Now. What'd ya think?" Dace asked as Allicia closed the door behind her. "Our names are gonna be on this sucker."

Allicia sat. "Well, the story is whatever a movie is supposed to be. Ripping. Exciting."

"A taut, edge-of-the-seat thriller?" Dace sipped her Allicia-made caffeine.

"If you say so. Politics and espionage and Treasury agents fighting bad guys. I didn't know Treasury agents were thus tasked, but I bought it. I was surprised that KANE was not the mole. Had he been I would have thought, Wow, that's so obvious, but then he wasn't and I liked that. The sex scene with AGENT ZED, though, is just ridiculous."

"It's supposed to be sexy."

"It's ludicrous. Making love in an abandoned stable during a thunderstorm? In wet clothes? With spiders and splinters and soggy hay? Who does that?"

"In movies, everybody all the time." Dace licked a dollop of super-chunky peanut butter that had leaked off her bagel and onto her finger. "And Ginny Pope-Eisler may be Agent Zed.* The studio'll want her naked, simulating sex in soggy hay. The crew will, too. Her body double'll make a few bucks."

"I love that the world is saved by Abbott Thorpe, but no one knows about it and no one ever will, and he goes back to his lousy apartment and government job without so much as Agent Zed's phone number to show for it. That illuminates the theme."

"Theme? You have an opinion on the *theme*? Let's hear it."

"The protectors of our freedom are unknown soldiers—the men

---

* Ginny Pope-Eisler's deal could not be made, so she passed. Maria Cross played AGENT ZED, as you know, a casting choice that infuriated Ginny the moment she heard of it.

and women who don't get rich or famous or celebrated. It's a sad comment on our modern times."

Dace sat back into the stiff lumbar brace of the rented chair of her rented desk. The thing was going to cripple her over time. "You actually got that from the screenplay?"

"Well, it's not stated in so many words, but I read between them."

"Bill Johnson is going to love you once he learns your name. But you and I are not here to wallow in the divide between text and subtext. We're in Production. We deal in problems. Such as, basic math. At two pages a day, how long will our shoot be?"

Allicia thought for a second before recalling that the script she read was 127 pages long. "Sixty-three and a half days."

"Ouch." Dace had again leaned back into the lumbar brace on her chair. "This thing hurts its occupant."

"Get out," Allicia told her. When Dace stood, Allicia spun the chair around and found the tension knob in the middle of the seat's back.

Dace said, "A sixty-three-day shoot puts us over budget by one point two million dollars and that gets our boss into hot water."

"Try it now," Allicia said, stepping away as Dace sat back into the chair.

"This is a thousand times better!" The chair was now as comfy as British Airways first-class.

"Want me to raise it higher?"

"Not needed." Dace took another bagel bite, another sip of her coffee. "So . . . ," she said, chewing, "we're budgeted for a fifty-five-day shoot. If we wrap filming on day fifty-two, our boss is a maestro. They throw him a parade down Fountain Avenue and he writes his own ticket for the next five years or three films, whichever comes first. Unless, of course, the movie tanks. Then, our boss is burnt toast and gets sympathetic looks from the people avoiding him. But, say, *Ask Dumb Questions (Soap in Your Eyes)* pulls in seven hundred fifty million dollars in rentals and is hailed as a benchmark in the history of cinema, Bill could have taken ninety-nine days plus a two-week reshoot to finish the movie, and no one'll care a whit. He'll still get his parade."

"So . . ." Allicia had taken up the habit of the vocal ellipsis. "If a movie shoots two pages a day? The math doesn't work then?"

"Shooting two pages a day is a canard. Some days getting an eighth of a page is a miracle—the actor has the flu, the rigging won't hold, the camera goes down. No matter what you try, that dog won't hunt. Are we behind schedule? Maybe. The next day, a seven-page dialogue-heavy walk-and-talk is finished before lunch, and the afternoon is nothing but Second Unit inserts and drive-ups. Are we ahead of schedule? *Maybe.* This is why this gig is NFP."[*] Dace sipped coffee. "What do you say about the night scenes? The rain?"

"Atmospheric preludes to the required sex scenes, I suppose."

"True. But to shoot? A hell train nightmare. They'll take a week. Call Times: five forty-five p.m. Monday: we work till the sun comes up Tuesday morning. Twelve hours later we're back at it, our body clocks out of whack. Everyone is miserable by Wednesday. Sleep-walking disasters by sunrise on Saturday. And add rain? Fake movie raindrops have to be as thick as chickpeas. Call in the water trucks, firehoses, and rainbirds. A crane to lift the sprinkler pipe a hundred feet into the air, with grips holding on to guide ropes like they're steadying a zeppelin. Add *wet* and *cold* to *exhausted*. Dress appropriately and avoid catching the flu if that's possible."

"I'll be there?"

"Oh, Tiny Alice, you're not escaping Night Shoots."

Dace's mobile phone bleeped. "Hey, Yogi." Yogi was Yorgos Kakanis, the DGA trainee who dressed like he was living out of his car. "Okay. Comin' at ya." She clapped her phone shut and rose from her now-comfy rented office chair. "The Film Office peeps are here. I'm showing you off as a local hire, so don't say 'fuck.'"

★ ★ ★

In the final week of Prep with the start of the shoot six days away, Allicia found herself seated behind Dace's spot at the big, square-shaped table arrangement for the much-anticipated First Full Read-Thru. The room was filled to capacity; extra folding chairs were brought in, and some folks stood to take it all in. The First Full Read-Thru, Allicia learned, was a big deal. John Madrid and

---

[*] Not For Pussies.

other studio execs flew in to claim ownership of the movie. The departments were all present. As many of the cast members as possible were brought in, even some who did not work for weeks. Ross McCoy and Maria Cross added grunts and moans during the Sex in the Abandoned Stable Scene. Everyone laughed. Some got aroused. The people who had made movies before knew that the First Full Read-Thru was the No-Turning-Back-Now date on the schedule. Except, of course, for those who got fired.

Allicia found herself swept up in the moment, breathless— something new to her experience was about to happen, and she was in the room as both a witness and participant. She was going to help make a motion picture. Her body felt a tingle. She lost a bit of her physiological balance, her spiritual equilibrium, sensing a part of herself rising, up—up—up and out of her body—a spectral version of herself was suspended in the room, there, in the PO on Ten Pin Alley. She saw herself, she saw everyone, sitting below her around the square of tables, under fluorescent lights, as Bill Johnson read his own stage directions, as the actors read their lines with varying degrees of certainty and commitment. When the lingering spirit of Allicia heard Bill Johnson say, "Fade to Black. Roll End Credits," the corporeal Allicia Mac-Teer found her eyes misted, her hands applauding. She felt *safe*.

She was run ragged all that weekend and the Monday and Tuesday before the film started for real. Wednesday morning, she was at the Base Camp in a parking lot fifty-two minutes before the crew call at 7:00 a.m. Dace arrived at 6:33. They were both on the set for the movie's first shot—at 9:26 a.m.—its first slate, rolling on scene 42, take 1, hearing Bill Johnson call out, "Action!" Ross McCoy as Agent Abbott Thorpe ran from an alley, across a street, and down another alley. The first shot of any movie should always be so undemanding. Why? Because Dace said so. Allicia had assumed, as do all civilians, that the first shot of making a movie was the first shot of the movie itself, that the film was made in the order of the scenes. Day 1, scene 1. Makes sense, right? But making a movie makes no such sense. Scenes are often shot in order of locations or actors' schedules or for all sorts of other convenient or financially oriented reasons.

Principal Photography was a vibrant, fervent, harried blur of time with moments of exhaustion, panic, weeping, and confusion balanced by major laugh bust outs. There were thrilling things to eyewitness (want to know how they filmed that multiple truck crash? they got multiple trucks and crashed them!), group activities (a Texas Hold 'Em tournament at Ross McCoy's rented farmhouse, where Allicia lost her buy-in of sixty dollars and Ross first showed his *dog* demeanor), and a near on-set brawl between a Greensperson* and one of the lesser-experienced local hires in the Grip Department. Allicia watched in amazement as Clyde Van Atta showed off his On-Set Control Technique that calmed everyone down to the point of handshakes. That Friday, no one was fired. Allicia likened the making of *ANQ(HNL)* to what Basic Training must be in the Marine Corps.

Years later, the memories of those weeks were still inside her bones, creating tactile feelings and revered emotions that buzzed like an electric current. Tasked with the organizing of food and drinks for the end-of-day viewings of the Rushes—the footage shot on the previous day—Allicia could, if she wanted, stay and watch. She certainly did! Seeing all that raw footage—the camera positions, the dolly moves, the over-the-shoulders and the close-ups—the shooting of a motion picture started to make sense.

On Day 52 out of 60 Shooting Days, Allicia was sitting with Dace in her rented Mustang—the woman needed an American muscle car so Transpo arranged one. A thunderstorm was passing over as the entire Unit waited for the skies to clear. They were on the set a mile and a half from Base Camp. The scenes were 86, 86a, and 87—"Thorpe Misses the Drop"—and rather than sit in the Video Village tent with the muddy floor, Allicia got coffee from Craft Service and took the shotgun seat. The steady rain was making loud tack-hammer taps on the Mustang's roof.

"So . . ." Dace waved her cup at the windshield, at the Set, the Unit, and the rain. "What do you make of this? The job. The motion picture racket." Dace looked at Allicia. "What have you learned, Dorothy." She took a look at her watch, at the sweep-second hand just rounding the number 12. "I'll give you ten minutes. And . . . *hack!*"

---

* The department that places trees, bushes, and plants.

Collecting her thoughts, Allicia tried to organize her mental note cards but gave up. She could not condense all she had been through on just one hand. "Making a movie, I think, brings pressures that'll crack the bones of lesser folks. So many moments that are just merciless . . ." Allicia talked without interruption for nine minutes, thirty-six seconds, without pauses of *um, ya know,* or *kinda like.* The woman delivered a monologue, like a CIA sitrep. *Creative Chaos and the Effects on Human Interaction, Business Practices, and the Impact on the Local Environment During Operation* Ask No Questions (Hear No Lies). All that was missing were bullet points and a laser pointer.

"Well put" was all Dace said. "So . . ."

The rain was letting up; the ball-peen blows atop the Ford had grown softer. In a few minutes the crew would be back at work on scene 86a. "You understand, there is no reason for you to move to LA."

The idea of moving to Los Angeles had never crossed Allicia's mind. When *ANQ(HNL)* was completed, she would thank Dace for the trust she had given her, for the opportunity to be a part of something so grand and exciting, for all she had seen and learned. She would make sure to say the same to Bill Johnson—who by now was calling her *Alice Mac-T-Bird*—to Clyde Van Atta, and to all the department heads. In eight more shooting days the movie would Wrap; Principal Photography would be concluded. She would no longer be a part of the cash flow, meaning she'd be unemployed. She was planning to seek a position with the Virginia Film Office.

"To keep the Virginia tax rebate, we'll keep a Postproduction office open." Dace rolled the driver's-side window down and tapped the drops of cold coffee out of her cup. "You'll be my proxy there. You'll ride this picture out until we lock. Then you can sit around, flip through fashion magazines for a while. Date aggressively but don't get knocked up. I'm feeling the odds are ninety-five percent certain *Sal Diego* will have his next opus in his typewriter before this one gets panned by *Variety* and cheered by *The Hollywood Reporter.* Then, look to the western sky, Alice. I'll send up a flare."

Allicia was confused. "I'm confused," she said. "A flare?"

"I'll be needing you." As she was rolling the window back up, Dace said, "You're in the Picture Business now."

* * *

Oh, Dace! Let's meet tonight for margaritas at El Cholo!

Al thought of the woman every single day, hoping, wishing, that every incoming call would be Dace needing her. Over the years that COVID-19 wreaked its wanton havoc, she pondered what Dace would have made of the lockdowns, closures, and cancellations that had stopped traffic on Fountain Avenue, shuttering the cinemas. Streaming services such as the Hawkeye and its competitors had become the arbiters of what films were financed, which movies were seen, and how the audience viewed them. Seeing movies at home turned out to be not that bad.

"Al-bania," Dace would have said. "It's the death of vaudeville writ large." She'd learned what was what on Fountain Avenue.

* * *

Years before, Candace "Candy" Mills had been working for her widowed father at Mills Office Equipment in the city of Orange, California, her hometown. After the era of one-thousand-key adding machines, then the ten-key desk calculators, Amos Mills sold and serviced copiers and printers all over Orange, the county. Because of the income stream from toner cartridges alone, the shop was never idle nor broke. Printers and copiers jammed and froze up all the time, and when they did, Mills Office Equipment was there. Her father also had a sideline restoring old typewriters. In the back room there were vintage writing machines in various states of disrepair, and on the shelves were Royals, Underwoods, Remingtons, Hermes, Olivettis, all in working order. Occasionally, some got sold.

One day, Amos Mills was out on a call so his daughter was minding the store when a beat-up Ranchero—one of those half-car, half-pickup-truck vehicles, loaded down with all sorts of tools in the back—pulled into the metered slot in front of the shop. The driver, a lanky, skinny guy in worn work clothes, dirty with sawdust and dried putty, came through the door asking about the typewriters in the window and up on the shelves. Were they for sale?

"For those in need," Candy Mills told him.

"Any one of them better than the other?" the guy asked.

"Let me see your hands," Candy said. He held his up. They were the gnarled and skinned hands of a man who worked with hammers and scrapers and putty knives for a living. "Spread your fingers." He did. He had long fingers, like those of a pianist who could cover an entire octave with no strain. "You have long fingers. So . . ."

"So, I need a big typewriter."

"You don't need a typewriter at all." Computers and word processors had been getting cheaper by the week. "No one does, except maybe for addressing envelopes."

"I'm looking for a mechanical muse. An inspirational tool."

Candy looked out the window at the parked Ranchero, at the motley collection of tools, tarps, and hardware this guy was driving around with. "You going to just chuck it in the back with your power sander and saber saw?"

"No. I'll wrap it up in fine linen and treat it gently. Depending on how much it sets me back." He waved his long-fingered hand at the wall of typewriters. "What will one of these set me back?"

"Oh, those are all gems. Collector's items. Rarities. As much as sixty bucks."

He laughed. "I've been saving up for a new old typewriter."

He went to the shelves and read off the brand names of some of the machines—none made earlier than 1961. "Do I invest in a Voss? An Adler? This little cutie—the Hermes Rocket?"

"With those big mitts of yours? That Rocket will bring you to tears. Tell you what . . ." Candy came out from behind the counter rolling a wheeled chair. She pushed it to a low table that had an HP printer on it, which she picked up and set on top of another nearby HP printer. "Here's paper. Grab that Remington Noiseless. Sit here and write on it. Take it on a test drive. Switch out machines until one sings your song. What's your name and do you want a cup of horrible coffee?"

"Bill Johnson and yes. What should I call you?"

"Candy. Short for Candace."

"No, it's not. Still two syllables."

The coffee in Mills Office Equipment was Yuban from a can, dripped from an appliance so old and so beat-up that its decal had faded to MIS ER COFF. He took it with two sugars and more nondairy creamer than was good for a person. One by one, he typed on every single working typewriter in the shop—and the guy could *type,* not just a line or two of THE QUICK BROWN FOX, but whole paragraphs, testing the tabs and the margins. He didn't need to be told that a lowercase letter *L* was the absent number 1 (l) or that the machines without an exclamation mark meant that to make one you hit a period, then backspace, then held down SHIFT and punched 8!

Candy walked him through some of the knowledge she had picked up from her father. The Hermes were Swiss machines. The Olympias were made in West Germany. Towers were Smith-Coronas sold by Sears department stores. The guy was fascinated by every detail—like the extra keys on the Olympia with German umlauts and their lack of a $ key. After going back to some of the typewriters in a process of elimination, he crowned a champion: the black-on-black Smith-Corona Sterling. It had the best action, easy-to-set margins, and a space bar that never skipped. The Sterling also had the loudest bell.

"I gotta have that loud bell," he said. "To pierce my ferocious, laser-like concentration."

"Another coffee?" Candy asked. This would be his third *Mis er Coff.* He'd been in the shop for almost two hours.

"My body says no, but my addiction says, *Gimme.*"

For another half hour, the two talked—a mutual flirtation. She was in the shop to help her pop, she told him. She was a local girl, so had worked both at Disneyland as a ride operator and at Knott's Berry Farm as a ticket taker, both fine jobs with good hours and decent pay but the costumes, she found, were humiliating, and she could not always fake the mandated good cheer.

He was in California from Cleveland, Ohio, for two reasons, he told her—the climate's lack of winter's misery and to get into the Business of Show. In fact, he'd found work in Hollywood almost immediately, hanging wallpaper, where he met a guy who knew a guy who helped him land an entry-level job on a Swing Gang.[*]

---

[*] The Swing Gang works overnight, preparing a set or location for the next day's shooting. The small army of carpenters, painters, paperhangers, set dressers, grips, and electricians is always exhausted.

That was three years ago and was why he kept all the tools in the bed of his car/truck. Thus, his presence in the city of Orange—a film was going to shoot there for a few weeks, using existing storefronts and the former movie theater, now a Pentecostal church, as a location and sets.

"I heard about that. A movie in my hometown." Candy Mills's idea of a moviemaker was someone with less sawdust in his hair. "Why Orange?"

"It looks a bit like Erie, Pennsylvania."

Candy had never lived anywhere but Orange. "Didn't know that."

This customer did more than prep sets. "My head is restless," he said. He was also a writer, one who feverishly wrote and wrote and wrote unsold scripts that were met with industry-wide silence, so many that he'd worn out his hunk-of-junk 1972 Brother typewriter. He had, miraculously, gotten an agent from a cold-submission screenplay he'd written. But having representation is not the same as having a job. At night he swung with paint and putty, but in the daylight hours, fueled by coffee just as bad as that served at Mills Office Equipment, he'd beaten out a screenplay with the working title of *Stenographers Can Be Heroes Too*—a period piece about a young woman secretary in New York City in 1939—the same year as the Sterling's manufacture—when there were Nazi spies on the loose. He hoped to type his complete first draft on a working, old-fashioned typewriter—just as his title character would use.

"You mean, you're going to actually write on this?" Candy was surprised. After all, Mills Office Equipment dealt in laser printers. No one wrote on typewriters save old-lady mystery authors on TV shows who also solved crimes. "Brave you! Get yourself some onionskin paper for easy erasures. And you'll need these." Candy supplied two extra ribbons of over-and-under black and red, a pencil-looking thing that was specifically a sharpenable eraser with a mini-broom on one end, stiff brushes for keeping the keys and guts of the Smith-Corona free of gunk, a large eyedropper of sewing-machine lubricant, and the card of Mills Office Equipment with CANDY MILLS—EXPERT added in ballpoint pen. "Call if you have any problems. You won't, as my pop does good work. But if you need more horrible coffee, it's here."

The next week, he did stop by the shop for some more horrible coffee as well as some chitchat with Candy Mills, whom he called the single-syllable Dace, and who chitchatted right back. He took her to visit the movie location to see not only the labors of his night job on the Swing Gang—the whole street had been made to look like something out of Erie, Pennsylvania, in 1964—and to see a scene being shot. You'd think a movie being made would be a treat to witness, but all Candy—no, Dace—saw was a bunch of vintage cars and a bus driving around in circles. Everyone on the crew looked like they were being kept from lunch. There was a camera up on a crane's swing-arm, but what was special about that? Some guy was yelling orders at a lady, who then yelled the same orders through a bullhorn.

Dace Mills and Bill Johnson dated for a while—as in they slept together quite a number of times and made each other laugh, especially when they were stoned. He allowed her to read some of his pages of *Stenographers Can Be Heroes Too* once he was satisfied with them, which is where she learned screenplay terms like the slugline INT. OFFICE—DAY, which told everyone concerned that the scene took place indoors, in an office setting, and during daylight hours, and the Page 30 Event, which closed act 1 with some kind of expectation of what was to come. They stopped having sex with each other after a long talk about neither of them being "in it for the long haul" then going out for cheap Chinese food at a place in Huntington Beach. The two stayed pals. They did things on occasion like go to Disneyland (thanks to her contacts) and hang out at parties in North Hollywood (thanks to his).

When Bill Johnson changed the setting of *Stenographers Can Be Heroes Too* from Manhattan in 1939 to Anonymous City in 195-X (Communist agents, now) the budget came way, *way* down, so far down that he was able to direct (for no fee). By shooting at some of the same city of Orange locations with some of the same vintage cars, landing Maria Cross in the title role, and wrapping Principal Photography of the sucker on Day 17 of a seventeen-day shoot, Bill Johnson became, truly, a *Film Director*. And, as the main set of INT. OFFICE needed multiple desks—each with a vintage typewriter—Mills Office Equipment provided them all *for no cost!*[*] Dace Mills solved Bill's problems and kept him in Yuban for the month of Prep and all seventeen days of the shoot. He didn't pay her a dime but did something much better—he gave her a credit. ASSOCIATE PRODUCER: DACE MILLS rolled by on a gender-neutral single card during the end credits of the film, which had been retitled *The Typist*.

★   ★   ★

The cancer that made Amos Mills a widower was in the BRCA gene silently carried by many women; a crooked bit of DNA the mother had passed on to her daughter and only child. Damn if it didn't take Dace Mills's life with the same relentless fury, rolling up and into her body like a slow-moving night train.

As Bill Johnson's single-card producer since *The Nova Bosses*, Dace had made sure Allicia Mac-Teer remained on her desk after *ANQ(HNL)*. The next production, *Darkness of Eden*, prompted Allicia's move from her native Richmond to Baton Rouge, Louisiana. After the months of Prep and Principal, as happens to even the best of humans, Al transferred her life to the picture-postcard chimera that is Los Angeles. *Darkness of Eden* did Post at the Radford Studio near Ventura and Laurel Canyon: a.k.a. the Valley. Mary Beech of Housing found her a rental cottage in the Hollywood Hills—on the Valley side—with a next-door neighbor who looked like Cat Stevens (he was not) and a killer night view. Optional Enterprises had half of a floor in the circular Capitol Records Building in Hollywood, and Al had an office in it—a little pie slice of a room with a desk, phone, and a corkboard wall adjacent to Dace's office, a large, curved room with a picture on the door of Frank Sinatra from his ring-a-ding days. When Bill Johnson's screenplay for *Imperion* was liberated from Development Hell with a Green Light, Al was bumped up to her own rolling end credit as associate producer. To many people on Fountain Avenue, that meant she had

---

[*] Amos Mills was aghast! Free rentals? Bill Johnson placated Pop with a small role in the film as Patron in Line at the movie theater who says, "What's the holdup? I'm missing the newsreel!" Pop was all done in one take.

gravitas. Her phone started ringing more and more often with calls from brownnosing influence peddlers who sought out a moment of her time, just a few words with her about *something that could mean a lot to her, and maybe to Bill Johnson as well!* Al didn't care much for the air of desperation, the never-satisfied search for significance that governed the actions of so many of the citizenry of H'wood. She saw those people as Act of God problems to be either ignored or told to go away.* Al was smart enough to write notes to those who had done a good job, made a good movie, or provided a service that made the lives of Dace Mills, Bill Johnson, and her a little less complicated. Those notes on Optional Enterprises buck slips with AL MAC-TEER embossed at the bottom were not typed but written by hand.

With *Imperion* in Post, Dace *finally* moved in with her boyfriend of three years, Andy, the estate lawyer, the guy who had been asking for her hand in marriage ever since he had divorced his wife three and a half years prior. Andy lived in a house in the flats of the Valley. He had a special-needs son who required twenty-four-hour care, so the onetime horse barn had been converted into living quarters for the angels who looked after Andy Jr. With her commitment to that relationship and her move from her little place on one of the Helena Streets in Brentwood to Van Nuys (who does that?!), it made sense that Dace showed up less frequently at Optional Enterprises at Capitol. *Imperion* had shot on location in Albuquerque, New Mexico, for sixty-five days. Finally home, Dace had a football-field-sized yard to landscape, a man who needed a knitted sweater, and a special little boy who brought a worthy per-

---

* Ignoring such fools was simple. Al learned how to tell others to go away by overhearing Dace do that very thing on a call: "Listen, cluck-wad, you are very close to thinking you can fuck with me. You perk up on a conference call and demand a two-million-dollar cut in the budget when we are talking about the completion bond? Here's what we are going to do. You and your services are no longer needed by Optional Enterprises. You are fired. Shut up . . . Shut up . . . Shut up. No, you were not advising us of your expertise, you were cutting us off at the knees on a call with the fucking completion bond company, currying the favor of lawyers under the pretense of protecting the vision of my boss. You are gone. Gone. Firing you is saving us close to half a million dollars, as well as having to ever bother with you again. *Vaya con dios,* have a nice day . . . Yeah? That right? I don't give a shit."

spective to the worldly concerns of the Cardboard Carnival. And she had Al Mac-Teer to get things done.

Much was going on as *Imperion* rounded third, headed for home. *Horizon of Eden* was in Development. *Albatross* was but a submitted screenplay that had landed in Bill Johnson's restless gray matter. One midmorning Al was at Optional Enterprises, on the phone with the studio dealing with the list of invitees to the Tastemakers screening of *Imperion* (with a new temp score)[*] when she heard Dace come into the big office next door. Absolutely nothing was amiss, nor was there any anticipatory vibration in the air. When Al was done with the call she hung up and crossed through Dace's office on the way to what she called the refreshment station, down, or *around*, the uniquely curved hall.

"Coffee or something?" she asked Dace.

"An herbal tea," Dace said from her chair at her curved desk that matched the arc of the walls. Thinking back on the memory of that day, Al wondered why she failed to notice that Dace was without her knitting bag. Or that she had asked for an herbal tea. With beverages in matching mugs (a Rat Pack Sammy Davis Jr. smiling on one, Dean Martin on the other), Al heard Dace ask: "Hey, can you keep a secret?"

If Al had taken a sip of her coffee, she would have spit it all over the blond wood of Dace's crescent-shaped desk. "Ask me if I can tell a lie, why don't you? I lie every day, to everyone but you and Sal Diego." Al sat in the Design Within Reach chair opposite her Teacher, her Guide, her Sensei. "Secret keeping is most of what I do."

"I'm leaving, kiddo." Dace sipped her almond herbal tea. Then . . . there was silence.

I'm leaving, kiddo. With those words the axis of the world shifted, the lights went a bit dim, and Al's head jerked to the left, but her eyes stayed locked in place.

Al had noticed the weight loss, of course, the effects from what had to be medications. And there was the loss of energy in Dace's carriage. Al had noted that as well. As with Dace's absence from

---

[*] A temp score is music, any music, slotted into the movie until the final score is composed. Temp scores are usually musical cues from previous films.

the office, nothing was ever asked; no explanation was expected. Dace had been coming and going/calling or not calling since ABQ. If she had wanted Al to know something, she would have said so, straight from her shoulders.

I'm leaving, kiddo. Al didn't need to ask what those three words meant. She understood their simple yet ballast-laden intent. *I'm leaving, kiddo* was Dace-talk for *I'm leaving . . . you.*

Both women cried—Dace less so than her protégée. Al reached across the desk and took Dace's hand in her own, in friendship, in honor, in solidarity.

Dace died before *Imperion* was in the theaters, an impolitely fast exit, the hubris of medicine routed by the physiology of cancer.

Few people knew of Dace's limited time: Andy, Al, Bill Johnson, and Clyde Van Atta. The quartet was crippled by the prognosis, emotionally bent at the burden. Yet, for the next few months, they never insulted Dace by wasting her time with questions like *How are you feeling? What can I do for you? What are your blood numbers today?* When she stopped coming into Optional Enterprises, neither Al nor Bill Johnson paid her any visits. Dace talked to them on their BlackBerrys multiple times a day, preferring her audio/email/BBM wit to the stark visual of her body becoming more and more sticklike.

The last time Al, Bill Johnson, and Dace were in the same place, it was on the Mixing Stage for a final rundown of *Imperion*'s reels 5 and 6. Dace walked in under her own power—a Teamster had picked her up and would take her home—using a cane, so very skinny she seemed to float in the soft, dim light of the stage. After running the last third of what was the completed film, she said, "Well, Bill Johnson. You figured out how to make *that* motion picture." The three of them talked for the better part of another hour, most of it spent laughing their asses off. Then the Teamster drove her off the lot, back to her home in the Valley, and to the shores of Elysium. There was a memorial service, but Al couldn't remember any of it.

LONE BUTTE

Because Dynamo had failed to fold Knightshade into the *Agents of Change* franchise, the company all but wrote a check to Bill Johnson the day he made the pitch. The execs at Hawkeye congratulated themselves for landing the esteemed filmmaker on what was their inaugural big-budget franchise. While Bill Johnson went on with the writing of his screenplay, the rights for the flamethrower character were being hunted out by Business Affairs (at the Hawkeye), and someplace other than Atlanta was being sought for the shoot (by Dynamo).

Baton Rouge came hard and heavy for the picture, crowing about the Cajun food, showing off all they had set and ready as the best location to make the movie. New Mexico, Virginia, and Ohio (if the budget was on the small side) offered their states as money-saving back lots. Out of nowhere, the former East German city of Dresden also published a packet for the studio and streamer. A movie studio lay fallow just outside the city with an attached amusement park—*Kino World!* The tourist attraction was funded and built in the heady years after reunification and drew crowds for the roller coaster, Twist-o-Whirl, and its Cowboy-Land section complete with a poisoned Water Hole—WASSER VERBOTEN! There were five sound stages at *KinoWorld!*—built to attract production, with financing, if the city proper was used for at least one location. The *KinoWorld!* stages were currently empty, available, cheap!

Bill Johnson found no need to scout any of those candidates. He'd shot an *Eden* in Baton Rouge. The summer humidity took a solid three steps out of his stride, and the flora of Louisiana was always jungle green, a verdant, primordial landscape that ran contrary to what was in his head for his movie. He did not scout Dresden, as he didn't need multiple sound stages, just one big room for Green Screen. Bill Johnson didn't consider any other location for his film after learning that a tax rebate was possible in California and walking the streets of the small, old-looking town of Lone Butte.

Everyone had been right about Lone Butte. Spanish Johnny—he of the California Film Commission and no longer such a moron from the studio—had his ducks in order. Once banished from the set of *Horizon of Eden* after one too many arguments about shooting over twelve hours (then taking a bit too much credit when the film grossed $1.2 billion worldwide), Spanish Johnny left the Executive Chorus, cocksure he could run his own production company. A disastrous move. He'd landed safely at the CFC and was delighted to hear from Optional Enterprises again. Al Mac-Teer had done her gold-medal job of prescouting, prearranging, preplowing and preplanting all production seeds well before Bill drove into see the town with his own eyes. Yogi had studied Lone Butte on his own, having driven up to survey the intricacies and environs of the small town without carrying so much as a script or a calendar. His report to Bill Johnson: "It's Kansas and Nebraska and Missouri all rolled into one." He downloaded stock photos of small towns in seventeen different states as well as Lone Butte and challenged Bill Johnson to pick out the one in California. Bill couldn't. "It's six hours in a car from Sherman Oaks."

"Okay," Bill announced at the office, sitting with Al and Yogi. "We make a run at Lone Butte. Send up flares to the team." With that, Al alerted Yoko Honda, the genius art director, and painting-with-light cinematographer Stanley Arthur Ming—a.k.a. SAM— that the game was afoot and not to take any jobs before talking with Bill.

Then came a stroke of luck and a ton of legalese. Long ago, an outfit named Diamond Club Publishers expanded to become the Dynamic Group and went on another spending spree to purchase, among other titles, all those created by Kool Katz Komix, including *The Legend of Firefall*. A decade went by. With the successful screen adaptations of *The Girl from E.X.C.E.S.S.* and the heroic duo of SENTINEL and CHAOS in the movie of the same name, the ramifications were enormous. The Dynamo Nation created the Ultra world, and the title of Bill Johnson's screenplay became *Knightshade: The Lathe of Firefall*; the motion picture would be shot in the North Valley town of Lone Butte, California, less than an hour's drive from Sacramento. One could get there via Uber, Lyft, or PONY.

* * *

A PONY driver, Ynez Gonzalez-Cruz, born in, reared in, and still a daughter of Sacramento, had just quit one of her jobs, leaving her with two modes of employ rather than the three she'd held on and off for the last five years, since postponing her studies at Iron Bend River Community College. She was no longer the night housekeeper at the Airport Garden Suites Inn—a job she would not miss, though the people there were wonderful, especially the crew of Vietnamese women who made up most of the department and kept tabs on how many guests left evidence of wanton sex in the beds, bathrooms, and carpeting of the hotel rooms. On Wednesday mornings, Ynez did the bookkeeping for the Delta Laundry Service, which ran one coin-O-mat, fluff-n-fold, dry cleaners in Woodland and others downstate in Lodi, Fresno, and Hobartha. She had started as an attendant helping load the washers and dryers. One of her many uncles owned the business. The math work was very straightforward, so she usually completed her accounting by noon. At one point in her life, she had worked four jobs over the course of a week including her part-time position at the Uni-

Mart in Fair Oaks. She was planning to return to IBRCC when she could, to finally complete her transferable credits, once the school opened again after all that remote learning, but until then she'd become a serf of the gig economy by becoming a driver for PONY.

Why all those jobs? So Ynez could finally have a room of her own. An apartment. The woman had never lived without her family on top of her, relatives and strangers in need all crammed into the tiny-roomed house in South Sacramento like too many cats in a box. Every job she took brought her a few dollars closer to an independence she yearned for, dreamed of. Her plan was to save up and move out, yet still come home for family dinner a few times a week.

Had she driven for Uber, Lyft, or the new SoloCar, fate might have been crazy different, as the dictates of those companies were not as free-form as were those for PONY. PONY car drivers were given leeway that brought human needs and nature into the driver/passenger/pickup/destination formula of transportation. Ynez had regular passengers who could text/select her and her alone for a ride. And, if desired, Ynez, or any PONY driver, could wait—at a discounted rate—for a passenger to complete a task, like a shopping errand or a teeth cleaning, and make the ride a round trip or one of a series of drop-offs and pickups. Had Ynez been a more aggressive employee of the company—a PONY EXPRESS, as the company hoped—she could have pounded her day, rushing each rider to a destination, and then pursuing the next text/request, banging out as many rides into her shift as made possible by traffic conditions, gas mileage, and COVID-19. But Ynez chose to live differently. She had enough pride to never be seen piloting one of the ridiculous two-seat minicabs that had SOLOCAR SOLOCAR SOLOCAR painted on them. She loved her slightly used Ford Transit too much. She'd financed the auto thanks to a distant cousin who was aiming to be Salesman of the Month at Sierra Auto Yard in Folsom. Despite the car's liftgate, which more than once conked her on her chin, her Ford made Ynez feel like she was a London taxi driver in one of those iconographic black taxis, with all the legroom and the knowledge of her city.

Originally, PONY car drivers and passengers were urged to signal their recognition by "shooting" each other with their fingers, as bad a corporate PR strategy as was imaginable. The world—and America—had too many actual shootings, so the idea was wisely abandoned. Now, a small LCD device in the passenger side of the windshield flashed the name of the hailing customer, who would wave their phone, give the driver a symbolic salute, and the driver would do the same. No imaginary bullets were fired. Ynez was on duty in her Transit the morning of Al's arrival for that first visit to Lone Butte and environs. Due to a bad-luck nail-in-the-treads flat tire, she had given Lucy Garces, one of her friends from her housekeeping days, an emergency lift, gratis, to Lucy's work at the Garden Suites. She was grabbing a coffee from the lobby's Day-Break Station, which was being stocked by Armando Strong, a one-time boyfriend who would be happy to regain that status, when a PONYTEXT from one Al Mac-Teer popped up on her PDA. This Al fellow was requesting a pickup at the airport and transport to a small town up north off the interstate—and a hold request for the day. Ynez immediately replied *On My Way Arrival in 8 minutes* along with her PONY ID emoji and the GPS location of her car. She added a friendly *would U like a coffee,* since the online training course for all PONY drivers admonished them to "Think Friendly and Be Helpful!" Twenty seconds later, Al replied *2 shot espresso w/hot 1/2 & 1/2 if poss.* Hot half-and-half was, in fact, possible, so armed with a refill of her own drip/milk/sugar and Al's order (both in Garden Suites HOT DRINK! takeout cups) Ynez was on her way to her first paying customer of the day. She pulled up to the arrivals curb in less than eight minutes.

★　★　★

A.MAC-T was the flashing LCD on the Ford's dash. A woman gave the salute. Ynez had expected an Al. Ynez was prepared to Be Helpful and get out to open the door for the lady. No need. The woman, who had no luggage other than a large dark green leather messenger bag on her shoulder (were those knitting needles sticking out the top?), opened the sliding door herself.

"Hey," Al Mac-Teer said, seeing the advantages of Ynez's domestic imitation of a London cab. "Legroom." Ynez had removed the middle seat of the Transit, which cut down the number of possible passengers from five to three, but the legroom was universally appreciated.

"Good morning. You didn't mention any sweetener, but I have some if you need."

Ynez handed the espresso back to Ms. Mac-Teer, who had to lean forward from her seat to reach it.

"I'm sweet enough, thanks." Al leaned back, one-handing her seat belt, noticing the source of her morning coffee. "Looks like someone visited the DayBreak Station. How are you this morning"— Al checked her phone for the PONY driver's name—"Ynez?"

"Lovely, thank you." Ynez pulled away from the curb.

"Are you familiar with where I need to be? A place called Lone Butte?"

Ynez hadn't really studied the location Ms. Mac-Teer had programmed into the PONY ROUTE on her GPS (which the company insisted be rebranded as "Great PONY Service." Ugh.) but knew right off the bat exactly where and how to go. "The old lightbulb factory. I can get you there as fast as possible or a few minutes later with a better view. Any preference?"

Al checked her phone. There was no need to be moving pronto. Spanish Johnny and other suits from the CFC might have to cool their heels a bit, but that was no pity. "You call it," Al said.

"I'll take the Old 99. 'Through the Heart of the North Valley.' That's what they call the former highway. Before the interstate, it was the main route all the way to Oregon and went through almost every town, the ones that mattered. The state has been hoping to turn it into California's version of Route 66."

"Will I be enthralled with the scenery and sights?" The coffee Ynez had delivered was beginning to go cool. Still, it was a cup of an addictive stimulant and it was free.

"Some of it. If you prefer roaring trucks, I'll take the interstate."

For the first of its miles, the Heart of the North Valley was not particularly scenic; the usual collection of exurban commercial parks and radiator repair shops looked like they had been in business for either two weeks or twenty-five years; it was impossible to tell. Farther along the two-lane sprouted gum trees on its shoulders and older businesses that looked art-directed, even if they were shuttered. Long driveways led to houses with porches and the occasional barn. An old root beer stand looked like it was still a going business. The Old 99 did have some charm.

Ynez had a policy with her passengers—she did not talk to them until they talked to her. She was not about to be one of those jabber-lipped, stream-of-my-consciousness people who couldn't respect another person's time or attention. This passenger—Al Mac-Teer, seemed nice enough, but no-nonsense. Ynez gave her no nonsense in return. The lady in the back was checking her phone, digging around in her bag for a pen to go with her composition book, writing down some notes—occupied, busy.

"Do you know anything about this factory we're going to?" Al Mac-Teer asked, with a rhetorical, time-blowing air.

"They made lightbulbs in it for a million years," Ynez said. "It was a major employer. Westinghouse closed it when they opened a bigger factory after the interstates all connected. Transportation costs were shaved too much to resist the move. Some people had worked there for generations."

"Sounds like you did."

Ynez laughed. "That all happened before I was even *born*!"

"But it's common knowledge?"

"We studied it in school."

Al looked at her driver. Judging from appearances, she guessed Ynez was not long out of high school. "What class talks about lightbulb factories? Was this high school?"

"IBR Community College. I lucked out with a great teacher— Ms. Woo. She taught Government and Civic Economics. Every class was a conversation about the places we saw every day. She taught the history of our town."

"Are you on a business track? Or government?"

"No. I just had a slot open and needed to take a class. I could have signed up for Intro to Oral Hygiene or Women's Rugby."

Al left the conversation at that. One had to be careful when it came to engaging drivers in talk about their troubled lives. She changed the subject. "So, are you available to stick with me all day, Ynez?"

"Sure."

*　*　*

From that first ride to Lone Butte until the opening of the Production Office for *Knightshade: The Lathe of Firefall,* Ynez was Al's one-woman Transpo Department. The legroom and waiting coffee were both pluses, but Al rode in Ynez's PONY car because the driver caused no problems and solved a few as well (warm half-and-half). She drove carefully, did not jerk into turns or exceed the posted speed limit, nor was she chatty. She didn't look at her phone too much. And she was always there, at the ready. Al never had to look for that Ford Transit and her driver.

As it turned out, the lightbulb factory would make a fine Green Screen stage—there was one large hall with a high ceiling and the square footage of a ballpark. The old offices in the hulk of the facility were like rabbit warrens—too many with no windows, but ah well. The parking lot was massive, level, and graveled, so there would be room for all the trailers of the Base Camp for the weeks of shooting the movie's VFX.[*] Johnny Madrid proved his worth, seeming to have tamed the cranky state officials beyond those of the Film Commission, having solid information about California's Incentive Program, a possible tax rebate, all but guaranteeing big savings on the budget. "Just as long as *t*'s be crossed and *i*'s be dotted," John said, trying to sound hip. Failing.

Her first gander at the actual town of Lone Butte was from the back seat of Ynez's Transit. Though the approach to the town proper was a mishmash of cheap homes and nonfranchise businesses, like a new Dollar General, a rusting Quonset hut with letters saying CERAMICS fading in its windows, the main crossroads of Old Lone Butte at Main Street and Webster Road was a marvel of All-American Anytown-ness, a time capsule, inside a snow globe without the snow. The storefronts were mostly empty, barely occupied, and looked unchanged for the past three decades. There was not a single operating café or restaurant in the down-

---

[*] Visual effects, a.k.a. CGI—computer-generated imagery. And SPFX, the special effects like explosions, super-fast running, and levitating kung-fu fights—none of which can happen in the real world, only the Reel World.

town area, but there was a large-enough customer base for a tattoo parlor and a smoke shop. What had been a Western Auto now housed a junk store, but with a squint, Al could see the ghost of Lone Butte as the town it once was, right out of one of the Bonnie and Clyde states: the old bank with pillars holding up the entrance, the State Theater was not open, but looked like it was still a movie theater, Clark's Drugs advertising itself in a once-neon-ringed sign, an establishment-looking building with THE ALMOND GROWERS ASSOCIATION carved in stone along its cornice, and a wide Main Street, as free of traffic as an old-time back lot in the Gower Gulch. Lone Butte would be a cinch to shoot in.

"There was a plan to go big on historical renovation here," Ynez told Al as she drove around, slowly. "The hope was to attract tourists and tech developers and artists to live downtown. Craft beer saloons and such. The timing was great on one hand—they did some work before the 2008 crash. But then? Here it is more than a dozen years later and the damage done by credit default swaps ruined everything. Harsh."

"Harsh," Al agreed. Ynez knew about credit default swaps? From Professor Woo?

"Let me show you the Historic Homes District," Ynez said, making a left turn, then another and another as the Ford tooled along streets named after presidents and trees. Some of the homes could be called historical, in that they were Victorian looking. There were many broad porches and second-story widow's walks. Tall, thick-trunked shade trees—they looked a hundred years old—cooled the home fronts and lawns. Most of the houses had occupants—or at least owners—who kept the yards nice and the houses painted and trimmed. Out of all the homes in the square miles of the Historic Homes District, only three stood out as common, the rest were well-kept gems, with one or two of them rubies-in-the-rough.

On the way back south on Old 99, Al felt very peckish—she hadn't eaten since an In-One Food Bar on the plane from Bob Hope.* "I'm hungry."

---

* The airport in Burbank was once called Bob Hope Airport. The name had been changed, but most folks still called it Bob Hope.

"How about a cheeseburger?" Ynez asked.

"I allow myself one cheeseburger a year, and I've had it already."

"Not like these. I know the owners of the root beer stand we passed on the way up. You will not believe what they do with a cheeseburger."

"Serious about their cheeseburgers, are they?"

"Ms. Mac-Teer," Ynez said from the front seat. Al's face was lined up in her rearview mirror. "I can't explain it, but I promise."

Al took a moment to ponder and give in—was she really salivating at the thought? A Pavlovian cheeseburger? "Okay." She surrendered. "I'll pass on the root beer to be a good girl and pay the price on a cheeseburger."

Ynez knew the owners—the Alejandros—from one of the voter registration drives they'd worked on for the first Obama election. She and Al sat outside under a portico on a slatted red-pine picnic table.

Had Al carried with her a trophy with BEST CHEESEBURGER IN THE WORLD engraved in gold, she would have handed the award over to Ricardo and Julia Alejandro right then and there. The two women had no fries—they didn't want to kill themselves—and Julia brought out tall, frosted mugs of cold, sweet root beer, on the house. Between maneuvering the everything-and-grilled-onions cheeseburgers from baskets to mouths, Al and Ynez chitchatted politely, revealing the PONY driver's life, work, and family; because she lived at home she had no space to call her own nor any privacy, ever. Work and school were the only reprieves she had, the only time with herself.

"What's so special for you about Lone Butte?" Ynez wondered.

When Al told the truth, that she was in Ynez's car to possibly make a motion picture, all Ynez said was "How cool." Al was prepared for the standard civilian reaction to the news that she was in what Fellini had dubbed the Cardboard Carnival—*You're making a MOVIE who's in it what's it called what's it about can I be in it?* She was surprised, then, when Ynez—a civilian, after all—had none of the responses that explode when the H'wood Bomb was dropped. Al thought it was Ynez who was "cool."

"When I come back, you're my driver, okay?" Al asked as she was getting out of the car at Metro for her flight back to Bob Hope.

"Sure. See you next time, then!"

With that, Ynez departed the airport in her Ford Transit with all the legroom. Al headed for the metal detector and shoe inspections at Homeland Security. On the one-hour flight to Burbank she pulled out her yarn and needles and knitted a beanie.

Al was back in Sacramento for an important face-to-face, come-to-Jesus meeting with the Film Commission and Johnny Madrid, a photo-op with the governor (if the meeting went in Al's favor), and an interview with a reporter from the *Sacramento Bee* (again, per the outcome of that meeting). Ynez had PONY'd her from the airport, a two-shot espresso with warm half-and-half at the ready, committed to driving her all day. The reporter from the *Bee* was to get the interview over sandwiches at a legendary market/deli place on one of the alphabet streets downtown.

"Ynez!" Al said as she buckled in. "Why am I so happy to see you again?" Al's good mood did not last long.

The meeting with the California Film Commission devolved very quickly. Al needed to pin Johnny Madrid down as to where *Knightshade: The Lathe of Firefall* stood with the state of California: Was the budget too high to qualify for the rebate? Was it too low for the incentive to kick in? Was there a lottery for the rebate, or was it first come, first served? Had they lost their place in line to some other movie and if so how the fuck did that happen? Johnny tried to explain the supposed glitches in the Hawkeye's application and, yes, other productions had come to the commission wanting the same rebate. Al asked what those productions were and if they were in Hard Prep like *K:TLOF* was *very-soon-to-be*. Johnny said he was not at liberty to divulge certain information. Why did Al feel like her chain was now being jerked? She wondered that out loud, along with if Mr. Madrid had somehow forgotten his lessons—his showbiz history—when it came to dealing with Al Mac-Teer. Was he turning into a glass-jawed pussy-boy before her very eyes?

"John-Boy!" Al hollered at him, loud enough to be heard down the halls of power, maybe all the way to the governor's office, where a photographer was waiting. "You are very close to thinking you can fuck with me!"

In her PONY, meanwhile, Ynez was dealing with yet another family crisis, one far removed from film commissions, tax rebates, and hard preps. Her nephew—little Francisco—was at her sister's house, and her sister had to leave for her shift at the Cheesecake Factory; there was no one else to look after the boy, so could she come? Ynez had committed to PONYing Al Mac-Teer to the Shumate's Market & Deli for that interview, then back to her flight at the airport. There was no way Francisco Perez could come with Ynez, not as she worked. What, was he going to stow away, in his car seat, sharing the back of her Transit with a client? Couldn't happen. Could she drop Francisco off with Mom at home? No. Mom was at the doctor for her thyroid.

Here was a problem with no solution—the idea of her sister missing her shift, of little Francisco, the most adorable little man on the planet Earth, having no one to look after him? That could . . . not . . . stand. So Ynez had to do the unthinkable, frowned upon by the managers of PONY, and against the grain of her relationship with Ms. Mac-Teer. She was going to have to bail.

Ynez typed out a PONYTEXT, which buzzed on Al's phone just as she was contemplating chucking her CSFC coffee cup at Johnny Madrid's glass jaw.

PONYTEXT From: YNEZ—Ms. M-T. Emergency. Will arrange a new PONY for you. Very Sorry.

"Gimme a second," Al said to the as-yet unconked Johnny Madrid. She pinched back **A.MacT: You ok????**

Despite Al's request, Mr. Madrid kept talking. Al needed to understand that his hands were tied, you see, and the way things worked was that he was not really the one to sign off on the bigticket items, you know. He was just a lowly state film commissioner.

"I asked for a second, sir." Al shut Johnny up with that and one scary look.

PONYTEXT From: YNEZ—Yes. Sister needs help.

A.MacT: She okay?

PONYTEXT From: YNEZ—No babysitter. Sorry. Will arrange new driver.

A.MacT: You baby-sitting?

PONYTEXT From: YNEZ—Yes. New Driver will be Julio— here's his info.

A.MacT: How old? The kid?

PONYTEXT From: YNEZ—16 months. Julio's PONY is a Blue Honda.

A.MacT: What's the name?

PONYTEXT From: YNEZ—Julio. Blue Honda.

A.MacT: No. The kid.

PONYTEXT From: YNEZ—Francisco. Julio will be here in 14 minutes.

A.MacT: Francisco cute?

PONYTEXT From: YNEZ—God, yes.

A.MacT: He in a car seat?

PONYTEXT From: YNEZ—Yes.

A.MacT: Fetch him and bring with.

PONYTEXT From: YNEZ—Not allowed.

A.MacT: I say it is.

PONYTEXT From: YNEZ—Big problem. Can't have him in front. He'd be in back with you.

A.MacT: Better than him driving.

PONYTEXT From: YNEZ—LOL. Canceling Julio. YMRT.*

★ ★ ★

Thanks to the understanding of Al Mac-Teer, Ynez could see the morning through with no loss of pay. She was at her sister's place in twenty minutes, had Francisco strapped into his car seat, which was buckled into the back of her Ford Transit, and was rolling to the Capitol Mall to wait for Ms. Mac-Teer to emerge from her meetings. Francisco slept; the ride was perfect for his midday nap. Parked in the shade of one of the thousands of huge trees in the downtown area, Ynez opened the side door of her car to let in the air and sat in the back with her nephew, taking a moment to call Shumate's Market to make sure they had a table set aside for Ms. Mac-Teer's interview. Marco, who answered the phone, spoke Spanish, and Ynez was able to explain the why and when of her request. Al would just have to announce herself to Marco, and she would be taken care of. When Marco asked if Ynez was "spoken for," she laughed out loud and thought that when she was down-town again and waiting for a PONY client, she'd grab a lunch at Shumate's.

* You may regret this.

Francisco did wake up. He did want out of his car seat, so Ynez unstrapped him, setting him free.

A.MacT: Victory. Governor is Hot. Coming to you.

Francisco was flopping around on a blanket on a patch of grass a few yards from where Ynez was parked when Al met him for the first time. "What a cutie-pie! He's a smiler!" Al bent low to lock her eyes on Francisco's brown soul-windows. "Oh! Those eyes! Flecked in gold! Francisco! Grow up fast and marry me!" Al was downright giddy! There is something about cute, grinning babies that makes grown-ups say everything in exclamation points! "Let's get rolling! Gotta speak to the newspaper-writing people!"

Shumate's Market & Deli was downtown, not too far from the Capitol Building, so had limited street parking. Ynez let Al off, told her to ask for Marco, and to let her know if he was cute.

"You called ahead?" Al was impressed. "You just made life a little easier!"

Ynez found a space on the opposite block right on a vest-pocket park with little kiddie swing sets and metal rocking horses on huge springs planted into the ground. While Al verbally fenced with a business reporter from the big local paper over deli sandwiches as thick as a roadbed (a Shumate's specialty), whole pickles, and bottles of the most delicious apple juice in the world, Francisco Perez was pushed on a swing, held on a rocking horse, and picked up fallen sycamore leaves with his tia Ynez. Could a child be happier? Ynez was having such a good time she was a bit sorry when her text chimed and she had to PONY back to pick up Al.

"That reporter was as clueless as a pickle!" Al said to Francisco. "He's going to write a dumb article!"[*] To Ynez she announced that Marco must be all of sixteen years old and was failing to grow a mustache. They were all buckled up and headed to Metro, Francisco rattling a ring of big plastic toy keys—a red one, a yellow one, and a green one.

"Ms. Mac-Teer?" Ynez asked, looking in her rearview mirror, seeing Al stroking little Francisco's head of curls. "Can I say thank you for understanding? Not everyone would have a kid in the car."

---

[*] "Streaming Services Take Advantage of Tax Rebate, Saving Millions"— *Sacramento Bee*.

Al was marveling at Francisco's hair, making a few of the jet-black curls stand straight up from his brown head. "*Too many* people don't know Francisco like *I do*! And it's time to call me *Al*! Let's check the time of my *airplane ride*! Oh, heavens! I have over an *hour* before I fly away! Let's get some *coffee* before I go! Where can we get good coffee for *grown-ups*? Does Aunt Ynez *know a place*? Will I ever stop talking *like this*?"

Ynez did, in fact, know a place with good coffee that was free of charge, and very close to the airport. Al was so busy cooing at Francisco and twirling the kid's hair she did not notice when Ynez pulled up to the lobby of the Garden Suites Inn.

Al laughed when they entered the place. "All Garden Suites smell the same," she said. The uniforms were no longer dark green but gray and of a hideous unisex fashion. The graphics and signage had changed fonts. There was the Afternoon Station with its snacks and drinks and, lo, damn good coffee-making fixtures. With the free HOT DRINK! they sat in low, comfortable chairs in what passed for the hotel's lobby. Francisco was holding himself up at the mahogany-like coffee table when the hotel staff began coming around—to greet Ynez and to confirm a question that had swept through the hotel the moment they had come through the front door.

"Ynez! Did you have a *baby*?" The desk attendant, the lobby manager, a parking valet, and two Vietnamese housekeepers swept by—all asking a version of the same question, delighting in how cute that little boy was, greeting Ynez like a member of the family.

After the coffee, driving to the airport, Al asked Ynez what *that* was all about. "Why are you such a beloved figure at the Garden Suites that everyone knows your name?"

"Come again?" Ynez was navigating the departures lane for the drop-off.

"You were the crown princess of the Garden Suites Inn. The employees flocked to you."

"I worked there," Ynez said. "I was a housekeeper."

Al was jangling Francisco's toy key ring in front of his face. "I did time at the Garden Suites myself."

"Really?" There was a big SUV that was going too slow right in front of Ynez. "In housekeeping?"

"No. I was front desk."

"If I could have been on front desk, I'd still be there. But once a housekeeper . . ." Ynez turned past some waiting cars and pulled up at the departures curb. "Here you are. Thanks for riding with PONY."

"See you next time. And *you*!" Al took Francisco's chubby little cheeks in her hand and flicked his lips. "Grow up quick! I'm saving myself for *you*!"

As Ynez and her nephew pulled away, Al trudged off to the security checkpoint, imagining a note card in her head—numbered 1, with a name—YNEZ.

★   ★   ★

The Hawkeye/Dynamo Nation/Optional Enterprises production teams began making runs into Lone Butte. Visiting locations, photographing the town, mapping out possible sites with each step they took. Yogi—who was now Bill's First Assistant Director and a genius with both a shooting schedule and a crew—went with his then girlfriend, Athena, to take iPad videos of specific angles and camera moves; Athena played KNIGHTSHADE, he played FIRE-FALL. After seeing their recordings, Bill Johnson made a road trip in his Dodge Charger, Dictaphone on his shotgun seat, driving from New Mexico to Las Vegas (Nevada), up to Reno, then down the Sierras to the eastern entrances to the upper North Valley. He met up with SAM, the art director Yoko Honda,[*] and Yogi right smack in downtown Lone Butte, where the four of them walked the streets around Main and crisscrossed the Historic Homes District.

"This place is ours three sixty," SAM said. "We've got shots in any direction." With a computer program, SAM would know the location and angle of the sun at any minute. Golden Hour shots—when the sun is setting and the light becomes an ephemeral spun gold—would be prepped to a T.

"We'll own Lonely Butte," Yogi said. "Traffic lockups will be cinchy."

"Good bones in this town," said Yoko. "The boarded-up, vacant

---

[*] Yoko Honda and Bill had worked together since the first of the *Eden* trilogy.

look is going to be free. And *there's* your coffee-shop set." She was pointing to a storefront with its in-place vintage sign for what had been a place called Clark's Drugs. "It's got a counter and booths. Dress it with drugstore shelves."

There were vacant lots hidden behind empty buildings for Base Camp. Motel and motor lodges for crew housing were out along the interstate. Airbnbs were all over. Complete homes in the Historic Homes District were available to rent. An old, restored building for the Almond Growers Association had rooms, offices, a dining hall, and a lobby, as though the building were calling out, *Use me!*

"Hey, let's put the PO here instead of out at the Green Screen stage," Bill said of the almond growers' former clubhouse. "If we can grab some of these old houses for the department heads, we can walk to work."

"Why not *live* on the set?" Yogi asked. "We can bring in some cots for the Swing Gang."

So. Lone Butte it was. Bang. Pow.

Bill finished the screenplay on his Sterling, then handed it over to Optional Enterprises to be converted into the Final Draft screenwriting software. Hard Prep began when Dynamo started writing checks, cash flow began, and everyone became employees of the entity called Lathe Productions.

Al Mac-Teer began flying into Sacramento often, and Ynez was her driver every time. "I miss Francisco," Al would say when she slipped into the legroom of Ynez's PONY Ford. "He's not seeing anybody, is he?" Ynez would share her iPhone photos with Al—pictures of Francisco and others in her family. Over many a drive to and from Lone Butte, the women talked and gossiped and laughed and stopped to quaff root beers and split award-winning cheeseburgers. With the opening of the Production Office mere weeks away, and the springtime day so lovely, the two women were sipping from frosty mugs when Ynez drifted into territory yet uncharted.

"Can I ask you a question?"

Okay, Al said to herself. Here it comes—the Hollywood stuff. Impressed that it had taken some time until Ynez inevitably broached the subject of *How do I get into movies? I mean, if you can do it, there must be a way for me to make it into Hollywood, right?* Al was all set to answer. Take Fountain.

"What's with those knitting needles?" Ynez had seen them sticking out of Al's carryall tote. "I've never seen you using them."

Al almost laughed out loud. This Ynez was without guile! True, Al had not done any knitting in the car while in Ynez's charge. She was always on her phone, on her iPad, reading pages from a thick binder, or making notes in a composition book. Or she was talking with her pleasant, interesting driver. When Al knitted, it was when she was alone—on the flights to and from Bob Hope, in her room at the Garden Suites (of course) on the brief overnights in town, after a cocktail, and with the TV on the cable news channels with the volume down. She had yet to get to knitting when she was with Ynez. The question led to telling the long story of learning to knit years ago, of the guidance, impact, and loving care of a woman named Dace, and how knitting provided a quiet, time-altering sense of calm in a job that was often a frenetic, nonstop panic for months on end. Al wove her verbal yarn right up to her drop-off at the airport. Exiting the Transit, she said, "Knitting and sanity go together."

★ ★ ★

So. Ynez had yet to ask about movies—how they were made, how Al had come to work in the Carnival of Cardboard, how, maybe, a person like herself could get into the movies, never saying the other thing civilians had declaimed to Al Mac-Teer once it was revealed she was from Hollywood: "You should make a movie about me!"

The Gonzalez-Cruz family, though, was not as tight-lipped or incurious. They were a clan. Depending on when you showed up at one of their houses—for a meal, a hang, a coffee, truly, any time of day—there would be up to seventeen family members present, all living complicated lives, working many jobs, any jobs, and/or going to school, making food for people, or cleaning up for people. The roster was the mother, Margarita, and father, Gus, four daughters (Ynez had shared a room with her sisters for her whole life), three brothers (who shared a room), two in-law husbands, one in-law wife, a girl- or boyfriend or two, little kids ranging in age from Francisco's sixteen months to little Esperanza's nine years. One could not call Carmen a kid anymore—she had just had her quinceañera. There would be cousins and friends from all over town, from out of town, from out of the country, all hoping to find some kind of job, some kind of living—some kind of life in America—after Gus put them to work temporarily in his gardening-landscaping business, but only as many as could fit in his truck on any one day. They slept on couches, on mats in the back room, ate at the kitchen table, all hoping to emulate Mr. and Mrs. Gonzalez-Cruz by getting their papers, raising kids who were born Americans, and obeying the laws of America. They had fled poverty and violence and hardships born of hopelessness, so sleeping on mats for a few months was nothing. Being in America was everything. Men who looked at the Gonzalez-Cruz girls with lust were some of the comers and goers. When she became old enough, Ynez left the house on any pretext and stayed away as long as she could.

When she was asked about her job, in Mexican- and Nicaraguan- and El Salvadoran–accented Spanish, Ynez waited for a moment in the swarm of vigorous table talk to report she was driving a busy lady who had knitting needles and yarn with her but never actually knitted. "She's an impressive lady," Ynez said of her semipermanent client. "She's calm and funny, has a crush on *this little boy* . . ." Ynez leaned over to give Francisco a kiss on his head. "So, I asked her what's up with the needles. She knits when I don't see her."

"*What is so special about a woman who knits?*"

"*Mom, didn't you use to knit?*"

"*I wish I could learn how to knit.*"

"*What says you can't?*"

"*There is a place on Howe that says* KNITTING CLASSES. *Go there.*"

"*How much does it cost to learn to knit?*"

"*In money or time?*"

"*Mama. Teach me how to knit. I'll make Christmas presents.*"

"*I'm too busy.*"

"She has a man's name—Al," Ynez interjected. "She has a tough job and it helps her stay calm."

"*I stay calm by taking a nap.*"

"*I stay calm by not giving a shit.*"

"*No talk like that at the table.*"

"Yeah, asshole."

"I'd like to knit things, but it looks complicated."

"What job does she do?"

"Where do you take her?"

"Lone Butte."

"Where is that?"

"Up toward Chico on Old 99."

"Ah, yes. Lone Butte. The Knitting Capital of America."

"She has meetings at that old lightbulb factory."

"Are they hiring?"

"What's the pay to make lightbulbs?"

"That place closed up years ago. Lightbulbs are made in, like, Vietnam now."

"And Chihuahua."

"She going to open up the place to make lightbulbs again?"

"She meets with a commission from the state," Ynez said. "And I take her to the Capitol Building downtown for meetings there. She met the governor."

"The governor would love to reopen that lightbulb factory. Or have it make electric cars or batteries."

"Yarn. Big yarn factory."

"I drove her to that Shumate's Market for lunch."

"I used to work there! Mr. Perenchio still own it?"

"I have no idea."

"He was nice. But then I got on at the Marie Callender's."

"Which Marie Callender's?"

"The one on J Street."

"Why didn't you take her to Marie Callender's? Donnie Garcez is the assistant manager there now."

"Not at the J Street. He's at the Arden Fair one."

"She had an appointment at Shumate's. That was the day I looked after Francisco. This man!" Ynez kissed that adorable head again.

"From the governor to that place?"

"She was interviewed there by the Bee. It was in the paper."

"What for?"

"She wants to make a movie. That's why we keep going to Lone Butte."

That last bit of dialogue was the Cue. After the briefest of pauses, a moment of silence as those around the table processed the word that had just come out of Ynez's mouth: *movie*. Then came the verbal explosion of the Gonzalez-Cruz Family Dinner Theater.

"*What?!*"

"*A movie?*"

"*A movie? A real movie movie?*"

"*What movie?*"

"*What's the name of the movie?*"

"*Who's in it?*"

"*What's it about?*"

"*What's it called?*"

"*What is this lady's name?*"

"She goes by Al. I call her that. Al."

"*Why does she have a man's name?*"

"*Ynez drives lesbians now.*"

"*Lesbians. LBGTQ. As long as they pay up.*"

"*And tip.*"

"*And give five stars.*"

Ynez's youngest brother, Jose, pulled out his phone and asked the lesbian's name.

"I don't think she's a lesbian."

"*Why? Because she hasn't hit on you?*"

"We've talked about boyfriends."

"*You tell her about Andre and how he cheated on you?*"

"In fact, yes, I did. She offered to have his legs broken."

"*I hope she wasn't joking.*"

"*How do you spell her name?*"

Jose looked her up on the IMDb.

"My God!" Jose hollered. "She's a producer! She makes movies with Bill Johnson!"

"*Who?*"

"*Lesbian movies?*"

"*Bill Johnson a woman too?*"

Jose knew movies. Jose was in high school and lived on his phone. "She made *A Cellar Full of Sound*!"

Ynez did not know that. She had gone to see *A Cellar Full of*

Sound with her sister Anita but was so tired that night she took a long snooze during much of the film. Ynez often fell asleep during movies, with her head tilted back, her mouth open, her jaw loose. She'd conk right out because she worked all those jobs. So she had slept through Al Mac-Teer's latest movie and had no idea what it was about.

"She was up for an Oscar!"* Jose could not believe that.

Ynez couldn't either.

"And look!" Jose was showing the table the IMDb photo of Al Mac-Teer. "She's of color!"

"But check out her boss!" Jose pulled up Bill Johnson's IMDb photo: as white as a man can be. "He made those *Eden* movies."

"Those were good!"

"Ynez! You're driving a major player, you know that?"

"A may-ja playa."

Ynez did not know any of that.

"Have her give me a job in that movie. I'm beautiful and of color."

"If she's a rich movie producer why is she in Ynez's car?"

"She should be in a stretch limo, like a Hummer with a hot tub."

"Lesbians are cheap."

"Save some dinner for your papa. He'll be home soon."

Jose pulled up the website for the *Sacramento Bee* and found the article that had come out of Al Mac-Teer's meeting at Shumate's Market. He read it out loud until it got boring—the stuff about the California Film Commission, tax rebates, and a new bill by a representative from Lompoc. That's when Anita, Ynez's sister, who had taken piano lessons since she was six years old, got up from the table to instigate the family's night of singing. At the piano in the living room, she pulled up on her iPad the sheet music for "The Place Is All Ours," the Oscar-nominated song from *A Cellar Full of Sound,* and figured out the tempo and melody.

Everyone has gone
No one's left around

---

* True. Had *ACFOS* won for Best Picture, Al, as a credited producer, would have taken home a statuette.

It's just you and me
The only folks in town . . . The place is all ours.*

Singing took over the living room, drawing in the family one by one as the dishes were washed, as a plate of food for Gus was covered and set aside, as other songs came out of Anita's fingering of the eighty-eight keys. The hullabaloo over Ynez's brush with the glamorous world of moviemaking faded, replaced by favorite Mexican ballads and requested songs. When Gus finally came home, he took his shower, then Margarita poured his one bottle of Pacifico into the cold glass she kept for him in the freezer and set out his full plate of warmed dinner. As he ate, Carmen Gonzalez-Cruz sang "The Heart Wants What It Wants," a song as beautiful as Selena Gomez herself. The tired, hungry, hardworking man sipped his single, ice-cold cerveza between bites. His family had once been so poor. Now they were so *rich*. He listened as his family filled his life with music; so many voices in tune as to blow the roof off his little house. Who would ever want to leave this home?

★　★　★

Bill Johnson stretched out his long legs, his not-too-fancy boots well short of the driver's seat.

Ynez was piloting the car out of the airport, bound for the Old 99, for Lone Butte. Al and her boss man had flown in together from Bob Hope, bringing carry-on leather day bags filled with binders, iPads, notebooks, and either knitting needles or a kitchen timer. Johnson also had with him an old, battle-scarred square case, the handle held together with wire. He had put it on the floor, sliding it under his seat.

The decision had been made to have the Production Office in the Almond Growers Association Building after all. There was a large-enough parking area behind the place for the trailers, which made Base Camp an easy reach. The possible locations for Eve Knight's house were all within a short hop, and Bill had revised his screenplay to have more scenes set in downtown Lone Butte to make as much use of the picturesque place as possible. The coffee shop/

---

* Permission to use lyrics granted by Ex Luna Vox Publishing Co.

diner, the old church, the intersections, the EDGE OF TOWN locations, even the NIGHT BATTLE would be right there. Catering could serve meals in the dining hall where almond farmers once held banquets and dances. When all the location filming was complete, the Unit would move the Base Camp out to the old lightbulb factory, its hulk of a building made into a huge stage enveloped in enough Green Screen to wrap the Berlin Wall. They'd use the factory exterior for the first Knightshade-Firefall battle royal.

On the drive to Lone Butte, Al and Bill Johnson talked business the entire way, so Ynez just steered the Ford. When they passed the root beer stand, it was Bill who asked if the place was operating.

"Ynez knows the owners," Al said.

"Who's Ynez?" Bill asked.

"Our driver, you dope," Al told him. "I introduced you."

"Sorry, Ynez," Bill called from the back. "I've been a dope for many a year. Your name is now permanently scarred into my brain."

Ynez just waved and drove on.

"I like root beer if it's draft," Bill said.

Other members of the movie company had reported to Lone Butte, staying at the King's Way Motor Lodge on the interstate or the BestAmerica Motel, driving their own cars, surveying the town's sites in these days of Hard Prep. All their expenditures would be reimbursed. The office furniture was scheduled to arrive that day. In less than a week, *Knightshade: The Lathe of Firefall* would begin the countdown to the start of Principal Photography on large, wall-sized calendars in the various Almond Growers Association Building offices—fifty-six days out . . . forty-two days out . . . thirty-one days out . . .

Al had booked Ynez on a day that might go so long that there was no reason to keep her around. She and her boss would be staying at the King's Way for at least three nights, then have Ynez PONY them back to a flight to Bob Hope.

Ynez dropped her clients off in desolate downtown Lone Butte and headed back south on Old 99. She hadn't made it past the abandoned ceramics place when she saw the delivery truck for Standard Rental Furnishings slowly heading the opposite way, into the town. The driver was looking at his GPS, wondering if he could possibly be in the right place. Ynez recognized the driver—Cazz Elbarr.

Ynez had been in two classes at IBRCC with Cazz—Health 1 and the College Reading Experience: Joan Didion. The two got to know each other, and Cazz turned out to be wicked funny, perhaps because he smoked so much weed, which made him talk all the time. She didn't know Cazz delivered for Standard Furnishings but was not surprised. Everyone needed to work, including the fellow who was sleeping in the truck's shotgun seat, wearing the same corporate-logo polo shirt.

Ynez tooted her PONY horn and flashed her Ford headlamps. Cazz looked up, recognized her, and stopped. Ynez edged up to meet him, and the two rolled down their driver's-side windows.

"The fuck you doin' here, Eenie?"

"Working, Cazzual. Are you delivering to the movie company by any chance?"

"If that's at 1607 Main Street, Lone Butte."

"Follow me." Ynez pulled a U-ey with Cazz following in his truck.

The only person now in the Almond Growers Association Building was a young woman named Hallie Beck who had something to do with the Art Department. Al and Bill Johnson and everyone else had left on foot to examine some possible locations so close by they didn't need the Teamster Sprinters.

Ynez introduced herself and Cazz to Hallie, then asked where all the cheaply made contents of Cazz's truck should go—the tables, desks, chairs, sofas, lamps, shelving units, wire dividers, and power strips. Hallie assumed the furniture should be divvied up between the various, empty offices, though the lion's share of the bigger pieces should go into the large, main office.

"You can figure it out," Hallie said. She was looking at the two of them. She was mighty low on the food chain and had neither the knowledge nor the authority to give instructions.

Cazz was flummoxed. "I'm supposed to have two guys with me, but one never showed, so it's just me and Casey Junior." Casey Jr. was the guy still sleeping in the truck, maybe in a coma, or at least very hungover. "This is going to take a million years."

"I'll help." Ynez thought, *Why not?* Cazz would make her laugh while they worked, even though he was not stoned at all, not at work in the morning.

The main room had space for six desks, the attendant shelving, and the long, folding tables with uncomfortable folding plastic chairs. Cazz had brought the truck around to the Main Street entrance. There was no traffic, so he backed in perpendicular to the building's front door. Ynez helped him off-load the truck, dolly the furniture onto the liftgate, and roll it all into the Almond Growers Association Building. She arranged the desks with plenty of space between them, making the main room look like the headquarters for a congressman seeking reelection. The warren of hallways and offices inside the Almond Growers Association Building was toward the back. As Cazz was moving the truck to the rear lot and backing up to position the liftgate, Casey Jr. woke up. So, not in a coma!

"We there already?" Casey asked.

With an extra body and Ynez plotting out how many offices needed how much of the rental stuff, the furnishings came off the truck a bit faster; by the three-hour mark they were nearly done. That's when a harried young man—a PA[*] named Cody Lakeland—barreled into the Almond Growers Building, took one look at Ynez, and barked, "I need your help on something."

Ynez was dressed in ordinary clothes; unlike Cazz and Casey Jr. she was not wearing the polo shirt of Standard Rental Furnishings. Lakeland assumed that Ynez had some position in the PO and could therefore be told what to do.

"Go get these coffees," Cody told Ynez, handing her a scribbled list of desired lattes, cappuccinos, drips, espressos, chais, and decafs. "When you come back, I'll have the food orders. Stat!"

Ynez wondered what *stat* meant and asked.

"Now, please! Pronto!"

There were no fancy coffee places in Lone Butte proper, but a Pirate Coffee drive-thru was out on the interstate. Ynez voice-called the order for what was fourteen special hot drinks while she was driving the seventeen miles. With her personal debit card, she paid for the mixed elixirs, served in skull-and-crossbones recycled-

---

[*] Production assistants. Not members of the DGA, but all hoping to be, unless they want to be producers, cinematographers, screenwriters, or, after working twenty-hour days on a movie, in some other line of work.

paper cups with compostable sleeves and tops, asking for a receipt. Twenty-nine minutes later she had them set out on a table she herself had unfolded in the Almond Growers Association Building's main room. Cazz had finished his job and was gone, having taken Casey Jr. with him. Cody Lakeland found his triple-espresso Pirate Coffee and was adding two sugar packets after handing Ynez a wish list for a grab-and-go buffet lunch. Salads. Sandwiches. Wraps. Burritos. Two pizzas—one double plain cheese, one pepperoni with sliced olives. Drinks as well. And all were needed *stat*.

She was exiting through the front door to drive the seventeen miles once more to the interstate's ubiquitous fast-food outlets just as Al, Bill Johnson, and the other production folks were entering the rear of the Almond Growers Building. The two moviemakers did not see their PONY driver.

The lunch options available were wraps from Wrap 'Em Up, some decent greens from the salad bar at the McDonald's, and individually packaged deli-like sandwiches from the FastGas SnackShack. She got cans of soda and flavored bubbly water from the place, too. She had called in the pizza-pie order to Big Stork, a franchise that was trying to introduce a by-the-slice drive-thru. They took whole-pie orders, too. A Loco Taco had burritos as did the Taco Mas on the other side of the interstate, so she split the Mexican food orders right down the middle. An hour and a half later, Ynez had lunch arranged buffet-style on the same main office table where she had landed the coffees.

Cody grabbed a burrito-like food from the Taco Mas box, saying "Here" to Ynez. He was charging her with yet another list, this one laser printed on three pages rather than scribbled in pen and ripped from a spiral notebook. "Buy as much of this locally, if possible, to make us look like we care."

The list was a long one. Ballpoint pens in bulk. Steno pads in bulk. Corkboards and pushpins in bulk. An order for printer/copier paper in bulk. Paper clips and staplers. Cups. Pencils. Electric pencil sharpeners. Whiteboards with colored pens. Microwave ovens and teakettles. The Amazon billing number for Lathe Productions was on the paper, so Ynez assumed she was meant to go online and make the order. But locally, the Uni-Mart between Bidwell and

Chico was close by, closer to Lone Butte than the Uni-Mart in Sacramento, her old part-time employer. "You need all this today?"

"*Duh!*" the boy-child said. Ynez took that as a *stat*. She grabbed a slice of Big Stork pepperoni and olive, a bottle of water from an open box—who arranged that, if not her?—and went back out to her Transit. She had just left the front of the Almond Growers Building when the production team came in to graze on their lunches. Again, Al did not see Ynez, only the food she had arranged.

The Uni-Mart Corporation was hell-bent on kicking the shit out of Amazon[*] and had developed a system of bulk ordering, which, along with her familiarity with all things U-Mart, made Ynez's task extremely easy. She had but to give the Order Service Desk her printed pages and, *voom*, the whole smash would be delivered to 1607 Main Street, Lone Butte, by 8:00 a.m. the next morning.

When Ynez returned to the burgeoning office of Lathe Productions, no one had policed the refuse and scattered leftovers, so she did. But there was a paucity of trash bags, paper towels, and such, so—after a quick, incomplete tidying up—she used her car once more to run to Dollar General for cleanup supplies. She kept the receipt. Back in Lone Butte she completed her own Operation Clean Sweep, wiping down the tables in the main room, bagging up all the refuse, and carrying it out to a rusty dumpster in the back lot that had not seen use in some time. Needing to use the restroom, she accurately assumed the need for toilet paper, hand sanitizer, and dry wipes—she'd bought such from Dollar—and stocked first the men's room, then did the same to the women's.

When she came back into the hallway, Bill Johnson was about to go into the Gents.

"Hey," the director said. "What's your name again?"

"Ynez."

"That's right. Ynez. What's up *wi'choo*?" Bill went in to do his business, not waiting for the answer.

Cody Lakeland happened to see and hear the exchange between the gofer and the director of the motion picture. "No. No, no, no, no, no," he said to Ynez. "You do not talk to the director. Understand? You do not bother the director."

---

[*] Good luck with that.

"He asked me my name."

"He's being polite. You are not the first. You are not the UPM. You are not a producer. You . . . do not . . . engage . . . the director. Understand?"

Ynez had no idea what a first or a UPM was.* "Okay."

"Stock these restrooms with toilet paper. Make sure there are extra rolls. Soap and paper towels, too."

Ynez had already done those tasks. She was going to explain that to Lakeland when Bill Johnson came out of the bathroom. The Boy Boss immediately averted his eyes, looking down at his shoes to avoid the director's attention.

"Ynez!" Bill called out. "I got it now!" The man disappeared down the hall having ignored Cody Lakeland, whose name he thought was Chester.

Ynez's phone went off with a PONYTEXT.

"Silence that thing," Lakeland said, exasperated. "All phones are to be on vibrate in the PO. Come *on*."

A.MacT: PLZ tell me you have my Boss's typewriter in your car!!!

PONYTEXT From: YNEZ—Will check STAT!

She hurried out to her car parked along Main Street. Ynez was expert at finding items her clients had left behind in her car. Phones were a constant mystery to solve, as she would hear their muffled ringers going off in a wide variety of tones. Abandoned, too, had been wrapped gifts, tote bags, expensive pens, luggage, laptops, travel mugs, an engagement ring in its Tiffany box, passports, and, once, a cat in an airline carrier. Some guy did not care much for his girlfriend's cat. A typewriter? This was new. Ynez couldn't remember if she had ever even seen a typewriter except in old movies.

She opened the rear liftgate, careful to avoid yet another chin busting, checked the rear cargo area to find nothing, then the passenger seats, still nothing. For the sake of certainty, she looked under the rear seat and saw a beat-up, black square box with a wire-aided handle and figured a typewriter must be in it. It was

---

* First Assistant Director—Yogi Kakanis. Unit Production Manager—Aaron Blau.

heavy. The twin locking clasps by the handle stuck a bit when she tried to slide them to the open position, but then she heard the two clicks and lifted the lid. Yeah. She had found the typewriter. The machine was old, black, and said STERLING on the carriage.

PONYTEXT From: YNEZ—Got it.

A.MacT: !!!!!! Keep til tomorrow XX!

PONYTEXT From: YNEZ—I can bring it now.

A.MacT: no need!

Seventy-two seconds later Ynez walked into the space Al had claimed in the Almond Growers Building, the office she would occupy for the duration of Lathe Productions. Earlier in the day, the PONY driver had set up the rental desk without knowing that by day's end Al Mac-Teer would be sitting behind it. Ynez was carrying the typewriter in its case.

"Shut the front door!" Al could not believe Ynez was in her office. "You drive at the speed of light?"

"This is it, right?" Ynez set the box on Al's desk.

"Explain this to me," Al said.

"Your boss left this in the car? You wanted me to get it to you?"

"Tomorrow. How are you here so soon? I'm curious."

Just then the Lakeland kid showed up at the office's door. He'd heard the voice of the to-be-attended-to Al Mac-Teer—the Big Boss Lady of Optional Enterprises—and thought he could help out. "No. No, no, no, no, no. I'm sorry, Ms. Mac-Teer."

"Why are you sorry?" Al was curious about so many things now.

"This should not be happening." Cody gave Ynez what he wanted to be a look of reproach but came off like an actor in a community theater production of *Boeing, Boeing.* "Do I have to explain *all* the rules to you?"

"Cody," Al said in her regular, non-ass-kicking, problem-solving voice. "What rules need to be explained?"

"Production Office protocol. This girl"—he gave a head juke toward Ynez—"doesn't know the job. Furniture setup. Coffees. Runner. She's done fine at that, but she needs to know who she should *not* be talking to."

"Do you know that *this woman* has a name? Do you know what her name is?"

"Ynez," Ynez told him, then and there. "I'm Ynez."

"I didn't check the names of the local hires," Lakeland explained. "That's on me. We'll leave you alone and sort out the confusion. Sorry, Ms. Mac-Teer. This won't happen again. Right, *EE-ness*?"

"Wait. I'm confused here," Al said. "Ynez? Have you been here all day running for Mr. Lakeland?"

Cody Lakeland *gulped* as a sudden, intense fear clouded his head, a discomforting tingle running through his limbs. Al Mac-Teer had just referred to him as "Mr. Lakeland." This. Did. Not. Bode. Well.

Ynez explained what her day had been like, driving out of town, seeing a friend of hers delivering the rental furniture that was now placed throughout the building. Her friend was shorthanded, which was a problem, so she helped move the stuff in. She was going to leave, but "Mr. Lakeland here"—Cody's eyes went wide at that—sent her to get the coffees, then the lunches, then the supplies for the office . . . so she did. She had never left Lone Butte, but for the trips to the local Uni-Mart up Chico way and Dollar General, which was why she had shown up so immediately with Bill Johnson's boxed-up typewriter. "Did I do something wrong?" Ynez had no idea if she had, and if she had, she had no idea what.

Al Mac-Teer laughed. Loud enough for her chuckles to echo through the hallways, stairwells, and offices of the Almond Growers Building. Her amused laugh bounced along the dimensions of the new Production Office in invisible, diminishing waves of sound.

"Cody," Al said, turning to the petrified young production assistant—petrified in the physical sense, as if he had turned to stone, immovable. "I'd like you to run out and grab coffees for *EE-ness* and myself. I'll take a double espresso with warm half-and-half. Ynez?"

"Drip. Milk and two sugars, please."

Cody produced a pen and a notebook to write this down, not that he could forget such a simple order, but to look like the whip-smart professional he so desperately hoped to pull off.

"And Cody?" Al added. "Go around the PO and take orders from anyone that would like a little bump in the afternoon. Get a receipt and get reimbursed through petty cash."

"Sure," croaked Cody. "Um, *Ee-ness*? Where did you go for the coffee this morning?"

"Pirate Coffee. Take Webster west, just this side of the interstate." She used her phone to ping Cody the GPS marker. "You can order online and time the pickup. That's what I did."

"Copy that." Cody left. He ended up having twenty-two orders for coffee, served in recyclable skull-and-crossbones cups with quick-composting sleeves and lids.

Al considered her PONY driver, the young woman she had known for months now. When Cody returned with their coffees—which took the kid an hour and forty minutes—Al would explain to him the Mac-Teer system of Production Office protocol. Until then, she had a private, door-closed talk with Ynez. Al needed her to work for her, to solve problems, to help her make the motion picture. Ynez would have to give up her job at PONY and be on call 24/7 for however long Al deemed necessary. Ynez was, Al explained, a nugget of gold panned out of the Iron Bend River—and Al was not about to let her go.

"So, you're going on the payroll," Al told the young woman.

Though her weekly salary would be pure entry-level for the Cardboard Carnival, it was still more money than Ynez earned working two, or even three, jobs.

More money, really, than Ynez had dreamed possible.

Eve Knight has Ultra Powers, and a very complicated past.
Hiding in obscurity with her elderly grandfather, avoiding all
contact from the Agents of Change, she is forever challenged
by what she *feels* and the lifesaving acts she must take on. Yet,
there is no joy in her life—only dread. The woman has not
been able to *sleep* due to the visions she has of a mysterious
presence known as Firefall . . .

Logline for *Knightshade: The Lathe of Firefall*

WREN LANE

No one knew where she lived these days, other than the few people
who enjoyed her friendship, had earned her trust, and who accepted
the burden of keeping her whereabouts a secret. Micheline Ong,
her representative, was one of them.

Not that Wren Lane was a nutty recluse who loved her cats or
parrots more than human beings. Not at all. Where the lady lived

was a closely kept bit of intelligence because of the stalkers. And the too-aggressive fans (mostly male) who insisted they and she were destined soul mates. And the paparazzi who sought real-life photos of the lady, who followed her like FBI agents on a surveillance, more like attempted kidnappers. If you considered, too, the merchants who wanted her autograph on posters, photos, memorabilia—to sell for profit—you would conclude that Wren Lane was being hounded like a female Jean Valjean by a squad of jerk Javerts.

Would it matter if Wren's love life was not the gossip-fodder shambles it is? She's beautiful. She makes movies. It's the territory. When she broke up with Whit Sullivan—who was not in for the duration—there were stories that she had moved to Scotland. When she divorced Cory Chase—who had anger issues—it was reported she was the one to keep the lake house in Austin. When she broke off her engagement to Vladimir Smythe (for the second time), a local paper in Salina, Kansas, reported that she'd bought an eco-farm to live behind its excavated berm. Not true. Currently she shares an isolated place not too far from Los Angeles with a good-looking fellow by the name of Wally, her twin brother. They'd split the cost of the former citrus orchard. There is a small airfield nearby where she keeps her plane, a Cirrus 150. She'd earned her pilot's license in Austin during her troubles as Mrs. Cory Chase, to get away from the moods of her husband. She found that flying a plane kept her grounded, occupied, and challenged, the sky giving her what no man had ever supplied (a confident safety).

"Before I date one more knothead," she told Wally, "please remind me of my past errors." She was living with her brother—for now, anyway—because they were cosmically close and Wally was wicked smart in business. Not only was he keeping his sister rich (and making her richer), but he also kept her safe.

Living on the property in a guest cottage was the team of Tom Windermere, LAPD Retired (her other trusted, sane male), and his wife, Laurel, a damn fine cook. When in Los Angeles's environs, Wren stayed in the small mother-in-law apartment in the back of the Windermeres' house in Eagle Rock. Detective Windermere was a constant presence in Wren's life, seeing to it she was never discovered, bothered, or threatened.[*]

And yet, Tom could not fend off all her offenders. At a NATO/ ShoWest convention in Las Vegas, Wren was receiving an Award for Female Star of the Year when a producer idiotically propositioned her from the dais with a repeat of what he'd said to Wren just moments before, in the elevator, on the way from the holding suite to the exhibition hall. He had mentioned two reasons she would not regret joining him in a shower, one being to save water. "Oh, come on, now. What's wrong with a little joke?" He said that both times.

So many little jokes . . .

Wendy Lank of Pierpont, Illinois, East Valley High School, class of 2012, heard them all the time. She was called When-She Yanks, Will-She Spank, Lank the Skank, and you get the idea. She was *the Girl* of East Valley. She left the place before her class graduated, ditching her cap and gown for some modeling gigs in Chicago. Wally joined her the summer of graduation, since Pierpont was a town full of dickheads. He was good looking enough to model, too, but he hated having his picture taken, so went to the Kellogg School of Management at Northwestern. Wendy moved on to New York, modeled a bit more, fought off a whole new set of dicks, got cast as Hot Office Bitch in one scene in a sitcom set in a small-town city hall. She did get an agent and came so close to getting the role of Best Friend in *Small Fryes* on Showtime that she decided to give Los Angeles a try. Wally set her up with two girls he'd met at Northwestern who rented a hillside house on Woodrow Wilson and needed a roommate. All three of the women had done modeling/acting and took improvisation classes; onetime *the Girl*s vying for a place in the Business of Show.

Wendy Lank studied, worked out, dated men with skin-care habits better than her own, dressed down to waitress, and went to all the calls her agent could arrange without much luck. She had a callback for Bill Johnson's *Horizon of Eden,* but nothing came of her reading. For a Buick national commercial, she rode shotgun on

---

[*] In the heady first years of her celebrity, two different predators made it onto her property—one into the house.

a winding road up near Lake Arrowhead, looked at her adorable children in the back seat, and suggestively stroked the neck of her fake husband. That guy was gay. Good looking and gay, the only man on the shoot who wasn't all over her, in attitude and eye-wise.

She changed her professional name to Wren Lane* and got a quick booking as a cadaver in *Victim #69*. She was dead and bluish but had a lot of screen time—even got to open her eyes in a fantasy sequence and deliver this line to Danielle Moore playing the pregnant, overworked woman detective on the murder case: "The girl they just brought in? Her, too." *Victim #69* was a damn good movie that did good business. And that moment with the cadaver! Casting people noted the dead blue girl, Wren Lane.

★   ★   ★

At her home in Where-Is-It-Ville, at 11:57 p.m., Wren was in bed with the TV on, heading for a Bette Davis movie on Turner Classics, when she came across herself, as HELEN† in *The Organization Man*. She remembered reading for the part—and loathing it—when was it? In 2016. She was not up for Best Friend, Caring Sister, Office Bitch, or Cadaver. She was reading for Helen. After so many lost auditions, she'd won. Yes, she was younger by fifteen years than the star—Porter Hovis, back when he was around. Older movie stars seemed to always play characters with wives fifteen years their junior. There in bed, Wren saw herself in the movie, saying:

```
                    HELEN
        Don't you see how much they need you?
        Your children miss you. I miss you.
```

Such a horseshit line in a bullshit scene in a fake too-pretty kitchen, in lip gloss and formfitting yoga pants and a stretch top,

---

* Wendy Lank could have become Wren Lake, but Wally suggested Lane, as it simply substituted the letter *e* for the letter *k* in the family name.

† Character names in film scripts are always capitalized. It seemed appropriate to do the same in these pages.

pleading with her husband to understand that his working too long, too hard, too much, was harmful to their family's wellness.

The Husband/Hero/Everyman, throwing his head back in righteous frustration, gave out with "What do you want me to do? Just walk away?"

```
                        HELEN
          I want you . . . to be here . . .
          for us.
```

The director-writer used take 7 of the performance—the one where he suggested she put in the pauses. He . . . had given her . . . the line reading.

Years later, the movie now filled up time on a basic cable channel at midnight. Still, the thing stung her. She loathed it, the experience of making it, and a bit of herself for taking the job. And yet she was now forcing herself to watch—up through the kitchen-in-sexy-yoga-clothes-and-lip-gloss scene (which had been the audition and test pages) to remind herself: No more. No more. Never. No more of the Wife (I want you . . . to be here . . . for us). Best Friend (Listen to me, you can do this!). Sister (He said *that*? On a *first date*?) or Bitch (If you didn't have your head so far up Mr. Valentine's ass, you would've learned *that* from the bullet points!). No more roles like that. No more roles . . . like that.

Before *The Organization Man* was released—to very soft numbers—she landed two generic programmers: the rom-com *You Were Going to Call Me* and the action movie *Actionable*. Neither film did anything for her. She turned down the sexy Psychiatrist in *Wayward* because, she had to point out, she was too young; no one would buy her as a criminal psychiatrist, and what criminal psychiatrist would not know the pool man was Gemini? It made no logical sense. Her agent at the time called her to yell, "Logic? Wren! Money! A movie! Logic? Who gives a shit?" She stuck to her guns and knew the phone call meant that she was going to fire her agent at the first appropriate moment—which turned out to be when she got to know Micheline Ong, fresh off the desk of Richard Fleisch and starting on her own as an agent at the Pacific Artists Group.

With Micheline battling for her, Wren landed two roles back-to-back—the *Gaslight* rip-off called *False Front* and the charming *Periwinkle*—two characters that could not have been more different, either performance warranting her name on the A-list. She had two Golden Globe nominations in the same year! Lost both, to Dame Sylvia Upton (comedy) and Ginny Pope-Eisler (drama). The SAG Awards passed her by, as did AMPAS. Still, it was a good run by any standard. And she saw a future within her grasp. Almost.

It was said that her versatility was her handicap. Was she the beautiful woman who took out her revenge in *False Front,* or was she the girl-next-door sweetheart of *Periwinkle?* The roles that then came her way lit no fires in her belly—each character was a version of what she had done before. *Sadie Foster's Fortune* and *Fury and McDowell* did well because both had Wren Lane in them. Then came *Sergeant Harder,* her above-the-title billing, and new status as a gorgeous, sexy, sexed-up sexpot who could carry a huge, megahit movie. People referred to the movie, and Wren, as *Sergeant Hard-On.** Her new era had begun.

When the pandemic began in March of 2020, the Business of Show closed for the duration, shutting down talks she was having with a pair of producers who saw her as a contemporary Lucrezia Borgia. Just as well, as another Borgia series beat them to the punch, shooting in Hungary until it was shut down by COVID-19's ransacking of Budapest. In her Fortress of Solitude throughout the lockdown, Wren doubled up on her fitness program, swam an hour a day in the jet-stream pool she had her brother install, flew her Cirrus to build up her pilot hours as well as for the healing exposure to clouds and the horizon. She went on a jag of watching nothing but old movies starring the legendary women of motion pictures—the powerful, badass women who deserved the first billing in their movies because theirs were the main roles—Vivien Leigh, Katharine Hepburn, Joan Crawford, Ingrid Bergman, Sophia Loren, Bette Davis. Garbo. Ava Gardner. Rita Hayworth. Greer Garson. Veronica Lake. She watched so many old movies her brother, Wally,

---

* Wren fought for a title change but was ignored. She no longer answered any questions about the role or the movie.

begged her to find something in Technicolor, so he could watch, too. She gave him Marilyn Monroe with Jane Russell in *Gentlemen Prefer Blondes*.

"These ladies ran their own show," Wren told Micheline Ong, her brother, the Windermeres, and her pilot/instructor Heather Cooper as they flew over the coastline, the desert, and the Valley. "They told men what was what when men controlled what was what. Like Willa Sax does now."

"Willa Sax is Cassandra Rampart," Micheline had told her during one long Zoom. "That's her franchise no matter what she does next, forever."

"Willa Sex. She and I are locked into those formfitting corsets, our cleavage leading the way. Bette Davis was Bette Davis. Between the two, I want to be Bette Davis."

Micheline got her client's point. Wren was soon to be twenty-nine years old and was tired of being Sergeant Hard-On. By her own clock, she had until age thirty-three to establish herself as the Bette Davis version of Wren Lane. She was going to give Ginny Pope-Eisler a run for the better roles.

On a hike along the public trails, dressed down for the exercise and unrecognizable, Wren and Tom were getting in five miles when Micheline rang in for a FaceTime. The agent was in her car, stuck in traffic on the 101.

Wren answered. "Hey, Meesh."

"Ready for this?" Meesh Ong asked.

"What?"

"The planets are aligning."

"You dropped out there."

"The planets are shaping up for you."

"You froze. Can you see me?"

"Can you stop walking where you have a signal?"

"This good?"

"Don't move."

"How'd you like to live the Ultra High Life?"

"Hold on. Hikers are coming by. Let me put my mask on."

Wren had a mask around her neck. She covered her mouth and nose just as a couple walked by leading a dog. They'd put on their masks as well. "Hey. Nice pooch."

"Thank you," said the hikers.

Wren turned back to FaceTime. "What was that?"

"There's been a shoe drop at the Hawkeye," Micheline continued. "They're making a Dynamo movie with a big female role as lead. That female should be you."

"Who's directing?"

"Bill Johnson. Writing and directing."

"Bill Johnson. Oh . . ."

A ringtone went off in Micheline's car. She picked up another phone to read a text.

"Bill Johnson is no fan of mine," Wren reminded her.

"Bill Johnson will do what he is told," Micheline said while reading her other phone. She tapped a quick, unimportant reply and set the phone down. "The Hawkeye will go direct to streaming with an Ultra movie. A big deal. The character will be yours for years."

"What is the character?"

"Nightshade, but with a *K*."

"When does it go? Is it in, like, Romania for eight months?"

"Let me get you the job first, then we'll dictate terms. May I?"

Wren thought for all of a moment. "Yeah. Sic 'em."

"Woof." Micheline cackled in happiness. "Hey, Tom!"

"Hey, Mooch," Tom hollered from off-screen.

"If there are comic books can you send them to me?" Wren asked.

"I'll send you the link. And the logline."

"What?"

"You can read them on the link. And the logline."

"You dropped out."

"I'll send you the link!"

"Can't hear you."

"I'll send you the link!"

"You froze again. Tom says he can get them for me. The comic books."

"I'll send you the logline, of the movie!"

"I love you, Moochie."

The image of Wren froze. In that conversation, Micheline had traveled ten yards on the 101, between Coldwater and Woodman.

★   ★   ★

Because of Bill Johnson, Dynamo had, at last, a track for Knight-shade in their Nation of films. In Postproduction at that time was *Agents of Change 5: Origins,* still months away from release. On the orders of the higher-ups, the film's final team of writers wrote scenes to be added, code-named "Death of the Knights." EVE KNIGHT would be introduced as an Ultra in the final version of *AOC5* with ten days of shooting a few cryptic scenes in Atlanta, all of which was top secret. And no small endeavor. The *Agents of Change* cast had to be rounded up from far-flung places, including locations of other movies they were shooting, lockdowns, and a silent retreat in upstate Michigan where one of the actors had taken a thirty-week vow of no talking. Those Ultras were to be squeezed back into their costumes and paid hundreds of thousands of dollars for two weeks of work at the Dynamo Studios in Georgia under COVID-19 protocols.

Bill Johnson made his casting of Eve Knight a deal breaker. He'd cracked the story and character, so he'd choose the artist to play her, or there'd be no Bill Johnson in the mix. The Instigator powered through his demand; Dynamo and the Hawkeye surrendered with a request to "consult" in the casting.

When Al Mac-Teer heard the word "consult," she did an old-school spit-take with her morning smoothie. Consult? With her boss? Bill Johnson would consult with the powers that be until they ran out of words, then cast Eve Knight as he saw fit.

When she saw the caller ID of the Pacific Artists Group, Al knew it was one of two people—either Micheline Ong or the agency's president, Phillip Bork. Micheline would be calling about Wren Lane being Eve Knight. Phil would be calling to complain about the Industry not knowing what it was going to do next and did she have any new theories or gossip. She hoped it would be Phil Bork, because his cynicism was often hilariously cruel.

"Hold for Micheline Ong, please," the new assistant said. The way these people were doing their jobs, making all those calls from their homes—the big offices were still on lockdown—was a marvel. Then again, Al was in her backyard, fragrant with those redwood trees, taking calls.

"We have got to talk, Al," Micheline "King K" Ong said. "It's that time."

Al wasted none. "She's on the list." Bullet point translation: *Wren Lane is being considered for the role of Eve Knight.*

"The list? Oh, goody! You're doing me a favor by letting me report to my only client that matters in this world that she is on a list. Not just a list, but *the* list. She'll ask me who else is on said list and what the fuck do I tell her, Big Mac?"

"Oh, jeepers, Micheline. You got me. You win. I cave to your hardball prowess. I'll hand the part over to Wendy Lank right now. How much money would you like us to pay her and forward me her Perq Package. Oops! Flag on the play. I don't make those decisions and that's not how this works and you know that and tell your spoiled client anything you dare."

Micheline cracked up. So did Al. "You know there's no one better suited for Knightshade, Al. I mean, come on."

"I love the idea of Wren. I do. My boss isn't against her, but Hawkeye signs the checks and Dynamo has a vote in this, you know."

"Your boss makes this call. The Hawkeye and Dynamo quake in fear of him."

"As well they should."

"And if there was some consensus among them all, someone else would have already been cast. I think BJ should meet with Wren ASAP so he can see the wisdom of giving her the role."

Al let a quiet beat pass, a silence over the cell signal . . .

"How about I let my boss know you just called him a blow job and you can start buttering what is left of your toasted career?" Al asked.

"I'm SORRY!" How is it that Micheline did not remember to never, ever refer to Bill Johnson as "BJ." What a rookie mistake! "Gonna wash my mouth out with hand sanitizer!"

The situation for Al was this: Jessica Kander-Pike had turned down the money and the role on the first offer, the money on the second offer, and the money on the third offer. Her no meant NO! Al admired that. Bill then wanted P'aulnita Jaxx, but she was leaning toward directing herself in her own, semiautobiographical movie for Oprah Winfrey's WinCast. Dynamo *suggested* Jo Annhalter, but she was flirting with walking away from acting to dedicate herself to glorifying the Lord Jesus Christ and having a lot more kids—of course, she may not have had it in her to go back into the gym and torture herself into Knightshade shape, not with a brand-new baby and, let's note, an offer on another film that would actually shoot in Los Angeles.* The Hawkeye telegraphed (admitted) they would approve whichever woman would fuel the fantasies of innocent preteenage boys and creepy men of all ages—a category that Al knew Wren "Sergeant Hard-On" Lane *owned*.

"Have her call me." Al offered this bone to Micheline. Al had met Wren at a Women in Hollywood breakfast, before COVID-19. They had been seated at the same table. Al knew Wren on sight, but when she introduced herself, Wren was caught up short. She was under the impression that a woman like Al Mac-Teer, who instilled fear in the eyes of most people in the town, who was a role model for most of the women in the Roosevelt that morning, would be a lot grumpier than Al was. But Al was nice. And funny. Acerbic but not cynical.

"Done," Micheline said. "Zoom or FaceTime?"

"Audio only. I don't want to have to look nice."

Eight minutes later, a blocked caller ID came in on Al's iPhone.

"Yeah?" Al said.

"Al Mac-Teer, Wren Lane."

"Hey."

"Want to know why I'm the answer to all your problems?"

"Sure."

Wren began, "Nightshade is a toxic plant or series of plants loaded with alkaloids and scopolamine and hyoscyamine that can kill you with delirium and hallucinations, or so says Google. Eve Knightshade, then, is a hipper character name than, say, Bella Donna, which would be too on the nose. But look, name aside? There is not a woman out there who doesn't need what she craves: a good night's sleep. Sure, she wants to make her bed with a decent chap when the time is right, but the time is never right! Nor is the chap. Something I am far too familiar with."

---

* *Whirlwind Season*. She crushed it. Jo Annhalter could do no wrong. Wren hated her. Admired, too.

Both women chuckled at that.

Wren continued, "Every woman in the world is *tired*. Take away Eve's abilities and you have every woman on the planet. She needs a nap a hell of a lot more than she needs a man. I know Bill Johnson has the pick of the litter right now. I do wonder why he's never so much as called Micheline about my availability. I get that I had no juice back in the days of *Horizon of Eden*. I could have played Maureen in *A Cellar Full of Sound*, and if he had shown any interest in me, I would have done it for scale plus ten.* I saw *Pocket Rockets* twice. I voted for *A Cellar Full of Sound* even though I never got a call, so all is forgiven. I think the man makes great movies and I want to make great movies. I'll waive the turnaround. Wrap me at eleven twenty-nine p.m., and I'll be in the chair the next morning at five forty-five and happy about it. I've learned the value of being low maintenance and don't care what side of my face is on camera. I assume you will repeat to Bill every word I just said, verbatim."

"I'll give him the gist." Al had put her phone on speaker.

"Will he meet with me?"

Because she liked what she had heard, Al said, "I can ask him."

"Will you?"

"He's not in town."

"I'll go to him."

"He lives in New Mexico."

"I'll fly to Santa Fe. I have a plane."

"You have a *plane*?" Al knew Wren and her ilk were loaded with movie money, but having her own jet was a level above.

"I have a pilot's license. I can be in Santa Fe in seven hours."

"He doesn't live in Santa Fe, but that's not the point. He's not big on meetings until he's at peace with his options."

"Al, no one else is going to be a better dose of delirium-inducing alkaloids than the woman you are talking to on the phone right now." Wren let that bit of rehearsed dialogue sit for a beat. Then she asked a genuine question. "Why does he want to make *Knightshade*, anyway? It's a franchise chapter for a corporation. He could do anything he wants. Why this?"

---

* A fee of the Screen Actors Guild scale salary plus 10 percent for Micheline Ong. A bargain for the likes of Wren Lane.

Al let that question hang for a beat, for it was something new to hear on such a call. Why won't he talk to me? Why won't he look at my tape? What do I have to do for him to see me in the part? Those were the questions that came from actors all the time. No one had ever asked *why* her boss wanted to make any movie. "The man is a mystery to me, Wren. I'll give him a nudge about meeting you."

"Thank you."

"Text me your number."

"Doing it now."

"Later then." Al pressed END on her phone.

Wren did the same at her house. Wally was sitting on the couch having listened in on the whole conversation.

"Nice at-bat," he said to his twin sister.

"Did I come on too strong?"

"You'll find out soon enough, won't you?"

From her backyard, Al speed-dialed her boss in Socorro, expecting him to pick up no matter what he was doing. He had a movie to move from the inside of his head to the outside of his person. Dynamo was building new sets for *AOC5* to be ready as soon as whoever played KNIGHTSHADE was fitted for her costume. The game was afoot. The clock was running.

"Yeah." He was golfing. Al could hear the wind over the phone.

"Wren Lane."

"Maybe."

"Meet with her."

"No."

"I think you should. She's got something. She can be there in seven hours."

"In seven hours, I will be having dinner."

"Tomorrow then."

"Why?"

"Because she asked me the same thing. *Why* are you making this movie? Not why won't you cast me."

"Hold on a second." Bill did something with his phone, then Al heard his bag of golf clubs rattle in that patented sound. Then she heard a grunt and the *whack* of club face meeting a ball. "Ah, *criminy*. Topped it . . . You say I should meet Wren Lane because of *why*."

"Yes, I am saying that," Al confirmed. "She says she'll never be late to the set."

"She's lying."

"Confirmed by SAM." Stanley Arthur Ming had worked with Wren on reshoots of *Sergeant Harder* and had texted Al; she was no trouble if everyone did their jobs well.

"Okay. Noon tomorrow. She'll be late."

"She flies her own plane. Be at the airport ready to tell her why you want to make the movie."

"Oh, I'll be right on *that*. Send her the script." Bill Johnson pressed END and swung his pitching wedge at a little white, dimpled ball that was not nearly as close to the green as he wanted. Then he picked up his gear and went back to the house to work.

★ ★ ★

At 140 mph, taking the Cirrus to the meeting with Bill Johnson would make for a long, poky flight. Heather Cooper had access to many planes, so wrangled a twin-engine Beechcraft King Air C90B for the day. To and from Socorro would be half the flying time of Wren's single prop and would give her a few hours in what her next aircraft *might* be. They took off before dawn, headed east into the rising sun (which is lovely, but a headache-inducing bitch after the first six minutes), leaving early due to the time change in New Mexico. Wren piloted some of the way to get the feel of the King Air's two engines, then gave the aircraft back to Heather and read Bill Johnson's screenplay for the third time. She had dressed neither up to a photo-shoot glamour nor down to a girl-next-door costume: her best vintage Levi's—meaning the pants that fit her ass to perfection—hiking boots, belt of wide leather in chocolate brown, a buckle with a turquoise lightning bolt, a white Tom Ford collared shirt with a dark green shemagh, a man's vintage, small-face stainless-steel Rolex on one wrist, a thick leather bracelet embossed with the word *SERENITY* on the other, and a pair of classic, reproduction Randolph Engineering aviator glasses. Heather Cooper wore a pair of Randolphs as well but was dressed in her pilot's uniform—dark blue pants and blazer, black necktie, white shirt with epaulettes, and her career-marking three stripes.

The landing at Socorro was timed perfectly. Circling the field at 11:50 a.m. local time, Wren saw the red Dodge Charger of Bill Johnson parked near the FBO. Wren landed the plane, then taxied to the Field Business Office, shutting down the engines at two minutes before noon.

"Mr. Johnson," she called, approaching his car as he leaned on the hood, his arms crossed, wearing Ray-Bans.

"Ms. Lane," he replied, opening the door to his shotgun seat. "You fly with style."

He drove her through the middle of Socorro at High Noon, pointing out the so-called landmarks. "Over there, the Walmart."

At Frank and Lupe's El Sombrero, he stopped to pick up their lunch.

"You have a big challenge right off the bat, you know," Bill said, driving to the house with the Jayco in the driveway. "Red or green?"

"Green," Wren said. She knew what the declaration meant. The chilies: red or green or, for some New Mexicans who like both, *Christmas*. She was told this by Wally, who had learned it all from a girlfriend who had parents living in retirement in Truth or Consequences. Green chilies were the choice of those in the know.

Dr. Johnson was teaching, so they were alone in the kitchen. Bill had plated matching orders of huevos rancheros and poured iced teas.

"So," Wren said. "You go first."

"No small talk?" Bill eyed her. Wren Lane was a beautiful woman, yes, but long ago, he had learned that beautiful women were a dime a dozen and paid a price for being so. Being beautiful put women in a lofty caste, worshipped no matter the setting yet begrudged for having their lives made easy by their beauty. Bill had learned to listen when they talked; to never bullshit a beautiful woman. He leaned back and spoke quietly: "I make movies because no other labor satisfies my quest to capture an unspoken truth, one so pure and undiscovered that the audience will slap themselves upside their heads for not having seen it long ago. This collection of moving pictures—about Knightshade and Firefall—is about men and women trapped in this purgatory we call *today*. There will never be equality between men and women—maybe someday the same pay for the same work, but even that is still an unpaved road. Do we dare hope for acceptance of the differences between boys and girls? Can we just respect each other's fragile humanity? When the hell would that, could that, ever happen, eh?"

"Simple enough," Wren said with a shrug of her perfect shoulders.

"That is *why* I want to make this movie. I get to use the vernacular of the superhero-action genre. John Ford had westerns. John Frankenheimer had cops in cars. Scorsese had Little Italy. Spielberg had family. I have Eve Knight. And you want to be her . . ."

Wren worried: *Is this guy now entering dickheaddom, the realm of three dots at the end of any question? Did that ellipsis translate as What are you willing to* do *for the part . . . ?* Long ago, back in New York City, a producer of a low-budget movie that was to shoot in Bulgaria said this: "You want the part . . . ? A quick hand job and it's yours . . ." To get out of there, Wendy Lank pretended to accidentally spill her coffee all over the dick's desk and apologetically beat a hasty retreat. Had it happened today, Wren Lane would have thrown the coffee on his chest, called in the assistant, and yelled, REPEAT WHAT YOU JUST SAID TO ME AND GET A LAWYER!

"Why?" Bill asked, straight from his shoulder. "It can't be just to hear the lamentations of your enemies."

"Because . . ." Wren could use ellipses with the best of them. "She can't sleep."

Bill chewed a bit, then talked with his mouth still full of some of Lupe's *huevos*. Al had told him about the sleep thing. "So. The superpowers? That's just eye candy, the fireworks to occupy the audience. If we do this right, Eve Knight has our attention and our miles-wide empathy. Wanting to see her, finally, getting some sleep will be the spine of the picture. The itch that needs to be scratched. The MacGuffin.[*] That she gets it in the arms of a man as fervid as Firefall? The surprise, eh?" Bill chewed a bit more and reached for his iced tea. "God, I hope we don't blow it . . ."

Wren was sitting completely still. Her fork was in her hand. Egg yolk the color of gold was mixing with *chili verde* on her plate. "Listen," she said, quietly, putting her flatware down and searching for the words she wanted to say next, words of finality, of con-

---

[*] Hitchcock's definition of a movie's key element.

crete, of understanding. "I don't want to sound like second-rate screenwriting right now, but did you just say what I thought you said?"

"What do you think I just said?"

"We. You hope we don't blow it. We. As in you and me. You the director and me as Eve."

"Yep." Bill lifted a fork of lunch to his mouth. "Why not?"

Wren exhaled, deeply and audibly, in a gust of breath that would have spread the coronavirus had she been infected with it. (She was not.) She heard a whispering in her ear—audible to her only—the words *Okay then*.

She repeated "Okay then" for Bill, sitting across the table. She lifted her iced tea. "That was fast."

"Ms. Lane, I've seen everything you've done since *False Front*. You are a very talented artist. A bit underappreciated and under-utilized."

Hearing that made Wren feel fucking wonderful.

"I wonder about something." Bill reached over to Wren's right wrist, the one with the leather-strap bracelet with the word *SERENITY* embossed on it. "When have you ever felt *this*?"

Serenity. Wren had picked out the accessory to complement her look, to balance the Rolex hanging loose on her left wrist, not to give her a subliminal connection to superheroes like Wonder Woman or Ursa Major, who both wore sexy bracelets. She had bought the strap on a whim, at a small shop run by local artists selling their wares. She could have chosen LOVE, HOPE, PEACE, or SURRENDER, but they all seemed common, like generic gifts for Valentine's Day. She chose SERENITY because she wasn't about to surrender to anyone. Serenity had been, and always was, her elusive hope ever since she'd been Wendy Lank *the Girl*.

"Don't do that thing that others might try," Bill said. "Don't stay awake for the duration of the shoot so you will actually *be* exhausted and sleepless like Eve. Those powers of hers make it so she doesn't just need the sleep but knows the lack is killing her spirit."

"She's *never* been at rest," Wren said. "She's never had a quiet mind nor stilled body. She's never felt the mortal, simple joy of drifting off to sleep, into the realm of the spirits where time has no measure and dreams carry her away." *Like* me, Wren thought.

Bill listened impassively, then said, "Yep."

★   ★   ★

Kenny Sheprock was driving up La Brea when his phone let out the special ringtone he kept for Wren Lane—"Bette Davis Eyes" by Kim Carnes with the raspy voice. The lady loved hearing that song every morning in the makeup chair on that *Sergeant* picture, charging the trailer with energy. Wren's energy. Kenny's era for music was the Carpenters, but a smart makeup man let the artist tune in the music.

He'd filled in for only two days on *Periwinkle*—that was a few years ago now—which was the where and when of his meeting up with the Lady Lane. Kenny had since slowed; fewer early-morning calls with sixteen-hour days and ten-hour turnarounds. The work—more than forty years of it—had roughed him up over three tough marriages, three now-grown kids, a mild cardiac arrest, and many, many moves around Los Angeles: his had been a standard makeup man's life.

Tina De La Vigne had been Wren Lane's makeup artist. She and Kenny had come up through the years side by side in many an H/MU* trailer. She needed a week off for a personal surgery smack in the middle of shooting *Periwinkle*—a procedure that could not wait—and asked Wren if she would be comfortable with Kenny, the man who had done a ton of movies over the years and had taken care of none other than Beatrice Kennedy for most of her films. Beatrice Kennedy was a raven-haired beauty, and even though Wren was more a blonde than brunette, the decision to have Kenny Sheprock tend to her for a week was a bunt, especially after he came in to meet over a pot of tea and finger sandwiches, which he brought. Tina came back to finish the picture, but with her health an issue, she called Wren a week after Wrap to announce that she was going to stay home with her family. Kenny, then, became

---

* Hair and makeup.

Wren's makeup artist—as stipulated in her deal—and worked only for her, with her, on her pictures.

"Kenny!" Wren sang out over the speakerphone. "It's that time again!"

"I love hearing that news," Kenny said. "Where are we going, kid?"

Wren adored being called kid by this man, this calming influence, this artist, craftsman, and, well, saint. Saint Sheprock, she called him. "First, Atlanta. Soon, but not for long."

"Okay. Atlanta." Kenny had worked in Atlanta with Beatrice Kennedy on two of her pictures. Atlanta was fine.

"Ever hear of Lone Butte?"

Kenny knew of the town. He'd served as makeup supervisor on *Offramp** around Redding in 1994. "I have. What's the picture?"

"A thing about me kicking ass and looking hot."

"Again?" That made her laugh—ah, that girl's laugh! "When?"

"As soon as my deal is worked out. A movie is already done, and they want to slap me into a few new scenes. Then the same role in a few months. We need to get cracking."

"Who's directing?"

"Bill Johnson."

"I know Bill." Kenny had done some of *Border of Eden* and had helped set up *Barren Land* but left to serve Beatrice Kennedy.

"So? You're in?"

"I am if you are."

"Kenny Sheprock, you make me a happy woman."

"That makes me a happy man."

What a racket, Kenny thought. He was on La Brea coming up to Fountain. Fifty years prior, half a century ago, he was of limited coin and had no contacts save a certain phone number in his slim wallet. He had slept in his car behind Mickey Hargitay's landscaping business, right . . . there.[†] He had the green light, so he passed

---

* "A piece of crap," according to Sheprock.

[†] Mickey was midcentury Hollywood royalty, by his marriage to Jayne Mansfield, being the father of Mariska Hargitay. He'd been a body builder and first-rate landscaper.

the spot, as always blowing a kiss to commemorate the site of his personal history—Kenny Sheprock Slept Here.

In 1973, he'd driven to Los Angeles from Bates City, Missouri, his makeup kit and boxes of supplies in the trunk of his used Impala, on the strength of two names in his wallet. One was of a distant half cousin who lived in Long Beach; the other was Fred Palladini, the makeup man who, two years earlier, had answered a knock on the H/MU trailer door when he was shooting *The Barrow Gang* on location in Independence, Missouri. It was 8:00 p.m., a Night Shoot, and Fred could not believe he had to go to the door rather than whoever it was just entering. There, not daring to so much as stand on the trailer steps, was a kid, holding a binder.

"Yeah?" Fred asked.

"Yes, I would like to speak to the person in charge of makeup?"

"What can I do for you?"

"I have done makeup and puppetry since I was a kid and would like to become a professional."

"Is that some of your work?" Fred pointed to the binder in the kid's hands.

"Yes, sir."

"Well, I'm kind of busy right now. I'll have time at the meal break around one in the morning. Come back then and show me."

"I will, sir."

"What's your name?"

"Kenneth Sheprock?"

"See you then, Kenny." Fred closed the door on the kid and went back to making up the actor playing Buck Barrow. Fred Palladini had started working in Hollywood as a bullpen makeup artist, putting fake beards on the extras on those old Technicolor Vista-Vision biblical epics and black-and-white B-movie westerns. He'd done *Lassie* when TV came along, and for the last three decades had worked constantly. He got into features in the early '60s, knew everything, worked everywhere, did everyone. He asked Ivy, in Hair, to grab a couple of sandwiches and Cokes for him and bring them back to the trailer before the meal break was called. At 1:05 a.m., another knock came at the door, and there was young Kenneth.

"Come on in," Fred bade the boy. "You eat? Have a sandwich. What's your name again?"

Kenny didn't answer right away—his senses were on overload, this being his first-ever visit to the makeup room of a major motion picture, of any motion picture. The lights around the mirrors, the wig blocks, the tall chairs, and the sponges and the palettes and the brushes and tools. The smell of the spirit gum and pancake makeup was the same as in the dressing room at his high-school plays. "Kenneth Sheprock?" Again, the kid uptalked his last name.

"Grab a seat, Mr. *Ship*rock." He meant one of the makeup chairs. "Fred Palladini. I'm going to eat while we do this. Help yourself if you want."

Kenny Sheprock was talking to Fred Palladini. *The* Fred Palladini who created the makeup for *The People of the Fog*. The credits of dozens of movies read MAKEUP . . . FRED PALLADINI, movies like *Margo, The Nine McCulloughs, The Fox of the Wind*. Fred Palladini! Sitting in his makeup chair! Kenny couldn't believe it.

Fred took a bite of his egg salad sandwich and nodded toward Kenny's binder. "Let's see your portfolio." By the time Fred had flipped through the photos of Kenny's makeup work in high school, the local playhouse, and the Children's Marionette Theater, the veteran had an idea of the young man's raw talent. He showed him a trick with glue and powder that held down the edges of fake noses and how to cut sponges for a razor-sharp application edge. He showed him the color he was blending on his palette and the different film bloods he was using depending on the wound, that lung blood needed to be darker than shoulder-wound blood. He told Ken *Ship*rock to keep at it and if he was ever on the Coast, to give him a call. A makeup man had done the same for him right after the war. Fred would show him around his garage workshop and give him a few more pointers. At 2:00 a.m., the actors started trooping back into the makeup trailer—coffee cups in hand, all of them—so Kenny had to leave. He hadn't touched his sandwich, but he did leave with the Coke and Fred Palladini's phone number. That was in 1971.

Two years later, Kenny was in Los Angeles and down to his last eighteen dollars. The half cousin in Long Beach was no longer in Long Beach, was no longer anywhere. The number Fred Palladini had given him had been dialed four times, but there had been no answer. So Kenny Sheprock from Bates City, Missouri, had neither a person to talk to nor a place to go in Hollywood. The bushes behind Mickey Hargitay's landscaping business were where Kenny had peed. His three meals a day were bananas and peanut butter right out of the jar. He would keep trying the Palladini number until, well, something happened, like being told he had a wrong number or Mickey Hargitay calling the cops.

Saturday morning, after a night of anxious sleep despite the wide back seat of his Chevy Impala (his dad had bought it used in 1966), tossing and turning to the sirens and traffic and hollering of the riffraff that populated the streets of that part of Hollywood in 1973, Kenny locked his car, walked to the pay phone at a gas station on Melrose, pulled out one of the two dimes in his pocket, and tried Fred Palladini one more time.

"Yeah?" It was Fred Palladini! He'd answered his phone!

"Mr. Palladini?"

"Yeah?"

"This is Kenny Sheprock? I met you in Missouri when you were shooting *The Barrow Gang*?"

"The kid with the makeup portfolio."

"You remember me?"

"Sure. Are you in town?"

"I am and I called this number like you gave me?"

"Glad you did. So, you're in town, eh?"

Kenny was in town. He didn't mention his financial straits, his diet, or the unwitting hospitality of Mickey Hargitay. Fred had been shooting on location down in Coronado for the week, which is why he'd not been around to answer the phone.

"Tell you what, kid. I can meet you here at the shop this afternoon. Are you free?"

Of course he was, and he found the place out in what was called the Valley. He had bought a Thomas Brothers Guide—the book of gridded maps, sold everywhere, that was a requirement for anyone new to town.

Fred Palladini's shop looked like a factory rather than a cubbyhole to tinker on movie magic. There were presses and molds, old plaster-cast heads, industrial-sized containers of chemicals and gear.

If you were not a makeup artist, or lacked the desire to become one, the place had all the charm of a pool-supply warehouse. For Kenny Sheprock, it was utopia. Fred showed him his wares, the old and the in-process, for a couple of hours, walked him to a burrito place for some food, then had coffee with him at his workbench until almost five that afternoon.

"Tell you what," Fred said as he was locking up. "I'll call a pal of mine who helps run the Hollywood Film Academy. They make student films all the time and need makeup artists because they don't teach it. You won't make any money but can get some work under your belt and meet some folks. Most of the film business is done by meeting folks." At Kenny's Impala, Fred could not help but notice the telltale evidence of the kid's living arrangements. "I came out in '47. Had to sleep in my dad's prewar Plymouth. But it all worked out. You'll do fine, as long as you're lucky and on time."

Fred Palladini was a life changer. It turned out some kids did need a makeup man for a student film that was shooting the very next day up by the Bronson Cave. The film was going to need blood. Kenny parked his car off Mulholland above the Hollywood Bowl, falling asleep with a view of the city lights that stretched to the horizon and beyond. That Sunday morning, he finished the bananas, took a shit in the bushes, brushed his teeth with water from an old Boy Scout canteen, and was on time for the production at the Bronson Cave, where the TV Batmobile had come roaring out of the Batcave. A million things had shot at those caves, just under the Hollywood sign, which in 1972 was so dilapidated and abandoned it read more like **H u l l j W a b D.**

Fifty-some years ago, that was what it took to get started. Kenny Sheprock had met some folks. He'd been lucky and was never late.

By the time Kenny got home to his place in the hills, a copy of the Bill Johnson script had been emailed to his in-box—K. SHEPROCK in light gray stenciled on every page—with a cover letter from Al Mac-Teer and Optional Enterprises.

Kenny,
    You know the drill. We're looking forward to working together again. Let me know your needs and questions.

                                                                    AM-T

Gail, his girlfriend, was showing some properties, so with her out of the house,[*] he made some tea and read through *Knight-shade: The Lathe of Firefall*. The screenplay was not a run-of-the-mill tentpole franchise to Kenny's mind, but a smarter story with less exposition, less shoe leather. Eve Knight was a helluva role for the Lady Lane—Wren would act the stuffing out of the part—and the movie would be one helluva production, makeup-wise, with all the battle scars from the fight scenes. With Kenny on MU and, as always, the two ladies known as the Good Cooks doing hair, Wren would look like the billion-dollar beauty she was. The big job would be the prosthetics on the Firefall character—some fun work to do there—but Kenny would just be looking on, maybe helping out, depending on who the MU vendor was on the picture.

Printing out a hard copy of the script, Kenny started marking up the pages for Continuity and the Time Line. He was working on another picture.

★ ★ ★

Wren never opened the leather three-ring script cover—the one embossed with w.l. in the lower-right corner—without two pens at the ready, one red ink, the other blue. Red was for notes regarding her subtext, what Eve Knight really meant by what she was saying.

EVE KNIGHT
I'm right here, Pop-Pop . . .

meant "I'm so very tired of taking care of this old, infirm man!"—at least on that read. On her next pass, she wrote in red *Never will I not be here!* Wren would fill the margins up with so many variants of subtext that her scripts took on the look of college papers that needed serious revisions. The blue pen was for any other notes that

---

[*] Gail's husband, Carl Banks, was a makeup man who had worked with Kenny often. He died of a brain aneurysm four years earlier. Kenny had been divorced, and Gail had always been a great gal.

came into her head like *medical drinks for Pop-Pop that she sips, scars on knuckles?*, and *head jerks: She hears things!*

Even though Micheline Ong was still fighting out the deal negotiations with Business Affairs at Dynamo/The Hawkeye ("Wren Lane is not doing you a favor by being Knightshade! You know you are the luckiest bastards in streaming to have her!"), Wally Lank and the Windermeres began the search for her housing upstate. Wren would need privacy, security, and space. A compound was needed, one with a fence, with gates, with passive barriers like trees and hardscape as well as beams and security cameras, to be installed if need be. A place with a gym would be ideal, of course, as Knightshade had the body of a superhero, so Wren needed access to a fitness room, a trainer, and a nutritionist—all items in her Perq Package, even though she never used them, since Laurel Windermere did all the cooking. Wren was an early devotee of the Dray-Cotter 40x6 PhysioSystem, the six-days-a-week series of workouts that took exactly forty minutes per session. The results were Olympian. The routine had been torture for the first three weeks, but by now Wren banged out Dray-Cotter as easily as reading Graydon Carter's *Air Mail* on her iPad.

The next Rubicon to cross—for everyone involved—was who was going to play Firefall? Was he going to be a star of equal stature to Wren Lane, like Rory Thorpe or Bruno Johns or Jason Hemingway? Wren would have smiled at the hiring of Rory Thorpe, who was currently unattached and, according to Willa Sax, a head-on-his-shoulders kind of guy. Turned out, Thorpe had signed to do a movie version of *Green Acres*. The other actors were unavailable, busy with their own franchises.

Contractually, Wren had approval on all casting choices—a paragraph that made Bill Johnson nod sagely, thinking, *Yeah, sure.* No one told him whom to cast or not to cast. Since the screenplay had very few scenes with the title roles mixing it up with each other, Firefall could have been played by anyone in the costume. But the Hawkeye wanted a BFS,* as did Dynamo, and the plan was to turn both superpeople into long-running characters with their own titles as well as appearances in the ongoing Dynamo Nation of

---

* Big Fucking Star.

films; the scenes putting Knightshade into *AOC5* were being generated at that moment. Wren would be playing Eve Knight until she aged out, as would whoever ended up as Firefall.

As often happens, the casting of Firefall came in the wink of an eye. Micheline Ong, Al Mac-Teer, Bill Johnson, and the bigwigs at the Hawkeye and Dynamo all asked the same question: How about O. K. Bailey as *Firefall*? The actor was just coming off shooting a modernized version of the old *Scarlet Pimpernel*, set in a stylized Paris of long ago, but with a wall-to-wall hip-hop/rock score, steampunk production design, and wildly choreographed fencing/kung fu/mixed-martial-arts fight scenes. The movie, boldly titled *Rapier,* was much anticipated, and OKB, as he was called by his agent, was one gorgeous dude. The Hawkeye wanted him very badly, Dynamo even more. Micheline made sure her client would be First Billing Above the Title, and all Al Mac-Teer said was "Hey, folks, this is my boss's decision!" Bill Johnson pondered his options.

Firefall was mostly a *presence* in the movie. The character had few lines but inhabited space like a physical manifestation of an idea, not unlike the very first Frankenstein's monster. In the early 1930s, the idea of the dead being brought back to life made some audiences faint and others outraged. Before the monster even walked, before Karloff was to rise and stomp around in what is now a familiar trope, just the sight of his trembling, once-lifeless hand made women scream, men cry out "*No,*" and the forces of religion and politics decry the hubris of life being created against God's will in a motion picture made for profit. When Karloff started doing the heavy-shoes, arms-out bit, some people fled the cinemas in terror. There was no way that Bill Johnson's Firefall was going to empty any theaters—the movie wasn't going to *play* in any theaters. But Firefall had to first repulse the audience in the extreme, to horrify if only for a millisecond, then prove to be of the same flawed, human tissue as did Frankenstein's monster; he was no undead zombie, alien, legionnaire of Hades, or unkillable dream-stalker like those who now inhabit a new movie every week. Firefall was no monster, but the Unknown Soldier, the casualty whose face and name are known only to God, a victim of war who seeks solace, peace, and eternal rest.

The Hawkeye was desperate to land OKB in the role and said so; an exclusive overall deal was in the works for the actor. At a Make-Nice meeting at Dynamo's offices in Culver City, Bill listened as the studio folks did their consultation dance. OKB was going to be a huge star after *Rapier* hit the streets, and they wanted to lock him up. And who would be better in the role, really?

Bill had seen OKB's work. The actor looked fierce in *Hands of Stone* and made off with the picture. In *Rapier,* the better moments worked when there was no dialogue, a fact in favor of seeing him as Firefall—who had very few lines. If there was any knock Bill had against the choice, it was in OKB's eyes. Dark eyes. There was a moment in the screenplay—in Bill's head—when Firefall's eyes are seen for the first time, and they needed to seem vulnerable. Firefall had to be vulnerable. Could dark eyes be vulnerable?

So, Bill pondered the possibility of OKB as Firefall, saw much of the reasoning to cast him, and suggested he and the actor have a talk.

OKB had recently fired his agent, having been poached by one of the two remaining super-agencies. OKB lived in Paris. OKB would like to read the script. Then, his super-agents were certain, he would love to talk to Bill Johnson.

Al Mac-Teer emailed an ultra-secure copy of *Knightshade: The Lathe of Firefall* to the actor. Three days later (three days? why the delay?) an email appeared in Al's in-box: *I dig it. OKB.* Bill liked that the actor's response was in so few words, in the same cryptic spirit as the character.

Neither man was big on Zooms or Skypes ("They hold no mystery," said OKB), so a half hour of international cell service was arranged. O. K. Bailey sipped red wine just a stroll away from the Trocadéro and its famous view of the Eiffel Tower, talking of the superiority of Paris versus LA or New York. Bill mentioned many of the famous Americans who had lived as expats in the City of Light. OKB brought up Firefall before the director did.

"You're going to get me in my third act, you know," the actor said.

"What's that mean?" Bill thought he was talking about the third act of the movie.

But OKB was talking about his career. "Act one was *Hands of*

Stone. I was killer, man. I was all over that. Act two, *Rapier,* which no one thought would amount to anything, but have you seen the Internet reaction to our teaser?"

Bill had. OKB, his swordsmanship, and his dark eyes were a web sensation for a few days. "I'm all classy and bon vivant and kill all the bad guys with style and people are going to laugh at how easy I do it. In *Lathe,* I'm like, stoic. Misunderstood. Relentless. Will not be stopped no matter how hard Wren Lane tries. We've got something there, don't we?"

"We do," Bill said. He talked about the Frankenstein mode, the man-of-few-words character, and of Firefall's vulnerability—his fabric of humanity. "He's a brand-new character for the studio, an Ultra we've never seen before. No prescribed powers or personality that we'll have to carry over from an earlier film. So we are starting from scratch."

"I like starting from scratch. FireFella will be me," OKB confirmed. "BJ, OKB is your man."

Bill Johnson flinched a nano-muscle of indignation at the nickname, writing it off as coming from a guy who referred to himself in the third person, with three letters.

The Hawkeye was thrilled. Dynamo threw a ton of money into the deal. Wren Lane bowed to the expertise of her director. OKB was good looking in a not-her-type way, not as tall as one might think, and, by opting to live in France, perhaps a bohemian sort. None of that mattered, really, because Knightshade and Firefall were together in less than a third of the movie—granted, in long scenes, loaded with fight choreography and SPFX. The two would, often, work on separate days. Bill Johnson called her—he was trusted with her top-secret cell phone number—to make the casting official and sound her out on a few other things.

"OKB is okay by me," she told him. "You can cast an Elvis impersonator and we'll still have a great movie."

"Excellent. How else you doing?" Bill asked. "Anything you need? Anything you worried about? Anything we need to do?"

"Bill," Wren told him. "I'm not one of those actors you need to check on to see if my mood is stable or if I have boyfriend troubles or if I'm cranky about the pages. You'll hear from me if such is the case."

Serenity. There it was. Bill Johnson never bothered Wren with a checkup call again.

Al did, though, a few days later because some lower execs at the Hawkeye were questioning the use of the word *lathe* in the title of the picture. They did not think the audience would know what a lathe was, since most of them had no idea themselves. Why not use *legend,* as in the original Kool Katz Komic? What did Wren think? Al wondered.

"Call the movie *Knightshade and the Motherfucking Cock-sucker.*" Wren was not prone to swearing like that, but she had just finished her workout and had been listening to some old Biggie Smalls.

Al Mac-Teer said she would suggest the title change to the powers that be.

★   ★   ★

Over six days of shooting in Atlanta, Wren busted into *Agents of Change 5: Origins,* as movie history now shows. The world saw the death of her parents, the Knights; the machinations of the team headed by AGENT LONDON; the other Ultras disagree on Knightshade's trustworthiness; and just how badass Wren Lane was as Eve. The planets had truly aligned with her in the role. The one scene between her and Ursa Major sent the Internet into a frenzy. That so much had been packed into so few scenes, filmed in ultrasecret, then mixed into the final print of *AOC5* showed what Dynamo could do with a billion-dollar franchise.

Bill Johnson advised the writers of *Origins* on a few beats, but otherwise was content to let Dynamo do what Dynamo did. The Hawkeye looked on with a diabolical, *heh-heh-heh* kind of pleasure as the character they now owned upturned the Dynamo Nation. The streamer took out ads blaring that Knightshade would soon be seen again, but only on the Hawkeye. Within twenty-four hours, 2.6 million new subscriptions had been sold. The trend continued.[*]

In the dwindling weeks before shooting her own movie in Lone Butte, lodging for Wren was a priority. Tom Windermere worked

---

[*] With 2.6 million subscribers at $15 a month for a year: $468 million.

with Housing, saw a half dozen possibilities, blew them all off for being too exposed, not private enough, accessible to anyone, and not safe. Tom never told the true reasons all those places were unsuitable, keeping to himself the list of known stalkers he monitored, the predators that he knew were threats to Wren. Wally was involved in the search, too, and he finally came up with a suitable compound for his sister; a huge expanse of land with, get this, a private landing strip for her Cirrus 150.* She and her squad moved in a month before rehearsals, in love with the place. She had her workouts, her wings, quiet nights of scene study, and her stunt-coaching routine all on-site in her leased Xanadu/Shangri-la/Sloppy Joe's. On occasion, she secretly slipped down to Sacramento for good Mexican food, arranged by a nice lady named Ynez who worked for Al Mac-Teer. The local hire knew everything, and everybody.

To build up her pilot hours, Wren and Heather flew often, all over Northern California, heading straight north toward Mount Shasta, the huge dormant volcano that towered over the top end of the valley, which had once been covered in snow year-round. Climate change had made it a big M-shaped mountain of brown. Mount Lassen, to the northeast, was a volcano, too, as well as part of a national park. Trips to LA were a breeze, for meetings and dentist appointments. Due to insurance demands, Wren was not officially allowed to fly her own plane. She did not care. Heather Cooper told anyone who would listen, "I'm her insurance."

One cloudless evening, the two pilots left just after sunset, flying west for San Francisco, making a figure eight in the sky as night fell and the lights of the Bay Area cities competed with the stars in the indigo heavens. Rivers of light—the cars on the interstates—ran below them in white and red, guiding them to and from Baghdad-by-the-Bay. Secure at the controls, Wren felt the plane separate from herself like she was flying on her own—not in a machine, but under her own native power, like a superhero. An Ultra. An Agent of Change.

---

* Owned by a Silicon Valley unicorn who bought the place from an almond farmer/widower. This new owner had a fleet of planes—a Honda Jet, a Cessna Caravan, an ultra-light, and a Beaver Sea Plane—so he'd built the runway.

OKB

The two stars first met in Al Mac-Teer's office in the Capitol Records Building. Wren had flown down to Hollywood from the compound in Lone Butte. O. K. Bailey was just in from Paris. They were left alone with coffee and healthy snacks for an hour of getting-to-know-you chitchat. He told Wren of shooting in Paris, living in Paris, asking how often she had been to Paris, and he was, in fact, going back to Paris until his contract dictated his presence in Lone Butt-plug—a joke of his that did not land, which he realized and covered for by saying, *Merde, my language!* Comparing notes on the screenplay, OKB told her he wanted to work the line "Here's your answer! What was the question?" into as many scenes as he could, since, as BJ had said, they were "starting from scratch" and OKB had a lot of ideas. Wren steered her side of the conversation to their characters' flaws, their being so taciturn and so fated to meet.

"I like that, too," he said. "We come off as superhero Romeo and Juliets."

Nonsense, Wren said to herself. Shakespeare's young lovers were kids who were in love with the idea of being in love. They took one look at each other and, *foom,* you had the classic story of star-crossed soul mates. Firefall and Knightshade were not kids at all, but she went gently in saying so. "We're not young lovers, though, are we? We're adversaries first, each with a history. I sense you without ever seeing you, I *feel* the oncoming conflict and get in your way. You try to sweep me aside but can't. We seek to destroy each other a few times, ending in a draw before we consider that the other is a damaged, tortured being. Not exactly the Capulets and Montagues. Maybe Petruchio and Kate?"

"Who?" OKB asked.

Their ensuing *chit* was about the shooting schedule, their *chat* about their time in the makeup chair each day—for her nonglam good looks and his scars. They compared notes on possible costumes. She would not have to wear some dumb cape; OKB didn't want to look stupid in an army helmet. "You and I can dream bigger than what's on the pages, yeah?"

A week later, Wren received a FedEx from Paris delivered by courier. Inside was a box of strike-anywhere matches and a note that had been wood-burned onto a bit of thin plywood. *Am I gonna light you up, Eve? Here's your answer! xx OKB* was branded onto the shingle, which was cute, appropriate. Wren responded in kind with an old Zippo lighter she found online with the eagle, globe, and anchor seal of the United States Marine Corps—a nod to the origins of his character. She sent it off to him via his agency with a handwritten note: *Thank you for your service, EK (WL)*

A week later, from Paris, came a handwritten note: *Thanks for the Zippo. Let's not ***k til we're done. OKB.*

"*Star star star k? Star star star k!* What the hell does *star star star k* mean?" Wren asked Wally.

"Well, the f-word ends with the letter *k.*"

There was a line in the screenplay, delivered by Firefall to Knightshade during a choreographed fight scene. (A long one— the rehearsals were grueling. Wren needed nightly physical therapy and mineral wraps to recover.) A line that had no *** in it.

```
The Warriors pause their battle, taking a
breath . . .


              KNIGHTSHADE
     This won't end well for you.


              FIREFALL
     Let's not talk till we're done.


              KNIGHTSHADE
     We're done when you're gone.
```

Let's not talk *till we're done!* If OKB's insertion of three *'s meant the f-word, Wren would not let that s*** fly. She took a photo of the note and texted it to Al Mac-Teer, who was aghast.

On a Thursday in Lone Butte, thirteen days out from the start of Principal Photography, Wren and OKB were called to the huge inner volume hall out at Westinghouse Light—this would be the Green Screen stage where the air-ballet fight scenes would be shot. The place was already rigged with cables and pulleys and carabiners from which the actors would hang for certain scenes, and their stunt doubles would dangle for hours. For the sake of all the pertinent departments a test of this fight rigging was going to show how long the setup would take, how much area it would cover, how the actors would take to being whipsawed by the wire team while they acted scenes of conflicted emotions, romantic notions, and punchouts. All this in the hope of heading off time-consuming cock-ups that could devour an expensive shooting day.

All week, Call Sheet Number 1 (Wren) and Number 2 (OKB) had been challenged, trained, and instructed separately. If Wren was in the rigging being supervised by "Doc" Ellis, the stunt coordinator (whom she had worked with back in her Sergeant Hard-On days), OKB was in the dojo being trained by Doc's enthusiastic team. Then they'd be switched out. Wren took to her training like a Cirque du Soleil hopeful, relishing the demands of her harnessed flight and ballet by way of kung fu moves. OKB was bored and sort of hated Doc's team because he thought the guys who trained him for *Rapier* were more in tune with his rhythms. Wren would stay after her sessions, fine-tuning her harness straps and adding airborne somersaults to her hang time. OKB did everything he could to be finished by lunch.

When Wren and OKB were laced and buckled into the constricting apparatuses, they were working together, at the same time, for the first time. Yogi and his seconds looked after the two stars, to get estimates of how much warning time would be needed On the Day. Ynez had laid out coffee, snacks, health bars and fruit, then hung around to make any needed quick runs. A good thing, since OKB asked for a smoothie as soon as he walked in—with pineapple, celery, egg-white protein, and kale. Ynez made that happen, somehow, then lingered to watch what to her looked like a trapeze act. Bill Johnson was safety-strapped into a cherry picker and lifted off the floor to be parallel to his actors, shooting video on his iPhone for possible camera angles. The EPK* crew captured more footage

---

* Electronic Press Kit.

than they would ever need. Two execs—one from the Hawkeye, one from Dynamo—had flown up from LA to make their presence known. Afterward, they held a two-hour meeting with Al and Bill that covered fifteen minutes of subject matter. They flew back on the Dynamo corporate jet, the hours, fuel, and landing fees billed to the production as overhead.

Wren and OKB were hung, swung, dangled, inverted, made to ascend like eagles, and to descend like lunar landers. There was no doubt that the two stars would be doing serious hang time once the company moved to the Green Screen stage for the two weeks of shooting after all the location and set photography was in the can/ on the hard drives. When both were raised twenty feet above the air-bag safety mat and were in each other's arms for a practice run of their up-close work, OKB suggested they have dinner together, just the two of them.

"Not sure I'm free," Wren said. "I have workouts." Since that ***k message, Wren decided she would never be alone with her costar, never in a room, just the two of them, without the door being kept wide open. When she told Al of her reluctance to meet solo with OKB, Ms. Mac-Teer agreed with *abso-fucking-lutely* never, seeing to it that no such meetings were scheduled.

"We do have to eat," OKB said from his harness. "We have a *relationship* in the movie. Let's work on it before those other actors show up."

Those other actors—playing OLD MAN CLARKE, the four INVESTIGATORS, Eve's wheelchair-bound POP-POP, etc.— were not yet in Lone Butte, saving production money on housing and per diem. For the first days of Principal Photography the only cast members on the Call Sheet were to be Knightshade, Firefall, and Day Players.

"Let me check my schedule," Wren mumbled.

"Do that," OKB mumbled back in imitation. Then he shouted, "This harness is hurting my *sack*! Can we rehearse the kiss now?" No one answered until Bill called over from the cherry picker, "No." Protected by Screen Actors Guild rules, the actors could stay bound up in the body harnesses only for a limited time. The pair was lowered to the floor and unleashed.

"An artists-only breaking of the bread is a good thing to do,"

OKB said on the way down. "Just me and you and our inner mono-logues. We can make it a celebration of our start date. A formal affair. Come on, Wrennie."

"We should have a kickoff thing," Wren, never "Wrennie," said, stepping out of her harness with Doc's aid. "I'm thinking of hav-ing a Two Weeks Out Dinner for, like, everyone this week. Let's do it then."

"Everyone?" OKB asked like a pouty child. "Goody. *Everyone.*"

★ ★ ★

The dinner was scheduled for Tuesday night. Due to security rea-sons the event took place at Wren's compound.* The invitees were Wren's team—Kenny Sheprock; Ronnie Goode and Goldie Cooke, a.k.a. the Good Cooks, who had overseen Wren's hair and wigs since *Periwinkle;* her brother, Wally, with Tom Windermere hov-ering as needed; and Laurel doing the cooking with the help of Ynez, once the menu had been set for a Mexican feast. From her mother's kitchen, Ynez arranged platters of dishes that could *never* come from a woman named Windermere. Al, Yogi, Aaron Blau, Bill Johnson, SAM, and OKB brought the total to thirteen with room still for a couple of plus-ones.

Tom met their cars at the compound's security gate; he had texted a GPS pin to their phones. There was a quarter-mile drive down a gravel lane lined with transplanted Monterey pines to the house, a low-slung architectural gem, built of rusted-looking steel, massive windows made of triple panes of gas-infused glass, and building materials that were also solar panels. Despite all that hoo-ha and a cost of close to $90 million, the house looked rather modest, what with the airstrip, barns, stables, baseball field, and pickleball courts all out of sight, as well as the man-made pond that was stocked with bass. Wren had the patio doors open and special lights that looked like fire torches but were just incred-ible simulations—no smoke, no danger of fire, no heat.

---

* Tom Windermere insisted it be so. Had the dinner been thrown in, say, the private room of a restaurant, the staff would post about it on social media—*Hey, movie stars are coming to my restaurant! I'm getting a selfie!* Who could blame them?

Wren made the margaritas. If anyone wanted a cocktail, they had unlimited access to the bar. Kenny brought three bottles of superb wine. Bill brought a six-pack of Hamm's Special lager. SAM made dirty vodka martinis just as he liked them. Aaron had a diet ginger ale. The evening started out just fine, despite (or due to) the late arrival of OKB.

"I think that's him now," Yogi said, drawing a laugh from the crowd after an hour and a half of taquito appetizers and four different kinds of salsa and chips. Everyone laughed because the roar of OKB's brand-new Audi echoed through the soft evening air. OKB came up the quarter-mile driveway at a speed that was all braggadocio and stupidity, turning a hot circle in front of the house, revving the German engine like a drag-strip funny car. Gravel spit from the spinning wheels, hitting the others' cars like horizontal hailstones, pitting the paint jobs of the company-leased automobiles. Ynez's Transit took a broadside of the bird-shot pebbles.

A woman was with OKB. He was the only guest to bring an unannounced plus-one.

"Nicolette, everyone!" OKB hollered by way of her introduction. Nicolette looked to be an exhausted seventeen-year-old Parisian girl, judging from her hip-for-Paris/odd-for–Lone Butte outfit, her skinny-in-an-unhealthy-way frame (she smoked, a lot), and from the fact that she had landed in an Air France jet in San Francisco that very evening after a twelve-hour flight from Paris's Charles de Gaulle—picked up by OKB and zoomed to the party. From that moment, the night took a turn for the just so *fascinating*.

Everyone was hungry and delighted by the quality and authenticity of the cuisine—this was no meal of burritos and red sauce. There was *molcajete*-style guacamole, crabmeat taquitos, slow-roasted pork, enchiladas *mariscos,* a mahimahi in *crema fresca,* and something called *sopa de viuda*. Bill was thrilled with the supply of green chilies (Wren had made the request), and everyone had had just the right amount of alcohol of choice. And, to put it bluntly, the dinner party was made most memorable by OKB's transition into an outright SOB.

Had the guy done cocaine that night? If so, he hadn't shared any with Nicolette; that poor girl was sleepy, made even more tired by having to listen and speak in English. OKB talked in a loud, high register, as though he wanted to remind everyone of his presence, as if someone, somewhere, were listening in on a speakerphone. He laughed for no reason after saying things that weren't meant to be funny. He commandeered the talk at the table by banging a glass with his knife and insisting, "One conversation! One conversation! I have a question I'd like to pose to BJ! *Beej!* Tell the table just what the fuck happened on *Albatross*?" Then, he cackled like Frank Gorshin as the Riddler from 1966.

Bill Johnson did not need to answer the question because OKB didn't give him the time to speak. The one conversation at the table was going to come from the mind and mouth of OKB.

Verbatim, here is a sampling of OKB's oratory that evening:

"Guys, you gotta admit that whole project was a boner, even you, right, BJ? You named the movie *Albatross* for Christ's sake. What, was *Shitstorm* taken? . . . When I got *Hands of Stone* everyone wanted to play one of the two winning fighters, but I knew MacGraw was the part they couldn't cut. No MacGraw meant no driver of the bus . . . I never use the automatic, not in a car like the Audi! Shift with the paddles, man! . . . If you read only one book this year, read this old book about a seagull from, like, the 1970s. It'll take you a half hour and change your life . . . I was locked into this two-shot on *Rapier* that went on for three days. Three fuckin' days, man. You gonna do that to me, BJ? Take three motherfuckin' days to shoot some fuckin' over-the-shoulder? I told them to tighten up the lens and let my double do the last setup . . . BJ, you gotta think of a part for Nicolette, don't you think? . . . I discovered the secret of shaving on *Rapier*. Never with a blade and lather, but get three different kinds of electric razors and rotate them across your beard every three or four hours. Kenny Shipshape, am I wrong? Is that not the perfect way to keep a cheek stubble-free and skin soft? I keep a Norelco in the car . . . BJ, you change your shoes at lunchtime? I heard that's what Scorsese does—changes his shoes at lunchtime. Nicolette is like a wild woman in Paris—models for *Le Globe,* was on, like, the most popular TV series that made all of France, like, stop what it was doing the nights she was on, she's everywhere . . . My place is a dump compared to this . . . you fly your own plane? Really? I almost took flying lessons from this guy in Kenya . . ."

The man talked and talked and talk-talk-talked until he and Nicolette abruptly left, again spewing gravel all over the parked cars and the front of Wren's $90 million rented home.*

Al and Bill lingered at Wren's place after the others had gone as Ynez helped Laurel Windermere clean up the kitchen. Wally gave them a hand. The hour was late, but another pitcher of margaritas was assembled and blended by Al, who made sure there was enough for those who remained. When Ynez took off with her Transit full of now-empty platters she had brought from her home, Laurel bade them all a good night, and Tom melted into the darkness to walk the perimeter of the compound. Wally was tired enough to go to bed but was not about to. No way! He'd been quiet the whole night—after some polite chitchat with his sister's movie people—but then came OKB and Nicotine from Normandy. A postmortem of the dinner theater show was due; Wally wanted to be a part of it. Hell, he would even serve as master of ceremonies.

"All I know about movies is what I've witnessed as my sister's civilian beard," Wally said, sitting down on the big custom sofa in the main room—the room with the Shepard Fairey painting that slid up to reveal the huge LCD TV. "But that OKB guy is going to be somebody's nightmare."

"We've seen this before, eh, Boss Man?" said Al, raising her glass of south-of-the-border delight to her lips. She thought, for just a flicker of time, that she saw Dace—dear Dace—sitting on the other side of the massive sofa, drinking her margarita with a bemused smile, knitting a pair of mittens.

"Well," Bill drawled. He was hesitant to delve into what had transpired over the course of the evening. Wren, his title-role actor, was in the room, had hosted the dinner party, had sat through the whole horror show put on by the guy who was going to be her above-the-title costar. Dear God, they were all going to start in a week, and if Bill did not carefully measure what was going through his head—the many worries he'd come to have about OKB—his

---

* LEGAL DISCLAIMER HERE: Nicolette is not her name. The woman in question was, in fact, twenty years old but looked so very much younger. Her notoriety is not due to the claims made here, but she is European and a celebrity of a *type*. We can confirm, though, that she was brutally exhausted due to half a day's flying and the accompanying jet lag.

lack of discretion might scare Wren into fits of preshoot jitters. But he studied her, saw that she was again wearing the leather wrist strap of *SERENITY*, weighing what he had seen of her since that green-chili lunch in Socorro. Wren was a hard worker with few complaints and a ton of ideas for her Eve—*I'm not saying we shoot this, but I'll just keep it in my pocket*—and Bill liked that. "Going Cone of Silence, here, okay?"

"What does 'Cone of Silence' mean?" Wren asked.

"What we are about to share is going to make you, Wren, a coconspirator," Al said, secretly relieved. Having Wren in on certain topics would make her life easier, giving her someone to vent to, someone other than Ynez.

"Really." Wren was not asking a question but rather confirming the statement. "If this is going to be about OKB, I have ideas for what to do with the corpse. I mean, if we're going to kill him and he disappears mysteriously, isn't that an insurance claim?"

Al hooted. Then looked at Bill with a quick head nod toward Wren. "She looks like one of *them* but thinks like one of *us*."

Bill agreed. It was usually better to leave cast members in the dark about the inner workings of the Production Office, the decisions made, the things that were said. But Wren Lane deserved better. "Yeah. We've dealt with worse than O. K. Bailey."

"Not worse," Al piped. "Just as bad. BOLDFACE NAME NUMBER ONE turned out to be microdosing heroin in his trailer, but we got him through NAME OF FILM. BOLDFACE NAME NUMBER TWO was getting a divorce, banging the gaffer, and hitting on me, but she showed up for work on time on NAME OF THAT OTHER FILM."

"We roll with the punches," Bill said. "We get them to the set, get them into the costume, get them to say the words in the right order, and no one is the wiser. It's all behind-the-curtain stuff. The show goes on. On ONE OF BILL'S GOOD MOVIES, we had BOLDFACE NAME NUMBER THREE, who was fine in the mornings but gone-baby-gone after lunch—after an hour and a half in the trailer with his personal assistant, Johnnie Walker Black Label. Argumentative all afternoon. Stumbling, slurring."

"Groping. Occasionally vomiting. A primo shit-faced artist," Al said, knowing that the amount of tequila she'd put into the blender had her on the road to being shit-faced herself.

Wren was aghast! "BOLDFACE NAME NUMBER THREE is a Boozilla?"

"Sorry to reveal those particular feet of clay," Bill told her. "Some of them are just so damaged, you know? Our art and science is too full of future twelve-steppers unless, first, they seal off the kitchen doors with wet towels and put their heads in the oven. Or if word gets out and no one wants to hire them."

That prompted a question from Wally. "So, you know firsthand that BOLDFACE NAMES NUMBER ONE, TWO, and THREE have behavioral problems because you've made movies with them. But then, on the record, you say such wonderful blather about them, their fiery passion, and their uncompromising work ethic. How they inhabit the role when the cameras are rolling."

"My God, Wally," Bill said. "You've quoted me verbatim."

"What happens when another director calls you up and asks what working with SHIT-FACED NAME NUMBER THREE is like?" Wally asked. "Doesn't a code of ethics of the DGA require you to tell the truth, the whole truth? Don't you have to warn them, 'Run away as fast as you can'?"

"You do tell the truth," Bill said. "That, yes, BOLDFACE NAMES are terrors to work with, but . . . they are worth the struggle. Given all the hassles, would you work with them again? Yes."

"I can't imagine there not being someone just as good as FUOKB," Wally said. "Who wants to work so hard just to make a movie?"

"Wally"—Bill laughed—"you don't do this for a living." Bill let that hang in the air, that one part statement, two parts accusation.

"Boss?" Al asked. "Shall we?" With raised eyebrows, she cocked her head toward Wren.

Wren felt the eyes of Bill Johnson upon her, much like she had all those months ago in Socorro, New Mexico.

"Yep," Bill said. "I think we're good."

"Okay." Al shifted her body on the couch to directly face Wren Lane. "Girl. You need to decide, right now, to either join the Brain

Trust or invite us to leave immediately. I'm talking blood oath, here. You'll be keeping secrets."

Wren laughed out loud.

"No laughing matter. You'll be expected to lie in protection of us all. You will become a liar. A dissembler. You in or out?"

"Is there a secret handshake?"

"No handshakes. Just the secrets." Bill had been nursing his second can of Hamm's Special lager, but now finished it clean.

"Let's get cracking!" Wren said.

Wally piped up. "Am I going to be a liar now, too?"

Al looked at the gorgeous twin brother. "Wallace. You don't count. No offense."

"None taken. I lie every day anyway," he said. "By the way, who are you people? What are you doing in this house? Has this conversation even taken place? No."

Bill got up from his section of the sectional to get a third can of Hamm's, talking as he did. "Is OKB the one, true Firefall? Nah. Is anyone? No. Firefall doesn't exist, does not yet inhabit a place in the space-time continuum. He has yet to be committed to film. Firefall is words on paper and iPad screens. He is a costume rendering and character sketch. He's not been image-captured in a camera."

"Friday," Al said. "Camera tests are Friday."

Wren knew that. She and Le'Della Rawaye had already been in weeks of passionate costume talks, fittings, refittings, and—did she have to say it?—more fittings to make sure the six costume changes for Eve Knight were Ultra-perfect. Friday, she would model fourteen different looks from which perfection would be evident and obvious.

Bill continued, "OKB has middle-child issues. He's uncomfortable in the prosthetics needed for Firefall. He won't work with the prop guys on learning the flamethrower because it's all going to be fake CGI. Doc Ellis says it pains him training OKB in the stunts because he can't lose the fake smile on his face lest he reflect his frustrations and OKB gets his feelings hurt. The star of the movie must never have any hurt feelings. Le'Della says he pouts during his fittings like a baby with a wet diaper. What am I missing, Al?"

"He talks about his two movies—all of his *two* movies—as

though they're groundbreakers. Like *Hands of Stone* is already on the Criterion app and *The Rapist* will be as big as all the 007s put together."

"*Rapier*," Bill corrected her.

"What did I say?"

"*The Rapist.*"

"Not far off."

Bill took a light sip of the Hamm's, not for the alcohol but for the cold, icy blast to his palate. "The possibility exists that OKB could become one of the biggest movie stars in the firmament, all because of Firefall. If so, his shenanigans, like tonight's, will be considered traits of genius. The audience will project upon him all their masculine suppositions, all their romantic notions, all their heroic ideals because he can sword fight like a master and then save *you*, Wren Lane, from Knightshade's lifetime of solitary exhaustion. His Scarlet Pimpernel and Firefall can be to him what Stanley Kowalski and Terry Malloy were to Brando.

"Or he may be yet another of the dozens worth but a dime," Bill said. "Damn good looking but in need of puppy training. I've dealt with worse examples of the Talent."

"The *Talent*?" Wren piped up. "Is that what you call us? Actors are the *Talent*? Like the Nuclear Waste? The Livestock? The Pathogen?"

"You had your chance to excuse yourself, honey," Al said. "This is how we talk in the Inner Sanctum."

"Ms. Lane," Bill said, sounding like Clark Kent of the *Daily Planet* talking to Lois. "Serenity." He pointed to her leather wrist strap. "That is a rare quality along Fountain Avenue. But you've got it. We've seen you throw your soul and sinew into Eve Knight without making so much as a ripple on the waters of Production. Since we met eleven weeks ago, I've seen in you an artist of intuitive drive and indomitable curiosity in pursuit of a vision, an inhabitation, a manifestation of the one character in this movie upon which all our fates hang. Now I know—we all know—how fortunate we are. Wren Lane *is* Eve Knight. Without you, what are we doing this for? You have solved the most existential of our problems: why we are all here. You are the miracle we dare not hope for."

Wendy Lank blushed, feeling a misting of tears coming on. Who had ever talked to her like this, made her feel so accomplished, so naturally worthy, other than Wally? And Tom Windermere? And Kenny Sheprock? She found Al Mac-Teer looking at her with eyes filled with surety, nodding in agreement with her boss.

Bill went on, "OKB is the problem we expect, like so many of his ilk—the New Big Star, the latest hunk of forbidden fruit with confidence born of bluster. We can only assume he is steerable, that he can be manipulated, flattered, cajoled, tended to, babysat, made camera ready, and delivered to the set all in goodly time. In my talks with the boy, I see red flags," Bill said. "He wants to try a country-hick dialect. He is not wild about how he looks in the helmet. He wants Firefall to say 'Here's your answer' for some non-intelligent reason. I'm confident I'll get him off such choices. His good ideas are not so plentiful, but he's offered up a flexibility that I'll rely on. So, Wren, let's make this *deal* . . ."

The room waited. Wally cocked his head. Wren stopped breathing for a moment. Al said nothing, waiting for whatever her boss was to say next.

"I'm not saying you have to respect the man," Bill Johnson said. "But you do have to respect the process. You will be a pro. You will not let OKB mar your work or block your creative path. Let us"—he nodded at Al—"deal with him. You let your costar be as inconsequential to your emotive tasks as the accountants at the Hawkeye. And for your service in the making of another motion picture masterpiece . . ."—Bill held two fingers up to his lips and made a spitting sound, *tfui tfui tfui;* Al did as well, to take the curse off any claim to greatness*—"you will become my creative partner."

Al raised her eyebrows. *Partner, huh?* Bill had used that term with only two other actors that she knew of: Maria Cross, of course, way back when, and the late Paul Kite, who played the Narrator of *Barren Land,* whose role expanded during shooting and in countless recording sessions during Post. Bill had invited Paul into

---

* They had learned to do that from Yogi, who is Greek and given to superstitions about such things. Spitting three times castigated the devil, taking the onus off prophecies of greatness.

the Editing Room to help him feel out the pace and intensity of the movie and help write the prose that guided the film. There were times when Bill was, finally, satisfied with the work they'd done and felt they were finished, but after screening the movie again, Paul Kite would ask him, "Why do you think we're done? We can do better, no?" And now? Tonight? Wren Lane was about to breathe in that same rarefied air.

Bill continued, "You and I will discuss any changes, any new pages, for all the characters, not just Eve. You can watch assemblies of the week's footage with me, Hector, and Marilyn" (respectively, Chew and Cakebread, who cut *The Typist* for no money on a flatbed while they were the editing assistant's assistants on the old TV show *Richie Horowitz: Mind Bender;* long ago, but Hector and Marilyn cut film like butter). "I'll open reels for you right up to when we Lock Picture. You can say anything you wish to me, any opinion you have—just like *that* woman." He pointed at Al. "I can't make a movie called *Knightshade Versus Knucklehead* without Knightshade as a partner. Do we have a deal?"

Wren's eyes had not left Bill. In fact, she hadn't moved while the man talked. She hadn't even put her glass down and was unaware of how cold her hand had become from the icy elixir in it. She was stock-still and yet her heart was racing; she could hear her blood coursing through her ears. Wren knew her life had just changed.

"Deal."

"Good," Bill said, pleased. "Now we can talk about what has to happen."

★   ★   ★

There was no Full Read-Thru of the movie due to COVID protocols frowning on gatherings of many people. And getting the full cast together for the one day was cost prohibitive. Bill would meet and rehearse with the Talent in private when the scenes were soon to shoot, as he had been doing with Wren and OKB. OKB had moved off the southern dialect choice and was now spit-balling a Brooklyn mobster *dem-deez-doze.* Then came Friday's camera tests.

Wren was driven to the set by Tom, arriving to take her seat in the Works* at 6:36 a.m. OKB was given a later pickup time, 8:00 exactly. His prosthetics would take hours to apply—all that scar tissue and burned skin—so the plan was to have him ready at 1:00 p.m., throw him on camera beside Wren as she was finishing her last look—and there they would be, for the first time, Knight-shade and Firefall. Planned thus, the day's work would be done by 1:30. They'd call lunch and Wrap and be finished for the day.

Alan "Ace" Acevido, a local hire, was parked outside the actor's lodgings in Franzel Meadows at 7:45 a.m., behind the wheel of the stipulated Range Rover. For a morning pickup, 7:45 was a layin, a late call for Ace, who had retired from driving on movies the year before. He and his wife had a lovely eight-acre place northwest of Yuba City, where she raised miniature horses and Ace got into looming—he wove his own textiles. He built his own loom, in fact, and took to the hobby like Gandhi at his spinning wheel. But once a Teamster, forever a Teamster, so when production called looking for a local hire, Ace took the job, of course, because the pay was great. A week earlier, when he had first met OKB for approval, Firefall told Ace that under no circumstances was he ever to ring the doorbell when picking up. Never. "OKB will come out when OKB is ready."

"You're the captain of my ship," Ace said. But here it was Friday morning, at 8:00, then 8:15, then 8:25, with no sign of the actor. Ace texted one of Yogi's ADs. **ACE: WAITING.** At 8:45, he trans-mitted **ACE: OKB NO-SHOW.** Yogi, then, was told, pronto, so he reported the intel to Al, who had been in the production trailer since 6:00 a.m. Al then called the actor on his production-supplied iPhone and left a message: "Hey, Mr. B, wondering if there is any-thing we can do for you this morning. Big day today, kinda-sorta. Base Camp needs ya! Call me back."

Nothing. At 9:17 Al's text alert chirped. **STONERAPIER: !#@^%^%**&!.** Al dared to assume that the garbled CAPS LOCK message meant OKB was OTW (on the way), that Ace was Romeo Hotel (rolling heavy). But he didn't arrive at Base Camp until 10:04, with Ace carrying for him a large, overstuffed duffel bag that had

---

* The Works: Hair and Makeup. The time is noted by the Base Camp AD for the Production Report.

been, judging from the *Hands of Stone* logo on the side, the crew gift for that movie.

Earlier, at 8:08 a.m., Ynez had set a fresh smoothie on the counter of OKB's trailer kitchen—pineapple, celery, egg-white protein, and kale. Overhearing Al tell Yogi that the Number 2 on the Call Sheet was not just late, but late-late, she stopped by Craft Service and made another OKB Special, replacing the hours-old smoothie with a fresh one. But even that healthy shake had matured by the time the actor reported for work. OKB didn't touch it. He called for Ynez to come to him, which she did the moment she was told that Firefall wanted to see her and only her. OKB wanted to know if she could get him some banana pancakes and that he wouldn't "hit the chair" until he'd tucked away a breakfast. By luck and the sophistication of those in Craft Service, a griddle was heated, an add-water-only pancake mix was whipped up, and a sliced banana arranged on top of the tall stack like a smiley face.

"I asked for banana pancakes," OKB said when Ynez brought the covered plate and bottle of syrup. "Not pancakes with bananas." It was now 11:02 a.m. In front of the camera, Wren had already shot tests for ten of her costumes, but OKB had yet to go into the Works.

The whole day went like this. No. Worse.

OKB did not like having glue applied to his face like so much tar on a brush—he hated the feeling of cold goop on his neck. The glue was needed to hold the latex prosthetics, the makeup that would turn him into Firefall. The bald pate that would become his scalded scalp seemed too tight to OKB, so it had to be removed, applied again, was still too tight, so removed again and reapplied.[*] During his time in the Works he was bent over his phone nonstop,

---

[*] Friday's Camera Test was not the first time OKB had gone through the transition into Firefall. There had been three prior sessions to work out the complicated process. OKB had shown up early for the first one, but the team was not quite ready for him, so he wandered off and came back an hour later. He was hours late for the other two sessions. He had already refused to do another life cast of his head, with its messy, suffocating bucket of glop covering his shoulders and encasing his head as he breathed through straws stuck in his nose. He'd done such a cast for *Rapier* and insisted it be shipped in from Paris. He hated his burned-hair wig, and if he was going to have to wear an army helmet, what was the point of a cap and wig?

sending texts and emails and reading Facebook and BiO posts while the three-person team maneuvered around him to apply the delicate appliances to his neck, shoulders, jaw, and onto his pate. They had to keep asking OKB to raise his chin, to look up, to not lean over *for just a second* as they applied glue and smoothed over the specially molded prosthetics. He did, under protest.

At almost exactly noon, Wren had on her final wardrobe option. Kenny and the Good Cooks had had her various looks settled, each one now in the camera. Bill had walked her through the motions so all the angles could be inspected—to a mark, then profiles, left and right, all the way around, walk back. Everyone was talking and commenting and joking around as these tests were only to see what was what, costume-wise. The lenses and lighting were adjusted, then she did the same moves again. One more lens change and some added moves on the dolly allowed some of her fight choreography, then they moved outside for a second camera in natural lighting.

At this point, according to the original schedule, OKB should have been in costume, made up, and camera ready, but such was not the case, as Yogi then reported to those on the set. His second second AD had gone into the H/MU trailer to get an estimate of OKB's readiness. Without looking up from his phone—which was playing TikTok videos on speaker—OKB said, "I'll be ready in eight minutes!" That was supposed to be a joke. The head of the prosthetics team pointed to still-uncolored appliances glued to OKB's head and said they had at least an hour and a half left.

"So that's the scenario," Yogi told Bill and Al and SAM and the crew. Getting both Wren and OKB on camera in a two-shot would mean a long wait and for what? A digital composite of the two characters would have to do.

"Break the crew for lunch," Al said. "OKB stays in the Works. He's just the one look, so we wrap by four."

"Can I go, then?" Wren asked. She had a workout scheduled, had been up since 5:30 a.m., and wanted to rise at the same hour the next morning to get some flying in her Cirrus 150. Wren needed some sky time, and the weekend would be her last chance.

"Bye-bye," Bill bade her.

When OKB heard that the crew had been broken for the meal, he leaped out of the chair. "Let's all enjoy an hour's lunch!" As he

walked back to his trailer, his makeup far from complete, the second second told him he was meant to stay in the Works to be ready
when the crew was back. "A man's gotta eat. Get me the lovely
Ynez."

Ynez happened to be with Al and Yogi in the catering tent; a
skeleton crew was throwing together a lunch for the twenty-two
people working that day. Yogi's earpiece squawked with the request
for Ynez, so he sent her off to OKB.

"He left the Works. For lunch," he told Al.

"Of course, he did," Al said.

OKB was in his trailer, scrolling through the TV's satellite grid
for either live sports or new porn, when Ynez knocked.

"Hey, *Consuelo*," he said to Ynez Gonzalez-Cruz. "Is there a
great place for a pulled-pork sandwich in this Lonely Butte?"

"I can get you a sandwich from Catering," Ynez said.

"Pulled pork? A good barbecue?"

"I don't think so, but . . ."

"I got a hankering for barbecue. Sloppy, juicy pork, dripping
with tangy sauce. There's gotta be a place, eh?"

"Let me see if I can find one."

"Do that. Beans and coleslaw, too." Just then, the TV screen
filled with an adult movie on some adult channel. "Oh, look at the
tits on Mother!"

★　★　★

As Costume Designer, Le'Della Rawaye had dealt with actors at
their most naked, literally. She had clothed self-loathing human
beings with severe body issues (even when they were stunning
examples of beauty and health), dictatorial professionals who
knew how they looked best (yet were so often so wrong), stars
who had a half dozen sycophants with their heads so far up their
employers' asses that costume fittings became hours-long contests
of influence peddling, stars who wanted to keep trying things on
and on and on, and stars who wanted to get it all over with in ten
minutes. Old muttonesque stars who wanted to dress like lambs.
Stars who wanted to keep the clothes. OKB was a combination of
all those troubled children and Le'Della loathed him.

In the few weeks of Prep, OKB had kept Le'Della waiting for hours because, he said, there was only the one costume, right? He canceled fittings, insisted she come to his place in Franzel Meadows, then forgot he had done so, only to sit, talking about "the best things he'd learned about being an actor in movies, such as there being no substitution for listening to instinct." He had no comments on the renderings Le'Della had worked on for the last five months and kept referencing the "mind's-eye alternatives" to the Firefall costume he had rattling inside his head; of starting from scratch. In the screenplay, Firefall wore the battle-scarred uniform of a World War II Marine, one still fighting his phantom war in the Pacific, but OKB, well, he *sort of* hated that one-note idea," especially the helmet.

"All he is is a dead Army Man," OKB kept saying. "I understand it's where BJ started. But what does that give me to play with? Let's come up with some mystery!"

On that Friday afternoon, for his camera test, OKB as Firefall did not show up in front of the lens until 3:56 in the afternoon. Yes, he was costumed as a Marine, with fake burns and applied scars. He had a prop flamethrower over his shoulder. He wore the helmet tipped far back on his head for a jaunty look. He rarely stopped moving. He jiggled a lot and kept up a fake soft-shoe tap dance. At just one point did he do as Bill Johnson—the director/screenwriter, the boss of the whole enterprise—asked. OKB lowered the lip of his helmet to just above his eyes, and he stood still. He looked left, right, straight at the camera, and then re-jauntified his helmet, walked back and forth in a lanky, jokey pace—about-face, pace, about-face again—yelling *"About . . . face!"* He didn't want to go outside into the natural light, since light was light and what was the point?

With that finished, he made a request. He had some ideas of his own. He had done some shopping on those drives of his to LA and the Bay Area, and Nicolette had helped. He wanted to test some of *his* choices, that day, with Le'Della having seen only a few pieces. All he would need from her were some bandannas. For the next two hours, he went back and forth to his trailer, digging around in his big gift duffel, modeling various pants, pullovers, hoodies, shorts, boots, flip-flops, and, yes, bandannas—a series of *looks* that *he* thought were rugged, manly, mysterious, and unique; good, instinctive options for *his* Firefall, beyond that dead Army Man. Never once did he put on a hat. In variations, he looked like a cop, a lumberjack, a hitchhiker, a welder, an astronaut, and a well-muscled surfer* who could, with just a few imaginative revisions to BJ's script, have come across that flamethrower thing by way of a Cosmic Twist of Fate. "Like King Arthur and his sword, you see!" Why go with just that goofy backpack and hose thing? OKB wondered. How about just, like, a *fire wand* or some specially designed wrist-cuff-gauntlet thing? What if he didn't even need a device but could just *conjure* flames? OKB had sketched some possibilities himself, or Nicolette had, since he couldn't draw very well; he was an idea man, and weren't they starting from scratch?

Bill, patiently, like a Zen master, let the actor test all the clothes, filming each iteration of Firefall as imagined by OKB. Once his duffel bag of costume options was exhausted, Bill told his actor that he didn't cotton to any of the options, but he'd look at the test footage with an open mind, and they'd talk.

"Thanks, BJ," OKB said as he was leaving his trailer, about to get into the back seat of his Range Rover with Ace at the wheel. "I can't help but think the Army Man look has been done to death."

Bill Johnson, Al, and the department heads watched the footage that night, back in the Almond Growers Association Building, in the space that had been turned into a digital screening room. Ynez laid out a buffet of Chinese food from Golden Harvest in Chico that tasted better than Chinese food from Chico should have. With Friday-night beers/wine/martinis, the talk about Wren's many looks was so positive with so many great and varied options that Bill toasted Kenny and the Good Cooks and was satisfied if Le'Della made the final wardrobe choices.

"Everything looks good on Wren," Le'Della said to no disagreement.

Bill then ran the test footage of OKB. He froze the image of him as the classic, beaten, and burned-up specter of a 1944 USMC flamethrower so everyone could see it—the helmet low over the eyes, the stilled body of Firefall dominating the screen, a formida-

---

* "Like the fucking Village People," Al said.

ble creature, an indelible image—part John Wayne, part Lee Marvin, part Charlton Heston.* In that one frozen frame, O. K. Bailey
was transformed from mere mortal to motion picture icon.

"There!" Bill shouted. "My God! That's Firefall and that's why
OKB has the job!" At 3xFF speed, he blurred through the rest of
the footage, the koo-koo choices donned by OKB, and said, "Guess
what wardrobe I approve," as he cracked another can of Hamm's.

The next day, Saturday, at midmorning, Bill called OKB's
production-supplied iPhone, getting him on speaker as he was
driving somewhere in that hot Audi of his.

"Talk to me, *Beej*," the actor said. "If I cut out hit me back. I'm
taking Nicky to the Golden Gate Bridge. *Le Pont d'Or.*"

"The test footage looked good," Bill Johnson said. The use of
Beej was ignored.

"Tell me more."

"You are mesmerizing."

"In which costume?" OKB wanted to know.

"In that first one. The first change. That's Firefall."

There was a moment of silence. Had it not been for the sound of
OKB paddling his Audi to a higher gear, Bill might have assumed
the call was lost. "You mean as G.I. Joe?"

"I mean as *Firefall*," Bill said in the upper register needed for
calls to a hands-free driver. "You hold the screen as only you can.
One look and the audience will be frightened and fascinated and
wondering . . . *Who?* Who is this guy?"

"Really." Something was whispered in French that Bill could not
make out. "I can tell you who he is," OKB said. "He's . . . oh, what
are they called, again? Oh, yeah. An *Army Man.*"

"A Marine. He's the reason for the picture and he's badass."

"The other changes, those other costumes? They are badass,
too. I know they aren't Le'Della's stuff but, you know."

"They're confusing. He's not a welder. Nor a surfer. The flip-
flops would hamper you in the fights."

"Lose the flip-flops, okay? I was giving you options. The first
change I brought, the one with the raggedy jeans and the V-neck

* Wayne, Marvin, and Heston were iconic movie stars before the advent of
streaming.

T-shirt and, yes, the ever-important flamethrower?" The one Bill thought made him look like an Abercrombie & Fitch version of a garage mechanic wearing a leaf blower. "You think you know where that guy came from? I have chiseled arms, man. I work out. I'm fit. And you want to hide them under Gomer Pyle olive drab?"

"I want the eyes of OKB to tell all," Bill said, ready to pile on the compliments to keep his actor happy. "You'll cast the shadow of a monster, but when we come in close and see your eyes? You have eyes that carry weight, eyes that have seen too much. When that helmet is pulled down and your face is partly hidden, isolated between those scars and the hard line of that steel helmet, your eyes are as deep as a moonless night. You're Mars—the god of War. Sentenced to roam until there is no more war to fight."

The phone was silent for a moment, then another. The Audi's engine droned on. "Did I drop out," Bill asked. "Are you there? Did you hear me? Did I lose you, OK? You there?"

"Yeah," came OKB's voice over the speaker. "Mars, huh? Didn't read that in my pages."

"The god of War. I'll text you a screen grab of what got us all hot around the collar. You'll see. You're a vision."

"Okay, BJ. Scratch the others. Text me whatever."

"Drive carefully. Enjoy San Francisco. See you Monday."

"Whatever."

OKB's iPhone went silent. Bill looked at Al, who had been right there listening to the conversation. They were sitting in the back-yard of the house Al had requisitioned as her lodgings in Lone Butte, in the downtown Historic Homes District, where some mature plum trees grew in a tidy row, matching those in the yard next door as if they had once been a part of the same orchard. Between those fruit trees in the back and the huge, spreading syca-mores in the front of the house, Al could almost imagine herself back under her blessed, calming coastal redwoods in Santa Mon-ica. The street was even named Elm. Everywhere, trees.

Bill pulled up a screen grab from the camera test, of OKB as Firefall, USMC, and sent it to the actor's phone.

"I did not hear enthusiasm on that call, Boss."

"He gave up on the flip-flops pretty easy." Bill knew Al was, once again, correct, as always. Then Bill's phone pinged.

STONERAPIER: Nice helmet.

"Boss, he either agreed or just told you to screw yourself," Al said, inclined toward the latter. As was Bill, fostering an immediate pondering between the two. They'd been through so very much in all the movies they had made together—the years of dealing with crybabies, jerks, psychological train wrecks, on-the-wagon alcoholics, off-the-wagon addicts, crew members going through divorces, child-custody cases, bankruptcies, and more than a couple of feuds between the Talent—too many trials over the years to not recognize the potential problem with OKB. Any actor unhappy with artistic choices *forced* upon them will cause problems on the set. Delays. A loss of enthusiasm, and thus momentum. Judging from his behavior just the day before, in *camera tests,* OKB had the potential to be another BOLDFACE NAME #4, who made everyone's life a living nightmare on NAME OF SUCCESSFUL FILM HERE, only to be rewarded with an AMPAS nomination and a series of multimillion-dollar contracts. Or he'd be that other thing: an actor whom he'd have to cut around in the Editing Room.

In the history of Bill Johnson's filmography, he had fired exactly one member of the Talent. It happened in the wink of an angry eye, was loaded with vitriol and threats of vengeance, and caused a halt to production that lasted a sinful three days. There were lawsuits. And it happened on *Shitstorm,* a.k.a. *Albatross.* That could never happen again. So, long ago, a contingency was devised at Optional Enterprises should the cause ever re-arise . . .

Al asked, "Shall I get Yogi on the blower?"

"Yep," Bill Johnson said. "Aaron and SAM, too."

That's when the Call Sheet changed for the first three days of shooting—this was now Saturday, there remained only three days left of Prep.

*　★　*

Bill always started his films on a Wednesday, so the crew could have a short week, loosen up, lay down some of the more basic footage with scenes that were never too complicated to set up nor too emotionally heavy for the actors. The One-Liner, the simplified, Cliffs Notes version of all 53 Shooting Days, called for Exterior Long and

Wide shots of Eve walking in the abandoned downtown, approaching Clark's Drugstore, entering the place but not seeing the inside. She'd walk past the church and the State Theater. There would be Townsfolk.

Day 2 of the 53 was going to be more of the same, but with low angles of heat waves rising off the pavement, the digital thermometer on the bank sign, reflections in windows and car mirrors, and the arrival of the Investigators—in a matte-black SUV and a matching van/unit bristling with antennas and gear. Normally, Bill would leave some of those shots for the Second Unit, but for the sake of the first week of shooting, he'd grab an excess of footage, some that he might later use for cutting pieces in the Editing Room. One big shot scheduled for Day 2 was going to be Knightshade sipping water from the drinking fountain outside the courthouse—there was going to be a Cablecam for a push-in and some long-lens ECUs (Extreme Close-Ups), always tricky for the Focus Puller, especially in the first week. Stanley Arthur Ming wanted the soft light of Golden Hour, when the sun is low in the west, in the late afternoon. Day 3, the Friday, was going to be a Split; the crew called at noon to shoot half the day with afternoon light, then a big setup for one of the few Night Shoots: scene 7, *Eve hears trouble and RUNS*. Wren would be doing some running, some major looks of fear, panic, and worry (for which Bill wanted to take plenty of time), then her stunt double would be doing some harder, physical stuff. Wrap the week at midnight and everyone would feel confident and secure. OKB would have the three days off.

By midnight Friday, those on the production who turned out to be inept at their job, who caused more problems than they solved, who should never have been hired in the first place, would be as obvious as lima beans in a bowl of carrots. Those people, those problems, would be let go at the Friday-night Wrap, replaced over the weekend, and forgotten by lunch on Monday. That's why the first day of shooting was always a Wednesday.

But . . . the new and revised Call Sheet for Day 1 of 53 Shooting Days was changed to front-load OKB to the Production Start mark. He was to report to the Works at 5:15 a.m., be on set at 9:30 for scene 4: *Who is that? Firefall!* and shots of OKB in costume searching around town. Day 2 would be scene 93: *Out of the Mael-*

strom: Firefall! Day 3 (Friday!) called for scene 93XX: *Elements of Fight #2.* Wednesday, Thursday, and Friday, then, would have OKB working full days, in full costume and SPFX, in complicated scenes with extra cameras for Coverage. Wren would be in some of the shots.

With some good juju, Friday would show OKB to be on the team, in the film, filled with the spirit of the character. He would be committed, calm, and all in as Firefall. Bad juju would show something very different.

Through all those weeks of Prep, every day of herding those creative sheep, Bill Johnson's office in the PO looked like it had never been assigned to anyone on the picture. The room was pristine. Spartan. There was the requisite desk and chair. A phone. Two other chairs for visitors. A sofa and coffee table. A low rolling table, meant for a typewriter, was shoved into a corner. Pinned onto the particleboard on the walls were only the list of intercom extensions and a page of emergency phone numbers. He kept no papers on the desk. A pen was in a drawer, along with a stack of buck slips, the long rectangular cards with the words KNIGHTSHADE: THE LATHE OF FIREFALL at the top and BILL JOHNSON at the bottom. Another stack of different buck slips had his name at the bottom and OPTIONAL ENTERPRISES at the top. He kept his space so barren, he said, because in Prep his head became so cluttered that he needed a void space or else he'd go mad. For most meetings he went to Al's office.

He carried with him, forever at the ready, a leather-bound copy of his screenplay, the pages dog-eared and wrinkled from incessant, random readings. There were no notes in the margins—no scratchings in pencil or pen—because whatever new idea or image that came from the study of those pages became forged in his skull. If he couldn't remember the notes, they were not worth keeping. Coffee stains were the only extant markings in his script. Bill Johnson's office, in the Almond Growers Association Building, was a place to read, to ponder, to palaver, and to make phone calls.

At the end of one of the Prep days, he sat in his fortress of solitude both dreading and wishing to hurry the oncoming, relentless tide. The Shoot. The beginning of his heavy lifting, as though all the work he'd done thus far had been light duty. Ha!

He was waiting for vanilla frozen yogurt with rainbow sprinkles. His door was open when Ynez appeared with bags from YouGo FroYo.

"Al said to bring this to you," Ynez said.

"Why not, Y-not?" Bill said. "Come in."

Al appeared an instant later. "That was fast."

"They know me now," Ynez said as she pulled the containers out of the bag. "I don't even get out of the car. They run it out to me."

"You are going to have some of this," Bill said, meaning Ynez.

"Oh, I'm good. Thank you."

"I didn't ask of your status. I command you. No less than a spoonful."

Ynez looked to Al for some guidance here, not wanting to do something wrong.

"Here," Al said, offering up an extra spoon and her own disposable cup of no-sugar-added raspberry dessert food. "This is a tradition we have. We pause for yogurt and to collect our breath before we go into the Blur." Al placed her cup equidistant between herself and Ynez.

"What is the Blur?"

"You'll know very soon," Bill said. "The moment we start the Shoot and our labors of Hercules begin."

"I'm excited," Ynez confessed. "All we have to do now is make the movie."

Al and her boss, Bill, laughed out loud! They laughed and laughed, gulping for air. "Oh, Ynez! . . . All we . . . have to do now . . . is make . . . the movie!"

Ynez grimaced, like a kid would do at Easter dinner after repeating some joke she didn't know was about sex.

"The Blur is where we all live for three months, Y-Not," Bill said. "You won't remember what we shot the day before. Other than the Crew Call, time will have no meaning. The most difficult crisis we solve on the set will be scattered chaff as soon as we move the camera. Every time we finish a task, we'll have another hundred million to wrestle down, and on every single one we may have sown the seeds of our own destruction and there ain't a damn thing we can do to change our fate." Bill cracked up like a crazy person who heard voices.

"You're scaring her," Al said. "Tell her about the accidents, Boss. The *good* stuff that happens."

"Not just yet," the director said. "Ms. Gonzalez-Cruz, we have a fifty-three-day shooting schedule. If we make it to lunch on day twenty-six, we'll be at the top of the bounce, the high point of our kinetic energy. The halfway mark. Between now and then we'll be living inside a whirlwind that comes about only in war, love, and football games on rainy days. What should happen doesn't and what does makes little sense. We'll be spent, running on fumes with overstimulated brain cells. But we'll be halfway through, right? You'll think, *Ah, now we can relax. It's all downhill from here.* No, it's not. Nothing we will have done to that point will matter a whit. Still to come, days of bitter compromise, of one-damn-thing-after-another during which we may be forging the weakest link in the chain, the one that will snap and send the movie into laughingstock status or, even worse, into a soft, nondescript acceptance worthy of nothing more than golf claps." Bill put his hands together in slow, barely audible applause. *"Hey, a friend of mine saw your movie. Said it was cute."* He spooned a mound of FroYo into his maw. *"Be dar wokk-ah thoo . . ."* He swallowed. "We are walking through . . . a minefield. One wrong step and *foom*."

Ynez had listened without moving her spoon. The expression on her face was the same as when, once, she had been stopped by a highway patrolman for speeding and the cop told her about all the lives she was endangering.

"Or?" Al shouted the word. "Tell her the *or*!"

"Or . . ." Bill let the word hang in the volume of air in his spic-and-span office. "We roll film and capture magic. We're Zapruder on the grassy knoll in Dealey Plaza. We have a take so arresting that we'll strut onto the next setup like cocks of the walk. Example: the ash can in *Barren Land*.* To make a movie is to stumble around the laboratory and accidentally invent vulcanized rubber or Post-its. We catch the Nazi tanks after they've run out of synthetic fuel. We throw deep from our own twenty-two-yard line and score six. We ask the prom queen out for chili dogs and she says, *Finally! I've been waiting for you to ask 'cause I've wanted to get my hands on your . . ."*

"I think she gets it, Skipper." Al patted Ynez on the arm. "In the Blur the great and the horrible will happen side by side."

---

* The famous moment in that movie—in the Sears parking lot—where the exploding ash can landed so perfectly on the hood of that Ferrari on the first and only take.

"We'll shoot scenes that take two and a half days yet will be in the movie for forty-eight frames, if at all. We'll grab shots that are nothing more than afterthoughts that will be the clip For Your Consideration. Tell Ms. Gonzo-Sea Cruise about the Distorted Emotional Continuum."

"The what?" Ynez was weighing everything she was hearing, trying to imagine only five *L.I.S.T.eN.* note cards but losing count.

Al explained, "We seem like a big family, the Unit, all on the same movie, all working every day. We never stop doing each other favors. We see each other at our best and worst. We laugh and keep a professional air—respecting each other, blah-blah. But we start shooting and we live in a crunch of time and effort and get worn down, ground into sand. We don't dare become enmeshed in any-one's private life because all that matters is finishing the movie. The actors hang out with each other and become friends and lovers, ex-lovers and rivals. For three months we are all in this together—working hard, working long, working so that we can all work again. You'd think the long trial-by-not-getting-fired would bind us, forge us into one being, right?"

Well, Ynez thought, so far, what Al was saying had been Ynez's experience exactly. She felt like she was tight with everyone on the crew and cast she'd had the pleasure to know. She knew everyone's name and could translate their body language. Even Cody, the PO PA who had been such a jerk way back when, had learned his les-son and become a friendly if nervous coworker whenever he and Ynez were on the same task. "We are all one. Aren't we?"

"Yes," Al said. "Right up until we wrap the picture, we're pio-neers in the same wagon train bound for the promised land. But as soon as you can say 'Hey, I got another job!' all this"—Al waved her arms around the office, meaning the whole moviemaking experience—"will be just a blur. Take the pace and the pressure you've been under, Ynez, since I tempted you into the traffic flow on Fountain Ave. Triple it. Then square it. Then add having your period when we're shooting nights so you won't be at your best friend's baby shower and she can't understand why you can't get off."

"Al," Bill said, "tell her about NAME OF ACTOR HERE."

Ynez perked at the mention of such a big celebrity. She had yet to have the courage to ask about some of the famous people Al had worked with—what they were like and if they were as special in person as they came off in the movies.

"Ah." Al shook her head. "I was assigned to look after NAME OF ACTOR HERE on THAT MOVIE WE MADE. My mentor, Dace, taught me how to sidle up to him, in the course of a day's work, how to chat him up and find out if there was anything he was pissed off about, anything he needed, to get his emotional temperature."

"He carried the movie on his shoulders," Bill explained. "He had to *go there* in every scene, whether he wanted to or not. If he was happy, he had to be an emotional wreck for the part. If he hated his life and everyone on the picture, he had to be funny and charming. It was as if the day's pages were specifically written to demand the opposite of his mental state. We needed him to show up On the Day and deliver the goods."

"So, I was tasked to be his actor-whisperer," Al said. "I brought him the chocolate pretzels I knew he liked. I ran his lines with him. I put his chair next to the heater when the set was frigidly cold. We had talked about old Donald Duck cartoons and I made sure some Disney Classics were playing on the TV in his trailer at five-thirty the next morning. I listened to his bad-mood chatter and agreed with his chagrins. I laughed at his good-mood repartee, for however long that lasted. I reported to this guy"—Al pointed to Bill— "and to Dace what I considered to be the mental state of NAME OF ACTOR HERE every hour on the hour as a forewarning of what to expect when he came onto the set. I did this every single day with check-ins on the weekends. It was exhausting. Like being an au pair charged twenty-four/seven with a moody toddler. Speaking of which, why are you keeping Francisco away from my arms?"

"I'll bring him around when I can."

"Please do. I need to adore that child for an hour or so."

"Don't lose your thread, Al," Bill said. "NAME OF ACTOR HERE."

"On a twelve-hour day, I spent eleven of them looking after NAME OF ACTOR HERE. If we shot long, say a fifteen- or sixteen-hour day, I spent every minute of overtime with him as an aide-de-camp. I gave him a manicure once to keep him in his chair on the set. I was like a worshipping little sister to the man for a sixty-six-day shooting schedule. Then, THAT MOVIE WE MADE wraps and the Unit breaks up, parting ways. One month later, when I happen to sneak in a dinner of steak and martinis with Dace at the Golden Bull, who's at the bar but NAME OF ACTOR HERE. I walk up to him and say, 'Look who's here! Hey!' And he looks at me like I'm a Hare Krishna at LAX soliciting money. Not so much as a blink of recognition. We are not on the set, you see. I am not catering to his comfort, so I'm not in the common element of work. I am not even some vague shadow from the Blur, but I am, in fact, happy to have run into someone I recently spent a shitload of time with as, together, we made another motion picture master-piece. I greet him by name, I offer him a hug. He stiff-arms me. He says, 'I don't do hugs. And I'm on private time here, so don't ask for a selfie.' I say, 'NAME OF ACTOR HERE, don't you remember me?' He doesn't. 'Help me out. How do I know you?' That's what the actors do. They don't remember anything but how they looked on the one-sheet. We Production folk remember *everyone* and rec-ognize them for the rest of our lives."

"And that's the Blur," Bill said, getting up, tucking his leather-bound script under his arm. "Ride the river like a fallen leaf." He stood still for a moment, eyeing Ynez. "For what it's worth, Ms. Ynez Gonzalez-Cruz, I have known only three people in your position who seemed born to play the game. You are one of them. I'm glad you're on the picture."

Al and Ynez were left alone. "Ride the river like a fallen leaf. What hooey." Al snorted.

"Who were the other two?" Ynez asked. "The ones born to play the game?"

"Me, I think. Dace, who you didn't know. But he's right, Ynez. You've solved every problem that a movie can toss at you. You sailed through Prep. You're a starter now." Al stood. "I'm serious about Francisco. Bring him soon. I miss the smell of that little man."

★　★　★

The Brain Trust rejigged the schedule and alerted the departments. Sunday, three days out, Bill spent the morning going over the story-boards and the Pre-Viz* for the now-moved-up Firefall sequences. Then he and SAM reconnoitered the new positions for the shots while Al alerted the representatives of the cast playing the Investigators that they were now to report to Lone Butte on Monday for fittings, tests, and rehearsals. Housing had a few scrambles on their hands, but they found the vacancies and booked rooms in the motels on the interstate. The morning of two days out had Bill pounding the workload with, first, the Art Department and Set Dressing, because scene 93XX called for a ruined, fire-damaged Main Street, second with the SPFX team for the needed fire FX, third with Aaron for the safety regulations required by all the unions, guilds, and OSHA, and last with the H/MU team to fine-tune the look of Firefall. Bill wanted to accentuate the horizontal divisions between the wounds on OKB's neck and dark eyes under that helmet, which meant more glue was going to be slapped onto his torso, head, and neck. The Swing Gang was going to be on full alert, so Al promised a delivery of pizzas each morning at 2:00 a.m. Ynez would arrange and supervise the pizzas' arrival and serving. She had become pals with the folks at Big Stork and knew they ran a teenage crew after midnight. On Tuesday, one day out from the Start of Principal Photography, Bill wandered the halls of the Production Office at the Almond Growers Association Building, making himself available to anyone with questions, poking his head into offices, reading his script again and again, and sitting with Al at her desk, pushing around odd ideas and possibilities for later in the shoot.

Around 6:00 p.m., Bill was sitting with Al and put in a call to OKB from his desktop hardline.

"How you doing, Slugger?"

Al looked at him and mouthed, *Slugger?*

"All right," the actor said. "How are you, Skipper?"

Bill laughed. "I am ready. To shoot. You cool with the scenes? It's a fast start, I know, but I say let's jump on it."

---

* Pre-visualization. An animated storyboard that is a version of the scene.

"Yes. Let's. Jump."

"I have to ask you, especially as it's the first day, to keep an eye on the time. Starting late on the first day is a bummer for everyone, yeah?"

"Yeah."

"Not that the first day ever goes according to plan. We're all nervous and edgy. But we have this buttoned up damn good. And scenes three and four will be one cool sequence. I'm looking forward to it."

"Me, too, BJ, sir."

"First rate," Bill said, catching himself from using *Slugger* again. "Bring Nicolette along. We do a ritual with a flag and the slate before the very first take and she should be in on it."

"Nicolette took off."

Bill's heart rate pulsed a few BPM quicker at this news. He could feel it in his carotid artery. A fear scampered through him like a lizard frightened by footsteps on a desert path. "She did?"

Al noted the rise in her boss's voice. He sounded like he said, *She DID????*

"Yeah. Took a PONY car all the way to San Francisco and went back to Paris. Or hell. Wherever she calls home."

Bill shot Al a wide-eyed look of *uh-oh,* then grabbed up a buck slip from the neat pile on her desk and a red Sharpie from the California Film Commission coffee mug. He scribbled a flash card to show her.

Broke up with Nic _Gone_

Al grabbed the buck slip and Sharpie and wrote.

He broke up with Nic Gone
S H I T!!!

Their lives as filmmakers had just been made more fraught. Any newly broken heart on a production became a too-turgid soap opera for all involved, a subject of way too much talk that reverberated through every department, every trailer, at every meal break. To happen to one of the main stars, on the last day of Prep? Disaster. OKB breaking up with his French paramour could turn into as big and costly a distraction as that which had sunk every production of *Cleopatra* ever mounted.

"I'm so sorry, Slugger." Again? With the *Slugger*?

"Don't be." OKB breathed in and out, heavily. "I'm better off starting from scratch lady-wise."

"Affairs of the heart . . ." Bill was hoping some other thought was going to come to him. Nothing did.

"Gonna go out for a run to clear my head," OKB said. "Then hit the hay."

"See you in the a.m." Ah! A quote came to Bill's mind! "This too shall pass."

"Copy that," OKB snapped. "Corporal Fire-fuck, over and out."

As soon as the call ended, Al picked up her phone to text Ynez: **help asap.**

Ynez appeared in the doorway. "Yeah?"

Al asked, "Can you find out the details of a PONY that took Nicolette from OKB's place to SFO last night?"

Ynez needed a micro-moment to process the request. Nicolette? OKB? She Let It Settle, Then . . . "Bet I can." She stepped out of the office as she raised her phone and started pinching out a message.

"He's been getting laid thus far, with regularity, I assume," Al said. "And still's been an asshole *royale*."

"He will go through a state of anger."

"Aimed at all women," Al predicted. Knew.

"He will be frustrated. And moody. And preoccupied."

"So different from thus far."

Ynez stepped back into the room. "Friend of mine got a PONY request for a home in Franzel Meadows to the SF airport at 3:37 a.m."

"Is that crazy late or insanely early?" Bill asked.

"Lots of bookings that time of night, mostly partiers who can't drive," Ynez explained. "So . . . a skinny woman with just one huge rolling suitcase comes out. A guy standing in the door, yelling at her, in his underwear."

"Boxers or briefs?"

"They were fighting. In French. My pal speaks the version they teach in high school. There was a lot of profanity. PONY drivers are taught not to get involved in such scenes unless there's a threat of violence. All there was was yelling. Until the woman just about gets in the car. She was screaming, had the energy to lever her suitcase into the back seat, then pulls a brick out of the walkway. Hurls it at the guy in the boxers or briefs, hits a window, smash. He yells more. She gets in the car and says, *Allon zee!* Next stop, SFO. Air France. Two-hour drive. And no client for the ride back to Sacramento."

"Thanks, Y-not." For the longest time, Bill had called her Y-not for some reason. Ynez didn't mind. He looked at both women and sighed quietly.

"Our lives have just gotten harder."

BASE CAMP

The Teamsters show up first, very, very early. In the gloom of the dark.

Teamsters live in a time warp ungoverned by such things as official sunrise or the graveyard shift. They don't just safely, reliably drive and park the trucks, they *transport* the picture, then spatially organize it all, *Tetris*-style, in areas of square footage that don't look to have room for so many trailers. And yet, there they all fit; a Base Camp laid out in geometric precision, a logical aesthetic and hierarchy, structured in the black as if by midnight raiders. The Teamsters are engineers by axle who inhabit a plane a part of, yet separate from, the rest of the motion picture crew. Base Camp would not exist without the Teamsters. With them, the show can go on.[*]

---

[*] There is no complaining when the Teamsters are fed before anyone else, nor any chastising of them for sleeping in their cabs while others work—they've been on the clock for hours already.

According to the license plates, the mileage on their tractors, and the wear and tear on the trailers, these trucks, which hold the kit, paraphernalia, and stuff of cinematic history, have traveled all of America but are from Hollywood—if not the actual city, the idea. Monument Valley of the Navajo Nation; the shores of the Puget Sound; the streets of greater Chicagoland; the studios in Wilmington, North Carolina; Atlanta and Savannah, Georgia; New Orleans and Baton Rouge, Louisiana; and the neighborhoods of Las Vegas—Nevada and New Mexico—have seen Base Camp trucks parked side by side or end to end, open all night, working all week, spilling out the gear, the tools, the hardtack needed for the making of motion pictures, television shows, or feature films.

While en route, the trucks don't appear to be laden with any special cargo; they are but more big rigs on the highway, carrying, what? Mattresses? Artichokes? Paper towels? No. Inside these trucks are the tools and dies of fantasy and magic: the lighting gear, the camera works, the full-length mirrors, fitting spaces, laundry machines, and racks for the wardrobe. The prop truck has so many varied goods in it, you could walk in and ask for a bottle-capping machine to make your own soda pop, vintage dueling pistols, an old-fashioned stock ticker, and organic cigarettes rendered relatively harmless to the lungs. If the script calls for it, you'll find it on the prop truck. There's a big drawer of batteries, too, any size you need.

There are trucks for every department on the picture—the Carpenters, the Special Effects, the Greensman, the Art Department, and Grip and Electric.* The crew in those departments know every hook and lash, each drawer and cupboard, built into those big trailers and what they hold because they put it all there, everything stowed in place. A crew person is assigned a post equal to a ship's lookout or an army's quartermaster, with one ear on the proper radio channel to be ready for the call, the other listening for footsteps coming up the ramp. Needed: a sheet of plywood for a *dance floor, apple boxes* in various thicknesses, more *flags* and *netting,*

---

* Grips move "stuff." Electricians move the lights and cables—whatever is electrified.

the proper holster for a fake cop's rubber pistol, a fresh espresso for the Swiss cinematographer—make that four espressos, to caffeinate the dolly grip, the operator, and the focus puller as well. Copy? Copy that!

Crew swarms the trucks for twelve-, fourteen-, eighteen-hour days, operating the liftgates with loud vocal warnings to bystanders to avoid injuries. Injuries must . . . be . . . avoided. If the on-set medic must call in the EMTs, the shooting day may be halted for as long as an ambulance is at Base Camp. A halt in the shooting day is a disaster. An unholy sin.

The locals—civilians—might think a traveling circus has come to town. And they would be right, since *the actors are come hither, my lord.*[*] Schlegelmilches and Star Waggons are trademarked makes of the holding quarters, some a one-bedroom apartment with quality bedding, a wide shower, and big-screen satellite TV meant for the comfort of the star actors at the top of the daily Call Sheet. Double bangers are two studio apartments on one chassis, with the same amenities, just not so top of the line. Triple bangers are for the cast known more by their character number than their professional name—Number 29 Policeman, Number 32 Lady With Dog. They have fewer workdays on the schedule and are without the credits or the clout to rate a trailer of their own—no shower, but a cot to lie on. The Honey Wagons are small rooms, lined up like horse stalls, which can be cozy on some days, prisonlike on others.

The Hair and Makeup trailer is a mobile beauty parlor, with the smells of drying hair and spirit gum, wigs, hair gels and sprays, assembled shades of lip glosses and instant tans. Music plays under the chatter and over the whispered gossip that is to be expected when a half dozen actors are in the Works. The H/MU trailer has photo printers, label makers, an espresso machine, and kettles for tea that serve all day. The makeup chairs sit before mirrors bordered by lightbulbs so that every crack, blemish, and wrinkle in a face will be skillfully masked by the H/MU artists. Shaped bits of latex are going to be scars, scabs, and broken noses once they are applied and colored by the Visual Enhancement Technicians,

[*] *Hamlet,* act 2, scene 2.

who have been ready at their stations well before any cast member has climbed up the trailer steps, still sleepy and often very cranky. Beauty is enhanced in the H/MU trailer, characters are created, and psyches are becalmed.

What about those expensive, custom-made RVs and tour buses? Who's in them? Just famous movie stars and accomplished filmmakers—household names the civilians would recognize if they could get a peek at them. Whoever has that shiny three-axle Airstream certainly takes good care of it or has a Teamster who does. In fact, always the latter.*

Movies are made everywhere. There are studios—just like those in Culver City, Burbank, Universal City—operating all over the world, in Rome and Belfast and Potsdam and Mexico City and Edmonton. Budapest has studio lots competing for productions. Base Camps of the moviemaking kind have been set up in Vietnam.

Being on location makes an adventure of the shoot. Base Camp anywhere is a place of *possibility,* no matter if it's set up in a parking lot in Austin, an abandoned casino in Camel Rock, beside the Serpentine in London's Hyde Park, or within walking distance of Florence's Ponte Vecchio across the Arno.

As the start of Principal Photography nears, the Base Camp swells with lesser vehicles, all Teamster driven. Step vans, Sprinters, and rented cars move people from leased villas and crew motels to the Location. Electric carts, stake beds, and shorty forties take gear up to and back from the Set—which could be five miles away or around the corner. VIPs are transported in SUVs with tinted windows. The Craft Service taco truck is close by the set, an assembly point for more coffee, instant oatmeal, ramen, smoothies, and, in the afternoon and evening, cauldrons of soups and chili, wedges

---

* There is this one actor who made a movie in the UK. His dressing room was a brand-new fifth-wheel trailer with a state-of-the-art sound system and TV. Five long years later, he was working in Helsinki, and he was given the very same caravan. Half a decade later, the electronics were no longer up-to-date, and the thing looked and smelled like it had been inhabited by squatters. Driven from England all the way to Helsinki on a rough road without missing a bump, the thing was now a dump on wheels. But the actor took one look at "his" caravan and burst into tears. He was home!

of quesadillas, or PB&J sandwiches. Crafty keeps the crew fueled with starches and protein, carrying trays of food right up to the camera dolly like friendly waiters at a cocktail reception. The offerings are both substantial, healthy snacks and stuff that is horrible for you but so very, very much appreciated.

Twice a day the crew is fed at Base Camp with meals served in a partylike atmosphere, in a tent, an empty hall, or in trailers that expand quadruple-wide with pneumatic, auto-opening doors, HVAC systems, and seating for a hundred.

The morning buffet is heavy on the high-calorie comfort foods—porridge by the vat, waffles off the iron, imitation McMuffin sandwiches individually wrapped, omelets made to order, biscuits and gravy warmed by cans of Sterno, trays of pancakes, scrambled eggs, bacon, sausages, fruit assortments—with the rule "Take all you want but eat all you take." For those with healthier nutritional needs, *anything* can be prepared for a breakfast. Ask for a bowl of loganberries and goat-milk kefir and you'll find it available the next day.

Breakfast is served in the run-up to Call Time that morning. For some, this allows an easing into the day with mini–planning conferences, silent contemplation over third cups of coffee, and telling funny stories of the hijinks at the karaoke bar last night. On the tick of the clock, everyone is up and gone to work in tandem, under pressure in the rain, in the sun, in a panic, in calm certainty.

Six hours later—halfway through the day—lunch lasts for thirty minutes from the last person in line. There are options aplenty, with themed buffets for Thai-Fusion Day, Mexican-Cuban Day, Pasta-Risotto Day, Saint Patrick's Corned-Beef-and-Cabbage Day. Thick meats are sliced to order by the chef on a butcher block. Fish are deboned while you wait. Quartered chickens, Flintstone-sized ribs, burgers, and bratwursts are grilled on open-flamed BBQs. Condiments are self-served. The salad bar seems a quarter of a mile long and never runs short of greens or dressings. For anyone with a birthday, the candles are blown out, the song is sung, and a cake with their name fashioned in icing is sliced up. Ice cream is scooped out of tubs. Squares of brownies and bowls of cobblers can be grabbed by hand, triangles of watermelon, too. Solo cups are stacked beside chests of ice and big glass dispensers of cold water, iced tea, and lemonade. The Arnold Palmers you mix yourself.

Anyone can opt out of the big meal, make do with a build-your-own sandwich or a fruit salad, then slink off for a nap somewhere. At Base Camp, lunch is what you make of it. The food and produce are fresh, bought from the stores and suppliers right there in town. Again, eat all you take. And recycle.

The caterers have been brought in from out of town, but they need additional staff who come from the area. A movie company counts on home-turf employees—local hires—to solve problems and navigate the territory. And since they live right there, they cost nothing for housing and receive not a dime in per diem.

But they are civilians no more! Now that they are paid professionals, the Base Camp is *their* Base Camp. The long days of shooting and the weeks of effort they put in on the movie will be talked about for the rest of their lives. They will be asked, *Where did you shoot that scene on the interstate? Did those jet planes hurt anyone when they dropped those bombs?* Answers: *On a big stage,* and *those were neither real jets nor real bombs.*

Their names will roll by in the film's end crawl, forever and ever, giving them a professional credit they deserve, and have earned. They helped make the motion picture.

DAY 1 (OF 53 SHOOTING DAYS)

Ynez decided to sleep in her Transit, right there at Base Camp, perfectly comfortable with a futon, a good pillow, and a nice comforter. She wanted to be in the PO as early as 4:30 a.m. to help make sure the caterers would have breakfast ready. And she was just too excited to drive home to Sacramento, force herself into her bed, beside that of her sister, only to toss and turn with anticipation and worry, get up, drive to Lone Butte, and, maybe, be late on the very first day of shooting. Ynez felt an excitement like back when her older sister had the very first Gonzalez-Cruz grandchild and the family had come from everywhere to help and witness the delivery. She now preferred being at work—focused and occupied

on the movie in Lone Butte—to the constant squabbles and duties
of the house, her family and the comers and goers. She felt special
making a motion picture. She'd gotten food for OKB! She'd been to
Wren Lane's house! Wren Lane had sent a note to her mom, thanking her for the *beyond belief delicious* dinner, written on thick,
robin's-egg-blue stationery embossed with a florid WL. That note
was now in a frame sitting on the piano in the Gonzalez-Cruz living room.

At 4:20 a.m., Ynez grabbed a quick shower in the women's lounge
of the Almond Growers Building (plumbers had been engaged to
make sure the hot water worked as in the olden days) and dried
herself with a towel she'd brought from home.

Al Mac-Teer was up at 5:15. She made her own coffee in her own
Di Orso Negro espresso machine, three pods of the purple kind—
she never bothered with the name of the roast, just the color of the
capsules. She frothed her half-and-half while her Italian Black Bear
dripped away, then took her first sips as she stood before the sink
in the kitchen of her rented house in the Historic Homes District,
looking at the plum trees out back. For the slightest moment, a
yearning to be home with her canyon redwoods made her wonder why she worked so hard for so long in such a nutty way, but
then she banished that thought from her body and brain—she had
a movie to make! She banged through some emails, checked the
Trades quickly, saw that there were no emergency texts from Yogi
or anyone else. Her *L.I.S.T.eN.* app showed but three cards:

1. A Flag: Meaning make sure the Art Department delivered the
   special flag for the ceremony and photo with the slate before
   the first shot rolled.
2. A Clock: Showing 9:00 a.m. exactly, which would be the
   time of the film's very first shot, even if it was just B Camera
   getting footage of the bank.
3. A Soldier with a question mark: Meaning, Will OKB show
   up on time, in costume, as Bill Johnson had written?

Al swiped her phone to another app, a jokey one, a digital version of the old-fashioned Magic 8 Ball toy. "We going to make our
day?" she asked the app. She shook her iPhone, causing the screen

to dissolve into a liquidy blue, then white letters appeared, telling her fortune: ONLY TIME WILL TELL. She snapped a screen grab and texted it to Bill Johnson. He'd see it when he woke up.

Bill Johnson was still in his bed at 6:00 a.m. He was asleep and remained so until 7:31 a.m. When his iPhone alarm went off with Sal Diego's "Java con Leche Cha-Cha," he immediately checked his texts for any emergencies. All he saw was Al's *Only Time Will Tell*. Then he FaceTimed Pat in Socorro, getting her at the kitchen table with a coffee.

"Head still on the pillow?" she observed.

"In this lonely, half-empty bed."

"Good luck today, Johnson." Their tradition was to not be together for the final weeks of Prep or Day 1. The workload was too great, Bill's attention was too split, and Pat had too many responsibilities she could not live up to on location, like teaching a class on aerated regolith. She would fly in for the weekend to be with her man Sunday and on the set Monday.

After a shower and stepping into what had been and always would be his moviemaking uniform: old, loose boot-cut jeans and worn leather cowboy boots with matching belt, a button-neck Henley, and a plaid flannel cowboy shirt with fake-pearl snap buttons, he drove himself, in his red Dodge, to Base Camp, tossed his keys to the Teamster who'd park it, wandered into the ballroom to grab one piece of French toast, a hard-boiled egg, and a bowl of fruit salad, then sat down to eat. Did the man have a care in the world? Not that anyone could see. Inside, his guts were as knotted as a ship's rigging.

Wren Lane was awake five minutes before her phone went off with a soft sound of crickets. Last night, she'd taken a low-THC gummy to still her brain. Today was her first day as Eve Knight, as the one upon whom so much was now hanging, and without that legal medicant, she'd never have drifted off. (Like Eve never did!)

She would have no lines on this first day, but she would be called upon to inhabit the woman—never mind the distractions of the crew, instructions from the director, or the shenanigans of OKB. The movie was hers now. Hers. She had so many ideas, emotions, and connective senses in her jam-packed head, her actor's pocket. She would be on time and know every moment of the text (which

she had committed to memory with constant rereads of her script).
Once that first moment of hers was captured in the lens, she could
let loose the creative fury inside her that had been and would continue to be tempered by her calm, professional exterior; her serenity.

She stretched. She did her twenty complementing Dray-Cotter
exercises. She walked around the paths of the compound in the
growing light of the morning with a green juice in one hand and a
cinnamon bun in the other. At 5:15 she was waiting in the car for
Tom Windermere to drive her into Lone Butte.

"Come on," she said to him as he buckled up. "Take me to
work."

At 5:42 she was sitting in the Works with the Good Cooks and
Kenny Sheprock ready for her, their tools, pins, glues, and oint-
ments, the lip glosses, and other star-quality makeup laid out in
precision.

"First day, lady," Kenny said to her. "Let's knock 'em dead. And
thank you for *this*." She had given Kenny and the Cooks wrapped
gifts—inside was a silver penknife engraved with EVE K. FEELS
YOU. XX WL. Wren warranted an H/MU trailer of her own—a private den where she and only she would be prepped for the day. But
Wren preferred the action of the all-hands unit—the chatter and
community of the beauty parlor. She wanted to be in on the gossip,
energy, laugh bust outs, and occasional meltdowns that came into
the trailer with every cast member and each H/MU artist. Golden
was the memory of the story of one female actor, who had an unre-
quited yet major crush on the male lead of one picture but was
never able to close the deal romantically (sexually). Lord, how the
girl had tried. Reporting to the Works on her last day on the picture, said female actor was at first sullen, then angry, finally in tears
as Kenny Sheprock and crew tried to make her camera ready. When
pressed—again and again and again—as to what was so upsetting
and if there was anything to be done to calm her down, she cried
out, "I just want to fuck him!!! Is that so terrible?!" In a trailer of
her own Wren Lane would have missed that!

Yogi, his ADs, and the PAs were assembling at 6:00 a.m. They
were allowed a quick breakfast in the ballroom, where Yogi delivered his Into the Breach speech, his special tradition. "Principal
Photography is our Theater of Operation. Ours. The ADs, the

PAs. We solve the problems before anyone even knows there is a problem. People who don't have one of these"—Yogi held up his walkie, with earpiece and clip-on mic—"tuned to channel one, the Production Channel, will wish they had! Years from now, those who are still abed will claim to have been here for the making of this motion picture. You . . . are loved."

The crew call was for 7:00 a.m. Lunch would be at 1:00 p.m. The final shot of the first day of shooting would be complete at 7:00 p.m. Of course, *Only Time Will Tell*.

Al joined Bill along with Yogi, Stanley Arthur Ming, Aaron, and the script supervisor, "Formidable" Frances DiBiassi, who did her complicated job with an old, sweep-second-hand stopwatch and an iPad Pro with a stylus, not with the thick-as-a-baked-ham three-ring binder, ruler, and multicolored pens of old. The talk was of what shots they hoped to get by lunch: Start on Eve's half of the opening pages, since the sun was perfect, in the suspension rig for some, but standing for most of it. Get Firefall's entrance to satisfaction, then the reverse on Eve with the afternoon light. Move to various easy shots within walking distance, then end in front of the courthouse. No dialogue, multiple cameras, the SPFX unit, five scenes, two and a half pages, and call it a *Damn Good First Day*.

★   ★   ★

Ace Acevido had no reason to send a warning-flare text to the set when OKB came out of his lodgings in Franzel Meadows at 7:45 a.m.—on the dot, a true pro—rubbing a Braun electric razor across his face as he hopped into the Range Rover's shotgun seat. Ace wondered what had happened to the front window of the house; a blue tarp now covered what was a busted-open rectangle.

OKB switched off the buzzing Braun and put it in his oxblood leather *Rapier* messenger bag. He then pulled out a Norelco triple-head electric razor and continued shaving.

Base Camp was in the big lot behind the PO with OKB's trailer just steps from the H/MU. Ynez had delivered first-day-of-shoot gifts before he got there. His agents sent a basket of flowers. The Hawkeye sent a vintage G.I. Joe action figure still in its packaging. Dynamo Nation sent him a vintage pair of binoculars with the Marine Corps eagle, globe, and anchor seal. Optional Enterprises—Al and Bill—gave him a pair of expensive leather driving gloves for that Audi of his. Wren Lane gave him aviator glasses made by Randolph Engineering. *No doubt you are going to soar!* she wrote on her personal stationery with WL embossed at the top. Ynez arranged the thoughtful presents on the dining table of his trailer and put his smoothie in the refrigerator with a Post-it attached, on which she'd drawn a smiley face. The attending Teamster had the seventy-two-inch LCD TV tuned to Fox News. The refrigerator was stocked with waters, sodas, juices, and dairy-free protein drinks along with bottles of oat milk, almond milk, milk, and soy half-and-half. A bowl of fruit exploded on the kitchen counter. A basket of nut bars blossomed like a brown-and-orange succulent and a HaKiDo coffee maker was at the ready, with pods for nine different roasts to choose from.

OKB climbed up the trailer steps and left the door open, quickly changed into sweatpants, Ugg boots, and a button-up flannel shirt for the makeup job, then grabbed the smoothie and headed back down the steps and directly into the H/MU trailer, the chair, the Works. Hey! Three minutes ahead of schedule.

Wren's team had finished with her, so OKB was the sole actor in the mirrors.

★ ★ ★

The First Day of Shooting started off as most movies do, with the sense an event was about to happen, missing only the hoopla of tooting horns and banging drums. A show was about to get on the road. Theory and planning gave way to Doing and Shooting.

The Production Office staff was relieved to finally, *finally* be *getting it on.* The entire crew was pumped for the start of Principal Photography. Some of the Executive Chorus had flown in for the beginning of "their" movie, and no one was more excited—or petrified.

Also new in Lone Butte on this first day were the actors who made up the Investigators—the team who was hounding Firefall around the world and that would soon mix it up with Knightshade as well.* They had all been Zoomed and measured remotely and were now on location for as long as they were needed. Al made sure Wren had a chance to say hello to each of them as a welcome on such an auspicious morning, glad they would all be in the historic photo. At 8:50 the entire Unit was assembled in the middle of Main Street—the PO staff, everyone from every truck, office, and tent. OKB was pulled from the Works, looking both gruesome and comical, the prosthetics and not-yet-applied burned-flesh colors contrasting with his sweatpants and Uggs. The Art Department had made a flag representing the movie, a banner of orange and red with symbols of EK, a flamethrower, and LONE BUTTE in big block letters. The A Camera slate was specially made with the logo for the movie, with Bill's name on it as well as SAM's. In erasable marker was ROLL: I SCENE: I TAKE: I. The Unit photographer was on a ladder, and everyone crowded around. The Teamsters left their trucks and vans; the Swing Gang had lingered for the first shot of their movie. All in all, ninety-eight smiles were aimed at the lens. Wren was picture ready and wearing a robe to hide her costume. For many of the crew, this was the first sight they had of the woman, and many manly hearts went aflutter.

Ynez positioned herself on the edge of the crowd, on the left-hand side of the frame, and smiled for the camera. How had this happened? What magic had gotten her here? She had to wipe away a tear.

After the photo was captured, Bill was given a pair of scissors. Like a kid at his own birthday party, he cut the flag like a cake, but only a little square.

"As is a custom at the start of these adventures we all share," Bill announced, "take a cutting of your own from this flag and keep it somewhere special. When we have all been wrapped from the Cardboard Carnival, finished our lives of artistic struggle and physical labor, and we are up in movie heaven, we'll sew the pieces

---

* The famed Cassandra Del-Hora reprising her role as LONDON—who met Wren in Atlanta during the Dynamo shoots. Nick Czabo was new as GLASGOW. Clovalda Guerrero as MADRID, a favorite of Bill Johnson from long ago. And, as LIMA, in his second appearance in a Bill Johnson film, was Ike Clipper (ROY THE BARTENDER in *A Cellar Full of Sound*).

back together and remember all we went through in these days to come."

One by one, everyone on the crew came forward for a slice of the flag, even the Investigators, who felt sheepish and new. Wren cut into a part of the E of EK. OKB, though, didn't bother. He went to his trailer to use the bathroom. The only first-day gift he bothered to open were the sunglasses from Wren. He put them on to check himself out in the mirror before going back to complete his time in the Works.

Video Village is an easy-to-set-up tent arrayed with TV monitors showing the view of each of the cameras, identified by bits of white tape with A, B, C, etc. handwritten with a Sharpie in bold and confident block letters. An assortment of chairs is lined up for lookers-on. In this airy, open-sided bit of shade sat the Executive Chorus and other such visitors, along with Wren, Al, Frances, and on occasion Yogi, although he was in constant motion, entering and leaving every few seconds. Ynez, who had been given no task and was not sure where she should be, found herself right there, a few yards from the camera.

The tent for the Digital Image Technician is not an inviting place, but a completely blacked-in square that in a Louisiana state prison farm would be the Box where inmates were punished. The flaps of the DIT closed with Velcro tabs to block out all the light. A portable AC unit kept the interior atmosphere suitable for the same camera video monitors and the four people who regularly occupied the DIT—Bill Johnson, Stanley Arthur Ming, Yogi (coming and going), and the technician, a fellow named Sepp, who spent so much time in the dark space he had no skin tone to speak of. Going in and out from the darkness to the sunlight wreaked havoc on his eyes, so he stayed put for most of the day. Between shots he'd open one flap to look out but remained inside like a puppy being crate trained.

The very first shot of *Knightshade: The Lathe of Firefall* was of a shadow: a long, morning-sun shadow of the revolving sign on the town's bank, cast down onto the pavement of Main Street. Neither the bank nor its slow-spinning sign was genuine, but creations of the set designer, the Construction Crew, and the Swing Gang. The sign was going to figure in a battle scene later in the movie. At

9:22 a.m. on the Production Report, the A Camera[*] rolled, with a slight push-in on a short track[†] and a slow rise on the dolly head[‡] for two takes. Bill was satisfied. SAM said he'd gotten what had been planned, and the camera was moved to the next series of shots, the first shots of Wren as Eve.

```
1 EXT. IRON BLUFF–MAIN STREET–DAY


EVE KNIGHT–AKA KNIGHTSHADE.


We know her from the previous Agents of Change
Story.


She FLOATS in the middle of the street. No cars.
No citizens. Blistering heat.


Her eyes are flickering like she is in a
deep REM sleep, so we know: the woman is
sensing–feeling–something.
```

Other stars of movies would have had a posse of aides, assistants, and influence peddlers in tow. Wren preferred her own company and, at a distance, Tom Windermere looking out for her safety. In the center of the street, she had a few words with Bill beside the camera, then removed her robe to hand off to her costumer.[§] She took her mark, a T of red tape in the middle of the crosswalk, ready for her first take. Kenny and the Good Cooks came forward for final checks.

Ynez did not know where to set her eyes. Should she sneak a

---

[*] The primary camera for the main shot. The B, C, and D Cameras, etc., are for other angles.

[†] A few feet of railroad-like track that allow the pushing or pulling of the camera, adding a dynamic motion for the shot.

[‡] The camera sits on the dolly head, which has controls for the raising or lowering of the camera during the shot.

[§] A woman named Billie, who had been Wren's costumer since *Periwinkle*. Billie is, perhaps, the most quiet human being this side of vow-of-silence nuns.

peek at the monitors of Video Village and watch what was called the video tap to see Wren's very first shot? Would she be allowed to stand closer to the camera? Should she be relegated to the distance to stand with the new cast members, who looked on, shyly, at the shot they were not in before they were herded away to their meetings, fittings, and motel rooms? Should she find a place on the sidewalk to congregate with some of the other crew? Some of them had iPads that showed the video tap since the technology of moviemaking put everything on Wi-Fi. Ynez was so unversed in the making of a movie she didn't know where to *stand*.

Al noticed. "Hey, Ynez," she called. "Come here." Al got up from her chair in front of the video monitors. "Take my seat." Ynez could not believe the offer and was confused, worried that she had done something wrong. "Do it. Sit here." Al was firm about it. "This is a moment." She put a set of very expensive headphones connected to a radio pack on Ynez's ears. Through them Wren was heard by way of the big microphone on the long extension pole, held by the female boom operator off camera. Ynez could hear the voices of the camera crew, of Yogi and the ADs. She heard Wren ask how wide the shot was and if she had a range of motion that would be no problem for the focus.

Ynez could hear the wind, her own heartbeat.

"We are rolling," Yogi said. At least a dozen people yelled *ROLLING!*

Sound speed.

Set.

The calm voice of Bill Johnson said *Action* in the DIT tent.

Yogi keyed his mic. Everyone on channel 1 heard the first AD repeat, *Action.*

A whispered voice Ynez could not recognize—a voice from neither the tent nor the radio headset—told Ynez to *watch and never forget.*

On the monitor, Wren was no longer present. She was gone. Eve Knight had taken her place in body and soul, behind her flickering eyes . . .

```
like she is in a deep REM sleep, so we know:
the woman is sensing—feeling—something.
```

Cut.

CUT!

Ynez's own eyes flickered and fluttered. What had just happened? Did Wren's first shot last only seventeen seconds? Or had seventeen minutes passed? The deed was done. The motion picture had started.

★ ★ ★

Seventy feet of track had been laid right down the middle of Main Street, looking north, for what was going to be a long-lens reveal of Firefall. B Camera was going into a storefront to get an angle of Firefall crossing through frame, something with some soft-focus *koombies* in silhouette in the FG.[*]

OKB was done with the Works, his look complete. His wardrobe had been laid out for him by an associate named Mario, who had worked with Le'Della in Costumes on her last three productions. OKB had approved Mario despite preferring a female costume assistant. Mario—who preferred the pronoun *they*—was standing by to help OKB into any part of the torn and singed Marine uniform, but the actor assured them that he could tie his own G.I. Joe boots, thanks.

"Give the Duke a fifteen," Yogi said as he keyed his radio on channel 1. The Duke was the radio code name for OKB as Firefall. The young members of the AD crew had no idea that the Duke was a reference to John Wayne in the *Sands of Iwo Jima*. The Base Camp AD—a woman named Nina who had been on Yogi's team for the last eighteen months—understood that she was to now softly knock on the door of OKB's trailer, wait a beat, then open it a crack to let Number 2 on the Call Sheet know that the set would be ready for him in fifteen minutes.

"Mr. Bailey?" she said, looking up through the crack, seeing the actor lounging on the sofa, looking at his phone, still in his sweatpants and Uggs. His makeup made him look truly frightening. "This is your fifteen-minute warning."

---

[*] The foreground.

"It is?" OKB said, not looking up from his phone. "My warning? As in *You'd better be careful, I'm* warning *you* . . ."

"Just wanting to let you know they'll be ready soon," Nina demurred. "Can I get you anything?"

OKB shut off his phone and got up to stand in the doorway of his trailer, his "burned" half face overwhelming in the light. "Come in here a sec, Tina."

"Nina." She climbed the three steps, leaving the door wide open, per instructions.

"Take the radio out of your ear," OKB said, which Nina did. "I am now going to *presume* to tell you how to do your job."

"Sure," Nina said. "What can I do for you?"

"You can take a look around and realize that you don't have to be one of those production stooges that robotically do whatever they are told. Look at my costume there." The Firefall wardrobe was laid out on the double bed in the trailer's bedroom section, just past the shower and sliding-glass-door closet. "I can put that stuff on in about a minute and a half, even with the combat boots. I don't need a fifteen-minute warning. So, what say you don't give me one. No matter what they tell you on that radio in your ear, I want you to wait until they are actually and truly all lined up and ready to shoot on the set. Then knock on my door. I will open the door myself. You will tell me they are ready. I will then close the door, take a piss, put on my army clothes, fix a drink to carry with me, and come out in three minutes. Then you can tell the overlords that I am on my way. That all seems pretty simple to me. Does it seem simple to you?"

"Sure," Nina told him. "No problem."

"Great. And stop asking me if there is anything you can do for me. If I need something I will ask. I'm trying to be nice about this, but it's hard when I have all this plastic and paint sticking on my skin and I know it's going to stay there all day, every day, for the next three months. When next we talk, it will be when they are all ready for me. But don't just say 'They are ready for you' like I'm already late and it's my fault. Come up with a code word that means the same thing."

"Got it." Nina stepped back out on the trailer steps. "How about 'anchors away'?"

"That'll work," OKB told her as he reached for the latch on the door to close it.

Nina replaced her earpiece, stepping away from the trailer just far enough to safely report to Yogi that "Duke is *stewing*." What Yogi wanted to hear was that OKB was on standby. *Stewing* was AD-ese for "Maybe ready but too cranky to tell. I'll do my best."

"Bring him fifteen," Yogi told Nina.

"Copy that," Nina keyed back.

Twelve minutes later, Nina knocked. OKB opened the door. Nina almost said they were ready on the set but caught herself. "Anchors away?" she asked.

OKB rolled his eyes and closed the door. Fifteen minutes later he came out, dressed as Firefall, carrying a big steel mug of HaKiDo coffee and oat milk. "Anchors fucking away," he muttered, slipping on the sunglasses from Wren.

Mario, who had been standing outside the actor's trailer for the last forty-five minutes, noticed that OKB did not have Firefall's helmet, so went back inside the trailer to fetch it.

"Walking," Nina said into her mic as they headed to the set to let Yogi learn of OKB's arrival.

"I don't want to hear that, okay?" OKB said. "Don't report on me like I'm some convict in the exercise yard."

When OKB arrived on the set, Bill Johnson yelled out, "Behold!" There was a smattering of applause, a great number of compliments about OKB's makeup and wardrobe, many looks from the crew to get a gander at the other Major Player, and a high five from Wren, who was still on the set to root for his first shot of the picture. He was wearing the aviator sunglasses she had gifted him.

"Well," Wren said to OKB. "Ain't you hot shit!"

"Present and accounted for, et cetera," OKB said.

Bill stepped up with all that he could offer as direction. "Your first shot is a doozy, OK. See down there?" He was pointing north, to the far end of Main Street, where an AD was standing beside a traffic cone. "CGI will have you enveloped in a whirling flame, like I showed you on the Pre-Viz. On action, walk forward. Be Firefall."

"What am I looking at?" OKB asked.

"Too wide a lens for us to see, really."

"That's not what I was asking," the actor said. "What am I looking *for*?"

"This shot is not part of the narrative, but a flash of malevolence inside Eve's head. Your spooky appearance is the thing here."

"I'm showing up in this little, hot town, though, right?" OKB was looking down at the spot with the traffic cone. "I must be here for a reason. What's the reason?"

Bill took a moment, thinking, *Okay, he needs something to work with here, a motivation.* Some actors come to the scene knowing the why and what of their place in the scene, in the text. And they know their lines. Other actors don't do any of that; they need direction from the director. Turns out, such was OKB. "You are here to scare the living daylights out of Knightshade," Bill instructed.

"Ah," OKB said, nodding. "Elvis has entered the building."

"There you go." Bill nodded back at him.

OKB, a few moments before shooting his first scene in Bill Johnson's film, turned his head over his shoulder to say, "He's gay, you know. Firefall is queer."

Bill heard what OKB said. That would not have been a problem if the part had been written as a closeted gay Marine during World War II, but there was nothing in the screenplay to warrant such an interpretation. In fact, there was the opposite. Had OKB ever mentioned Firefall being gay in the months prior to this first day of shooting, Bill would have said that *wasn't* his intention, but it was a good character dilemma that they should "keep in their pockets." The URST* between the main characters was the spine of the film's relational structure. There was, after all, the Kiss. Among the ton of other moments, other emotional beats, a conflicted sexuality to Firefall had not once been discussed between Bill and Number 2. For now, Bill just wanted to roll on OKB's first shot.

A golf cart picked up OKB and Mario, clutching Firefall's helmet, to save the steps to the cone a few hundred yards down Main. The Prop Crew was there with the M2-2 flamethrower to help rig the actor up.

Rolling.

Sound speed.

---

* Unresolved sexual tension. As much a plot device as Hitchcock's MacGuffin.

Camera set.

Action. ACTION! ACTION-ACTION!

On Camera A, the tiny figure of Firefall began walking. A few seconds later, in Camera C, a side view caught him full figure passing through frame on the other side of a window, outside in the warming sun of the summer morning. Camera C, the fuzzy blob, became Firefall's worn, burned combat boots, huge in the frame, trudging on the pavement step after step.

Cut! CUT! CUT-CUT!

There he was. The fully rendered Firefall. It was done.

"Were those sunglasses?" Al was asking the question. She was looking at the A Camera monitor as the dolly reset. Frances was looking at her notes. The Executive Chorus had stepped away to congratulate one another. Ynez was the only other person in the Video Village who saw that, yes, Firefall had been wearing some very modern, hip shades. Ah, wait. Wren had seen them, too.

"I gave him those," she said. "Aviators. A start present."

"Back to One,"* Yogi transmitted and a half dozen voices repeated for little reason. The Unit started regrouping for a repeat of that first take.

"Boss Man," Al said. Bill was in the DIT but could hear her. "OKB had his sunglasses on."

"He did?" Bill had been studying the camera moves and the framing. SAM had looked at the shadows and the angle of the sunlight. He wanted to make an adjustment on B Camera. "Run it back, Cubby."

Cubby was the playback guy, who recorded every take of every camera and kept track of it all. He was in his own station, his own little fold-up tent, listening on open mics in both the Video Village and the DIT. A squawk box allowed him to answer directly or, to save time, acknowledge the request with a *meep-meep* sound effect.

"Playin' back," Cubby announced. First, A Camera ran from the clack of the slate. From so far away, there was no sign of any sunglasses on OKB/Firefall until the push-in on the dolly. The dark lenses could be seen under the lip of the low-angled helmet.

---

* The start mark of the sequence.

"Yeah," Bill said. "Go to B, please." Just like that, B Camera was on the monitor—the shot SAM was now rejigging for the *koombies* in the FG. When OKB appeared in the right of frame, if you looked for the dark glasses, there they were. "Yeah." Bill saw them. As a director, Bill did not like to carry around a walkie—he gave orders to Yogi, who then broadcast what needed to be done/changed/fixed/altered to whoever needed to know. But to talk to an actor on a distant mark, a radio was needed, and there was one on the monitor cart. "Yogi, get a radio to OKB."

"Let's get a radio to the Talent, please," Yogi said on channel 1. At the other end of Main, an AD carried a spare for just this purpose. Visible on the A Camera feed, OKB took the radio from the AD.

"Whiskey Tango Foxtrot," the actor said.

"OKB," Bill keyed back, "you had your sunglasses on."

"That's affirmative, BJ."

"Let's take them off and do it again."

"Well . . ." The radio *squelched* between OKB keying the mic. "Starting from scratch here with a badass choice, sir."

"Nah. We need to lose them and go again."

"Lose them?" Now OKB was asking a question. "I feel pretty good about them."

Because this conversation was on channel 1, everyone with an on-set radio could hear what was being said. Channels 2, 3, 4, etc. were for other departments to talk freely to one another only. But channel 1 was the Production Channel—the On-Set Channel, the Let's-All-Be-Working-the-Same-Task Channel.

"I'm coming to you," Bill said. He headed toward the end of the street, where his actor and two of the Prop Crew, an AD, and Mario were, where the orange traffic cone had been. The distance was far enough to warrant the use of a golf cart, but Bill chose to walk it.

"The password is *shit-face*," OKB said over channel 1, then he handed the radio back to the AD. "Take this off me," he said to the prop guy and gal, who unstrapped the M2-2 backpack. He also took off his army helmet, handing it to Mario, who was preemptively reaching out for the thing; their job was to maintain the costumes and, if possible, keep the actor comfortable. If Mario failed either duty, they'd spend the rest of the picture in the costume truck doing laundry in its huge washer/dryers.

Bill's long walk from the camera to the first mark gave him time to ponder both the reality of the moment—an actor with a new idea for his character On the Day—and what language to use so he could get the shot. Firefall was not a gay Marine and he couldn't wear sunglasses . . .

In a well-worn on-set power-play move, OKB did not step forward to meet Bill to have a chat. No, the production supplicant had to come to the on-set royalty. The AD and Mario distanced themselves in the shade of the buildings on the eastern sidewalk. OKB stood, helmetless, in the middle of Main Street with his eyes shaded by the Randolph Engineering aviator glasses, in which was reflected the approaching Bill Johnson.

"Halt," OKB ordered. "What's the password."

"I don't see the sunglasses, OK." Bill got right to it.

"Just spit-balling, Beej."

"They aren't period."

"Authenticity is for pussies."

"They hide your eyes."

"The helmet hides my eyes. The glasses provide mystery."

"There will be reflections that CGI will have to remove on every shot."

"This is a big picture, no? You can afford it."

"I'm thinking about the Big Reveal, though. When Eve knocks off your helmet and we see your scarred head and your eyes—those windows into Firefall's soul."

OKB was not buying that. "With the glasses, the reveal will be superpowered, man. First the army helmet's gone, at last, right? But then, my shades. Check this out . . ." OKB reached up and s l o w l y removed the aviators—showing his dark eyes in a formidable squint. "Bang. Fireball XL-5 is *here*."

"But that's the problem. Only *then* do I get your eyes. All the rest of the picture I get some guy in dark glasses."

"Exactly," OKB told his director.

"We've talked about this," Bill told him back. "When I come in *here*"—Bill held up his hands, framing OKB's face in what the actor called a BFCUOKB*—"I need to see those brilliant things you were born with, your pin spots. The eyes tell us you are *seeing it all*."

"Yeah," OKB demurred. "But that's a statement. What's wrong with asking a question? Who is this guy? Is he blind? Does he *sense* it all? Is he gay? Is he straight? Is he angry? Is he in love? What scratch are we trying to itch here?"

"Gotta tell you, OK, I don't see it." Bill let that hang. "Sunglasses have never been a part of the character."

"Not in your script, no. But up here, always." OKB was pointing to his temple. "Why not try?"

"We've never talked about such a specific choice."

"I know. My bad, BJ."

"So . . . let's try without the aviators."

OKB looked down at his combat boots, pursing his lips. "Tell you what my process is here." Bill Johnson just could not wait to hear about OKB's *process*. "Instinctive leanings aside—I do see the dark glasses, fire and shade, right? But shelve that for now. Logically? Where is the logic of this very shot? Do I see something particular? Am I here in Bone Scoot for a reason other than like an eerie ghost? Not according to BJ, the boss man. I'm just a dream vision in Wren's little coconut. An imagined thing. A fantasy. Hell, mister, the lovebirds haven't met yet. Eve Milkshake has no idea what I look like. I could be in a straw hat and P.F. Flyers for all she knows."

"Eve sees what *we* see, though. Firefall defines himself—to *us*—in this shot. And sunglasses make no logical sense."

"If we choose to make it so, they make all the sense in the world!"

"No . . . they . . . don't."

Al saw it all from a distance and knew it all from the body language. One shot in—not even *two* takes—and here it was, the battle of wills. An actor not wanting to give the director what was called for. The director not allowing the line, the beat, the scene. The whole film could go off the rails. This rarely happened on a Film by Bill Johnson—save for that one instance on *Albatross* (which

---

* Big Fucking Close-Up O. K. Bailey. Other common names: Star-Maker, Big Banger, Momma's Eyes, a Lee Van Cleef, Shooting the Cookies.

was, actually, three instances rolled into one). A scene in *A Cellar Full of Sound* came very close to self-combusting when the female actor, Kikki Stalhardt, had been "musing" on her "internal heart-beat" (she had self-published her own character bible, printing out copies she gave to the H/MU Departments, Le'Della in Costumes, her co-actors, Bill, Al, and the Prop Department) and had taken a blue pencil to her dialogue for the day. Between shots in the Club—before her own BFCUKS—she approached Bill, who was sitting with Al, and asked if it would be okay if she altered some of her dialogue, to fit it in her mouth. Bill read her ink-penned version.

"I want this scene to be in the movie," Bill said to the actor, handing back her rewrite of his dialogue. "Don't you, too?"

What Kikki Stalhardt came to understand in that aside was: If she delivered her version of her lines, the scene would be cut, the beat would be cut. Her part would be cut.

"I'll go back to the original," she said. "Maybe we can work some of my subtext in later?"

"You never know," Bill said.*

In Lone Butte, Al watched as Bill paced the long block back to the camera and Video Village and the DIT tent, signaling with a look to her that some agreement had been made regarding the dark glasses on Firefall.

The slates on the three cameras *clacked,* and action was called for take 2. At the other end of Main Street, OKB stood stock-still. He was not wearing the sunglasses. He did not move for twenty-seven seconds on Frances's sweep-second-hand stopwatch. Then the actor reached into a pocket of his uniform, pulled out the dark shades, and ceremoniously placed them on his face. Then he paced forward down the street.

Bill called *Cut* from the DIT tent, the word being repeated on the company radios and at the top of many an AD's lungs. "We'll go again," the director said, heading back toward this actor, on foot, as the *Back to One* echoed, echoed, echoed.

OKB was waiting for him. "I gave you what you wanted, right? No glasses."

---

* Bill let her say her bit in a later scene between the Girls in the Ladies' Room. He gave her two takes and used one of her sentence fragments in the finished film.

"You put them back on, OK."

"Yeah, but you have, like, a ton of footage without them."

"You put them back on."

"If you don't want me in the glasses, don't use it."

"I have to use it. It's Firefall's entrance. He walks the street. We see him for the first time, head to toe. I'm coming in close to see him. The glasses are not going to work."

"You printed both takes, though, right."

"We're shooting digital. We don't print a take; we have all the takes. It's not a question of what we print, it's what we shoot. The glasses don't work."

"They help me, though. Let me start with them; when I get up to speed and, you know, *feel* like I'm here, like I'm *there,* I'll give you some takes without 'em."

Bill Johnson was already behind in his self-imagined schedule. The very first day of his shooting was slipping away from him—as he had feared—because OKB was *starting from scratch.*

What to do?

Al knew exactly what her boss was going to do. He was going to burn takes.

Take 3 was shot with OKB wearing his sunglasses from start to finish. On take 4, he lost the shades and did not put them on. That was what Bill Johnson wanted from this first setup, what he had envisioned, what he had written, what he needed before he could move on. But before "Moving on!" was announced on all channels, OKB asked for one more take, please, to work on an idea he thought was a viable choice. So . . . Back to One.

Al and Bill shared another look. Her: *Why are you taking the time for another take here, Boss?* Him: *Giving him the rope to hang himself, maybe.* Her: *Aren't you going to use the deep voice and the icy stare?* Him: *Going to try the calm and patient mode. I already have what I need.* Al pointed to her wrist, as though she wore a watch, which she didn't since her iPhone told her the time. Bill nodded: *I know, I know . . .*

For take 5: OKB zigzagged from one side of the street to the other wreaking havoc on the focus pullers, who had had no warning, no rehearsal.

Take 6: The zigzag after the pullers got their focus marks.

Take 7: OKB did not put on those sunglasses again, but as Firefall, he did a little dance down the street, a skip-hop-shuffle move, as though the ghostly Marine Flamethrower was now an eight-year-old kid without a care in the world . . .

Take 8: OKB came running down the street like he was attacking Lone Butte at full charge.

Take 9: OKB refused to wear the army helmet, leaving it in Mario's helpless hands as he walked down Main Street until CUT!

Bill took a golf cart down to talk to OKB about that. He never got out.

"That doesn't work," Bill told the actor. "Gotta have the helmet."

"I was just showing you what could be. Don't print it if you don't like it."

"It's not that. It's that you don't have the burns on your head and scalp, the makeup prosthetics."

"You could add them, though. With CGI. In Post," OKB said. "In Post you can add them, right?"

"Yes, but no. It's a budget problem. We need the helmet now. We'll have you in the makeup for the *reveal* when we shoot it, but for now we can't have the head of OKB but not the scars of Firefall."

"One more take. Just one, then I'm satisfied. One more take for OKB."

"Okay." Bill U-turned the golf cart and *whirred* back to the DIT tent. One more pass to keep his actor happy, and he would move the cameras. Three hours of the morning light, the first day of shooting, the crew's time, and much of the wherewithal of Bill Johnson had been spent.

Rolling.

Sound speed.

Camera set.

Action. ACTION! ACTION-ACTION!

With the helmet on his head, OKB robotically marched down Main Street—goose-stepping like a Nazi Storm Trooper—until "Cut" was called from the DIT tent.

Over the radio, Yogi announced, "Moving on!"

Al said to herself, "Eight burned takes."

So went the rest of Day 1 of 53 Shooting Days. Every setup on Firefall turned into nonsensical versions of what should have been, what was *written*. A twelve-hour day produced great footage on Eve but only a few seconds of Firefall. Bill Johnson was not getting what he wanted, what he needed.

"Let's wrap," Bill said at 6:51 p.m. If any radio announcement is loudly broadcast during the shooting day, none has the volume of "Wrap!"

Yogi added a channel 1–wide, "And thank you all for an epic first day of shooting. You are loved."

★ ★ ★

OKB walked into the H/MU without a care in the world—smiling and happy with himself for his steering of the day to his instincts, his variances, his creative juju. Firefall was on track to be a fascinating, one-of-a-kind film icon as only OKB could manifest. He sat in the Works chair to have all the prosthetics removed and his skin repaired in a process that would eat up an hour. With his eyes closed and the three-person team working to get all that sticky goo off him, he heard someone step into the trailer, then Al Mac-Teer's voice.

"First day, done," Al said. "Bravo, everyone." The others in the trailer offered "Thanks . . ." "Good day . . ." "Stuff looks great," etc. "OKB, how about a quick talk about tomorrow, in your trailer, with the boss?"

"Sure," the actor said. "Let's chat it up."

"See you then."

"Roger Wilco, Copy That."

For OKB, the meeting in his trailer was a six-minute explanation of his work process to his collaborators on his new film. "This is what I do, guys," he said to Al and Bill, whom he was now calling Bo Jo. "This is my process. All those hours you and I talked? I listen hard, man. I got it. Filed it all away into my sinews and brain matter. Now, out it flows. Spit-balling. Free style from scratch. I give you everything and anything I've got, and in there is the truth. Anything I do, I love and approve of. And you? Well, I'm a big boy—use what you see as what you need. I've got no ego here. I supply the raw materials; you subtract the nuggets and gems."

"That's all great," Bo Jo said to his actor. "And I see what you're going for, but there's some stuff that is so off base I don't want to handcuff you with lost time."

"What's that mean?" OKB was reading the ingredients on a carton of one of the substitute milk products from his trailer's refrigerator.

"I don't want to hurry you through so many options. Eventually we must move on."

OKB repeated, "What's that *mean*?"

"It would be helpful if, say, in the early takes, we approach Fire-fall with the adage 'Less is more' being our goal."

"In some movies, I've found that *less* is *less*. As in, not enough."

Al's cranium echoed with a silent *snort* of derision at this: *The kid has made two movies! Two!*

Bill said, "We could do with less optional takes and save that time."

OKB said, "But having enough *takes* time. I can't be hurried and do my job, guys."

"I don't want to hurry your process," Bill calmly explained. "But I don't want to waste your time. Or your efforts. Let's nail it, then we can rejig it and play around some."

"I need to be loose, see?" the actor said. "To let the character flow out of me, unfiltered, without a lot of *rules* laid down on me. Like we did today."

"We're already half a day behind," Al said.

"You're talking schedule, sweetie." OKB just called Al Mac-Teer *sweetie*. "Not my concern. My gig here is to walk and talk and strut and scare as Firefighter Army Man every moment I'm in the lens. That is what OKB does for you. Schedule is for production stooges with radios in their ears."

"Well, let's do this," Bill offered. "Tomorrow, you and I talk some before, so we are on the same page, so we can both feel good about what we get."

"You mean, like, in here before I go into the torture chamber?" He meant the Works.

"When you are comfortable, and ready to jump in. Say, on set for fifteen minutes, then we get a few takes, then we can play around."

"I think it would be better if we just do a half a dozen takes, see what's in the box, then talk some."

"Ah." That was all that Bill said, just that *ah*.

"It's how I work best. The truth is time independent. And there's nothing wrong with going deep and long to capture the truth, *n'est-ce pas*? And I gotta confess to you, I feel *great* about where we ended up with Firefly by the end of the day."

"I'm glad," Bill said, rising, moving to the trailer door. "Onward."

Outside, Ace had the Range Rover close by, ready to drive OKB back to his lodgings—where a set carpenter had safely boarded up the broken window. Tomorrow, the Art Department would install the new glass. A movie unit could solve any problem.

The key players—the H/MU team, Yogi and Aaron, the Sound Department, and SAM's camera operators, as well as the Executive Chorus—gathered at the Almond Growers Association Building to look at the dailies, where Ynez had arranged some sandwich platters. The truth is, with digital monitors being so good in these modern times, a communal viewing of *Rushes* was not necessary anymore—there was no need for the postmortem to examine the raw footage, since it was seen all day in real time. But this was the very first day of shooting, and OKB had been high maintenance, so the ad hoc screening room was crowded with fully invested spectators.

Save for the incandescent Wren, the footage was disastrous. Even the Executive Chorus was concerned, judging by their sudden lack of high fives for one another. With half sandwiches and crudités, they watched OKB's prancing and dancing and mugging and goofing in angle after angle, take after take, all wasted time and burned-up budgetary dollars.

When the horror show was complete, Bill remained to finish a plate of chicken salad, with only Al, Aaron, and Yogi left in the Media Room. "So," Bill said, crunching on a dill pickle spear. "What do we do to save our picture?"

Day 2 (of 53 Shooting Days)

Thursday's work went as off the rails as the day before, except OKB was late to Base Camp that morning by one hour and forty-seven minutes. He wanted changes in his smoothie ingredients, so had Ynez make three trips to Catering before he sauntered into the Works, only to fall asleep in the chair, leaving his drink untouched. His head kept nodding forward and the team had to keep waking him to get the job done, the makeup applied and textured and colored and highlighted with no seams showing.

Yogi had issued a new Call Sheet at 9:00 p.m. the night before—all the departments were told to look for it that evening—to start with scenes 4A (parts), which had Firefall in different sections of downtown, wading out of a roaring VFX cyclone of scalding-hot air and smoke. Some of the smoke would be real world practical, supplied by the on-set SPFX. Everything else would be VFX done in Post. The afternoon work would have Wren on the set for scene 5, which should have been shot on Day 1. OKB was not on set for his pre–first take discussion with Bo Jo until 10:51. To get some footage Bill had SAM roll on INSERTS, CUTAWAYS, and ESTABLISHING SHOTS that were not scripted but would be useful in editing, in Post.

Finally, OKB arrived at the camera. Bill talked with him before his first shot of Day 2, the actor saying only, *Yeah yeah. Got it got it got'cha,* before taking his mark. His first bit was scripted for Firefall to take a few steps, pause malevolently, decide on a path, and then walk off camera like a soldier on point.

Rolling. Rolling! We are rolling! Cameras rolling!

Sound rolling.

Markers.

Camera set.

Action. Action! Firefall lunged into frame, took off his helmet, scratched his head, then hopped-a-skip off camera like he was a kid playing Wag-a-Bump. Bill called, "Cut"—so did everyone on the AD team. The scene continued to veer off on similar odd tangents for another seventeen takes. Seventeen times, Bill talked with OKB before rolling. Seventeen times, the actor said something along the lines of *I see . . . Uh-huh . . . That's an idea . . . lemme come up with something . . . Yeah yeah. Got it got it got'cha,* then did whatever he damn well pleased.

Al was not on the set. She was in her office in the PO. Half of the Executive Chorus was with her. (The other half had returned to their HQ in Los Angeles.) Behind her closed door, with Ynez stationed outside to keep anyone from entering, she was choreographing an intricate dance of necessity.

"The actor we have hired was two hours late on the second day of shooting," she explained to the mini-chorus—a guy from Dynamo and a woman from the Hawkeye, both vice presidents of their holy orders. "He has no idea of the movie he's in. He has no ideas for his character other than Firefall is gay, looks great in aviators but bad in a helmet. We have about four seconds of usable footage from our first shooting day."

"Firefall is gay? I never saw that," said the woman from the Hawkeye. "But we could work it."

Al explained, "It'd make moot the screenplay we all decided was a go picture."

"Dynamo already has a gay superhero with Sky Angel," the Dynamo exec said in a monotone. "We don't need another. Would being trans work?"

Al ignored that. "If we have to reschedule to make our days, that means altering the screenplay. Revisions and cuts."

"I've got ideas for cuts," said Mr. Dynamo.

"We've discussed revisions in Creative at the Hawkeye."

"No to both," Al said. "Before we ask my boss to revise his screenplay, he works his ass off on our Number Two to manipulate him into a performance that makes some sense. We can rejig the One-liner to get Firefall and Eve together ASAP. We'll have to get on the Green Screen stage sooner than we'd like, but so that goes. Then we shoot OKB out as fast as we can. Hey, Ynez?" Al called to the door. Ynez was there in an open crack, immediately.

"What can I do for you?" she asked.

"Java boosters all around. How do you guys take coffee?" Al asked the executives.

"I know already," Ynez said, and was gone.

Al turned back to the execs. "If he keeps being so late, we could threaten his agent that OKB will have to cover the cost of all the time lost to his tardiness."

"I like that," said Hawkeye. "Teach him a lesson."

"Oh, I'm sure it will," Al said, knowing full well that OKB was unteachable.

Back on the set, OKB was very excited about an idea he had, one that *sprang* inside him on the spur of that very moment. He asked Props for a pack of Juicy Fruit gum, then wadded up half of the sticks in his mouth. Firefall was now a gum-smacking hunter-on-the-prowl, with a jaw working overtime as he sauntered through the scenes. "Bravo Johnny!" he called out to Bill Johnson. "This is it! This is the character!"

"I'm not so sure." In fact, Bill was very sure—of the opposite. "Let's do some without the chew."

"No, man!" OKB said, smacking his gum. "Let's be bold and go with it. It's a counterpoint! I've been having to jump and move and twitch to find myself as Gomer Pyle but with this . . ." He tried to blow a bubble, which one cannot do with Juicy Fruit. "Look, man. I can stand as still as you want, but now I feel like I've always wanted to feel."

OKB did stand still, in his helmet, with no sunglasses, looking as malevolent as an actor can with a jaw working at a wad of gum like Mr. Ed with a mouth full of peanut butter.*

"Let's go back and reshoot what we did yesterday!" OKB was very upbeat at the idea!

"Maybe later in the schedule," Bill said.

"Let's do it today! We're right here! Let's set up on Main Street and shoot my intro! Two takes and we'd have it!" With the gum in his mouth, OKB was spitting with each exclamation point.

"Too much equipment to move."

"Two blocks?"

"It's tracks and crane and three cameras," Bill explained.

"At the end of the day, then. Hey, Sammy?" OKB called Stanley Arthur Ming by a name the man hated.

"Yes?" SAM asked.

"Wanna get some badass Golden Hour shots from yesterday?"

"Aren't we shooting Golden Hour here today?" SAM was looking at Bill.

"I didn't have *this* yesterday." OKB pointed to his mouth and the gum in it. "I'm liberated now!"

---

* *Mr. Ed* is a very old TV show about a talking horse. Peanut butter was put in Ed's mouth. As he licked, he appeared to be talking. It has been said that Ed was a happy horse who liked peanut butter.

"Let's finish up here," Bill said, pulling what appeared to be a shot list out of his pocket and pretending to study it. "A couple more setups before lunch, then we'll look at the schedule."

"Copy that!" OKB went back to his mark. "Gonna need fresh Juicy Fruit!" The actor was calling to the prop crew.

Bill kept his eyes on a little card that was actually a game of Jotto, which he sometimes played during setups to bide the time. "SAM?"

"Yeah?"

"And Yogi?" Bill called to his first AD and told the two men that after lunch he wanted the cameras up on the roofs of the buildings around the square and the courthouse. Long lenses to capture the wide frame with Firefall small in the shot. Then they'd move to the crane and jib arm, put B and C Cameras on the towers, wait for the afternoon light, and shoot Firefall from behind.

Wren was to be told that she would not be working in the afternoon.

★   ★   ★

Wren didn't want the afternoon off. She wanted to work, even though the second-best thing an actor can hear on a movie—after "They are ready for you"—is "We won't be needing you today." So she did a full Dray-Cotter workout, her long-and-slow stretching routine, reread her script, pens in hand, had a light dinner with the Windermeres and Wally, and was about to invest her evening in an old movie. Badass Bette Davis played *both* Kate and Patricia Bosworth in *A Stolen Life* in 1946, and Wren wanted to see how the legend of Fountain Avenue pulled off two roles in the same film.

She was seated in the most comfortable recliner a tech giant's money could buy, in the Media Room, watching the massive LCD video screen illuminate into varying shades of gray for the black-and-white movie when her iPhone rang out with Al Green's "Let's Stay Together." That was the ringtone Wren had for any call from Al Mac-Teer.

"Pause," Wren said to the Media Room, freezing the old Warner Bros. shield on the wide-as-the-room-itself screen. "Yeah?" she said into the phone.

"How's your serenity on a night like this?" Bill Johnson—the only human being on the film of greater influence than Al—was calling on Al's phone.

"Bitchin', as they say in old high-school yearbooks." She was quoting a line from *A Cellar Full of Sound*. "What's with calling on Al's number?"

"I'm here!" Al called out, the phone set on speaker. They were in her office at the PO.

"What's going on?"

Bill spoke up. "Nothing that's about you other than being about everything . . ."

"That sounds ominous," Wren said, then added, "Lights on— half." That was meant for the Media Room, the lights of which then faded up to midbrightness.

"Forgive the man," Al said. "We need to have a talk, the three of us."

"Right now?"

"Yep," Bill said.

THE FRIDAY NIGHT MASSACRE

When OKB arrived at Base Camp, he was more than an hour late, yet was not asked to go into the H/MU trailer until after he had enjoyed a breakfast. Yogi had greeted the Range Rover as Ace pulled up, the first AD explaining that there was a possible change in the morning shot list, so there was no hurry to go into the Works. "We have at least an hour before the cameras are placed for shots that don't need you, so stay comfortable, sir."

"Where's Ynez?" was how OKB greeted that news.

"I can raise her on the radio," Yogi said.

"I can't stomach another warm smoothie today. I need some huevos rancheros with no cilantro and bacon so crispy it's made with an M2-2 flamethrower."

"Can do, sir."

"I wish someone had told me there'd be this delay," OKB said as he closed the door to his Star Waggon. "I could have stayed in bed instead of hurrying for no reason." Thus spoke the man who was over an hour late for his noon call.

When Ynez showed up with the foil-covered plate of his made-to-order breakfast, OKB answered her knock on the door, took the food from her, and said, "Many thanks, Sugar Bits. And notice I said *bits*. With a *B*."

★　★　★

The official anthem of the United States Navy is "Anchors Aweigh," not *away*—which didn't matter when Al finally showed up beside the camera whistling the familiar tune. Bill turned to her with a rueful, tight-lipped grin. She rolled her eyes as a comment on the gladiatorial matches she'd had all morning, but there it was: thumbs-up.

Bill left the set for the short walk to the Almond Growers Association Building, where the actors' Green Room had been set up. For the cast who would be waiting for their scenes to be shot, a room was provided with real couches and chairs, a big TV, their own Caffè di Multiplo espresso machine, and plenty of outlets for chargers. It was here that Ike Clipper was waiting for his first shot of the movie, ready as Mr. Lima, in his uniform/costume. Bill Johnson, he was told by Ynez, was coming to have a quick chat with him.

"All right-i-o," the actor said.

"Can I get you anything?" Ynez offered.

"Nothing at all. I just had a little snooze. I have free coffee. Gonna have a free lunch in a couple of hours. Ynez, I'm *good*."

Two minutes later, Bill Johnson came into the Green Room. For twelve minutes the two men were behind closed doors. When the door opened, Bill walked out, headed directly to the Base Camp, to OKB's trailer.

Al was standing by, phone in hand, watching her boss. In sixty seconds, she was to make the call that only Bill, Wren, and the execs from Dynamo and the Hawkeye knew was hers to make.

Bill triple rapped the aluminum door, then opened it and called out, "It's Bill. Can I come in for a few words?"

"You'd better," OKB said from inside.

Al hit CALL on her iPhone.

OKB was lying on the trailer sofa as *Judge Judy* played on mute, scrolling through TikTok on his iPhone. "What's the scenario, Blow Jack? Why ain't I shootin'?"

"That's what I'm here to talk about." Bill did not sit down but leaned against the kitchenette counter. "We are not shooting because I made a mistake and I have to cop to it. I had the chance—the responsibility—to set in stone the direction the movie was going to go. In how I needed to see Firefall. In how the character had to come to life."

It was just then that OKB put down his TikTok. "Yeah?"

"As you were pursuing your instincts, as I let you pursue them, I was going offtrack vision-wise. The role was changing, the character was heading into the creative hills, and the movie was shifting. What I should have done—from the get-go, so this is on me—is provide you a wiser and surer hand."

Judge Judy was saying something on the huge TV; the woman's head was nodding in what might have been silent agreement. "A surer hand," OKB repeated. "Okay."

"The end result, which is, again, all because of me, is not working out. This has nothing to do with, uh, with you or, uh, your process or any of, uh, your options."

"I agree."

"So, we're going to make a change. And this is my decision. Mine alone. I should have made this clear a while ago."

"Good!" OKB sat up on the couch. *Judge Judy* had given way to a commercial about a law firm specializing in personal injuries. "I say the first thing we do is revisit the helmet issue. I should have fought harder against that. My bad. That alone will get us on track and me being one hundred percent Firefella. I'll help you out with working a few Saturdays to make up the reshoots. The crew might bitch, but I'm game."

"No," Bill said. "We won't be shooting Saturdays."

"If I get into the makeup for the head scars—now that we've lost the helmet at last—we can treat today's work like it's our day one, yeah? Starting from scratch now!"

"No," Bill said, again. "We won't be shooting any more today."

"Good! My MU team will need some extra time for my no-helmet noggin. Gonna look cool, Baker John-John! Sometimes Night Shoots just become *magic*, don't they?"

"I'm sorry." Bill said, pausing. Pausing. Pausing. "We are making the change by letting you go."

"I'm wrapped for the day? I've been sitting here for hours and you're not going to use me today? *Shit*, man."

"We're letting you go from the picture."

OKB did not have the slightest idea what those words meant.

Bill continued, "It's not working out. We're making a change."

OKB thought he had heard something wrong—but then a five-letter Wordle flashed in his head: FIRED. "You think you can fire me?"

"It's my fault, OK. And it's my call. I'm sorry for my part in this. Again, I should have done things differently from our first conversation."

OKB was sitting on the couch, very still. His eyes were locked on the asshole pussy who had barged into his trailer like he was a big shot: the director, Bill "Blow Job" Johnson. "I'm *committed*. The cameras have rolled *on me*."

"I know how hard this must be for you to hear. You are one hell of an actor . . ."

"I'm the star of this movie and you think you'll survive without me? You can't eat three days of Principal Photography, Johnson. This is not one of your *Eden* movies with a built-in audience of teenage girls and sad fanboys. You need me. You cannot afford not having me."

"It's not working out."

"Dynamo has me signed for three more movies, man! You think you're talking to someone other than the whole fucking franchise? You're not. Firing me will be suicide for you. You want to re-cockup your career with an *Albatross 2*?"

Just then, as Judge Judy was reentering her TV courtroom, OKB's iPhone vibrated and hummed. The screen lit up with the logo of the agency that represented him, meaning that Al had performed her end of the firing sequence with her usual exactitude. OKB was about to hear mayhem rather than TikTok.

"That will be your agent," Bill said, leaving by way of the aluminum door he had previously opened. "He'll explain better than I. Sorry, OK."

The talk with Ike Clipper took twelve minutes—the firing of OKB less than three.

★ ★ ★

"What would you say to Ike Clipper?" Bill had asked Wren, just the night before.

"I would say, *Who?*" The name was unfamiliar.

"Ike Clipper," Al explained. "You've met him."

"I did?"

"You did," Al assured her.

"When?"

"Yesterday. For the first shot."

"Our first day of shooting?"

"He's in the cast," Bill said. "He's one of the Investigators."

"Oh! Playing Lima?" Wren understood now. "The Bartender in *A Cellar Full of Sound*!"

"Yep," Bill said. "Ike Clipper."

"Ike. Clipper," Wren repeated. "Whoa."

"Is that a hesitation on your part?" Bill asked.

"No," Wren said. "It's a comment on the risk you are taking, Boss."

Al looked at Bill, eyes wide. Wren was right. Wren knew.

"I'm imagining that bartender, Ike, in a Marine uniform," Wren added. "Good set of shoulders on him. Tall enough. Enigmatic to my experience. Nice eyes . . ." There was a pause over the phone. "Why didn't you just cast him in the first place?"

★ ★ ★

Outside, Al was waiting for her boss to emerge from the metal box that housed the onetime Firefall. She fell into stride with Bill as they headed toward the PO. No words were exchanged or needed. Caesar was dead. They had a republic to save.

Ace had been told to stand by with the Range Rover, parked and idling. The meal break had been called. With the crew eating in the big ballroom of the Almond Growers Association Building, the Base Camp could be kept free of crew members for the sake of saving OKB his face, from leaving his trailer, the Unit, the production, without anyone witnessing his walk of shame.

Al asked that Ynez pull her PONY car up to the lot's entrance and sit in the back, hidden by the Ford's tinted windows, to keep an eye out for OKB riding away. She hadn't been there long at all when the car appeared, Ace at the wheel, OKB in the shotgun seat yelling into his phone, then driving away west of town toward Franzel Meadows. Other than Ace, Ynez was the last and final member of the crew to set eyes on OKB in Lone Butte. There are some citizens who later saw a silver, two-seat Audi speeding out of town, down Old Webster Road toward the interstate, doing at least seventy-five in a forty-five mph zone, but they didn't know who was behind the wheel.

Ynez keyed her radio, set on channel 4, to raise Al.

"Hey hey," she said over the air.

"Yeah?" Al had been waiting for the transmission.

"An anchor is away." She had given the signal, as instructed. OKB was GBG.[*]

"Copy that. Come to the set ASAP," Al squawked.

Ynez hopped up behind the wheel and drove the right turn, three blocks with another right turn to the set, parking behind the taco truck as the crew was returning from lunch/dinner. She hadn't had lunch with the crew—she was never able to take the time to sit and eat—so she made herself a quick Crafty PB&J on toast. She had set her radio back to channel 1, when Yogi broadcast an announcement for all to hear.

"All crew, everyone on the crew, every Unit member, please assemble in front of the camera for a brief announcement. Everyone. All the trucks. The PO staff. All hands come along to the set for a meeting. You are loved."

The massing took the better part of fifteen minutes. Some of the Teamsters were awakened from naps. The caterers' presence was not required, but many showed anyway. The collection of people was not much different from the assembly that had been called two

---

[*] Gone, baby. Gone.

292 THE MAKING OF ANOTHER MAJOR MOTION PICTURE MASTERPIECE

mornings prior—way back on Wednesday—for the crew photo, the cutting of the flag, and the first shot of the picture.

Bill Johnson stood on a platform Yogi had the Key Grip put together, made of four connecting apple boxes and a square of plywood. With him raised thus, all could see their film's writer-director. Everyone could hear him, too, so there was no dramatic use of a megaphone or Voice of God PA.

"Hey, everyone, this will only take a minute," he announced. "We are pausing production to make a change in our cast. In the role of Firefall . . ."

Someone in the crowd gave off what could have been called a rebel yell of relief.

"Firefall will have a new actor in the role. We have bid a professional, courteous, and respectful adieu to the talented Mr. Bailey, who will, I am sure, go on to continued success, with all our wishes for that to be so. In the meantime, that is it for today. We are going to wrap our first three days of shooting—"

"Shooting? We've been shooting?" someone yelled. Many laughed.

"And enjoy a well-deserved restful weekend. I am indebted to and in awe of your hard work and dedication. See you all on Monday."

A cheer went up—a loud cheer with applause and whistles and that rebel yell again. Everyone likes an early Wrap on Friday. Yogi keyed his radio mic to tell the crew to look for a new Call Sheet for Monday in their email in-boxes by midnight at the latest.

A few members of the crew were anxious, worried of the possibility that they might not survive the Friday Night Massacre themselves. The Firefall H/MU team might be let go since all their work had been with the now-cashiered OKB. Ace Acevido wondered if he would be driving the Base Camp Sprinter van or maybe a golf cart, or simply told to go home to his looms and little horses now that the prime cast member he'd been ferrying about was prime no more. Even Ynez saw the possibility that Al might sidle up to her and bid her a professional, courteous, and respectful *adios,* and off Ynez would go, returning to her PONY car and babysitting duties. She had, after all, answered the constant beck and call of the now-defunct OKB. But other than the loss of Number 2 on the Call Sheet, the only person of the Unit to leave permanently was one of the production accountants who learned that her mother had received some very bad medical news, and she needed to take care of her extended family. A local replacement would be hired over the weekend.

Once the company had been wrapped and all the gear was stored and the trucks all locked and secure, the Unit began a Bonus Weekend, one longer than usual. Folks took off to Sacramento and San Francisco, to campsites in the mountains, to a kayak trip on the Big Iron Bend River, and there was a Gamblers' Special carpool headed to the casinos on the Nevada shore of Lake Tahoe.

THE WEEKEND

Saturday and Sunday were workdays for the picture's key players, a nonstop labor of herculean, epic proportions. The momentary sense of relief that came with the beheading of OKB the Terrible gave way, in a nanosecond, to the realization that the nation-state of *Knightshade: The Lathe of Firefall* had to be governed out of this chaos. The department heads were a mere twenty-four hours in front of their staff—none of them would be kayaking or shooting craps.

AL MAC-TEER cornered every department head to gauge their wherewithal, to make the needed shifts and changes due to the giant hiccup of a recast, but not a one flinched. She talked to the casting folks about a replacement for the role of Mr. Lima. There had been talk about cutting the role entirely—simply giving the leftover business and dialogue to the three remaining Investigators—but Al vetoed that, saying recasting the role gave them the opportunity to bring more diversity to the production. She had a web link of every actor who had auditioned, so started scanning faces for the next Mr. Lima, making her own selects before going through them with Casting. By 10:00 a.m. Saturday Al was Zooming with Polly Kates of Miller Thompson & Kates—lining up possible candidates. At 1:45 p.m., Al was in her office at the PO pounding out every dent that came across her desk, which included a long, panicked, expletive-filled phone call from an exec at Dynamo who was having second thoughts about the whole damn thing.

STANLEY ARTHUR MING pored over the shot footage to

determine what, if anything, could be offered up to Bill Johnson—and for the chance to make changes. If SAM had to reshoot all of what was on the hard drives, he'd put cameras in two other positions and play with reflections.

LE'DELLA RAWAYE was not panicked by the casting change. From the measurements she had taken of Ike Clipper he'd fit just fine. She knew Ike from *A Cellar Full of Sound* and found him to be low maintenance and willing to "bow to the expertise" of the costumer, since he admitted to having no fashion sense. The only problem he offered Le'Della was his self-consciousness about his feet. He had small feet, he said. He would appreciate combat boots that did not make his feet so tiny. The headache soon to come Le'Della's way would be in whoever was cast as the new Lima, which would call for fittings ASAP.

AARON BLAU and YOGI were enmeshed in the rescheduling of Days 4 to 14. Some of Wren's work could be moved up, but only some. Other cast members—those in the scenes at Clark's Drugstore—were not yet in Lone Butte. They decided on working Splits for Days 10 to 14—from noon to midnight—a week away.

YNEZ GONZALEZ-CRUZ drove from Lone Butte to her home, leaving a few minutes before midnight so she could wake up and have breakfast with her family for the first time in weeks. She kept little Francisco on her lap through the meal, taking a selfie with him and sending it to Al with **Possible new Lima?**

AMacT: heart heart heart heart heart heart!!!

Then, seconds later.

AMacT: Next week will be nuts. No driving home for you. Pack a bag and stay in a spare room at my digs.

DR. PAT JOHNSON had had enough time without Bill around. Rather than fly to be with him, she had hitched up her Jayco on Wednesday morning, the first day of shooting, to take three days of driving and camping and be in Lone Butte around the time her man woke up on the first off Saturday of his shoot. She stayed at campsites she'd booked on a site called Care-a-Van, the last of which was a compound run by Buddhists; though she never saw them, she did hear some gongs. She was not within a Wi-Fi signal until Friday morning when Bill reached her with the sad yet necessary news of chucking OKB. She'd be in Lone Butte by high noon on Saturday, she vowed.

BILL JOHNSON started the weekend early, with a massive dose of caffeine as he reread his screenplay yet again. With Ike, now, as his Firefall, he let the familiar text wash over him like a physiologically cleansing rain. Then he took a walk around the still-sleepy streets of the Historic Homes District of Lone Butte, carrying with him his flea-market nine iron like a cane. He took swings at leaves on the sidewalk and bits of branches that had fallen on the grasses while letting rattle in his head any movie-related thought that came to him. There was a veritable flood.

His morning was to be meeting after meeting after meeting, then a Recce of the locations that were going to be put in use much sooner than scheduled. Most important was going to be his time with Ike. The director needed a prolonged meeting of the minds with his new star because God help him if Firefall remained as maddeningly wrong as had been the case. Bill had gone all in on Ike Clipper. If there was so much as another single day of shooting lost to idiocy, there would be hell to pay; a horrible mistake would have been made, one that the Instigator would have a tough time cleaning up. Fucking up a sure thing is frowned upon on Fountain Avenue.

★   ★   ★

On that fateful Friday, minutes before OKB's firing, Bill had found Ike in the Green Room. He was doing burpee exercises as the director closed the door behind him.

"Ike," the director said. "I wonder if you can help me with a problem."

"What can I do for you?" Ike was panting, wiping off a sheen of perspiration with a sweatshirt.

"Step into Firefall for me."

Ike had no idea what those words meant. "You mean, Lima becomes the flamethrower?" Ike was imagining his character going through some Wolfman transformation, due to some curse or cosmic rigmarole that made his Defense Department/CIA/Investigator character become the Phantom Marine.

"No, we get someone else for Lima."

"Someone other than me?" Ike felt his throat constricting.

"I need help here, Ike. I need you to be Firefall. I'm going to ask OKB to, uh, step aside. If you are up to it, and I have no doubt that you are, I'm asking you to take over the role."

"Of Firefall."

"Yep."

"Me."

"Yep."

"As Firefall."

Bill nodded.

"I'm not sure what is going on here."

"The favor I am asking you is to *be* Firefall. Inhabit the character. I've run through a list of possible artists, of actors who could make Firefall as I see him, as I wrote him, as he is in the picture. No one is better suited than you."

Again, Ike did not understand what any of those words meant. Not right then.

Bill continued, "You're an instinctive actor. You comprehend. You listen. You react. You don't ask for a rundown of procedure. You provide your own motivations and you behave as the character would in the situation, in the moment. You don't steal focus but create it. In *Cellar,* I asked you to come up with some business in a scene—some beat I hadn't written or had time to think about, and on action you started Windexing the mirror behind the bar. You went to Props and got a bottle of Windex on your own and used newspapers to wipe the mirror, then a story in the paper got your attention and you started reading it as you wiped the mirror with it.* You gave me four beats when I asked for one. I asked you for an idea and got to sit back and watch what you came up with. You solve your own problems. And mine."

"Okay . . ."

"You hit your marks and tell the truth, even as Roy the Bartender. My mistake here was not realizing this three months ago

---

* One of the best cutaways in the movie—around the forty-seven-minute mark.

and going to the studio and saying, *I've got your Firefall—he's Ike Clipper and I want him and him only.* I'm sorry I didn't do that, but I'm coming to you now. Last minute. Sudden death. You've read the script?"

"Yeah. Of course."

"Mostly your own dialogue? Lima's scenes?"

"Of course, yeah."

"Read it now for Firefall. Read it a hundred times, every chance you get. Find the truth for me."

"Take the role away from OKB? I don't want to rob a guy of his job."

"You won't be. No matter what you say, he's being replaced. Gone. This happens in pictures. Buddy Ebsen was allergic to the Tin Man makeup so Jack Haley joined up with Toto and the others. You know baseball? Lou Gehrig?"

"Buddy Ebsen not able to hit the curve so Gary Cooper got the role?"

"Wally Pipp didn't have it in him to play one day. Gehrig went in at first base and stayed there for over two thousand games."

"Two thousand one hundred and thirty. Heard that on a Final Jeopardy. OKB is Wally Pipp and I'm the pride of the Yankees?"

"If you got the game."

"I'll try."

"Don't try. Just be. The bigger challenge for you will be a year from now, when the picture comes out, your life is going to be altered. The attention will feel white-hot and caustic. Or maybe so much fun you'll become a crazy person. Celebrity is not a natural human state. There's no training for it. You'll be fine if you plan a bit. You'll be rich, maybe, if you watch your money."

Inside Ike's head: *Foom!*

Bill went on. "There will be some back-and-forth with your reps and Business Affairs. The Hawkeye and Dynamo will have you for more movies—not a bad thing. Keep your head straight and your shoes tied. We have some schedule shifting to do, so I can't say when your first day will be, but sometime next week you become one with Firefall."

Ike was silent, but then said, "Wait." Bill had no choice but to. "Wren? Does she know about this?"

"I wouldn't be asking this of you without her full approval."

"Really?"

"Word."

For a moment Ike felt his body stretching, like his head was elongating to the height of the ceiling in the Almond Growers Association Building. His ears went fuzzy with a seashell ocean roar, and he could not make out the words Bill Johnson was saying: "Stay in here for a bit, as I'm going to talk to OKB now. Once that's done, you'll begin." Bill headed for the door. "Be cool, Ike. Be Firefall."

IKE CLIPPER had the feeling one has when skydiving—the exhilaration of flight being one thing, the reality of falling at terminal velocity being another. He was both giddy and terrified, sure of his self-worth and positive of his fraudulence. The only certainty in his life was that his most recent Five-Year Plan had gone out the window. The only two words that came into his head and made it to his lips were "Watch this."

★   ★   ★

Ike FaceTimed his wife from the Almond Growers Association Building. Thea Cloepfer was busy with the baby, of course. When he told her what had happened, she needed to hear the order of events three times before she could process what it all meant. Then she laughed. She held up the phone to show Ike their daughter, ten-month-old Ruby Cloepfer, kicking on a blanket on the floor.

"Wait till I tell her about her daddy," Thea said. "She might burp and have a poop. How are you going to react, honey, once this settles in? How are you?"

"How am I?" Ike repeated. "I don't know if I've been kissed or punched."

Years ago, Ike had been with Thea, standing in a line for a Locals Casting Call on a top-secret movie called UNTITLED 1970s PROJECT. She put her name on a list, so Ike did, too. They both had a ninety-second interview with an off-camera voice. Bill liked his looks, and the guy had said something funny to the disembodied voice of the casting director: "Nice office you have here. Where's the gift shop?"

Ike was a good, if minor, presence in *A Cellar Full of Sound*, a member of the ensemble who showed up on time, knew the pages, and had subtle motivations that he acted out on his own. He was quiet, he listened without comment, never left the set without telling an AD, and played well with others—even the aforementioned Kikki Stalhardt. On the weeks of shooting *Cellar,* the actor had been at the ready, a thin reed whipping in the wind. Bill ended up cutting to Roy the Bartender in the final edit for beats, laughs, and commentary because Ike was always in the moment. For that, Ike was the first actor cast in *Knightshade: The Lathe of Firefall,* because as written Lima was little more than a placeholder role, a spouter of exposition, a presser of buttons on keyboards. Ike Clipper, Bill knew, would turn a cipher into a someone.

Saturday was jam-packed for Ike. First, he had a medical exam for insurance, then was taken to the Stunt team, then Costumes, then H/MU, then the SPFX Wire Crew at the lightbulb factory, then Props, then back to Costumes. Kenny Sheprock asked him if he could spare the time and discomfort for the taking of a quick-drying plaster mold of his head, so he was back with the H/MU team, now set up for that messy process in an empty room in the basement of the Almond Growers Association Building, a room with a sink and no carpeting. A big bucket of water had been drawn to mix up the molding matter. When the stuff was goopy, Ike shut his eyes, and the cold gray mud was poured over his head, then slapped into place by hand while he breathed through two straws, one for each nostril. His ears were covered, too, and suddenly the world sounded very, very far away—almost like when Ike used to get stoned, but without any groovy visions. In that sensory-deprived state, time seemed at first to stand still, then ebb away into the past.

THE LIFE OF IKE

Like all of humanity, he was the result of many a cosmic fork in the road. His conception occurred on a lovely, inebriated night when his mother wanted to become expectant and his father was willing to make her so. Larry Schmiddt and Addie Cloepfer were neither married nor heterosexual, just good friends with a deep, yearslong connection. A few shots of tequila and wherewithal made the biology possible after but one session of intercourse.

"We're like fruit flies!" Larry yelled when Addie came to his place, waving the drugstore test kit with its thin red line.

Nine months later, on a September 11, before that date was etched in terror and crisis, Irving Cloepfer came into the world surrounded by a crew of gay men, lesbian women, straight members of the Schmidt and Cloepfer families, a ton of hoopla, and all the baby-raising gear required by experience and the law. Larry lived nearby. Addie had planned for the hard work of single motherhood. Irving was named in honor of her grandfather, whose body was never found after jumping out of a plane over Normandy the night before D-Day, in World War II. The boy was called Irv, Irvy, Little Ving, many different names, and all of them worked for him.

He was an only child, but he did not grow up alone. He had cousins, playmates, and a procession of the finest babysitters and caregivers to have ever read a book on child-rearing. Two sets of grandparents (one, a step-grandparent; Grandy and Grammy and Nana and Boxo were a quartet of delighted grand folks). He had, forever and every day, two dads, Larry and Greg, and, after some mispairings, two moms, Addie and Claire, who read books to him, rolled balls to him, and colored with him for more hours than he ever sat in front of a TV. It seemed, sometimes, that the adults in Irving's life were hell-bent on entertaining him, engaging him, investing time in him. It wasn't until he was in grade school, when he began going to other people's homes for sleepovers, that he found out not everyone lived in the same whirl of identities, ideas, actions, and parental units as he. He was often bored but not boring, unlike so many of his friends who became so as soon as they got an Xbox, a PlayStation, and a phone. In school, the dull, required classes were the times he'd study the holes in the acoustic ceiling tiles, letting his imagination range wide. The interesting subjects were so compelling, he didn't need to take notes to ace the class. Math was a lost cause for him, as was chemistry, but so what? His report-card grades were nearly constant: A. A. A. C. C. C–. Until high school, when a C was a cause for celebration.

He smoked his first joint waiting for a bus and spent the next few years *laughing*, dissolving into chuckles, idleness, cut classes, and days he never even made his way to campus. He was asked to leave high school and did so, laughing. Addie was livid—with the school and with the mush-head her son was becoming—but since she had done some of the same when she was a high-school sophomore, all she could do was find him another school and say, "I hope this works out for you." Larry and Greg were against all drugs—Irving was welcome anytime but couldn't get high at their house.

He ended up at the Banning Academy, a progressive, for-profit high school in an industrial park, his school hours so concentrated that he was free for the day by noon. He could wake-and-bake and go to class under the influence with afternoons as free as a seaman on shore leave. He went to movies, made videos, wandered around town, then started working the jobs given to teenagers: scooping ice cream and unpacking the stockrooms of bookstores. A friend of Addie's with a restaurant got him a busboy job, then a gig as a waiter, where he was called Server Irv.

He was then running with a pack of dopes, friends who were not interesting at all except when all of them were weeded out. That led to a run-in with some state troopers and a night in the slammer, a few hours that Irving and Co. found *hilarious* until the THC wore off. Then, nothing about being held in detention was funny. When Addie came to collect her Angry Young Man—almost a full day after she could have sprung him—she told him she was not fond of this circle of friends. He mumbled, "Too fuckin' bad." She slapped him then and there, one hand on the steering wheel, the other leaving a red welt on his face.

"*Too bad* I'll take," his mother said. "*Too* fucking *bad,* no."

That motherly *whack* was a fork in Irving's road, one of those moments when he turned this way instead of thataway, one that he wrote down in a notebook. He had been en route to being one of those too-hip-for-the-circumstances guys—a cutup, a smart aleck, a wiseass, the guy who ragged on anyone in authority, who laughed at anything on social media, who said, "Check this out," and showed videos on his phone despite no one wanting to see them. By the time his face had faded from slapped-red back to his usual off-white, he had given up weed, his taste for drugs finite. He took up long, purposeful walks listening to new music, even if the records were forty years old, and reading books he'd seen in class but never picked up. He reworked his Five-Year Plan—there was no longer an entry that said only *Jamaica!* He decided to talk less but listen more, to take the web browser off his phone, to move into his own space, to develop some decorum, some panache.

When his dad and Greg moved to Florida and his mom enrolled in Moore Community College for paralegal classes, Irv, at nineteen years old, was fully independent and free to do something as glamorous as moving to Paris to draw in charcoal and write stories on an old typewriter for the *International Herald-Tribune.* His mother offered to pay the one-way fare.

Instead, Irving Cloepfer took up more restaurant shifts, hooked up with the girls and older women who left their numbers on their checks, thought seriously about joining the Coast Guard, became a barista at Café deTête, quit, then took a steno pad and a ballpoint pen and wrote out a new Five-Year Plan.*

He put the date on the top of a page, from this year to five years hence. Then, he wrote *CERTAINTIES:*

Restaurant-Service Worker

Time my own. Too much?

Then, *POSSIBILITIES:*

Manage Restaurant—Salary not Tips

Find a Life, not an Occupation

College? Shorthand/auto repair/airbrushing/juggling/Hospitality Studies?

Next, *HOPES:*

Commit to extended study of course/subject

Be no longer Server Irv.

---

* A teacher at the Banning Academy was big on Five-Year Plans. The keeping of Five-Year Plans was, perhaps, the only takeaway from Irving's school daze.

Finally, Irving wrote out his mission statement.

The first line said, *Year One: I confess I am at the offramp for either the Promised Land or the Great Beyond.* His pen continued for another twenty-two steno-sized pages ending with *Year Five: Watch this*.

★   ★   ★

Moore Community College was big enough to hold his attention all day, the Pie Pan Restaurant his nights. At MCC Irving took Botany 101, Introduction to Tolstoy, Health and Wellness 1A, rugby, Stage/Exhibition Lighting, and American History I. His second semester had him studying human biology, the College Reading Experience, public relations, Health and Wellness 1B, badminton, Advanced Stage/Exhibition Lighting, and American History II. That summer he applied at the new theme restaurant that was opening at the Kirkwood Mall in a vain attempt to bring business back to the Kirkwood Mall.

Dr. Sore's Dark Emporium of Gore was to be an immersive dining/theatrical experience for the whole family and/or mandatory corporate off-site bonding events. A dinner-theater kind of thing with a full menu of creepy-sounding dishes and desserts: Boris Ghoul-ash, Pasta alla Vulture-ah, Ghost of Caesar's Salad, Blood Pudding. An emcee/host—Dr. Sore (his head was covered in bloody bandages)—would lead the patrons in games, competitions, and puzzles, then present musical acts for an hour-long show that made possible two seatings a night. All the acts were celebrity rip-offs done up as monsters and ghosts and banshees. Their songs and patter had been written by medium talents at the corporation with the hope to franchise the Emporium of Gore all around the nation and the world. The music was prerecorded. Evils Presley, Aorta Franklin, Slipped Disco, Blank Sin-a-lot-tra, Gray Slick—these and other trademarked characters would sing terrible parodies of songs in the public domain or altered just enough to avoid payment of royalties.

A risqué version of the *Hour of Gore* boosted the bachelor/bachelorette parties. On Monday nights, the whole place was booked by companies, clubs, family reunions, and, with a very special, watered-down show in script and song lyrics, by some church groups.

Irving was hired to hang the lights and stage manage the nightly shows. The food-service staff knew how to bang out the prescribed menu like clockwork, the desserts served just before the show began, and the tables cleared and reset within a half hour of the show's end. What made the job so special for Irving was the fun of interacting with the performers. The cast had a few folks in their thirties who considered themselves professionals. Dr. Sore was also the voice of Food Prince Supermarkets and did radio ads. Aorta Franklin was in a commercial for Supreme Burger, playing a woman staring in awe as a giant, new Sloppy Cheese & Rib BBQ Sandwich hovered over the city, a gig for which she was paid enough to buy a new Kia. And that lady could *sing*!

As could Gray Slick, a.k.a. Thea Hill, who sang two numbers and was a part of the all-hands finale to the show. Irv and she began a flirtation that he was sure would lead to a coupling once he was done with a few of the waitresses and Thea dumped her boyfriend who had some boring job doing boring things and was forever waiting for Thea to get out of her Gray Slick makeup. Thea hated the way he drove, but she didn't mind his Mercedes twin-seater.

Running the light board was simple, by rote and computer cue, anyone could do it. Irving sat in the lighting booth every night, laughing with the improvisations the cast was sneaking into a script—the inside jokes and subversive digs at the corporate over-seers. The crowd never caught on, the gang backstage would be laughing, the onstage actors would often break into giggles, but everyone dropped that stuff when someone from the corporation showed up.

★ ★ ★

One Saturday, noonish, the actor playing Dr. Sore pulled a very bush-league move. The guy called the Emporium to let loose a ton of expletives about never again entertaining "breeders' offspring and drunken Republicans." He quit then and there with the busi-est day of the week looming over the staff. There simply had to be a Dr. Sore for two sittings of birthday parties plus two evening shows. Blank Sin-a-lot-tra was an informal understudy for all the male roles, but the poor actor was going on with an ear infection, so was in no shape to take on Dr. Sore's hosting duties. Guess who could? Because he had been present for every performance since the place had opened and knew not just Dr. Sore's role by heart but could rattle off every line and every lyric of every moment of the show, Irving Cloepfer became an actor that very night.

He showed one of the waitresses named Meghan—there was a Megan and another Meghan—how to run the lights. Dr. Sore's costume pants were short enough to be clamdiggers, and the jacket was small at the shoulders and cuffs, but that only made the character more ghoulishly comical. The cast helped make Irving up with the scars and white makeup—Gray Slick/Thea Hill added the stitch-like lines around Irv's mouth to create a Día de los Muertos look. Irving went on as the emcee, a bit self-conscious for the breeder offspring, but by the final show for the inebriated Republicans, Dr. Sore was scoring big laughs. Bigger than ever before. The theme restaurant had a new cast member. Irving Cloepfer had come to a fork in the road and picked it up.

Soon after, the inevitable happened—Thea dumped her Mercedes beau just as Irving's hookup with Meghan ended (in tears). Dr. Sore and Gray Slick began their congress. On their very first night alone together they made out, made omelets, made love, and she spent the night at his place. Irving's most recent Five-Year Plan immediately went the way of a recycled newspaper.

"I think you should change your name." Thea was naked beside him in bed.

"You got a problem with Irving?" Irving asked. The bedroom was dark. It was almost four in the morning, this being the pause between their first and second bouts of *l'amour*. Thea liked going at it, and Irving was one young buck.

"My reps think so," Thea said. A lady who said she was Thea's agent had seen the show and introduced herself to Irving afterward, though was she really an agent? Were there really agents in town? Her firm set up photo shoots, PR blitzes, produced small-market ads for radio and TV, and when a convention came to town and spokespersons were needed, the lady booked those, too. Did that make her an agent? Thea had made fifty bucks one weekend modeling different wigs at a hair-care jamboree, so, *maybe*. And there was that diabetes medication square-dance spot that paid.

"I am offended," said a proud Irving Cloepfer.

Thea liked this man; she saw a reflection of herself in him, of what she wanted to be in a life so very free of standardization. She explained, "If you go out, your name will be on a list: Clopefer? Irving Clopefer? Klepfer? Cleo-pa-fer? No one will know how to pronounce it."

"I get that a lot, actually. You're lucky. Thea Hill. Simple, but is it a name or a place? Gonna climb . . . Thea Hill."

"Your self-tape will have you saying 'Irving Cloepfer' and the casting people will wonder how it's spelled."

"By your advice, I'll have to be Dick Jones. Stan Pock. Jim Town. Simple easy names that sound like gunshots."

"Anything other than Irving Klopp-feer and I want you to kiss me now."

"*I am climbing . . . Thea Hill . . .*"

Casablanca

WREN LANE gave her new costar a call to impress upon him her own glad tidings that the change had been made in his favor. Her caller ID was COMPANY PHONE, which Ike answered without knowing who it was.

"Yes?"

"It's me," she said. "Wren."

"Well. Howdy." Ike ran out of things to say until "What's new?"

Wren laughed. "I just want to tell you that I am thrilled to be working with you."

She suggested that he come to her place for dinner on Sunday night, along with Al and, if possible, Bill, just so they could approach Monday with some sense of familiarity with one another. "Let's get the getting-to-know-you out of the way."

"Yes, let's. Getting to know you will be a pleasure." Had he actually said that? What a dope.

Because Wren Lane's lodgings were kept secret, Ynez was the

one to take Ike to the Sunday dinner. Ike didn't sit in the back seat like a PONY client but came out of the motel and hopped in at shotgun, right next to Ynez, and the two yakked as she drove. They didn't talk about the movie or the schedule or the sudden change of fate for him but about kids. Ike shared iPhone pics and videos of his daughter. Ynez showed him photos of the babies in her family—Francisco was growing new teeth—all of the babies had more hair than Ike's little girl. She showed him the app on her phone called *L.I.S.T.eN*. He was going to need organization in this new life of his.

At the gate, Ynez punched a button and said, "Anchors away!" into a squawk box, then the faux-rusted iron barrier slid open. A quarter mile later Ynez pulled up in front of a house that looked like the lair of a James Bond villain, complete with a henchman standing at the faux-rusted iron hatch that was the front door.

"Tom Windermere," the henchman said.

"Clipper. Ike Clipper," Ike said. He refrained from following up with *Shaken, not stirred*.

Ynez's job was done. "Al is going to take you back after dinner," she said. "See you!" As she drove off, Ike followed Tom inside.

"Nice place," Ike said, taking in the vast expanse of tech-titan décor. "Where's the gift shop?"

"Wren will be out in a second." Tom had yet to crack a smile. "Something to drink?"

"What will the lady be having?"

"Tea, surely."

"Shirley tea for me, too." Still, no smile out of Tom Windermere.

Wren's voice was then heard. "Here's the man of the year." Ike had to look around to find the source, the room was so huge and there was no sign of a hallway or portal to some other part of the house. Oh, there she was, coming past a redwood column. She was wearing a man's black Tom Ford V-neck sweater and dark green straight-legged pants that cut off midcalf, and sandals that were oxblood red. She had an expensive man's stainless-steel watch on one wrist, a wide band across the other wrist. She wore no rings. Her hair was in what Thea had once told Ike was a French twist—the go-to hairstyle a woman used to send the signal of *this is all business but get a look at* me.

"Want to sit outside?"

"If you know the route." Ike followed her out of the big room, around a curved hallway to an opening in the house that seemed to have no doorway—just a wide absence of walls, like a carport. Some complicated wooden furniture was under the open, crimson sky, soon to fade in the west to blue, to indigo.

"I'm Laurel," said a lady who was putting out a serving of tea and snacks.

"Hi, Laurie. I'm Ike."

"*Laurel*. Heard a lot about *you*, lately."

Wren sat. "You've been the lead story here since Thursday. Is sage okay?" She meant the tea.

"I'm good with sage."

Laurel asked if he wanted something else to drink, but Ike demurred. "Are you a vegetarian?"

"I am not." Ike looked to Wren, thinking he might need to explain himself. "I do eat many vegetables. Swiss chard. Bok choy. Corn—on the cob or creamed. Kale."

"Radishes?" Wren asked. "You eat radishes?"

"I never turn down radishes."

"Yams?"

Pause. Pause. "Don't like yams," Ike confessed. He wondered if Wren Lane was a vegetarian or a vegan or some combination. If so, what would she think of his dietary practices? Was he suddenly a disappointment to her? New lead story: *My Costar Eats Flesh!* Was the dinner going to be all natural, garden grown, raw? "Forgive me my distaste of sweet potatoes, too."

"Squash? Squashes in general?"

"A zucchini cut thin and well fried. I'm game."

"Well, tonight it's build your own burger. Laurel can make a beet patty if you don't want beef. Or turkey, as requested by Al."

"Can't see beets replacing beef."

"They *don't*!" Wren was vehement about that.

It was then, right then, that Ike Clipper felt his place on the surface of the planet solidify, sensing an easing to the torque of Earth's axis. Since Friday he had been shot through a cannon of attention and activity, needed in another place just as soon as he was done in the room he was in. An exec from the Hawkeye and another from the Dynamo Nation reached him on his production iPhone; both said they were "thrilled and confident" to have him as Firefall: Ike could not remember either of their names, but he now had their numbers. That morning, Bill Johnson and Ike had talked for three hours about the fact that lacrosse was the first true North American sport because the First Nation tribes played violent matches that went on for days, long before the white people came to Plymouth Rock; about Jacques Cousteau being key to the invention of the self-contained underwater breathing apparatus; about how Stanley Arthur Ming was going to use a dioptric lens for a ton of shots; about some of the fabulous accidents that had occurred during the filming of *A Cellar Full of Sound;* landing on many more topics than that of the movie at hand or the screenplay they were about to shoot. "Firefall," said Bill, finally touching on the job, "is stoic. He's a Marine living up to his vow to never leave a brother in the field. You can do that for me, can'tcha?"

Ike vowed to do so. Since Friday—when he found out he was no longer Lima but was being bumped up on the Call Sheet—Ike was a nervous, if compliant, employee, an anxious underling, a cow on the farm smelling the slaughterhouse. Firefall? Okay. *Do these combat boots fit okay? They are okay. Goop being poured on his head until it hardened? Okay. Does this body harness hurt and are you okay with being suspended up high like that? I'm okay. Here,* he was told, *we want you to jump into the raging sea and hold on to this wild torpedo until it either runs out of power and sinks or hits a ship and blows up. Okay,* Ike said, already holding his breath.

On Wednesday he'd been introduced to the star of the movie, back when he was lowly Lima. Now as Firefall, he was agreeing with Wren Lane that sage tea would be fine and that he liked radishes. His newly surreal world now included talking cheeseburgers with a movie star who hated beets as much as he. Finally, Ike Clipper's world slowed down from a red-lined RPM to an all-systems-fine *purrrrr.* Because Wren Lane had made him laugh.

The two actors had some time talking, just the two of them, with scattershot topics.

Her: I spent high school avoiding jerks, then I left.

Him: I spent high school laughing via a controlled substance and was asked to leave.

Her: The most solid of beings? My brother, Wally. You'll meet him.

Him: Thea, my bride. You'll meet her.

Her: Turner Classic Movies. Bette Davis.

Him: *Jeopardy!* I record it.

Her: Music. Emmylou Harris. Lucinda Williams. Margo Price.

Him: Esperanza Spalding.

Her: Who?

Him: No idea but wanted to sound cool.* In my haze daze "Dust in the Wind" was a profound treatise on displacement, on the theme of ennui.

Her: Ennui? You pulling *ennui* out on me?

Him: Bucket list geography—Vietnam.

Her: Phuket. Iceland.

Him: I do burpees.

Her: Dray-Cotter is like magic.

Him: You go to a gym?

Her: There's one in the house.

Him: The house? The compound, you mean. The Installation.

Her: I wake up at three in the morning sometimes, look in the mirror, and think, *Who is this face looking back at me? Why is she here?*

Him: Want to quadruple that feeling? Have a wife and infant and then go away to pretend you're a flamethrower for a few months. Why am I here?

Her: To save us!

Him: I'll do the best I can. No pressure there.

Her: Best OO7?

Him: Roger Moore. His hair never mussed.

Her: Idris Elba.

Him: He's not a James Bond.

Her: He should be.

★   ★   ★

---

* Esperanza Spalding is a jazz vocalist and is great.

Al arrived and, a few moments later, the Johnsons came down the lane in a red Dodge Charger. Wally Lank walked in from a guest-house on the property and it was time for the burgers. As the newest member of this club, Ike held his own. For much of the evening, the dinner conversation sounded like an indecipherable code—nicknames, references to Fountain Avenue, stories about coworkers that Ike did not know. Had the dinner been only Al and Wren, alone, the personage of OKB would have been raked over the hot coals of Satan, but for the mixed company all that was said of the fired actor was Bill Johnson's wish that "he go on to better things."

Ike wondered when the director or producer or star would bring up what was going to happen on the movie, the work that was going to restart as of the next morning, but they never did. The only other talk of moviemaking was a story Bill Johnson told about Humphrey Bogart and the making of *Casablanca*.

Bill Johnson: The movie was for Warner's and like all of them had a schedule of only a few weeks—they cranked them out factory-style. The director was Michael Curtiz, Hungarian, so he's got an accent. The shoot is hot, with the lights back then being carbon arcs and the film stock needing the brightness and everyone dressed formally to gamble and drink and escape the Nazis at Rick's. Based on a play, you know. *Everybody Comes to Rick's*. Four screenwriters. Two Epsteins and Howard Koch among 'em. New pages are flying, getting tossed out, dialogue being tried out. Contract players wanting to score in their scenes. Ingrid Bergman seducing everyone just by being there. Claude Raines above it all and perfect. And Bogart at the top of his bounce—no more thug-heavy roles or second bananas or potboilers for him. As big a star as ever in the Cardboard Carnival. Smoking nonstop and needing a drink as Curtiz keeps him flattered in that Hungarian patter of his. A day comes midway through the schedule, Bogart is in this white dinner jacket, but no one knows what to shoot. The pages are still due, it's been a long day, and the guy playing Rick wants to go home, have a few highballs, then head off for dinner at Ciro's or Slapsie Maxie's. Curtiz has gotta shoot something or Jack Warner will be all over his European butt. The set is lit for day. "Heer is vat ve do! Bogie. Enter off, hit de mark, yes? Giff a nod left of frame. A serious nod, like you are sayink *Ho-kay* to Sam or whoever you like." "You want me to exit?" asks Humphrey Bogart. "Vye not?" says Curtiz. Bell. Roll. Speed. Action. Rick enters, stops, serious as a heart attack, gives a nod—to what? A passing cat? Exits frame left. Cut! Good. "This I vill use someplace in dis pick-cha. Bogie iss wrapped for to-day." The movie comes out and who is Bogie nodding to? The band. Giving them the go-ahead to play "La Marseillaise," Viktor Lazlo leading, pissing off the Nazis, drowning out their "Horst Wessel" knockoff, making the place stand at attention and sing their hearts out for France, sending the kind of chill through the audience that comes along once a decade. Ingrid has love in her eyes, glowing. Rick's gets shut down by the Krauts, Claude collects his winnings, shocked, shocked to discover gambling is going on. The whole picture turns on that nod of Bogie's, a shot grabbed for no reason other than to kill time, to roll film.

Al to Wren (whispered): He tells that story all the time.

Wren to Al (whispered): It's the second time I've heard it.

Pat to table: You love that story.

Bill to table: It's moviemaking in a nutshell.

Ike to table: You had me do that very thing in *Cellar.* Stand behind the bar, look off left, shrug my shoulders like *I dunno,* and it turns out it's me letting in the kids with the fake IDs and got a huge laugh. I was shrugging at Stanley Arthur Ming.

Bill Johnson: Yeah. I needed to shoot something and you were there. I need to shoot tomorrow morning, too, so, Wren, thanks for a great burger. We're on the clock tomorrow. Ike, be on time or I'll clobber you.

Ike: Screw you, you big jerk.

Pat: Attaboy. Don't let him push you around.

Al: First, a toast. To our survival, our picture. To all who dodge the potholes of Fountain Avenue.

Ike: Where's Fountain Avenue?

★ ★ ★

Thea was saying, "I'm so glad you and Wren Lane had a great night at Wren Lane's headquarters with Wren Lane." Her face filled Ike's iPhone. He was in his motel room, she was at her mom's, in bed, having accepted the FaceTime from her husband despite the half consciousness of only a few hours' sleep. "The most beautiful movie starlet in the world made you a cheeseburger and giggled at your jokes while I watched my fat thighs grow wider as the baby burped up on my sweatpants."

"I don't recall her laughing at a single thing I said."

"How long were you alone with her?"

"Never. She had a henchman, a cook, and a brother there. And Al and Bill. Pat Johnson."

"But over the tea? Just you and Wren Lane."

"Yeah. We were on a patio, in the moonlight, with a wisp of jasmine in the air. Soft music was playing from an orchestra down by the beach and a shooting star passed overhead. We made wishes—she for a renegotiated contract for her next movie, me to get my girls here in Lone Butte."

"What was the orchestra playing?"

"'Tequila' by the Champs."

"How many shots you do?"

"None. She did fourteen and later burped up on her sweatpants. Her brother held her hair for her."

"Didn't want to ruin that French twist. He runs her corporation. She flies her own plane."

"I did not know that."

"Divorced. She's never been with any guy for very long."

"She has a thing for Idris Elba."

"*I* have a thing for Idris Elba."

"My reaction to that is this fake 'buffering' face." Ike held a look as long as he could without blinking.

"Did I lose you? Did I lose you? Buffering. Buffering . . . How did you get back to your digs?" Buffering Face was a steady bit between Thea and Ike.

After another four seconds of his frozen look, Ike said, "Al."

"Do they even remember me from *Cellar*?"

"They said, 'Give our love to Girl Number 2 in Bathroom.'"*

For the next three minutes they talked about logistics—of when and how they'd get to Lone Butte for the duration—and the baby and her mom and her needing to walk more and him getting a

---

* She was a FEATURED EXTRA in the club scenes with a scripted line.

lot of steps in as he paces the floor of his room trying to calm his heart rate because he cannot imagine how he is going to deliver a performance in a role as important as Firefall. Thea said she was exhausted; she told her husband she loved him and said, "You'll figure it out, Irving," which was the best she could do at the late hour. She then clicked off, set the phone on the nightstand, closed her eyes, but lay awake for the longest time thinking of Wren Lane having tea with her husband.

In the motel in Lone Butte, Ike put the phone on his nightstand, picked up the script that lay on the bed. He read it straight through, this time not lingering on any lines of Lima, but the very few of Firefall. He read all the CUT TO moments: *The eyes of Firefall—his angry laser-sharp focus.* Ike read for an hour, pacing occasionally, script in hand. He came to the pages of the big action scenes, the mano a mano fights: Knightshade v. Firefall, with its martial arts choreography, trapeze wires, and body harnesses. The last fight culminated in the Kiss, a Cinematic Big Whammy Kiss, a kiss so overloaded with meaning, passion, and physical contact that both actors would go through a mandatory session with the Intimacy Coordinator, required by the Human Resources Department of the Dynamo Nation and the Screen Actors Guild. Ike wondered just how he was going to pull off that kiss with Wren. In bed and under the covers, he fell asleep after the longest time listening to the big trucks hauling north and south on the interstate.

Wren Lane dreaded kissing scenes. She didn't like the hygiene realities, the forced/fake emotion, the repeated takes, and the cleanup repair that Kenny had to constantly perform on her face from all that squishing of lips. Kissing in the movies was a mechanical process. But she'd get through it. When the day came and the cameras were rolling, Eve would kiss Firefall, and they'd move on to the next shot.

Worse were "hot sex" scenes, where a man and a woman tore at each other's clothes so they could hurry to the deed. Screenwriters wrote that all the time. Directors thought it looked passionate. This was nonsense. Unless lovers were inebriated, no one ripped off their clothes and lunged headfirst for a hungry kiss, not without chipping a tooth in the process, then having to dress in rags.

After everyone had left the house that Sunday night, Wren compared notes with Wally on Ike Clipper. The man seemed sane to Wally, and what was glibness to some was witty to others; Wally found Ike to be the latter. The movie may indeed have been saved by the change in the cast, as though a volatile, drunken brother-in-law had been disinvited to the family reunion.

Heading off to bed, Wren had nothing but positive feelings about Ike, his personality, his presence, his lack of neediness. When the schedule had them working together, Wren felt sure they'd make good partners in front of the camera. The only tinge of hesitancy she felt about him was this: Why did he have to be married?

DAY 4 (OF 53 SHOOTING DAYS)

The first shot of the week rolled at 8:57 a.m.

```
16 EXT. IRON BLUFF—STREETS—SAME

Eve Knight is the only pedestrian.

She passes by some old folks on their porch.
Greetings exchanged.

A teenage boy mowing a lawn. Greetings
exchanged.

Little kids in an aboveground pool playing
Marco Polo.

                    EVE KNIGHT
        Polo! Polo!

CORNER OF MAIN STREET

We recognize it from the Opening . . .

Eve walks past closed stores and shops.
```

```
The Bank Sign says TIME TEMP SAVE CONSERVE

She jaywalks (no traffic) to enter . . .

CLARK'S DRUGS
```

Wren Lane was *incandescent,* simply walking down the street.

At 7:45 a.m. Ike Clipper was deposited to Base Camp by Ace Acevido, then placed in the biggest trailer he had ever seen outside a Boat and RV Show, hard by the honey wagon—last week, one of its cramped stalls had been his changing space. This morning, he had a dressing vehicle bigger than his first apartment, supplied with all the food and drinks imaginable, a wide-screen TV tuned to Fox News, which he turned off, and, sitting on the kitchen table with multiple balloons attached, a basket of yams, zucchini, and radishes with a handwritten note saying, *FIGHT THE ENNUI! XX WL.*

Ike ate a bowl of nutty cereal and drank a V8. When Nina knocked on his door and pulled it open, she told him they were ready for him in the Works. He walked across the Base Camp, reached up to knock on the door of the H/MU trailer, then climbed its steps with the vocal warning of "Stepping in!" to let the artists be prepared for a rocking of the floor and to put down the eyeliner for a second.

Ike was met by three different versions of himself. One was in the bank of mirrors on the wall—his reflection. The other two were plaster casts of his head—grim faced, eyes closed, mouth clamped tight from the goop session on Saturday. One severed head was applied with the scar appliances of Firefall sans helmet; the other Firefall had the helmet from the Costume Department.

"Take a seat, kid," Ken Sheprock said. "We're going to fix you up, good."[*] Ike closed his eyes and let the makeup team layer him with glue and piece together the latex appliances that turned his shoulders, neck, forearms, and scalp into one scary, stitched-

---

[*] There, too, was the makeup team of Sean *(Connery),* Jason *(of the Argonauts),* and Brittany *(which is a part of France).* Ike needed the italicized identifiers to remember their names. Kenny had to leave to tend to Wren on the set.

together dude. With a couple of breaks to stand and stretch his legs, this first camera-ready application of his character took the better part of five hours. Right up until the 1:00 p.m. call for lunch.

The first shot after the BBQ chicken and salads (tomorrow would be Poke Bowl Day) was Firefall's camera tests. Walking to the set, in makeup and costume, Ike was greeted with applause. The sound mixer piped up the PA with the US Marine Band playing "From the halls of Montezuma," which some of the crew (former Marines) found either touching or inappropriate.

Bill Johnson had Ike walk, turn, pace, cross, as the camera pushed in and pulled out on the dolly. Helmet on. Then, all over again, helmet off. Coming in tight for a close-up, Bill told his actor to do anything but smile, which of course made Ike crack up. The test took all of twenty minutes. Wren came to the set just as Ike was finishing. She, like all who had the chance to hold this Firefall up to inspection, recognized the differences in demeanor and gravitas from the previous cast member. This Firefall carried weight, presence, and his place in the picture as surely as he did that M2-2 flamethrower. Wren told him, "Holy shit, Ike. I can't take my eyes off you!" Ike could not stop the tingle-feel of hearing those words from Wren Lane. His fake scars masked his actual blush.

After his digital scans, the makeup took nearly an hour to remove—a process that surprised Ike. He thought he could just tear the rubber pieces off his face. Had he done so, a few layers of his skin would have come off as well, and he'd have been sent to the hospital with scars lasting a lifetime.

At 3:00 p.m., the Unit was shooting on Main Street—Eve Knight in various costume and MU changes. Ike stopped by to watch from the Video Village long enough to have Ynez bring him a Diet Coke.

"What kind of ice would you like?" she had asked.

"Crushed," Ike had said. As a joke! And yet, crushed it was, in a red Solo cup.

At 3:50 and wrapped for the day, Ike felt like one more hanger-on, there only to ogle Wren Lane, so he asked Ace how far away his motel was. He thought to get exercise and a bit of experience on a mock G.I.-style forced-march in the valley heat. Calculating the distance and time required, they figured where the actor could be dropped off to allow an hour's walk to his lodgings, say five miles along Webster Road/CA 122. Ace insisted on continuing to the motel to make sure the actor made it safely. Were he to be absent too long, should fatigue and heat get to Ike, his Teamster was a text away. Seventy-six minutes was the time Ike needed to complete the march, enjoying the alternating stripes of shade thrown by the gum trees along the two-lane's shoulder. He strode along in a straight line, hiking at a natural pace, in a soft-footed cadence, imagining himself as an exhausted, haunted, restless veteran of too many wars. With a timer set on his iPhone, every ten minutes he stopped for a set of six-count burpees, right there on the shoulder of Webster Road. The long walk in the afternoon heat was a meditation, time spent alone with his thoughts, pondering the work ahead of him, his metamorphosis from Irving to Ike, from Lima to Firefall.

Crossing the parking lot of the motel/inn—giving Ace an *I made it* wave—Ike knew he would be taking that hike again and again. He'd ask the Prop Department for a World War II–era backpack and Wardrobe for a pair of combat boots, twin talismans of his vision quest for Firefall. He'd wear in the boots slowly, and weight the backpack with bottles of water, his copy of the script, and a few big rocks for the physical burden to match that on his spirit.

Day 4 was wrapped at 6:58 p.m. with everyone on the shoot exhausted by the heat.

Day 5 (of 53 Shooting Days)

The Porch Ladies—Cast Number 11 and Number 12 on the Call Sheet—had but one job on the movie. To sit in twin chairs of the cheap, fold-up variety and wave at Eve Knight as she passed in front of their porch. Their names were Shelley Margold (Porch Lady 1) and Macaiah Vellis (Porch Lady 2). They had never met each other but had both thought it would be a hoot to investigate a Casting Call for a "Local Hollywood Production" to be held in the Lone Butte Almond Growers Association Building. Shelley drove in from Chico as Macaiah came up from Maxwell to spend a morning following posted signs for CASTING, standing in line, getting their pictures taken, then sitting in a big room with free bottled water and snacks until their names were called. Each woman had spent a few minutes with a polite young woman named Ynez who chitchatted about how hot it was and how close they lived to Lone Butte. Then, both women were told thank you and drove back to either Chico or Maxwell. A week later, they were notified of their being cast and were told when to report for costume fittings—where they met for the first time.

Now here they were, sitting on a porch, surrounded by lights, camera, and *Action!* And there was Wren Lane walking by, looking fit and pretty. The movie star waved at the Porch Ladies. Shelley and Macaiah waved back. They were told not to vocalize any words— to say nothing, but to simply wave. Then, the man who was the director of the movie—Mr. Johnson—sidled up to the porch while the camera was being moved for some reason and introduced himself. A woman named Al was with him. Al asked if either Shelley or Macaiah knew how to knit. Both women did.

"Great!" Al said. She called for Ynez to come to the set. When Ynez arrived, she was told, "Ask Props for some yarn and needles for our Porch Ladies."

Then Mr. Johnson told the ladies to not only wave at Wren Lane but to say "Morning, Eve," which was for Shelley to say, and "Hello, you!" which was Macaiah's line. Mr. Johnson had them each practice the words a couple of times. They did "just great," he told them.

The Ynez girl came back with a prop man, who handed each of the actresses her own bag of knitting yarn and needles, with a few inches of scarf already started. Shelley had blue yarn. Macaiah had white. The Al woman told them to "just keep knitting" all through the shot, even as they said "Morning, Eve" and "Hello, you!" Which they did.

There was more Lights, Camera, and Mr. Johnson said *Action!* Shelley and Macaiah knitted. Wren Lane walked by, waved, and said "Hi!"

"Morning, Eve," Shelley said.

"Hello, you!" Macaiah called.

Mr. Johnson said *Cut.*

There was some chatter around Mr. Johnson from some of the crew. Evidently no one in the Sound Department was ready for the lines of *Morning, Eve,* and *Hello, you!*

Back to One!

A lady named Betsy with a long pole and a fuzzy bulb on it,* wearing headphones and talking to someone only she could hear, asked the Porch Ladies to say their lines again at the same "level" as they had just now.

Morning, Eve.

Hello, you!

Someone then yelled out, "Okay!"

We are rolling! Sound speed! *Action.*

Wren Lane walked by again and waved.

"Morning, Eve . . . Hello, you!"

Cut.

Mr. Johnson said, "What's wrong with that?"

Shelley and Macaiah were told they would be held, as a new shot had been added of Eve walking home from her breakfast, and the Porch Ladies might appear again. They were escorted to the Holding Area in the Almond Growers Association Building to relax until they were needed again in the afternoon light. Ynez asked them to do the movie a favor by taking the time until the next shot to keep knitting with their props so that the camera would see the progress they had made. An extremely if overly polite young man named Cody came to Shelley and Macaiah with some paperwork to sign for their "bump," as he said. Because they were given on-screen dialogue by the director, they were no longer background artists on the picture, but Day Players. For speaking, they were paid more!

"Are you members of SAG?" Cody asked.

"What is SAG?" Shelley asked.

"No," Macaiah said.

"Can I get you anything?" Cody offered, as he had been ordered to ask of anyone in the Holding Area, no matter the hassle.

Well, after the very nice lunch provided to all the crew, Shelley and Macaiah returned to the porch set with a good four and a half inches of scarf added to their knitting. They were ready to film

---

* Betsy "Boom" Luntz was one of two boom operators on the sound crew, made up of the legendary mixer Marvin Pritch, boom number 2 Kent "Bulldog" Arragones, and Jillian Patterson on cable, a former dancer who had met Marvin on a music video and was married to him for just a short-enough time to end the union as good friends. Marvin kept his ex-wife on his crew for the health plan.

the return of Ms. Lane, but due to the company shooting on Main
Street, they did not work that afternoon. They were invited back
for the next day's shoot, their knitting taken to be kept by the Props
Department.

They drove to their homes in Chico and Maxwell, respectively.
They would both be paid for another day's work.

Day 5 wrapped at 6:56 p.m. as Yogi announced that everyone on
the Unit was loved.

DAY 6 (OF 53 SHOOTING DAYS)

Ace Acevido was in the parking lot of the motel at 4:30 a.m. with
two large cups of Pirate drip coffee covered by lids: one for him,
one for Ike. Ace had always taken his coffee with nondairy creamer.
Ike's morning coffee had been near equal parts espresso, hot water,
and whatever milk was handy. To get into his role as Firefall,
though, he started his morning with Marine Corp–style joe. Black
coffee tasted horrible to him, but he stuck with the experience; the
G.I. joe jump-started his system like kerosene in a carburetor. At
4:44 a.m., bound for the Works and his first shot in the movie, Ike
had hardly slept all night. He'd gotten up to vomit at two in the
morning. Nerves. He'd done 250 burpees already.

With the first swab of the spirit gum glue on his neck—that first
application of the cold, sticky *goo*—Ike flinched. The sensation
was disgusting.

Sean (Connery) asked, "You okay?"

"Yeah," Ike said. "It's just that, man. That first batch of glue. In
the folds of my neck. I have to make peace with that icky feeling."

"Yeah," Jason (of the Argonauts) said. "You'd better. It's going
to be every day."

"You can do it, Ike," assured Brittany (a part of France). "Unless
you're a wimp."

Ike laughed. He liked this trio.

That glue was slathered all over Ike—his neck, face, shoulders,
arms, chest, and in his scalp—like so much cold corn syrup. Then
came more layers of glue as the many different latex appliances
were stuck in place, pressed over his now-gummy epidermis. Each

prosthetic then had to be colored, the scars and burns built up and painted. Over the course of the shoot, the process would become a few minutes faster, but every single day Ike worked as Firefall, the Works took more than four hours. To somehow escape the discomfort, Ike tried a meditation app on his iPhone. He'd drift off to sleep, but if the team needed him upright, Brittany had to hold his head in her hands, in her delicate fingertips, without waking him. This was every single day.*

The crew was setting up, once again, for the dreamlike appearance of Firefall with the long dolly track in the center of Main Street, the camera inside the antiques store with the *koombies* in the FG, and a long lens on the sidewalk to get the boot shot. SAM added a fourth camera up on a platform just behind the revolving bank sign that would reveal Firefall with every turn.

At 6:50, Bill Johnson met with Al in the PO to pull the trigger on the choice for recasting of the Lima character. A stand-up comic by the name of Hang To had a great face and handled the test scene's gibberish in a style like no other candidate, so that was that. The Investigators, now, would be a collection of American diversity: actors who were Black, Hispanic, Vietnamese, and Nick Czabo, who is as Caucasian as Jerry Mathers as the Beaver.

"Get Hang To here, ASAP," Al told the folks in Casting, Business Affairs, Travel, and Housing.

Because Wren was on a Will Notify, Ike was alone in the Works. At 9:02 a.m. he arrived at the Main Street set, Firefall top to bottom. Crafty was serving churros from carry-around trays, so no one really noticed Ike's presence.

"Okay, Eye Clipper," Bill said to him. "See that traffic cone down the way?" He pointed to the start mark at the other end of the street. "On action, you wait a beat, then walk toward us."

"Hmmm," Ike murmured. "Action. Beat. Walk."

"Yep," the director said.

"Watch this." Ike headed down Main. His attitude of confidence was a show, a pantomime. In his mind's eye, he saw only terror,

---

* IKE CLIPPER: "It was that very first mop of the glue in the morning—every morning—that I came to dread. The thought of the primary *slopp* of spirit gum, the feel and the smell, made my flesh crawl. Once that first sponging was over, I took it like a man. No wimp, I!"

of his hearing the call for action, then tripping on his own combat boots and falling on his chin. The prop team helped him into his M2-2 flamethrower, then retreated out of the shot, leaving Ike alone in the middle of the entire world.

Action!

Ike did not trip. He did not fall on his chin.

After three takes, they moved on, able to complete the shot list of Firefall's first day.

Wren was called into the Works after lunch. She came into the H/MU trailer as Ike was being touched up for the afternoon shots. She put her hand on his shoulder, looked at him in the mirror, and said, "Ike," not looking at him, but directly into his eyes via the mirror. "I'm sleeping better because you're here . . ."

Ike found himself dumbfounded as he did-not-trip his way out of the Works and back to the set for more of Firefall's pacing. Wren Lane's touch and her eyes and her fragrance were, er, affecting.

As Wren was prepped, the Unit readied two little kids in an aboveground pool that had been filling up with water all morning. Barry Shaw, the lawn-mower kid, was called in to play Marco Polo and splash around with Neighbor Kids. Shelley and Macaiah were reinstalled on the porch.

When the light was right, Wren walked past the porch, gave another wave. After three takes, Yogi announced a "Picture Wrap for our fabulous Porch Ladies! Let's let them know they are loved!" which caused a round of applause. Wren, the director, and Al wished them well and let them keep their knitting. Props wasn't happy.

At the house with the pool in the yard, Barry Shaw, a little girl, and a younger boy were in the water. Barry had his eyes closed, calling out, "Marco!" The kids called "Polo" and dodged his tags. Wren walked by yelling "Polo!" as well. Seven takes and a few flips of the lens later, the scene was done.

"Al?" Bill called. "Yogi?" The Main Unit was on the move to the Knight House for an exterior beauty shot. "Let's have the VFX unit get Knightshade splashing through this little pool, to and from the first rescue."

"You mean in scene 9XX." Yogi had a brain that knew not only the script pages but the scene numbers. As he was the first AD, he had to.

"Yeah. Keep this a Hot Set."* Bill turned to Al. "Hey, we're going to go faster thanks to Eye Clipper. Let's warm up the Clark's cast, pronto."

"Copy that."

Day 6 wrapped at 7:02, during the twelve-minute "grace" period (no overtime) at the end of the day. The last shot was of Wren and Ike having a face-off in the fantasy moment seen only in the mind of Eve Knight and was important as hell.

DAY 7 (OF 53 SHOOTING DAYS)

The Investigators were in Lone Butte, On Hold, ready to appear on camera anytime, as long as the work wasn't scenes 13 and 14. Nick Czabo (Glasgow) had driven himself up from his stone-made house in Topanga Canyon, where he and his husband had isolated all through the COVID-19 war. Clovalda "Lala" Guerrero (Madrid) was flown in from Albuquerque, leaving her family to fend without her as she made another Bill Johnson movie—this time, one the kids would enjoy. As dictated by her history with Dynamo, Cassandra Del-Hora (London), was flown in from her house in Nyack and put up at an available townhouse in Franzel Meadows.

With only seventy-two hours of notice, Hang To landed at the Sacramento Metro Airport and found his PONY car at the curb, "To" flashing on the dash. He hadn't had breakfast and was starving, so the driver, Ynez *something-something,* took him along the Old 99 route to a food stand for a mega-cheeseburger and a mug of good old-fashioned root beer. The movie company was not expecting him to report until 3:00 p.m. Ynez would deliver Hang directly to the set, in front of the courthouse in Lone Butte on the dot.

"Everyone is excited for you to arrive," Ynez told him.

"Yeah?" Hang had to speak loudly as he was so far in the back of the PONY car. "Yesterday I was writing jokes with my out-of-work pals and today I'm meeting Wren Lane to be in an *Agents of Change* movie. Can I shout a question to you, lady?"

---

* Hot Set—a set still in use, to be filmed later. Not to be touched, altered, or changed in any way. Even the water would remain in the pool.

"Ynez. Sure."

"How the fuck did this happen to me?" Hang To was only twenty years old. Before COVID-19, he was one of the funnier guys on Open Mic Night and did fifty-dollar gigs in Laugh Land and the Brew Ha-Ha, not using his given name of Henry, but going unique and Vietnamese. Now, *Hang* To was in a movie and every one of his friends asked him: *How the fuck did this happen to you?*

At 3:00 p.m. Hang was in the Video Village tent in front of the courthouse, talking with Al Mac-Teer, who introduced him to Bill Johnson. It was hot as blazes.

"Glad to have you," the director said. "See that Marine over there?" Hang saw the character of Firefall, sitting in a shaded chair with a fan blowing on him because the guy was in a ton of costume and makeup. "He was you but now you're who he was. Things work out, don't they?"

Al then escorted Hang to the Production Office, where a steady stream of people came to ask him questions and tell him what to do. Hours later he was sitting alone in a motel room out by the highway.

Hang took his personal phone out of his pocket, opened the BiO app to his My Saga page, and hit the NOW button.* The selfie camera started recording.

"Hey, Facebook resisters. Hang To again. Here's what's happening now. I got this damn fine dish of authentic south-of-the-border Chal-u-pita from a fast-food place that is freeway close (he gave the folks a view of the mishmash of Mexican-inspired food) and am enjoying what I can of it in this lifelike setting just off the interstate not far from a town called Lone Butte. Ever hear of it? Me neither until a few days ago . . . Remember how I told you something was *up* for the Good Hang? Didn't dare spill the four-one-one without putting a hex on what is now only *the greatest moment of my life,* second only to this Chal-u-pita . . ." He took a bite. "So good. I like the way it tastes in my mouth . . . Here's why I'm here, Dogs. I'm in a movie! Hell-a, yeah! Gonna be in the next *Agents of Change* picture. Gonna mix it up with them Ultras! Gonna rub shoulders

---

* Hang had been assigned a production iPhone as well. He was to always carry both.

with Wren Lane. Who? Her? You kidding me, Hang To? No! Oh yeah. It's happening, homies! That is what is happening . . . now!"

Hang didn't bother to review what he had recorded. He pressed POST and the video was sent to anyone on the BiO app who chose to see it. The consequence of this act would prove terrible. Just terrible.

The company wrapped at 7:00 p.m. on the dot.

Day 8 (of 53 Shooting Days)

If Thursday was not a good day for Tom Windermere and Wally Lank, charged as they were with the safekeeping and calm welfare of Wren Lane, it was a *terrible* day for Hang To.

Hang was not accustomed to being mega-popular on BiO. He had always topped out at a few thousand YEAH! responses to his NOW posts, but his last blast about working with Wren Lane on a movie in Lone Butte gave his social media footprint a major up-size. His one NOW had 374,565 YEAH!s and the news of the movie, the location, and the whereabouts of Wren Lane spread at Warp 9 Speed, faster than Ursa Major through the cosmos. The information was aggregated onto every showbiz, fanboy, and entertainment e-news site in the ether world. Hang To had given the Internet a scoop.

Wren was unaware of all things on social media and was concentrating on her work, trying to be as quiet and preoccupied as Eve herself. Hang was thrilled since such attention was the coin of the realm in his world of stand-up gigs. Tom Windermere wanted to find him and throw him onto the ground.

Wally Lank wanted to have a talk with the funny man. He'd seen, in real time, the exponential growth of the knowledge he had worked to keep top secret. That morning, his Wren Lane Alert was flashing red, the color code for the heavy, heavy volume of the online mentions of his famous sister. Along came the posts, comments, and security threats to his twin.

WL is where? LONE BUTTE? I'm going . . . Gonna drive smack down the middle of Wren Lane! . . . That WHORE will ruin the

AOC! Ursa Major 4ever . . . When will W.Lane answer me??? . . .
Die Bitch! Die Bitch! Die Bitch! . . . Be my Baby Mama Wren . . .

While Tom delivered Wren to Base Camp for the start of her
day, Wally ran through the comments and posts. He used security software that automatically took screen grabs of every online
threat. A database cross-referenced them all with other posts from
other times, assembling a digital trail for every threatening possible
predator. Keeping such a record was standard operating procedure
since the arrest of that one trespasser and the need to build legal
cases against any in the future. What was extra-standard was the
information Tom collected from various other sources.

Thursday morning at 6:44, Wally Lank texted Al Mac-Teer.

WLank@SkyPark: Got time?

AMacT: Call me.

WLank@SkyPark: Private in person.

AMacT: 114 Elm. Coffees on.

Wren's brother was a calm, class act, sure, but a face-to-face
meeting at 7:00 a.m. on the eighth day of shooting had Al steel-
ing herself for a problem that might be hard to solve. What was
Wally—and thus Wren—unhappy about? She hoped it wasn't Ike
Clipper. If Ike was a cause of concern she and her boss were fucked.

"Nice old place," Wally said, coming in through the front door
off the concrete porch. "Those trees must be as old as America."

"A perk of the job is getting first dibs on the better housing," Al
said. "I live mostly in the kitchen. This way."

The old dinette table had matching leatherette chairs in a fake
marble swirl pattern. Al's coffee maker was as big as an industrial
sewing machine. She pulled espresso, added her warm half-and-
half, and got to the point. "What's the scoop?"

"What is the company policy about social media?" Wally seemed
curious.

"None is allowed." No one who works on the picture is to post
about the film, not in any way. No social media—of any kind.
Every Call Sheet has these words in a little box in the top left corner: DO NOT POST ANY SOCIAL MEDIA REGARDING
THE WORK WE DO HERE. Dynamo Nation and the Hawkeye
are rabid about controlling all the news and messaging that comes

out of Lone Butte. No member of the cast or crew has permission to put a selfie up on the web for reasons legal, promotional, insurance-wise, and security driven.

"One of your cast members posted about being here and working with my associate. I mean my sister."

"Who?" Al grabbed up her phone to SEARCH the name Wren Lane and in the time it takes a quark to pass through a steel girder, there Ms. Lane was—all over the goddamn Internet. After a few scrolls of her thumb, Al landed on BiO, on Hang To's NOW video. "This is not good," Al said. "Sip that coffee while I get into this."

"Got any Ovaltine?" Since the script called for Eve Knight to take her coffee with Ovaltine, Wren had started doing the same. Wally blanched at the habit at first. Now he never took his coffee without it.

"No, sorry." Al then called out, "Hey, Ynez?"

Ynez was heard from an upstairs bedroom. "Yeah?"

"Can you get to the motel and bring Hang To back here?"

"How quick?"

"STAT."

"Need any breakfast or such?"

"No. Just Hang To."

"Copy that!"

Ynez came through the kitchen with a cup of coffee already in her hands. "Oh! Good morning, Mr. Lank." She left out the back porch with a slam of its screen door.

"'Just Hang To'?" Wally said. "Sounds like a murder conviction."

"It may be. This is one major cock-up. How is Wren taking it?"

"She doesn't know, and if we handle this, she'll be serene." Al kept texting.

AMacT: Mr. To? You awake?

TO2TO: Yes but no.

AMacT: I'd like to invite you to a chat over coffee pronto.

TO2TO: ? & ?

AMacT: My place. Ynez will pick you up as soon as you are ready.

TO2TO: !

Ynez delivered Hang to the back porch of 114 Elm Street with alacrity and a *slam*.

Al greeted him with "There's our man from Lima." Then she sat him down in her kitchen with a coffee, an introduction to Wally Lank, and a question. "You haven't seen a Call Sheet yet, have you?"

"Should I have seen a Call Sheet?" Hang yawned. The only reason he was up so early was that Cassandra Del-Hora had ordered the Investigators to meet at her place to start memorizing the dialogue for the nine pages of scenes 13 and 14.

"I printed one out for you," Al said, putting the recent Call Sheet in front of him and his coffee. "Here's today's. Let's walk through it together, okay?"

"Okay," Hang said with a sip of the strongest coffee he'd ever had.

"Starting from the back . . ." Al flipped the papers over—three stapled pages, printed on both sides to make six in all. "These two pages are boilerplate safety warnings about our fire FX. Insurance stuff . . . These pages have all the crew names and department heads, everyone working in the Unit. Here's a ton of information no one ever reads . . . Now, this front page has, at the bottom, the advance schedule for tomorrow—all the work we must be ready for . . . Working up the page we see the number of meals we need, the Call Times, and here . . . The cast and when they are due for the set. Look, there's you! Number 9 on the Call Sheet, officially ON HOLD. You have the day off."

"I wish. I'm rehearsing with Cassandra, Nick, and Lala," Hang said, adding so much sugar to his coffee Wally wondered if the kid was a former heroin addict.

"Here's the scenes we are shooting today . . . Here's the date . . . Day 8 out of 53 . . . The time of sunrise and when the sun sets. Pretty straightforward, no?"

"Ms. Mac-Teer," Hang said, setting down his coffee. "I know what a Call Sheet is. I got my SAG card as a Vietcong soldier in that miniseries about 1968."[*]

---

[*] *1968*, streamed on EnterWorks. Don't bother looking for Hang To. You never see his face. He yelled obscenities from a tree line.

"You were in that?" Wally Lank watched mostly nonfiction entertainment. "That was well done."

Al continued, "So, you're familiar with the words in this little box in the upper-left-hand corner of our Call Sheet." She pointed:

DO NOT POST
ANY SOCIAL MEDIA
REGARDING THE WORK
WE DO HERE.

"See?" Al asked of Hang.

"I do." Hang could read. Granted, he'd not yet seen a Call Sheet for *K:TLOF*, as he was not working until . . . OH, SHIT! "I put up a NOW on my BiO page!" Hang had *crowed* over the huge traffic the post had generated. All his friends were congratulating him and his manager was sure his newfound Internet presence would get him gigs.

"Yes, you did," said Wally. "Please take that down."

"Pronto," Al added. *"Stat."*

Hang fumbled for his personal phone to make that happen. "Am I fired for not knowing I wasn't supposed to post on BiO?"

Al explained, "I think your managers must have known, but I didn't confirm. My bad. I will read them the riot act later this morning."

Hang thumbed through the process to delete the NOW. "Is it some legal thing?"

Al looked to Wally, to let him explain.

"Let's understand this," Wally said in a calm, friendly, and *chilling* tone. "We don't want fans showing up in Lone Butte who only pretend to be fans. It's one thing to take pictures of the trucks and the city limit signs and maybe linger at the motel and try to get a selfie with the guy playing Lima, but honestly, the less people know about our secrets, the better. You cool with that?"

"I am now," Hang said. This Wally Lank fellow was either slimy as hell or as suave as an assassin. "Who are you, by the way? And why are you talking with me?"

"I've been an associate of Wren Lane since conception."

Because he kept a database of Threat Assessments—currently, there were twelve TAs—Tom Windermere brought in a team of ex-cops who had second careers in the security industry. He worked with Al to establish a perimeter around the locations in Lone Butte and made sure the crew ID badges and the Transpo dashboard cards were registered and up to date. He would be changing out the cars used for Wren every other day so that no one would recognize her current mode of travel. There would be a plainclothes guard at the Base Camp and on the set, an ex-cop who would keep both an eye on the comings and goings as well as enough distance to not be a distraction. He had Laurel go to the dog shelter and pick out two canines for adoption and arranged a trainer to make sure the animals were well behaved but barked at strangers. The simple fact had always been that barking dogs scared the shit out of most predators.

All this added security costs to Dynamo of close to a million bucks over the course of the shoot. When Meghan Bachmann-Seritas—the MBS of Dynamo Business Affairs—complained to Al that these costs were already part of the signed-off budget, Al informed her of the opposite and, well, tough titties, as the men used to say about such details.

Day 9 (of 53 Shooting Days)

Friday was as smooth a workday as a unit could ask for. Wren and Ike shot EXT. DAY* in Downtown Lone Butte/Iron Bluff under Bill's Main Unit, then had isolated shots with the Second Unit and the SPFX gang. The Investigators were called in for a Drive-Up to Clark's.

With only slight changes to the camera, the Investigators ran right out again, piled back into the SUV, and roared away for the end of scene 78.

Friday also saw the appearance of Clancy O'Finley as OLD MAN CLARK. Some on the crew saw his name on the Call Sheet

---

* EXTERIOR SHOT. DAYTIME in script parlance.

and expected a ginger-haired Irishman. That was not Clancy. Bill remembered him from his role as Precinct Sergeant Adams in *Rush and Roll*, a good cop show from decades ago. When he came up as a submission for Old Man Clark, Bill was surprised Clancy was still alive.

"I need Clark to have a face that equals his past," Bill said when he gave him the job. "I need the audience to ask themselves, *What is this man doing in Iron Bluff?*"

"There a specific answer to that question?" Clancy said.

"Whatever you provide," Bill told him. Clancy decided then and there that he liked Bill Johnson a hell of a lot.

Friday, Clancy's first day on the picture, required two lines.

1A CLARK'S DRUGS AND COFFEE SHOP—WINDOW.

OLD MAN CLARK . . .

Watching from his drugstore window. He's seen
this happen to this beautiful young woman
before.

              OLD MAN CLARK
        (a whisper)
    What is it, girl? . . . What trouble
    is chasing you?

And:

3 THE DUST DEVIL

Growing in size and speed—and color . . .

It's no longer a funnel of dirt, but of . . .
smoke.

              OLD MAN CLARK
        (seeing)
    What . . . the . . . hell on earth?

Three setups in thirty-three minutes.

The final wrap of the week was called at 6:58 p.m.

"Thank you all for a dynamic five days," Yogi broadcast over the radio. "Enjoy the weekend and remember that you are loved."

THE PLAYERS

Cassandra Del-Hora has played Ms. London in each installment of the Ultra/*Agents of Change*. The fans expect her appearance, in the films and at Comic-Con. The most screen time she shared with the Ultras had been in *AOC2: Renaissance;* since that chapter, she's worked just weeks as Lieutenant Colonel London USMC (now retired). For *K:TLOF,* Ms. London was called back in to run her half of the show.

She'd had conversations with Bill Johnson, expecting him to be under constant pressure from Dynamo to deliver what Dynamo wanted according to the Dynamo master plan, and to not fuck up Dynamo's billion-dollar franchise. And yet Bill Johnson was a calm fishing trip with Grandpa beside a quiet stream.

"What do you think?" Bill had asked her over a Zoom. She was in her little house on the Hudson. He was somewhere in Texas or Arizona on a golf course.

"Mr. Johnson," she said. "No one in the history of these movies has said anything to me other than to hit my mark and speak faster."

"I could tell." Bill had seen all the *AOC*/Ultra movies. "And make it 'Bill.'"

Cassandra went on. "You've written London the most interesting she has ever been. Why is she no longer in the Marines? Why the whole now-a-civilian scenario?"

Bill said, "I've seen the military uniform thing too much and convinced Dynamo that a between-movies change would open creative possibilities in later stories. You don't like it?"

"On the contrary," Cassandra said. "I get to wear something other than dress blues and camo. Can I ask you an honest question?"

"Only if you can take the honest answer."

"Was there any talk of aging me out and recasting younger?"

"An underling at the studio said something about London's days of being a MILF were numbered. But the Executive Chorus views you, Ms. Del-Hora, as the embodiment of Ultra continuity. Can't say the same for the guy who plays Sea Lion. You know what to do in our picture. I'll stay out of your way as long as you're on time, know the text, and kick some ass when we're rolling. I'll ask that you don't get pissed off for being Rain Cover* in the middle of summer."

Cassandra was Number 3 on the Call Sheet—the highest number in her history. London was a *huge* factor in *K:TLOF*. She *was* going to kick some ass.

★　★　★

CASSANDRA DEL-HORA (Agent London): "What do I do on weekends? When I'm working? Sleep in. Take a walk. Recover from the week—just like you. But not this weekend. Have you seen scenes thirteen and fourteen? Nine pages of dialogue. And all that computer data on screens. Nick, Lala, and Hank, I mean Hang, are coming to my place, and we are going to learn that scene.

"People ask, *How do you remember all those lines?* By learning them. Over hours and hours, with help from each other, by repeating the scenes again and again if the scene is long—and nine pages is long. If we were to show up on the set the day of shooting without fully knowing the dialogue it would be a disaster. Irresponsible. A one-day scene will take two, a two-day scene will be cut down, and the word will go out: those actors don't learn the text. Of course, when we finally shoot, we'll mix up the beats to fit the dialogue into the scene. That work is to find the truth. But have you seen thirteen and fourteen? As a grande dame of the theater once told me, 'There is no substitution for familiarity with the text, so learn your goddamn lines.'

"The shoot in Atlanta—those scenes with the rest of the AOC—were reunions for us all from the other movies. The way it works is Bill and the studio discuss the needs of this movie and Dynamo

---

* Rain Cover is the interior work that is held ready in case rain makes exteriors impossible to shoot.

protects the overall arc of the Ultra series. Wren came in brand-new, a freshman in class, for the flashbacks among us old hands. She held her own, fit the costume, and claimed her spot. She and I were the only cast who'd read the complete script—the others had only the sides. Dynamo keeps the pages very top secret.

"I've been a professional actor all my adult life, yes. Theater. I did a guest shot on *Rush and Roll* with Clancy O'Finley when I was a kid and he was a legend—not that he would remember. That was a huge break for me, as I was just coming off a run on Broadway in *The Wheel and the Wind*. I'd moved to Los Angeles. I didn't care for California. I'm called in for some superhero movie, next thing I know I'm in a Marine uniform running around the desert in Morocco! I fired that machine gun. Major London becomes Lieutenant Colonel London—one of the mortal Agents of Change. Here she is now, running things, kicking ass. I love London. Lone Butte? It's hot. Dry."

CLANCY O'FINLEY (Old Man Clark): "I confess. I did not remember Cassandra. Not that I recall most of *Rush and Roll*. Cocaine, you see. God gives you some sweetness in life, the devil gives you a sugartooth. All drug-addict stories are the same, at some point. Some low point. Then come the Twelve Steps, if you're blessed.

"What saved me? In a single word? Golf. Don't laugh. I played eighteen holes of golf every day for a hundred and two days—in a row—in a foursome with a former heroin dealer, a twenty-four-year-old alcoholic who had his first drink when he was age nine, and a fireman who did so much blow his nasal passages were like Silly Putty. I was the only actor in the bunch. How I kept working is a mystery of God.

"Cassandra said I was legend? She must mean because of Hamlet—in Philly, at the U.P.L.* That was a hell of a production—sixty people onstage at one point, more than in the audience at first. Then the word went out about this Black Hamlet. Black Hamlet? Bullshit. I played *Hamlet*. Period. Did a Broadway run. Did a lot of

---

* Urban Performance Loft. Now defunct, but a major force in the day.

Shakespeare festivals. Othello? Malvolio. King Henry. I got tired of never owning more than I could fit in my car. Tried my hand in LA. Played pimps and drug dealers. Never a Hamlet. Then came *Rush and Roll*. Then my troubles. Got sober for the last two seasons. Had three years on *I.C.U.* as Dr. Theo. Made a lot of money back. Met my wife. Had two kids. Kept getting this role and that part. Did movies in Romania no one in America saw—maybe on video when there were video stores. Here it is the year 2525 and I'm working with Bill Johnson and Cassandra again. Huh? What? Me? Really?

"One thing I'd like to change, if I could? The name of my character. Old Man Clark. Wish it was Handsome Man Clark.

"What do I do on the weekends? Fore!"

CLOVALDA (Lala) GUERRERO (Agent Madrid): "I live in Albuquerque. I used to work in the school system. I was an administrator, but now I'm a performer. I do commercials and I'm on a billboard for a Jacuzzi company. I'm here as Ms. Madrid because I was in a movie called *Albatross* that Bill cast me in as a local hire. I played the Police Dispatcher. I was there on the night there was almost a fistfight. It was a fistfight. I thought the movie was great. Of course, I was in it. Bill had me in for a week on *A Cellar Full of Sound*—I was the driving instructor who fails the bass player. I don't know why Bill keeps giving me these jobs. I don't even have to audition for him.

"Madrid is in every scene the Investigators have. Cassandra is so forceful and Hang is funny. Nick has this face that seems to be made for listening. Have you noticed that? Then he delivers his lines like he just thought of them. Bill wants me to sound like a police dispatcher who now teaches driver's education. He's so funny.

"Nervous? About being in a movie? No, not really. Bill always tells me to say everything straight out of my shoulders and there's nothing I can do wrong. He won't use anything that doesn't work so I shouldn't worry about what I do. I don't think I've ever had a bad day on a movie set, as long as there are no fistfights.

"Weekends I spend talking to the family on Skype. And rehearsing. Cassandra is a wild woman about scenes thirteen and fourteen."

NICK CZABO (Agent Glasgow): "Glasgow is the first job I've had since COVID locked us down. I was going to be in a miniseries for WinCast but it was postponed for six months, then canceled altogether. I spent the year in the house I share with my husband in Topanga. It's a house made of flagstones and rocks that some nut built in the 1960s—way up the canyon and perfect for us. It's all but fireproof. Floodproof, not so much.

"I started acting in college, getting sidetracked when I learned how to eat fire as I roller-skated. I went to Vegas and worked as an entr'acte in the big production shows. I made AGVA money.[*] Went to New York to study at the Civic Playhouse and got on film in a commercial for Bayer aspirin. I think Bill gave me Glasgow because I'm still carrying around my lockdown weight, and everyone else in the movie is so fit and trim."

HANG TO (Agent Lima): "Should I even be talking to you? I don't want to get yelled at again. I don't need to have Wally Yank look at me with those neck-slitting eyes of his and lecture me in that 'this won't hurt at all' tone of voice. If you have questions for me, clear them with Al Mac-Teer first and submit them to me in writing.

"I don't have time for you anyway. Cassandra has ordered us to her place for more line learning. Have you seen scenes thirteen and fourteen? I'm learning that dialogue as easy as I can memorize the ingredients on a can of Diet Mountain Dew."

ELLIOT GUARNERE (Amos "Pop-Pop" Knight): "Son, I've been an actor longer than you've been on solid food. If you were to get me started telling stories I'd go on so long your ears would fall off. Don't blink and you'd see me in *Star Wars*.

"Oh, I can't say enough about Ms. Lane. She had me in her trailer for tea and conversation and I didn't want to leave. We talked like

[*] American Guild of Variety Artists.

we've been friends for years. I've seen her movies, yes. Her performance in *Periwinkle* reminded me of, oh, who was it? What was her name . . . In that picture . . . Oh, dear. I'll shout it out in a minute or two.

"Ms. Lane asked me about Pop-Pop, who he is and what he has seen in his life. She had so many questions. She didn't talk about her character, but mine. Who does that?

"This is my forty-seventh picture. Of course, I'm counting the ones where I had few lines and worked but a day or two. I've not had a role as important as Pop-Pop since . . . Meryl Streep! In *Sophie's Choice*!"

AEA KAKAR (Nurse Sue): "Mr. Johnson cast me over a Zoom. He'd seen me in *M*A*S*H*Ghanistan*. I played the Woman Who Would Not Say What Happened. Said my face asked more questions than any speech or dialogue. I've played many nurses. I must look like the type. I flew up on the same plane with Elliot Guarnere from Los Angeles and we sat next to each other. We hadn't met, but when we discovered we were both working on this movie? We were talking a mile a minute. I helped him get to the lavatory, and the flight attendant assumed I was his traveling nurse. Yeah, I'm the type."

DAYS 10–14 (OF 53 SHOOTING DAYS)

The VFX unit worked all over Lone Butte starting at the Old Trestle Bridge with the Drone Cam for hovering, swooping shots that would include a CGI Knightshade—running, swinging, and leaping at her superspeed. The C Camera was getting inserts and setups independent from the Main Unit but golf cart close so that Bill could give his okay to the composition, including Eve splashing in that Hot Set wading pool from the game of Marco Polo. Barry Shaw was on the Call Sheet, along with Clancy O'Finley and many TOWNSPEOPLE to collect the nuts and bolts of the picture's second week.

Splits had the Main Unit working half the day in light—there were two sumptuous Golden Hour shots—making SAM work frantically in the narrow window of time. After the meal break, the pavement and stone buildings of Lone Butte cooled from the day's direct exposure to the sun, the evenings edging off into T-shirt cool and baggy shorts pleasant. Wren wore flip-flops between shots. Then came the dark work, scenes 93 and 93XX, the elements of Fight number 2 between Eve/Firefall, the battle in downtown Iron Bluff with SPFX napalm and VFX flames. Small, practical fires were controlled by the Fire Department in their trucks from Chico. Some of the aerial rigging was needed, work that had Wren and Ike hanging like marionettes, laughing like kids.

For the last three hours of Friday night's work, Crafty booked a soft-serve ice-cream truck. Ynez saw to it that the crew who could not step away from their duties were delivered cups and cones of vanilla, chocolate, or swirl. If the crew was asked what was *the* major event of Days 10 to 14, they'd say it was the chemistry between Wren Lane and Ike Clipper, especially in 93A, the moment when Firefall was bareheaded. Eve kicked him in the head, sending his helmet flying, and there he was, hurt and vulnerable. No longer a monster, but a scared kid.

The Unit wrapped at 12:46 a.m. Saturday morning. A few hours later, Ace delivered Ike to Metro Airport to catch the first of many flights home; for a short weekend to pack up Thea and baby Ruby and bring them to Lone Butte at last. You see, there was no way Thea Cloepfer was going to raise their little girl all by herself. No way. Not while Ike was becoming a movie star working shoulder to shoulder with Sergeant Hard-On . . .

Days 15–19 (of 53 Shooting Days)

Monday's work—the Knights on the front porch—was nothing short of a dream. SAM screened in the set with nets and a silk topper for diffusion. Elliot and Aea, together, were like a showbiz couple with decades of nightclub experience under their belts and fast affection for each other. Pop-Pop and Nurse Sue were so fluid a pair that Eve felt like a spare left glove for the first two setups. Not until Elliot complimented her did Wren relax.

"You curl your lines, Ms. Lane. Like Debra Winger." Debra Winger on the movie screen had left Elliot Guarnere a liquid mess. Being compared to Debra Winger (the Bette Davis of her day) made Wren melt with gratitude. The morning had been one of extra care and worry put in by the Good Cooks and Kenny—fine-tuning for the day's close-up work. The shooting day was as smooth as a windless sea. Bill was able to overshoot coverage, a luxury.

Tuesday was just Pop-Pop and Nurse Sue in the backyard, so Wren shot with the Second Unit for the morning, then reported to the Green Screen stage at Westinghouse Light for the first fight elements in the rigging. Wren was disappointed seeing on the Call Sheet that she'd be working without Ike.

At 1:44 that afternoon, Ace had a Sprinter van at Metro Airport for the arrival of Team Cloepfer. Ike, Thea, and baby Ruby came off the plane rattled, exhausted, and plum out of any sense of adventure. They had so many bags and bits of baby gear that the first attempt at fitting it all into the Sprinter was aborted and rethought. Ruby's car seat was not easy to properly belt. The same had been the case on the plane.

And Ruby was not a happy baby, having been in that car seat long enough. The little girl fought, wept, and screamed for most of the ride to the motel. Ace kept a smile on his face the entire route, so very glad his kids were over thirty years old. Thea felt her head about to explode. Ike kept shaking a set of toy keys in front of the complaining infant, sensing the hassles coming his way as a family man/working actor. He looked forward to being called early, being on set all day, or hiking down Webster Road with breaks for burpees.

He'd arranged adjoining rooms at the motel, one with an open door connecting two standard rooms, each with two queen-sized beds. Thea took one look at the living space and shook her throbbing head.

She noticed, "There's no kitchen."

"There's the coffee shop, and a pool," Ike pointed out. Yes, there was. Behind the motel's main building, just a few hundred yards from the trucks roaring north and south along the interstate. Next to it, too, was a playground: a wooden swing set with splintered beams and a plastic tube/slide that had been hot-bleached and discolored by the sun. Biscuits could be baked inside it by convection.

Thea was not happy with the realities of the family lodgings. Ike knew this because his wife had gone *quiet*. When his phone beeped with a text from Yogi—"Moving you to Will Notify for rest of week for VFX at Green Screen. See Call Sheet and welcome back. YAL,"[*] Thea took the news with a narrow-eyed glare. "Notify me, too, would you?" Then she asked another question. "How long is this movie shooting, again?"

★ ★ ★

The next day, Wren, Elliot, and Aea were working at the Knight House. Clancy O'Finley needed to redo his digital scans then meet with Doc Ellis to figure out what stunts he was comfortable with and to match up a look-alike double.

"Old Man Clark does stunts?" Clancy asked. During one of Bill Johnson's many rereads of his own screenplay, the director started a wish list of shots for the action-packed encounter between Eve and Firefall on Main Street at night. Old Man Clark would put out some flames that threatened his shop and take a tumble while doing so. If, that is, Clancy could manage the stunt and not get hurt. "No, I can't," the actor said. His stunt double took a padded fall On the Day, wrenching his shoulder, an injury that would have been Clancy's.

Ike reported to Westinghouse Light after being made up at Base Camp—a glorious 6:00 a.m. Call Time. Later, to get them out of their adjoining rooms at the motel, Ace brought Thea and Ruby to lunch at Base Camp at the Almond Growers Association Building. The newcomers were ushered around by the helpful Cody. The Hill women ate in a nearly empty dining room because the Main Unit had not yet broken for lunch and the Knight House was an eight-minute walk away. Ynez, grabbing an early fruit salad, recognized Thea and Ruby from Ike's iPhotos.

---

[*] You are loved.

"Is that little Ruby?" began her conversation with the Hills. Thea seemed none too pleased, as she thought Irving would be joining them for lunch but was not even in the building.

PONYTEXT From: YNEZ—VIP Family @ PO.

AMacT: ?

PONYTEXT From: YNEZ—Ike's family.

AMacT: ! Bring to set!

PONYTEXT From: YNEZ—Baby?

AMacT: Coming 2 U.

A Teamster dropped Al off—she was alone in the huge van—so she could greet Mrs. Firefall ASAP.

"There's the Girl in the Restroom," she called out. "Hey, Thea!" Remember, Thea had been in *A Cellar Full of Sound*.

Al sat with the VIPs and poked at an ersatz Cobb salad. At Base Camp, Nina happened to tell Wren that Ike's wife and baby were at Catering, and there was no way Number 1 on the Call Sheet was not going to meet Mrs. Number 2, in the flesh. When the crew began trooping in for the meal everyone was surprised that none other than Eve Knight had joined them. Wren always retreated to her trailer at lunch—so she could first meditate, then make herself a protein shake.

"Hello, Thea," the movie star said. "I'm Wren. It's wonderful to have you in town."

"Wren, at last we meet," Thea said. Wren was gorgeous but not nearly as willowy or statuesque as she was made out to be. "You've been awfully good to my husband. Or so he has said."

"Ike tells me you're an actor, too."

"I was an actor before Ike was an actor," Thea informed her. "So, yes."

Wanting to bolster Thea's status on location, Al piped up. "She was the Girl in the Bathroom in *Cellar*."

"Oh," Wren noted. She sat with them. While the chatter and hum of the meal filled the dining hall, the women talked and poked at salads. Ynez tracked down some dry Cheerios for the baby to finger to her lips, one at a time.

"Where are you guys living?" Wren asked. Al wanted to know as well, assuming Ike had gone to Housing on his own to find a place big enough for his brood.

"The motel," Thea said.

"What!?" Al could be heard over the din of the crew eating. Some folks looked over.

"We have adjoining rooms. A restaurant and snacks in the lobby. Mexican food and pizza and such across the parking lot. And a pool. I've seen it."

"The motel?" Wren raised a perfectly shaped eyebrow. "You can't live in a motel."

"I don't disagree."

Al said, "I'll get into this with Housing."

"We don't want to cause anyone a problem," Thea said, happy to be making a problem. The motel was not a dump, but she wanted a place with windows that she could open.

"Not a problem at all," Al said, standing up from the table. "But is Ike such a cluck that he doesn't let the production arrange better accommodations?"

"*Cluck* is not the word I'd use," Thea said.

Al saw index cards in her head.

One: Ike Clipper's face and a huge question mark. Why had he not asked the production for help taking care of his family?

Two: A rental car with a baby seat strapped into the back, which the production would cover. No more Teamster pickups for baby Ruby.

Three: A house. Better lodging for the Firefall family.

Four: A kitchen pantry stuffed with food. Ynez would do a supply run of groceries once a place was found.

Five: A Call Sheet with Thea Hill in the role of AS CAST so the woman would have a part in the movie, something to look forward to other than her husband coming home from a day spent with Wren Lane.

Ynez saw a card in her head as well: an image of her cousin Lupe holding little Ruby in her arms. Thea was going to need a babysitter.

Wren had an image floating around in her mind, of the empty guesthouses on her compound, specifically the big one by the pond.

Back at work at the Knight House, Wren found Al sitting in Video Village, talking on her iPhone with Housing.

"There has to be some joint available in town," Al was saying.

The townhouse in Franzel Meadows, once home to OKB, was where Cassandra Del-Hora was staying. Too bad, as that place would have been a giant leap up for the Clippers. "We have the technology and manpower to make a place babyproofed. Okay. Okay. But this is top of the list, okay? Let's fix, pronto. Call me."

"Hey, Al," Wren said. "I have an idea."

"I love ideas."

"The living situation with Ike? He needs a place, right?"

"Him? No. His wife and child, yes. Ike would be happy in a war surplus tent down by the river."

"Well, I've got an extra guesthouse."

"I know."

"Tom and Laurel are in the cozy one, Wally is in the yurt. The vacant one has three bedrooms and a hot tub."

"And it's a *guesthouse*?"

"I know. Embarrassing."

"I don't think it's a good idea for them to be living, essentially, with you. Close proximity could bring . . . discomfort."

"I was thinking you live in it."

"Me?"

"Yes. All you and I do is work every day. We wouldn't ever see each other unless we wanted to. You'd come and go and have your own kitchen. Let Ike and, you know, his great wife and adorable baby have your place. You stay with me and the production would save a few bucks, no?"

"You are as kind as you are smart, lady," Al said. "But I've got Ynez sleeping over on the weeknights so she doesn't have to drive back to Sacto. Or sleep in her car, which she did a few times."

"She could use one of the bedrooms."

"You'd allow such a thing?"

"Why not? We all work hard and none of us smoke."

"Lemme ponder this," Al said. Her digs at 114 Elm Street were in walking distance to the PO, pleasant enough, and tricked out with all the gear a movie producer needed on location. Al did most of her living in the kitchen. As both lodgings were already in the budget, the extra cost of a Clipper house would be saved. "I can walk to the set from 114. Which I like."

"Tom gets me to Base Camp in twenty minutes."

"That's a commute of half a podcast. I could use the distraction. But promise me that anytime you don't want my company, you say so."

"I won't even see your car. The guesthouse is over by the pond."

"Lemme think this through," Al said. "You go and act now."

That night, Al called Tom Windermere at the compound to make sure the move was kosher with Team Lane, then talked with Wren in the affirmative. Wren was happy to have someone other than her posse living inside the berm, within strolling distance. Having done a good deed, the actor took her script and iPad out to the pickleball courts to prepare for Friday's filming of scene 34. Thirty-four was unlike any other in the movie, and key to the heartfelt connection of Eve to her Pop-Pop, a heart-to-heart talk they share after she comes out of her visions of dread. She used the *ACT-1* app that robotically read out her lines and cues, then once she had her lines down, just the cues.

★ ★ ★

SAM had the Knight House tented in black canvas, the place looked to be termite controlled by a goth pesticide company—so the company could shoot the interior night scenes during daylight hours. A huge HVAC unit pumped cold air through monster-sized yellow tubes, so effectively that the on-set crew needed hoodies. Elliot and Aea wore thick cotton robes during setups. The Digital Image Technician, Sepp, had a space heater in his little black tent—a tent within a tent.

There were gaps in the black tenting that caused SAM lighting problems. Bill's shot list grew exponentially when blocking the scene—three dolly moves and coverage. Had the Knight House been a set on a sound stage, the walls would have been wild—removable for a camera crane. Impossible in a real house, a practical set.

And Elliot had trouble remembering the lines, an embarrassment for such a grand old pro.

"We can put the dialogue on cards for you," Bill offered. "Brando and you can have that in common."

"I'm no Brando," Elliot whispered. "You'll see me reading them."

To help the old veteran save face and be his best, Bill shot calmly, slowly. If Elliot needed a line, Frances quietly fed it to him, he'd pause, then deliver the words in his own cadence. Wren showed grace and patience during the coverage, off camera, sitting right next to the lens for Elliot's singles and close-ups. The man was exhausted by the final hours of the week, a fatigue he attributed to the quality of the work Bill was getting out of him and, "Matching you, Wren, dear."

The movie was now behind schedule. Scene 67—INT. NIGHT—AMOS'S BEDROOM was pushed to Monday. To guarantee speed and comfort three teleprompter screens would be placed in easy eyelines for Elliot to read his dialogue—a two-page scene that was almost all Amos. Sixty-seven could not be rushed. Nor given up on. Sixty-seven explained the whole movie.

Friday, Ynez moved Al out of 114 Elm and into the Pond House on Wren's acreage, putting her boss in the big bedroom while she took the smaller with two twin beds. She stocked the Pond House pantry with what she knew her boss needed to live, then did the same for the Cloepfers' kitchen; the many needs of a family of two-and-a-baby. Al had Transpo get the Cloepfers a rental SUV and had it parked in the gravel driveway out back, by the plum trees. Thea and Ruby were then moved in by Ace and Ynez. There would be no rumbling from the interstate underscoring their day, no more breakfast in the lobby, no more half acres of queen-sized beds. All this while Ike was at Westinghouse Light, shooting fight elements, but without Wren.

The week ended at 10:17 p.m., costing the production hours of Golden Time and a half. Ynez arranged a delivery of two dozen Big Stork pizzas and Crafty set out coolers full of soft drinks and flavored waters. In the backyard of the Knight House, an impromptu block party was held with good wine in the H/MU trailer and cold beers in most of the trucks. Wren and Elliot sat, each splurging with a single slice of pizza to celebrate a damn fine week.

"Dear girl, you are a grand artist and a true professional," Elliot said quietly to Wren. "You are a gift to all these people on this movie."

"Elliot," Wren said, a bit emotional. "Thank you."

"Look at them all." Elliot waved his plain cheese at the assembled Unit. "I've worked with some stars who prompt the crew to escape the set the moment the camera is cut."

Wren looked at the gang, eating and drinking and laughing.

"Because of our enchanted leading lady, they linger and enjoy . . ."

Yogi thanked the crew for another excellent week of shooting and told everyone he loved them loads.

A WEEKEND

Compared to that motel, 114 Elm Street was 114 Eden Avenue. There were fruit trees—plums that could be picked by hand and eaten when they were made ripe in the summer sun. The house had central AC but Thea preferred the air drifting in through the screens, through the open doors and windows, cooled by the shade trees out front, carried through the house and out the back porch door. The house was old but not creepy at all, with the creaks of the floorboards marking the family footsteps like cracker crumbs signaling anyone awake, coming or going. The only demerit of the old house was the back porch screen door with its tendency to slam shut.

Very early Sunday morning Ynez drove back to her hometown to pick up her cousin Lupe and her nephew, Francisco, then returned to Lone Butte. She bought an inflatable wading pool shaped like a big turtle, which took Ike some time blowing up with his lungs as Thea and Lupe talked over coffee. Later, one of the production accountants who had a fifteen-month-old boy—Karina Druzemann, the local hire—came by as well to make a kids' fun day. With less than an inch of water, the three little ones were wildly excited, making noise and smacking the safe and shallow pool with splashing hands. They *loved* having a trickle of water poured on their heads from a plastic pitcher, the three of them laughing to the point of unstoppable belly-giggles, which made the adults all do the same.

With the women and kids around, Thea felt like her time in Lone Butte now had the promise of pleasantness. With four grown women there to lifeguard, Ike donned his combat boots.

"Are you going somewhere?" Thea asked.

"Gonna hike around Lone Butte."

"Why?"

"You don't need me here."

"That is not an answer to my question, though," Thea said. "Is it?"

It wasn't. "I mean, you've got help with the kids. I thought I'd go meditate on the work ahead. And get in a workout."

Thea cocked her head. "Rather than spend an afternoon with your family? Rather than watch your daughter play with pals?"

"I won't be gone long."

"No," Thea said, walking away. "But you'll be gone."

The town was all but abandoned, so, like his character, Ike walked down the middle of the streets, pausing to drop and burpee every quarter mile. He crossed the Old Trestle Bridge to the other side of the Iron Bend River to explore the old park on the Little Iron Bend, circumnavigated the signs marking the town limits, not returning to 114 Elm Street until after three in the afternoon. Did he spend all that time meditating on the week's coming work? Sure.

"Four hours?" Thea asked him when he returned. Everyone had gone by then and Ruby was napping.

"The scene is a beast. I come for the old man and it's the end of the whole movie really. I want to be prepared."

Thea had read the screenplay. She knew the work her husband was preparing for—scenes 96, 97, and 98. He had eleven words of dialogue. Of course, he'd also be on his feet all day—standing next to Wren Lane. For three scenes. For eleven words of dialogue. Exhausting.

"Ynez's cousin is going to work for us," Thea told her husband.

"Doing what?"

"Helping with the baby. From eight to four. Some weekends. Four hundred a week."

What could Ike say to all that? "Okay."

DAYS 20 AND 21 (OF 53 SHOOTING DAYS)

Ike was called into the Works very early to spend the day in the wires at Westinghouse Light. He was in H/MU when Wren came in.

"You just might have saved my marriage," Ike told her. "Our move outta the motel is huge."

"I'm *so* glad," Wren said of her counseling-by-lodgings. "Elliot!"

Her Pop-Pop had stepped into the trailer. "My Little Pea," he said in greeting. "And you are the redoubtable Ike. Elliot." The two men had not met, somehow. "I understand there is a fine fellow somewhere inside all that gruesome body-work."

"So nice to meet you," Ike said.

"So nice to *work* with you," Elliot corrected the young man. "If you can call what we do work of any kind."

Ike's becoming of Firefall continued as Wren and Mr. Guarnere were made up and invited to the set. The Knight House was still tented, cooled, rigged, and ready for Elliot, Wren, and Aea to shoot 67. Four teleprompter screens were stationed around Amos's Bedroom with the operator set up behind Sepp's DIT tent.

"I'm not going to need them!" Elliot crowed, pointing to the prompters. He'd been running the scene since mid-Saturday and the words were now locked in his noggin. He and Wren had spent a lovely Sunday afternoon at her house running the lines and talking about Elliot's days in regional theater, before he settled in Los Angeles and began his other acting career. "The Picture Business," he called it. He would not gossip with Wren about the lovers he'd known until Wren pried a name out of him that made her cry out, "Shut the front door!"

"Not such a conquest," Elliot confessed. The woman, a VERY FAMOUS ACTRESS, was "anybody's easy company."

Of the teleprompters, Bill said, "Nothing wrong with the insurance of having them." The director knew the day was going to be a long one with coverage and angles, overs and inserts that would eat up the wherewithal of Elliot Guarnere. The man had a ton of dialogue in 67—as Pop-Pop finally shares with his granddaughter the secret history of his past—his time in the war—his old photographs—his connection to Firefall . . .

By the third setup Elliot was using the prompters as guides, surprising himself that he could. Al was relieved that he'd started using the monitors, that his eyes would land on the screens with an effortless glance to read the supersize print. "Here I thought it would be a crutch," he said to his boss, his costars, and the teleprompter operator. "But I'm feeling a luxury!" The old fellow laughed, swinging his legs out of the bed to wrap himself in a robe against the air-conditioning and warm up with a cup of tea.

His energy faded over the course of the day. Ynez offered to bring his lunch to the set so he could eat out of the heat. Elliot stayed in the bed, barely touching a cup of soup. Propped up for a snooze, he blamed the pillows for giving him a crick in his neck and a headache. The good news, for the veteran actor, was that he'd be off camera for the rest of the day. He could read the words from his script pages as dictation, giving Bill and Wren plenty of time to wrestle with the Eve side of the scene.

There are some that say the work Wren did simply *listening* to her Pop-Pop as he describes those photos is the best she has done in all her career.

★　★　★

Tuesday was another day in the bedroom of Amos Knight. Ike was to return to Westinghouse Light for the afternoon. As research for Firefall, he'd spent the night in a canvas tent in the backyard of 114 Elm, as Marines would do on bivouac.

"I thought Firefall never sleeps," Thea said. "But you do? In a tent?"

"Before he disappeared, Falls was a Marine like every other." Sleeping in a tent to get into character sounded like a thing other actors would do as prep. "Spending the night in a tent is kind of a prep."

And a way to leave me with the baby, Thea said to herself.

First thing in the morning, Thea deposited Ruby through the flaps of Ike's tent, with a bottle, Kleen Wipes to clean her messy bottom, and a change of her diaper. Ike was barely awake.

"Could you bring me a coffee?" he asked his wife, who was heading back through the screened porch into the house.

"The Marines made their own," she called back, letting the door slam behind her.

Ike gave Ruby her bottle and tried to sit up in the tent with his daughter in his lap. His back ached from sleeping on hard ground.

On the set of the Knight House, just before lunch, with the work in scene 98 due up after the break, Elliot admitted to Yogi that he had a headache "about as bad as a headache could be."

Those were the man's last words.

THE HOLD

There was music: a soft, Enya-like strain echoing like waves at sea, inducing a gratifying sense of calm . . .

There was a photo montage.

Still photographs from a lifetime—more than seventy years . . .

ELLIOT GUARNERE as a baby, held in the arms of his mother on what must have been his day of christening . . .

Then, a toddler, standing at a coffee table with four grown-ups—each one either smoking or drinking, all smiling—as Elliot looks up at the camera lens with such a confused expression it could be mistaken for a smile . . .

At the age of five, he pushes a toy wheelbarrow in a backyard . . .

His third-grade class picture shows him standing with his classmates on a riser. He is grinning like a bobcat . . .

He was on the high-school track team, the starting runner in the mile relay, passing the baton. So, he was an athlete . . .

. . . and an actor, of course. On the stage, his eye makeup is too heavy, his hand gestures too broad in Noël Coward's *Blithe Spirit*. Anyone who saw either of the two performances (Friday or Saturday night in the spring of 1964) would tell you, the best performance on that stage was that of Elliot Guarnere . . .

There are no photos in this montage of Elliot's college years because he could not afford to go to college . . .

But there he is, in some pocket-sized production of *As You Like It*. His eye makeup is no longer heavy, his gestures now subtle.

His hippie wedding had so many flowers and guitars, the photo looks like it was staged. His new bride is gowned and is as glowing as Mother Nature . . .

The roles he played over all his career fade in and away, one after another . . .

The photos of his stage career were taken from the seats. They don't look like real life, but are moments of captured performance, seen from a distance . . .

His on-camera work, his Reel Life, are shown with crystal clarity . . .

Oh, look! He was in a McDonald's commercial!

And in the Cantina in *Star Wars*!

He was in an episode of *M*A*S*H*!

He had scenes, then, in so many TV shows . . .

And movies . . .

And he went back to the stage. A national tour of an adaptation of—is that *Sweeney Todd*?

NBC's *Mid-Town Follies* for six years as Officer Vance.

His house in the Valley . . . His move to the Palos Verdes bluffs . . . his kids . . . his second wife . . .

Ah, gray haired now, as that neighbor on that long-running sit-com *Wanna Bet?* He'd be in only one scene in most episodes, but those seasons added up.

His third wife was the love of his life—she was a dozen years younger and had kids of her own, but love is love, eh?

Look! They traveled the world—the Tower of Big Ben, the pyramids of Tenochtitlán, at sea in one of the seven, at Masada, in Sydney Harbor . . .

Finally—Elliot as we knew him. On set as Amos Knight, between takes, a cup of tea and a smile for the Unit photographer . . .

★ ★ ★

Everyone was a mess.

The older members of the crew—those in hailing distance of their sixth and seventh decades—were shaken with a sense of their own mortality. The Good Cooks and Kenny Sheprock had gathered for a few bottles of wine and a long list of all those who had been in their trailers and chairs, folks no longer "working," as they put it. The three seasoned veterans mused that this movie might be, could be, should be, their final commute along Fountain.

Ike and Thea had yet to experience the sudden, natural death of a friend or colleague—like Elliot. They talked long into that Tuesday night. They made love.

Wren wept in moments of unbound sorrow. She had come to see Elliot as her true grandfather, a binding that happens when artists work so closely, so intimately, in scenes of dialogue as cryptic yet loaded as those between Eve and Amos Knight. She and Wally drank and talked of their parents—long gone and as mercurial in death as they had been at home—and wondered what either of them would have found in life without their molecular bonding as twins. Wren wished she had a lover again—a man to be there in her shadowed grief over the loss of kind-eyed Elliot. She thought to call Ike for a talk—they were all a part of the cast, right? But she didn't pick up her phone. Instead, she and Heather took to the sky in the Cirrus to escape the sad hang-fire of Lone Butte.

After the Thursday memorial—the entire Unit had filled the Almond Growers Ballroom*—Ynez went home to her family for as many days as possible. Her father had taken a fall on one of his jobsites, dislocating his shoulder yet not letting the pain create complaint. Once again, Ynez slept in her childhood bed, aided her mother in her duties to look after the rest of the family—for every large meal, every babysitting need, every cousin, and every migrant passing through. She wondered if the movie could go on after something so horribly sad. She would miss being in the movie unit so very, very much.

Al Mac-Teer walked and walked and walked around the compound she now shared with Wren Lane and Co. Yes, she had her iPhone with her at the ready, since the making of the movie had to continue. The shock and chaos of that Tuesday—when poor Elliot sat in his bed on the set and quietly passed—through all the emergency machinations and protocols with the EMTs and com-

---

* A few of the Guarnere family attended—some of whom had not spoken with one another for years.

panywide instructions, to that moment when, finally, the conversation had to turn from "What a terrible thing!" to "What do we do now?" had Al walking, alone with her thoughts for a meditation on the meaning of living, the mourning of a dear, sweet man. Al traversed the compound again and again—the landing strip, the ball field, the stocked pond, the mowed meadows, the perimeter fence, the berm, the pickleball courts. For a day, she did so silently. Then she began the calls a producer of a motion picture must make.

On Saturday, Al spoke with Wally in the main house's cucina-like kitchen to answer the big question of what the next week would be like and how the film would be completed and, well, what came next.

Dr. Pat had flown in for the memorial, was holding the hand of her man, her filmmaker, knowing full well that Bill was affected by the shocking loss, the death of an actor he'd cast in what would forever be the man's last role. Bill was not a young man, of course, so there was no way he'd not thought *that might have been me.* While Pat prepared breakfast and set the table with flowers, Bill left the house with his old nine iron, walking around the long block, circling the neighborhood again and again, pondering not only his mortality, but also how to keep his movie on track.

He and Al talked on his seventh trip around the sidewalk.

★   ★   ★

"Hey . . ." Wren had seen the caller ID. She'd had but a few talks on the phone since arriving home. Execs from the Hawkeye and Dynamo had put in calls that she let go to voice mail. Micheline Ong had spent an hour with her, soothing and listening, and Kenny called from Lone Butte to "check on my girl." Bless them all. Now, Al.

"Oh, Wren." Al sighed. "I'm so sad. How you doin'?"

"Present, is all. Is this the call to determine when we start up again?"

"When you're ready."

Wren felt herself tear up again. "How are we supposed to keep shooting without Elliot? Are we going back into the set to look at the bed he died in and pretend he's there?"

"Nope," Al said. "We will not do that. We'll move out of that house, build a double at Westinghouse Light, and save that last scene to shoot on the last day. No one is going back to that location but to wrap it."

"Thank God. What do we do about . . . ?" Wren had to pause again.

"About replacing a man who cannot be replaced?" Al asked. "For a scene that sends his character off to heaven, for the ending of the whole damn movie?"

"Yes . . ."

"We'll figure that out." Al let out a breath, as one does when one has to *get on with things.* "Whenever you feel comfortable coming back."

"Is it up to me? Not, like, Bill or the Dynamo Hawks? They going to sue me for being too fucking sad to go back ASAP and act like Elliot didn't die?"

"No. You tell me when you want to come back and then you'll come back."

Wren, now, let out a breath, as one does when one dictates unalterable terms. "Next week."

"See you then."

Days 22–26 (of 53 Shooting Days/Post 3-Day Hold)

Dr. Pat Johnson steadfastly refused to be the earthy blond National Park Ranger despite Bill's sincere request. She'd only have to work a *Monday.*

"There is some earthy blond actor who needs a job. I don't," she said, in the bed of their lodgings in Lone Butte, after the memorial for Elliot. "A talented professional will make much more sense of your written dialogue than I ever could."

"The Ranger is explaining geology, Doctor," Bill protested. "You're a geologist. The dialogue would be a bunt for you."

"Your dialogue is a first-year student's gobbledygook. Sorry, Cowboy."

"Damn." Bill gave up. "I wanted to see you in that park ranger uniform . . ."*

Hang To had kept his inner-comic-self clamped shut since the tragedy, as no one is more cynically funny than a professional comedian. His Vietnamese heritage had him dress in clothes with little color and light incense for the service held for Mr. Guarnere. Laughter is prohibited at Vietnamese funerals. Even little babies weep as if they know the weight of sorrow. By Tuesday he was yearning to be funny again, so turned that desire into very odd repetitions of his lines in scenes 72, 76, and 78. His delivery of "It works! Hey! My mass thermo-register works! If you'd had it in Cleveland, young lady . . ."—with the ad-lib of "young lady"— was so goofy even Cassandra laughed.

Clancy—as Old Man Clark—ran the shooting as though he truly was the owner of Clark's Drugs. All morning he spoke in his dialogue cues—making for a stream of conversational rehearsals there in the Works—and introduced the boy playing Carl Mills, a thirteen-year-old Down syndrome actor, to everyone on the set as "the star of our show."

The elderly Dishwasher/Busboy was played by Bill Johnson, who, as an actor, is credited as Lucky Johnson.

Friday, with both Wren and Ike still not on the Call Sheet, Bill had the units working around the downtown area of Lone Butte. When the light allowed—it had to be dark enough—the Investigators were called for scene 98, the EXT of the Knight House, where, using high-tech laser microphones, they listened to what would be

---

* The Park Ranger was played by Riva Osgoode-Bent, a community theater actor in Sacramento who, a month before, had sent her self-taped audition for any role available to the Locals Casting service. She got a text the night before notifying her that she had been cast. At 5:45 the next morning, she had the dialogue memorized, was put in her ranger costume and into the H/MU Works, then reported to the LAVA PITS set, which had been built beside the bluff in the Little Iron Bend River Park. The GROUP OF TOURISTS were extras. There was no LITTLE KID cast, but just a line yelled from off camera. So, for all of this one Monday, Riva Osgoode-Bent was the star of the movie. Ms. Osgoode-Bent would never be confused with Dr. Pat Johnson, as the woman is five feet, two inches, and heavy-set.

Firefall's face-to-face with Amos and Eve—the INT of which was now pushed to the final days of the shoot—on a new set at Westinghouse Light.

★ ★ ★

By Saturday the Cloepfers were restless. Ike had had the week off and without working being in Lone Butte was pointless. To Thea, anyway. They left 114 Elm Street to go shopping in Chico—things for the baby as Ruby was getting bigger—then kept driving north on Old 99 all the way to the town of Shasta on the mountain of the same name. They ate at the Shasta Inn, then headed back south. Ruby slept all the way home, as did Thea, using her sweatshirt as a head cushion, the passenger seat reclined back as far as possible.

Back in Lone Butte Ike announced he was going to head off for a Firefall hike in his combat boots and rucksack.

Thea wondered if he was going to roll up his tent and take it with him to do bivouac research down by the river and disappear until Monday. His attempts to inhabit Robert No-Middle-Initial Falls had grown tiresome.

Ike was twelve minutes out of the house and in his second set of burpees when he thought about his costar in the movie, wondering how Wren was doing with it all. He didn't want her to be sad . . .

He texted her.

Iklip: You OK?

In a nanosecond his phone bleated with an unidentified number. "How are you?"

"Oh, Ike . . ." Wren's voice trailed off. "How are we going to *do* this . . . ?"

Ike slowed down his Firefall pace. He had naturally turned down Webster Road, heading west, walking along the shoulder of the old route under all those gum trees. "Somehow."

A single word, and yet, what Wren needed to hear. "He was such a wonderful man . . ." Wren was weeping now. "And I keep crying . . . and I've talked to *everyone* about him . . . except you. I know he was old. I know his time had come. I know. But *somehow.*"

"Somehow. Together." Two words this time, more out of inexperience than empathy. A woman in mourning was new turf for him.

When the woman was Wren Lane he was in the weeds, not sure of what to say, how to say it, when to say anything. But he wanted to be an aide for Wren.

"Help me, Ike," she whispered. "Help me get through this . . ."

"I will." Ike had heard that line in a TV show once.

"You and I . . ." Wren was almost pleading. "*We* . . . are going to have to go into the Works and get made up and put on our stupid costumes and say our lines as though Elliot is still here. He was my Pop-Pop, Ike! I can't just say the lines to the space he used to live in . . ."

"I know." Ike said all that came into his head. "Me, too." *Me, too?*

After a long silence: "How are you dealing with this?" Wren really wanted to know.

Ike was not *dealing* with anything. He'd lost his footing and felt purposeless and silly. He was waiting to be told what to do with little to do but take up space at 114 Elm Street, look after the baby, knowing Thea was less and less enthralled with his status as the guy in the movie. Al Mac-Teer had said something about putting her in the film, giving her a role equal to Girl in the Restroom, which Thea appreciated but had since ceased to anticipate. Since the memorial, the question in Ike's mind always came back to Wren, and what he could do for her.

"What are you doing," Wren asked, with need in her tone, "to *cope?*"

All Ike could think of having done to cope was taking pen to paper a few nights before—when he was up with Ruby to change her and hold her in the night kitchen of 114 Elm. "I've rethought my Five-Year Plan . . ."

"Your Five-Year Plan?" Wren's voice became ever so slightly altered by hope. A hope Ike had offered, which made his heartbeat accelerate.

"Living life is being on a ship at sea. Course corrections are constant."

"Like flying, often," Wren said.

"You should know, yeah. I start by writing down all the Certainties. The obvious stuff."

"Like being contractually required to finish this movie," Wren said.

"Yep," Ike confirmed. "No matter how sad things are."

"Oh, that is certainly a certainty. This is helpful, Ike. Let me get a pen and paper." She kept a ton of notes from the conversation.[*]

The two actors talked fast and over each other for the next mile of Ike's hike. Of Possibilities, both great and disastrous. The movie could wrap on schedule. She could be injured doing some of the wirework in the fight scenes. The movie could come out great. The movie could be horrible. Anything can and would happen.

"New friendships could come from the job, or some jerk could break your heart again." Ike tried to toss that off with some casual nonchalance, but Wren wrote down: *Fall in love???*

Next, Ike explained the Hopes, which were both in and out of one's control. The two costars talked a lot about their hopes.

Finally—and most lengthy—was the Mission Statement. "Your sermon to yourself," Ike explained. "Your *why I am here* credo, your vow, your *Who Dares Wins* battle patch. I've written a million pages of Mission Statements."

Wren wanted to know Ike's current Mission Statement. "Are you kidding?" he asked. "To show up on time, know all the text, and have some idea to show Bill. The first two are bunts, but that idea thing is a toughie."

Wren was incredulous. "Are you shitting me? Ike! You are marvelous just standing on your mark!"

Ike stopped in his tracks out on Webster Road. Stood stock-still, silent and breathless.

Wren then offered up her own Mission Statement: *To be present and honest and let go of any expectations.* This came from a conversation she'd had with Elliot on the set between setups, back on the Porch EXT. "My dear heart," he'd told her. "Do as the great ones do. Show up and tell the truth without concern . . ." On her notepad, Wren wrote *Be like Ike.*

The two artists kept up the exchange until Ike had hiked more than halfway to the interstate—he'd been talking with Wren for

[*] And still has them.

so long that time and distance had passed in the purr (the Blur) of easy conversation. He turned on his heel and headed back to Lone Butte and 114 Elm Street.

Wren was not anxious to get off the phone. Nor was Ike, not until the State Theater was in sight and the two actors wrapped up the professional exchange, the personal intercourse.

"I'm so lucky you reached out, Ike," Wren said. "I need . . . needed you to bring order to my head."

"Glad to," Ike said, thinking, *Shit, I was gone too long! What am I going to tell Thea?*

"Give my best to Thea and that soft blanket of love, Ruby."

"I will."

"Hey, you know what would be fun some weekend? Let me take you flying." Wren's voice had noticeably brightened.

"In your plane?"

"No, Ike. In my '62 Pontiac."

"That would be fun. Would be Ruby's second time in an airplane."

Wren had not been thinking that Ike's little girl would come on the ride. Not the wife either. "I'll let you take the yoke."

"I've never flown a plane before."

"I hadn't either until I did and the sky became a whole new world."

Both of them sang out the Disney song of the same name. Both of them laughed. Both of them felt relaxed and unburdened for the first time in a week.

"See you on the set," Wren offered.

"Sure will."

"Thanks again."

"Anytime."

"Count on *that*."

"Look forward to it."

"Me, too." Wren pressed END on her phone. *Me, too?* She'd actually said that?

When he got home, Ike said nothing about the call with Wren.

★　★　★

On Sunday, Bill was on the second hole of a golf course up Chico way, he and Clancy taking in a round of the Goofy Game That Is Good to Play to Get Away. The second is a dogleg to the left, a par 5, calling for their Big Bertha Mega-Wood Drivers. His phone rang.

Al was calling. "Yeah," he answered.

"We gotta talk now," Al said. With the tragedy, wrapping the movie in fifty-three days was no longer in the cards, not that finishing spot-on schedule was ever guaranteed.

"I know. We're foxtrotted.* Any solution?"

"Meeting up with Aaron and Yogi when the latter returns from church." Yogi, to pay homage to the death of Elliot, had driven to Redding, to the Orthodox church there, to ponder again why bad things happen to good people, as any good Greek boy would.

"Hold on a second . . . ," Bill said. During the pause, there was the sound over the phone, of a *wooosh,* then a *klock.*

Clancy could be heard in the background yelling, "Go down the hole, Alice!"

"My God." Bill sounded despondent. "Clancy just hit the ball straight as Bud Abbott for miles and miles. I'll be at the PO in six holes . . ."

Al had called from a bench by the pond, from the compound where she was alone but for the extra security Tom had arranged, guys who lived in an Airstream trailer near the front gate behind the berm. The dogs that now lived on the property were not trained guard dogs, just a couple of big mutts that were allowed to bark at strangers—which Al no longer was. She kept a can of tennis balls and a Chuckit! for when the dogs came around to sniff her out, but as of this morning they hadn't.

Al pinched out a text.

AMacT: Y?

Moments later, Ynez was on the phone from Sacramento. "How can I help you, Boss?"

---

* Of late, Bill had been using military-style call words rather than expletives. *Fuck* was Foxtrot. *Asshole* was Alpha Hotel. *Cocksucker?* Charlie Oscar Charlie Kilo Sierra.

"Want to learn something about the business?"

"Yep."

"Gonna meet to solve problems. Join us."

"Today?" she asked.

"At the PO, pronto. Think of what can be cut, pushed to other units, or smooshed into fewer days."

"You want me to do that?"

"Why not you, too?"

Ynez felt an inner glow—the kind of warmth when trust has been passed on to you. Ynez had thought the movie would be put on indefinite hold due to the loss of Mr. Guarnere. But no. She was still a part of the effort, entrusted to help the production. But her father was not able to get any farther than from his bed to his living room chair. Her mother wore a poorly hidden look of fear and worry. One of the cousins, Antonio, had been arrested in a DUI. With the family's weekend work schedules as they always were, this Sunday called for Ynez and her sister to babysit three of the little girls, and Francisco, of course. What could she do?

She imagined the index cards of the *L.I.S.T.eN.* System and saw the obvious fix: five little kids in a wading pool under plum trees. Make that four little kids, all girls. "Could you stand it if I bring Francisco?" she asked Al.

"My lover? My angel?" Al smiled for the first time that week, thinking of little Francisco, brown eyes, a mop of black hair, smelling like a bag of muffins. "If you don't, I'll be crushed!"

By 2:10 p.m. Ynez was in the backyard of 114 Elm Street making introductions of her sister and nieces to Thea and little Ruby. The wading pool was collecting two inches of water from the garden hose and toys, towels, and blankets were spread out with cut-up snack foods, juice boxes, and comfortable folding chairs for the grown-ups. Ike was not around. As Thea put it, he was off on another An-Actor-Prepares-By-Walking-Out-Walkabout. "He usually comes home before dark," she said, sipping from a can of Hamm's Special Light. "But you never know."

Ruby was clapping and laughing in the company of kids just a bit older than her and the plan was for the pool party to last a couple of hours. Ynez put Francisco in his stroller and pushed him along the shaded sidewalks of Lone Butte to the Almond Growers Association Building.

They met in Bill's spartan office with the door closed.

Al held Francisco in her lap first, and for the longest time her eyes were on no one else. Yogi took him for a bit, as did Bill, who remembered doing the same with some of his ex-stepkids. Al insisted Aaron Blau take Francisco as well, which he did, treating the toddler sitting on his lap like some creature of the woodlands, a beaver, or a pine marten. Funny, then, that it was there Francisco fell asleep.

There were many problems needing solutions from this Sunday meeting. First . . .

Item: the loss of a key actor.

Bill Johnson: "Amos Knight will be in scenes ninety-seven and ninety-eight. We find someone to lie in bed with the CGI markers on his face so we can digitally make him into Elliot from the scans we took. If we need two days for the scene, we take them. Firefall, Eve, Nurse Sue, and Amos are all together and, hell, *that's* the movie right there."

Item: the emotional wherewithal of Number 1 on the Call Sheet. Everyone on the Call Sheet, sure, but come on. Wren.

Al Mac-Teer: "Asking Wren to perform to some guy with dots on his face? Bidding her Pop-Pop farewell like that? Why not just put a C-stand in bed with a tennis ball for her to look at? Mercenary. But, by pushing ninety-seven and ninety-eight to the very last scene we shoot, on the last day, we wrap the movie then and there. I'll wager Wren will use all that emotional weight and crush it."

Item: the crunch in what was left in the schedule.

Yogi: "We've got, still, Eve in Clark's, Eve rescuing the dog, Eve rescuing the kidnapped family, Eve meeting FF at the Lumber Mill. The three big fights, between them. Every Investigator scene save the stuff with Clancy. Scenes eleven through fourteen are thirteen pages. Saturday shoots, looks like."

Ynez: "Aaron, should I take Francisco now? He's drooling on your shirt."

Aaron: "Nah. Let's not wake him . . ."

Yogi: "There's Knightshade and the Investigators when she flips their car over, and when they mix it up on the interstate, plus the Kidnapping Rescue in scenes eight and nine."

Al Mac-Teer: "The Exteriors of Baton Rouge and Cleveland. The Interiors of Baton Rouge and Cleveland. And, plus, still to come, need I mention, I have to bring this up, and it's a pickle . . ."

Bill Johnson: "Oh, stop the buildup."

Al Mac-Teer: "The Golden Hour in the Field? One hundred and one and one-oh-two. The location is an hour away and the scene is a full day."

Aaron: "And Ike and Wren, the both of them, have to *get there*. Emotionally."

Bill Johnson: "We need some fresh eyes on this pickle."

The little office was quiet.

Bill Johnson: "What say you, Y-not?"

Ynez: "Me?"

Bill Johnson: "Give it to us straight from your shoulders. A solution for this pickle."

Ynez: "Really?"

Bill Johnson: "Why not you, Y-not?"

Al had had Ynez read the screenplay when she had been first hired. She'd since read it many times over just for the pleasure of seeing the movie in her head, a new vision of each scene with each read. From the creative moments she'd witnessed—in Rushes or on Al's iPad—the real movie looked better than the one in her imagination.

Bill Johnson: "We gotta omit scenes. Which ones, you think?"

Ynez: "None."

Every eyebrow in the room, save Francisco's, went up.

Ynez: "I watched you shoot different scenes at the same time, when we were on Main Street, one camera here, another over there."

Bill Johnson: "Those were shots in the same scene. Coverage. Added setups."

Ynez: "Pretty complicated, though. I know that the Interiors for Baton Rouge and Cleveland were going to be practical. Is that the right word? *Practical*?"

Aaron: "In the location houses, yeah. Not sets we build at Westinghouse Light."

Ynez: "Right. Real rooms in real houses. Could some rooms upstairs, here in the Almond Growers, be . . . dressed? Is that the right word? Dressed as a bedroom and the Rest Home. Could we shoot those scenes simultaneously when you do Eve in Clark's Drugs? You could just walk across the street to the Almond Growers Association Building and get the footage."

Everyone in the room, except sleeping Francisco, looked at Ynez as though she had just gone back in time and killed Hitler.

Days 27–31 (of 53 + or – X Shooting Days)

After more dealings with budget and schedule and production needs, Bill pulled the trigger to shoot the Rescue on the Interstate at Westinghouse Light, in the square footage of a football field and enough height for a circus. Wren and Ike had been at the place for elements of their fight scenes, but only individual shots, work that had been piecemeal compared to what the week would bring.

They shot in sequence, to minimize confusion and allow the VFX teams to get their Postproduction work in order. Overnight, Teamsters moved the Base Camp to the gravel parking lot of the old lightbulb factory. The Swing Gang, Lighting, and Set Construction crews worked eighteen hours.

Early Monday, the Unit assembled in the middle of the vast expanse of Green Screen. Doc Ellis's stunt team was ready to get it on. Wren was glad to shoot a very physical, angry scene with no dialogue and new people. The cast for scenes 7XX through 9, set weeks before, were given their calls overnight. The BAD GUYS were two of the stunt crew. The SINGLE MOM was an actress from San Francisco who used her Monday off from a production of Anton Chekhov's *The Cherry Orchard* at the American Conservatory Theater to make more money from two days on a movie than she made in twenty-eight performances as Varya. The kids were siblings who had been cast in Los Angeles.

Everyone had a great day and there were a ton of laughs, as well as applause for when the punk kidnapper crashed into the windshield of the stolen car.

★   ★   ★

Al swung by 114 Elm Street, not to talk with Ike, but with Thea. Mrs. Cloepfer was on the house's front porch, sitting in a beach chair she had moved to the front of the house to get off by herself.

"Ike's burpee-ing in the backyard," she called to Al, assuming she needed him. "Or practicing his close-order drill in the foxhole he dug with his Ka-Bar. Whatever a Ka-Bar is."

Uh-oh. Al could see the woman's body language—and tell from the tone in her voice—that she was not a happy spouse, but idle, on a dull location with her partner working long hours on a big, fucking movie with Lady *Periwinkle*. All day Thea had a baby to look after and only Lupe to talk to; that was it for distractions. Al knew the scenario; once the hullabaloo of getting the movie started became the routine of getting the movie done, the main squeeze/life partner of the producer/department head/and more often than not member of the cast discovered that time passes on location like a long, slow trek on a rocky stretch of dull road. What too often happened was the actor came home every night to a bored and/or pissed off partner. In the haven of work, then, some love affair would blossom, a *showmance* between two goo-goo-eyed lovebirds that would bring the other relationship crashing down. Many lives—and the production—went off the rails. Al sent a prayer upward: don't let Ike get the goo-goo eyes for Wren (although what man wouldn't).

Al could tell—she knew—that Thea Hill Cloepfer had had enough of her husband's movie-actor Sierra Hotel Indio Tango. "I gotta talk to *you*," Al announced. *Just in the nick of time.*

"Would you like a coffee?" Thea asked. "A mug of Marine Corps joe?"

"I'm caffeined up enough, thanks. I'm here with my producer hat in my hands."

"Yeah?"

"Would you act in a scene this week?"

"Doing what?"

"The key role of PONY TREATS DELIVERY WOMAN. It shoots, like, tomorrow and we need you."

"In a scene with Ike?"

"No."

"With the fabulous Wren Lane?"

"Nope. With Cassandra and Lala."

Thea spat out two words. "I'm in."

★ ★ ★

Wednesday's work was on a practical set in the former Management Office of what had been the Westinghouse Lightbulb Plant. The scene was the movie's introduction of London, in her crappy office, being summoned by Madrid.

While Bill shot the scene as though it were a procedural cop show from 1966, Thea had gone into Wardrobe, then the Works, then was assigned to Ike's massive trailer to wait to be called into the set. Alone inside the RV, wearing the uniform of a PONY Treats gigger, she went through every drawer and cupboard. In one pile of old script pages and call sheets she found a note, written in a woman's hand, on blue paper monogrammed with a florid *WL*.

FIGHT THE ENNUI! Xx WL

Thea read the note aloud to herself. "Fight the ennui exclamation point. Kiss kiss. Double-yew Ell." There was a black Sharpie in the drawer, too. She uncapped it and wrote *HOW CUTE!* under the XX's. She tossed the note back in the drawer, covering it with old Call Sheets. Nina, the Base Camp AD, happened to knock on the trailer door just then, and three beats later opened it a crack.

"Ms. Hill?" Nina called.

"Yes?"

"We would like to invite you to the set."

"I hereby accept the invitation."

Scenes 12 and 12A had been quickly shot; London and Madrid passed through security doors and into an elevator.

Thea was led to the camera set up in a hallway by a pair of art-directed elevator doors.

"Hello, you," Bill said as a greeting. "Ready for your close-up?"

"I know the dialogue, so, yeah."

"Looking at you, I have a question."

"Shoot."

"Do you look a little too, um, together. Or, too *collected* maybe?"

"I was given the costume. I put it on."

"I don't mean the costume. I mean the demeanor. What say you are one exhausted woman trying to make ends meet with this delivery job. You have a sick kid at home. Your husband drinks a little too much and has been laid off. You're in debt on all your credit cards and pizza delivery is one of three jobs you're working. You also clean houses and wait tables on weekends."

Thea thought for moment. "My mother told me not to marry this guy and hold off on having kids. Our rent is too high but we can't break the lease. I have six more deliveries to make then get home to tend the baby 'cause my husband will probably go out with his idiot pals. I'm exhausted, bitter, and just barely surviving the day. How about I play all that?"

"In seven-eighths of a page, yeah." Bill walked away glad this lady was in one of his movies again.

Thea made that last look of hers an angry glare at Madrid, counting out the cash tip, thinking it cheap, measly. As the elevator doors closed on her, Thea shook her head and muttered an expletive.

Bill laughed out loud and Yogi asked for a round of applause, for Thea Hill was Picture Wrapped on *Knightshade: The Lathe of Firefall* and very much a loved one.

SCENE 13

The scene was scheduled for two days of shooting. The preparation done by the cast, all those enforced rehearsals, allowed for the scene to be completed in thirteen and a half hours. Overtime was paid to the crew, but a day was taken off the schedule.

Cassandra, Lala, Nick, and Hang had shown up on time, knew the text, and had ideas. They were solid professionals. And heroes.

Oops

In the house at 114 Elm at 5:32 a.m., the baby had been fussing and Ike was in the shower. So, again, Thea was awake in bed. Ike's company iPhone was charging on the nightstand in the bedroom and buzzed into life with a text message.

COMPANY PHONE: FF—hear you are dangling on wire today while I save a pooch. CUITW.

CUITW. See you in the Works. Reading the text was simple, as was thumb-scrolling up through the text chain; a very long chain, going back over a week, before even then.

Thea scrolled to the recent calls made/received. There were some to and from **THEA**.

There were many—many many many—to and from **COMPANY PHONE**.

Thea then checked the voice mail. Not a single message left from **COMPANY PHONE**—just all those RECENTS . . .

PHOTOS were easily scrolled onto the screen. One after another:

Ike and Wren in the H/MU—sipping lattes.

Ike and Wren clowning at Base Camp.

Ike and Wren selfies as Eve and Firefall, oh the smiles!

Ike and Wren.

Ike and Wren.

Ike and Wren.

With Ike still in the shower, his wife leaned over, got the charger cord for the iPhone, and plugged it back in.

Then she threw it onto the floor between the bed and the nightstand. Checking to see that the screen had not cracked, she collected the phone by the cord and again threw it on the floor between the bed and the nightstand. Thea had to repeat the action three more times before the screen cracked enough to make the phone unusable.

"Oops," she said before rolling back into the blankets to get a bit more sleep.

THE MAN AT THE GATE

The Art Department, Construction Crew, and Swing Gang had converted rooms of the Almond Growers Association Building into working sets. The Day Player Cast had been brought in over the weekend. Stanley Arthur Ming had B Camera prepping those scenes while his A and C Cameras were in Clark's Drugs for the crucial, story-establishing scenes at the top of the movie. The work began in the Almond Growers—scenes in a hallway and hospice room with Ike and Cassandra making scripted appearances. The plan was to shoot the hallway, then move back to Clark's, then return to the Almond Growers bedroom set. This meant the H/MU trailer was busy all day, and that Wren and Ike would overlap at Base Camp.

COMPANY PHONE: We both work today? Coffee?

COMPANY PHONE: I'm in @ 9. I'll brew . . .

COMPANY PHONE: You must be in the chair getting glued up. Will find you . . .

COMPANY PHONE: If you wrap B4 lunch, I'll stop by with a Shave Ice.

COMPANY PHONE: Hey, FF! You ghosting me????

Ike never saw the texts because his phone had fallen off his nightstand. He'd given it to Ynez, who was going to get the screen replaced, the whole phone if necessary. He explained his silence to Wren when she showed up to the Works.

As they were past the halfway mark in the schedule, the shoot was now all downhill, causing a sea change in the Unit. The mood was upbeat. As Kenny Sheprock said to Wren, "We've broken the back of the picture."

Bill was stretched, no doubt about that, going back and forth between the two sets, even though the walk was a short one. So it went for the week, hard work for Bill, but done with an alacrity that kept the movie on schedule.

★   ★   ★

Thursday night, with a later call in the morning, Wren invited her guesthouse squatters—Al and Ynez—to join her for a light workweek dinner. Al made margaritas, Ynez kept trying to lay out the food options, and Wren kept ordering her to sit down. Laurel and Tom Windermere joined the group, but not Wally, who was in Los Angeles.* Wren had thought to invite Ike and Thea as well but didn't. She did an imitation of Ike doing his six-count burpees in between shots—her grunting out the way Ike kept count: *Hun . . . Hoo . . . Hree . . . Hoor . . . Hive . . .* Everyone laughed.

When Tom received a call on his ever-present radio from Craig, one of the ex-cops hired for added security, he excused himself. He took his car down the quarter-mile driveway to the front gate, where an older Honda had pulled up. Craig was standing beside the open driver's-side window. Using the side pedestrian entrance so as not to open the main automobile gate, Tom joined Craig and asked if there was anything he could help with.

Behind the wheel of the Honda was a baldheaded fellow.

Tom knew immediately who the man was, for he had code-named him Knife.

Knife was one of twelve Threat Assessments in Tom's database.

Knife had been in Atlanta just after Wren shot her earliest scenes as Eve Knight. He had taken the tour of the Dynamo Studios, jumped off to wander the lot, looking for Wren, until Security found him, noted his information, and escorted him off the property.

Knife had been trying to contact Wren since the Sergeant Harder years.

With security software and procedures that Tom is unwilling to divulge, he had a TA file on Knife—as well as eleven other Threat Assessments—that was constantly being updated.

Fueled by the information that was now on the Internet, Knife had made his way to Lone Butte. To talk to Wren Lane.

A security camera recorded his appearance. "This fellow here," Knife said, pointing to Craig, "thinks I'm an idiot."

"I'm sure that's not the case," Tom said politely. "Right?" Tom looked at Craig.

---

* The man was running three different enterprises. His own, the financial aspects of his sister's corporation, and the investments in place for the two Lank children. Wally often used Wren's plane and pilot, Heather (he had no license), to fly to LA for business and romantic liaisons.

Craig spoke up in a voice so dispassionate he sounded generated by artificial intelligence. "I've informed this gentleman that there is no one here who matches the description of his query."

"Guys," Knife said. "Everyone knows Wren lives here. The guy at the convenience store. The self-serve gas station lady. The taco stand. They tell everyone she's living here. Look . . ." Knife held up his phone. "This place is on Google Earth, right? Wren's staying in the big house, *right here*." He pointed to a screen grab of the entire compound, the big main house.

"Well, sir," Tom said. "We're telling you that no one here goes by that name. So, we'll ask you to turn around in the space right there and be on your way. Will you do that for us, sir?"

"Jesus Christ. You don't fucking get it," Knife mumbled, reaching across the seat for a thick folder of papers he then waved. "Wren needs to talk with me. Right now. Or else there is going to be serious shit going down."

"Again, sir," Tom said, without any rise to his voice at all. "We ask that you use the turnaround and be on your way."

"Look . . ." Knife was exasperated by this runaround. "I'm related to her, okay? My mother's maiden name is Lane, okay? I've sent Wren letters and documents detailing my connection to her. I am the cowriter of two of her future movies. If she ignores all the work I've done she is going to have a world of legal problems that will cost money and goodwill in her life and profession, okay? She has to talk to me and the sooner the better. For her own good, guys."

"Once more, sir"—again, no rise to Tom's voice at all—"we ask that you use the turnaround and be on your way."

"You'd better give her these and tell her to read them over." Knife held the folder up to the window.

"Sir, we have no reason to accept such a delivery. We ask that you use the turnaround and be on your way. There is no reason to escalate the matter."

Knife shot daggers at Craig and Tom. "Okay, bungholes. You're blowing it." Knife reversed the Civic, made a Y-turn, and drove off.

Tom went back to his car, started up, pulled through the gate and off the property to follow Knife in the used Honda.

★ ★ ★

Wren and the gang were now sitting outside on the front patio, finishing off their drinks, making vows for a compound-wide pickleball tournament over the weekend. Ynez needed to know the rules
of pickleball. The spirit of the Unit had spread to the house, like
in the final weeks of the school year—all that was left were a few
tough exams, the return to the Knight House for the scene with
Amos and Firefall, then the wrapping up of the whole Cardboard
Carnival.

"Most of the picture is behind us, PONY-girl," Al said to Ynez.
Both ladies were enjoying their margaritas. "You made it this far
through the Blur. All once so endless."

"You guys get to feel that way," Wren said. "I don't have that
luxury." Wren meant her emotional duties were still in play. Every
day, still, she had to *get there*.

"Of course," Al said. "I'm not talking as an artist. I'm talking as
a shipping clerk."

"I feel kind of sad." Ynez was confessing. "For all the complaints
about movies being crazy time? After we started shooting? Everywhere my eyes landed, every word I heard taught me something I
didn't know. It's hard work, but it's fun, too."

"That's making motion pictures." Al was smiling.

Laurel had a question. "Who works the hardest, do you think?"

"Her!" Ynez pointed at Wren. "No one knows how you do it!"

Wren gave an *aw-shucks* look and held up her right wrist, her
leather band of *SERENITY*.

"Bill Johnson must explode at some point," Laurel said.

Al spoke up. "He did back in the day. But by now he's seen everything that can happen on a movie and he still gets the movie done."

"Everybody works the hardest," Ynez said. "Does that make
sense? At some point, and there's no telling when that moment is,
someone is responsible for the whole movie, right then and there.
Props might not have the Ovaltine. The generator will go down. A
carabiner on a safety harness might not be clicked and Wren falls.
Everyone on the movie has to do their job well or they become a
problem. They have to work hard. And keep their word, too. Every-

one has the most important job on the movie. Oh, I'm not making any sense . . ."

Al smiled to herself. Ynez *got it*.

That's when they heard a man shouting.

The shouting was distant, so the words were garbled and impossible to make out, other than "Wren!" Over and over, "Wren!" came out of the darkness along with some loud, indecipherable gibberish. The tone of the shouting was angry. Frightening.

Wren's blood drained from her face. She'd heard this kind of shouting before, from crowds trying to get a peek at her, from aggressive fans on the other side of barricades, from outside her home at two in the morning. From paparazzi trying to get a rise out of her. That she was hearing such yelling here, in Lone Butte, suddenly depressed her spirit. She did not feel safe. Nor did Al and Ynez.

★　★　★

Footage from the night-vision security cameras, installed on the perimeter at Dynamo's expense, shows that Knife had stopped at the curve in the road that was closest to the main house and got out of the Honda. He can be seen screaming, then throwing a large package over the fence and onto the property. Tom Windermere then pulls up in his car, his hazard lights flashing, his headlights illuminating the scene in harsh gray light. Tom steps out of his car and approaches Knife, who obviously turns his wrath on him. Knife shouts, gestures, points. Tom is seen making no moves. Knife stomps back to his car, slams the door, and drives wildly away into the night. Tom returns to his car and follows him. All the way to the interstate.

In the morning, shooting continued with a slight rejig of the schedule. The Investigators were called to Westinghouse Light to shoot car interiors. Wren was given the day off. Al called Thea's number and told her what had happened at Wren's place. They should not be surprised to find her shaken up. Thea was creeped out.

Though the appearance of the man at the gate was kept a quiet secret, when Yogi called the Wrap to the week's shooting, his "You are loved" was meant for Wren.

THE MAN WITH THE CANE

The first check from Dynamo surprised the hell out of Robby Andersen, but there it was, waiting for him in the old coffee pot, nailed to a tree, that served as his mailbox. He'd named the house Coffee Pot when he bought the ramshackle place on Martha's Vineyard because he'd found the rusted, oversize appliance in the barn. Now his return address read Coffee Pot, Chilmark, MV, MA. The postal workers knew the Andersen-Maddio place.

Dynamo paid, first, for the option for the work known as *The Legend of Firefall* published by Kool Katz Komix, created by *TREV-VORR*/Robert Andersen, then paid again when the film known as *Knightshade: The Lathe of Firefall* began production. The two checks together came to a lot of money. Robby was glad to have a lot of money again. Not that he'd been hurting.

His work still sold and was still celebrated in many quarters—the Riverscapes of *TREV-VORR* had made their splash in the art scene go-go days of the 1990s. He'd bought Coffee Pot for the famed soft sunlight of Martha's Vineyard, lived in the barn, and kept painting—moving away from his Riverscapes. These days, he painted whatever was in his head.

Firefall had not entered his mind since 1989. Not since Uncle Bobby had died.

*   ★   ★

In 1977 to '78 he designed the sets for a summer Shakespeare company outside San Luis Obispo and wintered in Los Angeles, where the art scene was on the vibrant side and Lady Ophelia kept him company. When she broke up with him, amicably if firmly, he took to the road, heading east, painting as he went. He still had much of his Iron Bend stuff—all those studies of the river back in his hometown—and worked them up into realized Riverscapes. His used Ford pickup with the even-more-used camper (the propane did not work, so no stove, and an ice chest that needed ice) was his home and studio. He'd set up in a spot, put out a large folding table, chest high, then lay out his materials and tools, paper, canvases, paints, brushes, pencils, and a hand-crank pencil sharpener mounted on the Ford's tailgate.

By the time he landed in New Mexico, near Albuquerque, he had quite a portfolio. When he walked into the Gold Dragon restaurant—smack on old Route 66 on Central Avenue—he introduced himself to Angel Falls by saying, "If your name is Angel, I'm your nephew." Uncle Bob was in the kitchen. There was a moment of confusion, but then Uncle Bob saw the boy in the man standing before him for the first time in thirty years. Angel laughed out loud.

★   ★   ★

Robby stayed over a week, helping in the kitchen, going to church on the Sunday, showing his aunt and uncle artwork he'd created. At a spot under the cottonwoods of the Rio Grande, Robby drew more studies and Bob let him ride his motorcycle—a big fancy thing—around the dirt roads. The two men sat by a fire, talking under the wide sky, telling each other about some of their pasts, sure, but more of their learned lessons; all they had given up, what remained that they carried with them. Robby learned of Uncle Bob's drift-free simplicity. Bob Falls learned of his nephew's wandering bootheels.

Leaving them with some of his less completed work—and one finished piece of the Old Trestle Bridge on the Iron Bend, with the small figures jumping off into the river—Robby continued east. In '82 he landed in Manhattan. His work began to be appreciated in '87. Rather than letters, he'd send Angel and Bob hand-painted postcards in watercolors, sometimes arriving in bunches, days in a row. Those cards are valuable now. Angel gave them to one of her nephews.

Seven years later, when Bob fell sick, so very fast with a stage 4 cancer that had never been checked, Robby flew to ABQ just in time to get to his uncle when he still had the ability to speak. The funeral had quite a mix of mourners—the Lum side of the family, locals, bikers, ex-Marines. Robby was the only Andersen present, as he'd been the only one in contact with his uncle.

The family minister sang out a simple refrain, graveside, after his oratory and the gospel selections.

All will be well.
All will be well.
All will be well.
Wait for tomorrow.
All will be well.
Robby Andersen wept without shame.

★ ★ ★

Coffee Pot expanded in 2002 when Stella Andersen Maddio bought the lot next door, cleared out enough trees, and built her divorce-settlement house. She kept her married name for the kids, using Coffee Pot as her mailing address. The gravel drive from the highway now buttonhooked around Robby's barn/studio and her modern saltbox two-story house. Of her four kids, Gregory and Keli were back on the Vineyard to work for the summer when the Dynamo checks landed like lit firecrackers.

Robby was walking with a bad hip, thus a cane, and came over for most meals. Stella, fourteen years younger than her brother and a colt to his plow horse, had mastered her Instant Pot and organic garden and was ready for any number of drop-in diners.

"You wrote this?" Keli asked. She'd pulled up images of the fifty-year-old Kool Katz Komic on her phone.

"Wrote it. Drew it." Robby spooned black beans from the Instant Pot onto brown rice from the rice maker. "Cashing the check."

Gregory was eating a Popsicle, looking over his sister's shoulder. "*The Legend of Firefall.* I can smell the weed over the web browser. What in the world prompted this work of genius?"

"I remembered an uncle of ours who'd been in the war and set down a story about him in a kind of fever-dream homage."

"You had an uncle in Vietnam?"

"Not Vietnam," Stella said. She'd eaten. "Our mother's brother was in the Marines in World War Two. I never met him." She left the kitchen for the upstairs, for a storage room where she kept the family's very old photo albums, an inheritance from her mother, and transported all the way from Lone Butte many years ago.

"He was a flamethrower, that I remember," Robby said.

"Was he killed?" Keli asked, nearly done with the comic.

"No. He rode a huge motorcycle into town once, then was gone. Then I got a letter from him out of the blue. A nice letter. Which made me create *that*." Robby pointed to Keli's phone. "I tracked him down a few years later. Stayed with him and his wife for a week. Kept in touch. Went to his funeral."

"Okay," Keli said, having finished her reading, then swiping her phone to dig deeper into the Internet. "Your uncle is a character in a movie with Wren Lane."

"He is not!" Gregory was getting another lemon Popsicle out of the freezer. "You're talking about the future Mrs. Gregory Maddio!"

Keli listed the information from a lazy Google search of *firefall dynamo movie*. Wren Lane. Dynamo Nation. *Knightshade: The Lathe of Firefall*. Bill Johnson.

Stella came into the kitchen carrying a cracked, faded photo album open to a middle page. Some small, old letters marked V-Mail were loose on the inside with a small photo kept in place, having held its glue.

"This is him," Stella said, laying the binder on the kitchen table.

In a small black-and-white snapshot from 1942, Robert A. Falls, USMC, wore his dress blues uniform.

"I was named after him," Robby said.

"In Lone Butte?" Keli asked, an upturn in her voice.

"Yep," Robby answered, bending over the photo album, looking for his uncle Bob in the tiny photo of a kid dressed in a white hat, black tunic, and shiny buttons. Ramrod straight, he stood.

"Wow." Keli had a flat tone in the word.

"What?"

"That's where they're making the movie. In Lone Butte," she said. "According to the Internet."

Robby looked at his niece, then to his sister. "The Internet says Lone Butte," he said. "Then it must be true."

★   ★   ★

The drive from San Francisco had been a hoot for the kids, but a near-dystopian vision for Robby Andersen and his sister, Stella.

They remembered a less urbanized Northern California. And the rental car was an absolute shit-box, but it was all that was available.

The stretch of California from the City—from Oakland—to Lone Butte was the same geographically as decades before, but hardly recognizable now. Only the route up Old 99 had any feeling of familiarity, of enough of the old landmarks to connect Robby and Stella to the landscape of their youth. To get out of the car for a break from its body-bending confines, they'd had cold root beers at a stand north of Sacramento, then continued to Lone Butte itself, which, when entered from the south, looked *almost* unchanged to an eerie degree. CERAMICS was just visible. Main Street. The State Theater. Saint Philip Neri. Clark's Drugs. The trucks and trailers sitting near the Almond Growers Association Building were the only visible signs of the twenty-first century. Stella said the trees even looked the same size.

Robby could have steered through town with his eyes closed. He could have pulled up in front of the house via instinct alone. All those years had passed, and the only thing truly different for Robby was the need of his cane to get out of the car.

Standing on the sidewalk, in front of 114 Elm Street, Robby could see a good-looking fellow in his twenties, the current tenant, who was working up a sweat on the porch with sets of squat thrusts.

Ike finished his fourth set of burpees, then saw the fellow standing on the front sidewalk, supported by a cane, looking up at the house with a noticeable interest, most likely a fan who showed up to get close to a movie star.

"Good morning," Ike said with all the volume his burpee-breathing allowed.

"The same," said the man with the cane.

"Anything I can do for you?" If the guy so much as mentioned Wren's name, Ike would call Wally immediately. Tom would be there in six heartbeats.

"Not a thing. Just looking at my home."

"This your house, is it?"

"Not anymore. But I grew up in it. Plum trees in the rear, a line of four when I was a kid. If the back porch is still screened in, there might be a hand-cranked pencil sharpener screwed in about three feet up by the kitchen door."

Ike blinked. There was, in fact, a rusted bit of hardware a yard high off the back-porch floor that could have once been a working pencil sharpener. "Sounds like you did once live here."

"This your place now?" Robby asked.

"No. Just renting." Ike glanced at the car, saw a lady driver and two grown kids in the back. "They once live here, too?"

"My sister, yes. Keli and Greg, the kids, no. Their first visit to Lone Butte. They are not impressed. Rob Andersen."

"Ike Clipper."

"Ike Clipper?" Rob's voice went up an octave. "Really? You're playing Firefall in the movie."

Hearing the reference to the movie made Ike square up on the porch. Why hadn't he said he was Irving Cloepfer? Knowing there was a pencil sharpener by the back door didn't mean this old coot was anything more than some interloper who wanted to brush up against a celebrity, even one as newly minted as Ike. In those first days of shooting, Wren, Bill, Al, and even Ken Sheprock had told Ike to be ready for run-ins with this kind of yahoo.

"What movie are you talking about?"

"The one on the Internet. I read your name as playing Firefall."

"And what's your name again?" Ike was just about to step down off the porch and posture himself defensively.

"Rob Andersen. Robby. But you may know me better as *TREV-VORR.*"

Ike stopped. *"TREV-VORR?"*

Inside the house, on his laptop and in the three-ring binder of his copy of the script were digital scans of two vintage comic books. Pages of the comics were pinned up on the walls of the Costume and Art Departments. One was from World War II. The other was from fifty years ago, written by an artist by the name of *TREV-VORR.* "You're *TREV-VORR?"*

Robby was looking up at the roofline of his childhood home. "Yep."

A Homecoming

Al had a text from Ike on his new company phone, an odd query on a Sunday morning.

Iklip: What is name of artist who drew that old hippie comic book that Bill used as FF?

AMacT: Dude. Sunday . . .

She opened her laptop and scrolled through enough deep data to find the Dynamo Nation correspondence about copyrights and royalty payments—stuff she hadn't opened since Prep.

AMacT: Trev-vorr. Kool Katz Komix. $$ paid.

Iklip: I know. What is real name of Trev-vorr.

AMacT: Dude!!! Sunday!!! After cursoring through the documents again: **Robert Andersen. WTF?**

Iklip: Trev-vorr is sitting in my kitchen right now . . .

AMacT: WTF???!!

Al pulled up to 114 Elm in less than a half hour. The Andersen-Maddio clan had toured the house, with Stella and Robby offering up story after story, anecdote after anecdote, of life within those old walls. Thea and Stella compared notes on the oddities of the house. Coffee was made. Some 3-IN-ONE oil was found and applied to the three-foot-high pencil sharpener on the back porch, and the thing sort of worked. Robby always had a small sketchbook on his person with a pencil, which he pushed and cranked into a bit of a point. He was drawing Firefall for Ike Clipper— a Firefall for Firefall.

"What a pleasure meeting you!" Al said, joining them at the kitchen table. "You were born in this house?"

"No," Robby said, tearing out a page of his sketchbook to give to Ike. "We moved here after my dad got back from the war. I lived here until I went to art school in Oakland."

"I was," Stella said. "And grew up here until we moved to the new places out Franzel Meadows way. Funny how a kitchen table always fits right *here*."

"He was an artist from birth," Ike said, pouring more black coffee, holding up the sketched image of Firefall. "This is his uncle."

"Yeah." Rob Andersen was sketching Thea, who came in and sat down. "Uncle Bob showed up one day when I was a kid."

"Before I was born," said Stella.

"I visited him in Albuquerque."

"I never saw him," Stella said. "He and Mom wrote back and forth. Was he really that good a cook?"

"He was. He and his wife had a Chinese restaurant on Route 66. He'd learned all the secret recipes. I hung around there for a week. His wife, Angel, made me do the dishes in the restaurant to earn my meals, as a joke, really. Gave me and Uncle Bob time together in the kitchen. He told me some pretty wild stories of when he was a kid, when he was a Marine, when he was a biker. He'd become sort of religious. Said he was steered by a holy trinity—his wife, his Harley, and his Higher Power."

"Get this," Ike said. "The man had no idea he was Firefall."

"No?" Al asked.

"I'd forgotten about drawing that comic." Keli came into the kitchen. Ruby was passed from her into Stella's lap. Robby started a sketch of the baby. "I'd done a million others and had moved on to my Riverscapes."

"Painting rivers," Stella explained. "Want to know how to spend all your life savings and live hand to mouth? Riverscapes."*

"He still rode motorcycles?" Ike thought that was way cool.

"He took me to Clark's Drugs the first time I rode one."

"Clark's Drugs?" Al asked. "On Main Street?"

"Yeah. Bought me Cokes and comic books."

"Will you show us around the place?" Al asked.

"We can get into Clark's Drugs?"

"Yep!"

★   ★   ★

Al had the set opened for a Sunday Recce, with Ynez showing up with platters of fast Mexican food. She told Bill to get his golf-ball ass down to the set to meet the originator of his movie

---

* Those in the art world now pay six figures for some of Robby's Riverscapes, due, certainly, to the release of the movie and its introduction of Firefall.

and composed a text to Wren: **You might want to meet a VVIP at Clark's!**

COMPANY PHONE: ?

A MacT: **Firefall's nephew.**

Though not officially a Hot Set, Clark's was being kept ready for additional shooting, if needed. The only cars on Main that morning were those of Ike and family, the Andersens' shit-box rental, Ynez's PONY Ford, Al's Mustang, and Bill's red Charger.

"Wow," Stella said. "Good repro of the place. At least the diner section."

Robby agreed. "The fountain counter and the booths are just as they were. Crazy they never changed them. Over there," he said with a wave. "That was the five-and-dime section. Back there was the pharmacy. This was the newsstand." He meant the nook right by the front entrance, where they were standing.

Tom Windermere pulled up in the latest car from Transpo. Wren was riding shotgun and hopped out holding a small box bound with pink ribbon. When she came into Clark's, Gregory Maddio found his throat had gone dry—Wren Lane was in the room. Wren Lane was introducing herself. Wren Lane was shaking his hand. Wren Lane.

The food and drinks were laid out on the counter. Wren went right to Thea, handing her the ribboned box. "For the birthday girl," she said. Inside was a cupcake and candle, with a blue stationery note to Ruby saying, *Always be as old as you are! Xx WL.*

Ruby was turning a year old later in the week. Long ago, Ike had mentioned the birthday, and Wren made it a point to remember.

"Thank you," Thea said.

She appreciated the gesture and followed up with hopes that Wren was all right after what had happened with the man at the gate. Wren gave Thea a hug and whispered, "Thank you." Thea was not certain Wren was sincere. But when she added, "I was so . . . scared . . ." Thea cut the woman some slack. Who wouldn't be scared? Thea would have been terrified.

"I sat right here," Robby said, taking the very same stool he was once too small for. "Uncle Bob here. We read comic books. He smoked some. His motorcycle was right where Ynez's car is parked. He got bored and had to do an errand. He never came back."

"You walk home?" This was the first Stella had heard of any of this.

"The guy who ran the newsstand gave me a ride." Robby had an out-of-body moment, sitting at the counter in the same exact space as then.

"I sat where you are for my scenes in Clark's," Wren said. "On that same stool."

Bill asked if, for his own sense of purpose, everyone would crowd into the booth where he'd shot the Investigators when they first sit in their search for Firefall. They did: Ike, Thea with Ruby, Wren next to Robby, Stella on the corner. Keli and Gregory mushed in.

Ynez was mightily aware of the serendipitous history at play, there in Clark's. She had said to Al, "I bet this doesn't happen very often on a movie." Al just gave her a wide-eyed look of wonder and awe, meaning, *No, it doesn't.*

"We have the R-E-E-L Knightshade and Firefall, and the R-E-A-L Firefall," Ynez announced. "If only we had the R-E-A-L Eve."

"We do," Wren said. She reached across the table and took hold of Ruby's foot. "Here's our Agent of Change!"

Everyone laughed, including Thea, who cut the woman even more slack.

As is the case with coffee shops and the simulacra of a movie set, Clark's Drugs bade the group stay for a while. The thermoses that kept the coffee hot were a plus. The women stuck to the booth and talked. Bill and Ike sat with Robby, listening to stories about growing up in Lone Butte.

"Tell me," Bill asked of Robby. "About your uncle. Why did you make him Firefall?"

"He was a kid. They made him a Flamethrower. Went to war, did horrible things. Came home, then vanished," Robby said. "And one day, he was here. Like a specter. A phantom." At the counter, for the next hour, Bill and Ike heard all there was to know about Bob Falls. "The man was a god to me," his eighty-plus-year-old nephew said.

The Sunday filled with visits to the stages at Westinghouse Light, a drive-by of where the family printing shop had once been, which only recently had become the site of a Dollar General, a look at the now defunct Union High School, a drive across Old Trestle Bridge and a return to 114 Elm Street. A photo of everyone posed in the backyard, the plum trees behind them, was taken with Bill's phone on self-timer. Ynez printed up a copy of the script with a *TREV-VORR* ID, which everyone signed with a pencil. The old sharpener was pried off the doorway so Robby Andersen could take it with him.

Hugs were exchanged when it was time for the VVIPs to leave for the drive back to Oakland. Keli offered to take Ruby for a week. Gregory's heart stopped when Wren threw her arms around him and said he could be an actor if he gave it a shot. Robby Andersen waved from his seat, riding shotgun, as the car drove away from 114 Elm Street, a parting that would last forever.

THE REMAINDER

Nina (Base Camp AD): Running Base Camp is independent of the progress on the set. Time stands still there even if I don't. An unwritten rule for the Base Camp AD is that you never sit down anywhere but in the Production Trailer, so all day I'm on my feet with an ear on the radio. I get a sense if things are going well or if there's tension that could spill over to my area. I have folks to instruct, to inform, to move around, to keep tabs on, and to keep happy. I predict, give warnings, get the cast moving into the Works, to the set, back from lunch. I ask the Talent to let me know if they're taking a nap so that when I come knocking I'll do it gently. There are code words and numbers for situations. *Anchors Away* means "all is well." The worst is *Falcon 109*. That means "motherfucking disaster."

Ynez: I made Base Camp as nice as I could, but at Westinghouse Light it was just a big gravel parking lot. No shade like at the Almond Growers Building. I had a picnic table and camp chairs set up right at the door of Ike's trailer, which was right next to Wren's. The Art Department gave us some padded Astroturf and, you know, baby gear like a playpen, another wading pool that the Teamsters inflated with their compressed air. Thea and Ruby and my cousin Lupe would often come midmorning, so I had Set Dressing bring over umbrellas for later in the afternoon, when the trailer canopy couldn't block the sun.

Yogi: The grand fact of a movie's final weeks of shooting is that every day more of the work is behind you. You don't have to plan and meet and schedule a million shots to come. Every day you cross one task off the to-do list, and once that scene is shot, it stays shot. You can't relax on what remains, of course, there is never a day of coasting, but the workload thins.

Al: Moving into Westinghouse Light was a trade-off—you're inside, air-conditioned, and can shoot with no regard to climate or time of day. But there is a cost to the momentum and spirit. Everything takes longer to work through all the technical glitches so . . . What's the word Wren uses about how boring some days on a stage can be? *Ennui*. That's right. An ennui sets in.

Wren: The stage work is shots—this look, that move, a push-in or crane rise. But I still have to *go there*. I can't tell you how. I won't tell you how. Process is a secret. Mine is anyway.

Ike: We had three fight scenes. The Day Lumber Mill. The Night on Main Street. And at the Knight House. All in the wires. That was a lot of hang time.

Wren: Fight One, I want to stop Firefall. Fight Two, I want to kill him. Fight Three, I'm screaming at Fate, all alone and broken. Each is different.

Ike: Weird that each fight did have a different pace and emotional confrontation to them. That's something else. The acting and performance parts of each fight needed a new factor that, um, took me by surprise. Working in tight and close with Wren? I couldn't help but be, um, drawn into the moment. She does that to you, you know? Even with the harnesses and the wires and the VFX and stunt teams all over you. Wren, well, she doesn't just look at you, she *searches* you. Yes, having my family right there, most days was, uh, good. Kept me grounded, you know?

Aaron Blau: Second Unit was all over Lone Butte when the first was on the Green Screen. Those last weeks are all about getting the shots. Bill has a list two arms long of all he wants, of the beats the movie needs. We didn't have a moment to waste and every time we rolled on Second Unit we had to get what Bill the Writer-Director Johnson wanted.

Cassandra: Saturdays were our Investigator scenes—dedicated to just our pages.

Hang To: Who wants to work on Saturdays? I don't. The crew didn't. For car interiors and that bitch of a scene on the interstate. We weren't on the interstate but on a slab of pavement laid down in that big, dark stage. Wren was all worked up for that one. I thought she hated me, personally. Has she said anything to you?

Nick Czabo: Ike came by to watch that Saturday. The guy had hiked all the way from Lone Butte to Westinghouse Light—then hiked back. It was fun to watch Eve and London snarl at each other.

Hector Chew and Marilyn Cakebread (Film Editors): We'd been cutting every day, and we knew, even from the first scene with Eve and Falls, that something was brewing between those two . . . Their characters, yes . . . Those two in the footage were just smoking. Individually, Eve is singular and Firefall was cryptic—both of them so lonely . . . They carried loneliness in their eyes . . . When they finally are together they come off as love at first sight . . . After hate at first sight. I think Eve has been waiting for a Firefall all her life, but he's taken by surprise . . . There is one shot of Ike in the lumber mill fight where he looks like *Uh-oh, I'm in trouble,* but not because Eve is kicking his ass. Because she's taken his breath away . . . We put together a three-minute reel of their best moments, just to show what lightning we had in the Editing Room and put it up in the PO screening room one night after Wrap.

Ynez: I'd gotten FroYo. But once the footage started rolling no one lifted a spoon. We watched it four times in a row.

Al: I won't take anything away from my boss or SAM or Yogi or the whole Unit. But. Wren and Ike! Those two were like lovers in a two-seater Audi.

Dr. Pat Johnson: Bill put on music that matched the emotions on the screen. He called that a cheap trick, but oh Lord, did it work. I've seen how movies are made and I've known for years how fickle the process can be. Bill tells me dumb luck is the only reason he has a career. But there was nothing in those scenes that was the product of good fortune. Wren and Ike were, pardon the pun, on fire.

Al: If your world is expanded by going to the movies—if you're one of us who need films to make our lives wider, more complete—a great film has the same transformative power as hearing soul-filling music or being spellbound by, say, great oratory like a sermon. The three minutes of that reel made you feel glad to be alive and very lucky to work on Fountain Avenue. Because of Wren and Ike. Ike and Wren.

Yogi: Fight stuff. Some dialogue. Close-ups. But nothing prepared us for the look in their eyes. Ike's reveal. Wren's reaction.

Le'Della Rawaye: Fight Number 2, downtown with the flames. Then the very first look we got of Ike when Wren knocked the helmet off? We dove deep into that man's eyes. And the reverse, of Wren? Seeing his full face for the first time. Looking into his eyes. Like she wanted to cry. She had something, went somewhere. I said "Yes!" out loud.

SAM: We had them in silhouette, and shot overs, and ECUs and the one long Pogo-Cam angle. Worked well.

Ynez: And this was before we shot the final fight—after Amos Knight has passed and Eve is alone for the rest of time.

Al: We still had the Kiss to shoot. If Wren and Ike were that *enthralling and connected* as they slugged it out with no K I S S I N G, what would happen when the moment came? We found out the next day. Oh, man. Man, oh man. Man. Wow.

Thea Hill: I stayed home when Ike shot Fight Number 3. I'd had enough of Base Camp.

Ynez: There in the middle of that huge space with all the crew rigging and setting up, they might as well have been all alone, by themselves. The script called it "a kiss for the ages." Between the takes, they talked quietly, Ike and Wren. Not whispering, but in low, close tones. Heads together. Lots of smiles.

Hector Chew and Marilyn Cakebread: Those Rushes were extraordinary. Ike and Wren might not have once taken their eyes off each other . . . Even over the slates, they were in the moment . . . Kissing scenes are so often perfunctory . . . Or too blatant. The kisses are oversold and the actors look like they're faking it . . . But

Knightshade, the moment before she kisses Firefall, and his reaction? Bill and Al came into the Editing Room and ran the footage again and again and again . . . What was it Al said?

Al: I'd like to kiss a man like that.

BARRY SHAW

On Day 49 (of 53 Shooting Days) a meeting was called in the all-but-barren office of Bill Johnson. The door was closed.

Monday morning. 7:06 a.m. Per the Call Sheet, the day's work would be odds and ends; VFX needs, inserts, more of the Investigators in the SUV and sedan and a Stunt Unit shot of Eve overturning the Investigators' sedan after tearing off the door of the SUV and tossing it like a newspaper; a day to chop wood and carry water. Ike was pulled from the Works the moment Wren arrived at Base Camp. Aea Kakar had been On Hold for so long she'd gone home to LA but was now back, reporting to the Green Room at Westinghouse Light. Ynez had the usual breakfast orders lined up and everyone had their chosen coffee. Wren had a glass of a probiotic green liquid. Al was there. Bill was serious.

"How do we wrap our picture, guys?" he asked.

Everyone knew what he was talking about.

Scene 97. The finale. The end of Firefall's search. The passing of Pop-Pop. The completion of the story. Nurse Sue. Eve. Firefall. And Amos Knight. How do you shoot a scene with an actor who has slipped the mortal coil? How can you film a scene without the man being there?

"If we don't have ninety-seven we don't have a picture. The best I can come up with is two choices," the director said. "We have to call it."

"It's up to us?" Wren asked.

Bill spoke dryly. "We're soul mates. We've been through so much together no one of us can dictate terms. Technically, it's a bunt. A few setups with Frances reading Amos's dialogue. You three looking at an empty bed. With all the audio we have of Elliot in the hard drive we can reverse engineer much of his dialogue in Post with a sound-alike. VFX can animate any action we need from a CGI Amos Knight. Physically—technically—we can get the shots we need."

An exact replica of Amos's bedroom had been built on an adjunct space at Westinghouse Light—a set so authentic Wren had yet to visit, the memory of dear, sweet, magical Elliot Guarnere still too tender in her heart.

Bill continued, "I don't doubt you guys will dig deep. But I can't help but wonder if there isn't a mystic element to this challenge. Al and I have been talking in secret for weeks. This meeting is the result."

Ike was listening. Aea was in awe of Bill's reach at a moment like this—in the face of a production nightmare. Wren felt like she had very long ago, in Socorro, when Bill Johnson called on her for *Serenity*.

"Here's what I've been thinking . . ."

After hearing him out, the vote was unanimous.

★   ★   ★

The Investigators were done with all their dialogue in the picture on Day 50 (of 53 Shooting Days). They shot Exteriors in Lone Butte and finished up the fourteen-hour day inside Westinghouse Light. Hang To kept joke-doctoring his lines. Nick Czabo and Lala worked out a lovely bit of business in the back seat of the sedan on some needed cutaways. Cassandra was word perfect and attitude magnificent, knowing that this recent AOC chapter would refine, and redefine, the course of the Ultra Universe. Dynamo, Al reported, was surprised by the strength of the Investigators' on-screen chemistry. She'd had several conversations with the Executive Chorus about their pleasure and carried the message to the others.

"Let's not blow it on our last day," Cassandra warned. They had one scene left, the last page of the screenplay, with no dialogue but a ton of pressure. "They might keep us together in the next movie."

"Agents of Change 6: Lima's Revenge?" Hang asked. "I ain't coming cheap."

They were On Hold for Day 51. Per the Call Sheet: scene 97.

Bill ordered a ten-hour day to keep the focus tight and momentum rolling—no lunch break. He and SAM had talked through all the camera moves and each bit of coverage, which would not be the short, interrupted cuts, but the full scene from start to finish on every take, each angle. Talks with VFX had put everyone on the same page.

Ike was called into the Works at 5:00 a.m. for that first slathering of cold and sticky goop into the folds of his neck. Kenny Sheprock had suggested his skin might take the glue better if he shaved cleanly, with three different types of electric razors. That seemed to work.* Ike'd be camera ready at 9:00. Wren and Aea joined him in the H/MU trailer at 7:30. Everyone worked quietly, but to break up the stilted, tense atmosphere, the pressure from the work awaiting them all, Wren asked if they could run the lines in a hushed tone—as flat as could be, no acting allowed. Nurse Sue was all but silent in the scene, so Aea monotoned Amos's lines.

★   ★   ★

In another room in Westinghouse Light was Barry Shaw—the kid from way back in the shoot who had mowed grass and played Marco Polo in a wading pool as Eve walked to breakfast at Clark's.

Barry had a birthday during production, back on July 10. He was eighteen years old but looked too young to vote. He lived outside Redding, in the house he grew up in. He'd graduated from high school in June but had no college plans other than to attend Shasta Community and work part-time jobs as a FedEx/Amazon driver. He hoped to become an emergency medical technician and go to the California Highway Patrol Academy. He'd heard about the movie being shot in Lone Butte, had been in his high-school production of *Rent,* knew all the rap lyrics of *Hamilton,* and proved it in his short meeting with the local casting folks. They loved the kid.

After his Marco Polo scene, he'd been called in to work many of

---

* The daily glue was the only part of the movie Ike was looking forward to ending. Even though Sean, Jason, and Brittany had all been great folks to see every goddamn morning. Still, no more. No more!

the nights on Main Street as one of the citizens of the town when Firefall and Knightshade were fighting and all but burning down Iron Bluff. In the Rushes he had a particular bearing, a natural physicality as though he were not performing for the camera but behaving in the moment. There was one particular close-up—in front of Saint Philip Neri, a.k.a. Our Lady of Sorrows—when he was looking off camera at imaginary flames—that hit Bill Johnson smack in his heart. That night, Bill added a shot of Firefall's helmet, knocked off during Fight #2, rolling to the gutter, being picked up by the Marco Polo kid. There was something in Barry that sparked joy. Hector and Marilyn had flagged the footage the moment they'd seen it.

Some days ago, Barry's phone rang while he was washing his dad's Ford F-150, which would be his once he started classes at Shasta CC.

"Mr. Shaw, Al Mac-Teer from the production. How you doing?" said an official voice.

Barry had met Ms. Mac-Teer during the Night Shoots. "I'm okay. How are you?"

"Got a minute to talk to the boss?"

"Now?" Barry had no idea who "the boss" might be. "Yes." Bill Johnson's voice came through on his cell.

"Barry! How are you, lad?"

"I'm good, I think."

"You missing us?" The Night Shoots had been some time before. On the last morning of the shooting, the first AD had gathered all the Townsfolk in a group in front of Clark's Drugs, thanked them for their positive attitudes and work ethics, told them they were all loved and appreciated, and bade them an exhausted farewell with instructions to return all their props and costumes in the Holding Area. Making the movie had been, to Barry, about as much fun as making a movie was supposed to be, despite working all night.

"Yes. I kind of do."

"Ah, *kind of do*, eh? I wonder if you would consider coming back to join us for another bit of filming . . ."

Barry was a bit flummoxed. He was originally going to work a day with some kids in a pool, then was brought in to witness a huge sequence, then given a protracted bit with a rolling helmet.

And he'd stood next to Wren Lane at Crafty a few times. Who wouldn't want to do that again?

"Sure. Yes," Barry said. "I'd kind of like to."

"Great. Come in today so you and I can chat. But tell me something," Bill Johnson said. "Can you keep this all a big secret?"

"Yes," Barry said. "Sure." He did not ask why.

"I believe you. Al will tell you when to be in the PO."

Ms. Mac-Teer got back on the phone. "Barry?'

"Yes?"

"Come in right now."

Barry took the time to hose down the Ford F-150, then drove to Lone Butte with the truck still dripping.

★ ★ ★

His youth was the reason Barry was in a separate, secret room in Westinghouse Light at 7:47 that morning with the VFX team huddled around him.

Bill had explained it to his soul mates two days before: "Those Marines who fought the war were mostly kids right out of high school. If you were twenty-four, you were called Pops, or Old Man. No college. No career yet, not with a World War starting when you were still cheating on exams in algebra and Latin at Union High. Ike, Robert No-Middle-Initial Falls was a kid. Wren, Amos Knight was how old, do you think, when he fought in the war?"

Wren had long ago thought out this bit of her backstory. She'd talked about Amos's history with Elliot, on the first days of shooting. "Pop-Pop was nineteen when Pearl Harbor was attacked. He enlisted the very next day. He'd gone down to join the navy but a fellow in line talked him into signing up to be a Marine."

"Okay," Bill said. "Knight and Falls, two children sent off into hell. Only one kid came home. So. What if, instead of imagining that your age-appropriate grandfather is in that bed for ninety-seven . . ."

Bill paused. Ike and Wren and Aea leaned in. Ynez held her breath.

"You all see Amos as he *was*. On the day he first met Robert Falls." The room was silent. "Before they went into hell." Wren raised her eyes to heaven, imagining the sight. Ike bowed his head, imaging the moment. Aea nodded. Al waited for the answer. She and Bill had spent hours talking about this turn, wondering if the cast would see the same possibility they did.

As stated before, the vote was unanimous. Three in favor. Four. Ynez's vote had been tallied.

Barry was given a Marine Corps haircut by the Good Cooks. The VFX/CGI team marked his face with guide dots, so that in Post the digital scans of Elliot Guarnere's face would replace his own. He'd been given audio tracks from the finished scenes of Amos, so he could approximate the tenor and cadence of Elliot's performance.[*]

On the Day, he climbed into the bed in the set of Pop-Pop's room a half hour before Wren, Ike, and Aea were invited.

★ ★ ★

Yogi: The stage was kept calm and quiet. No one talked, except for the instructions to the crew. Everyone had walkies with headphones so chatter was muffled. Barry never got out of the bed. He simply closed his eyes between the shots and setups. The Talent never saw him get in or out. I usually watch the monitor to make adjustments as needed, to gauge when a problem arises that I can help fix. But for 97, oh man, there wasn't a moment we weren't witnessing something grand. I couldn't take my eyes off the monitor.

SAM: Bill and I thought simple was best—each setup was static; every size was still. We'd been shooting with a dynamic, subjective camera, with designed shots in sequences—always moving, pushing in. But for 97, we locked off the lens, really. Used a remote head so the operator and focus puller were not in the set but out of sight. The bedroom had only Wren, Ike, Aea, and the kid. That's right. Barry.

Frances: Their eyes. They were listening with their eyes. Aea had two words—"Yes, Amos?"—but she said them with so much *love*. Wren asked to do her coverage last. So, Aea went first and set a high bar.

---

[*] He drove around Redding each night, in his F-150, listening to those audio tracks and running the dialogue for 97 for hours and hours.

Yogi: We started with the intimate close-ups after a perfunctory rehearsal, just the blocking and marks. Aea's were a few takes, two sizes. Ike was next, and the guy was a wreck for the first few takes.

Frances: Bill wanted Ike to remain Firefall through the scene—stoic, right? And all "Mission," as Bill put it. Ike came undone a couple of times, not that Bill cut the camera. He let Ike roll along to wherever the scene took him. There were a few moments when I thought he had dropped a line, but what had happened was, Ike couldn't speak. He was forming the words but couldn't get them out.

SAM: Wren went somewhere else. I'd grown used to her specificity, all the detail she put into her choices in the movie. But in 97, she walked on some other plane. She spoke straight from her face—no embellishment, no nod at an emotion. No "performance." She didn't have much dialogue, but she spoke with a desire, a will. Few actors can do that. They all try.

Frances: That's when I saw that Ike had the same color eyes as Barry Shaw. Not blue as blue, but a combination of blue and gray. I was shocked by the match. Barry didn't say the dialogue. He thought it out loud. He came up with repeating the line about steak and eggs. He'd read that detail of preinvasion breakfasts of steak and eggs. He asked Bill if he could add it a second time. What a brave kid! Bill told him to go ahead and if it didn't work he'd cut around it. The moment is fucking priceless.

SAM: Barry would be replaced in Post, yes. But he'd studied Elliot's voice. Damn if he didn't sound like Elliot. He was Amos Knight. Wren gasped when she first heard him.

Marvin Pritch (Sound Mixer): I have my little monitor so I see what's on camera. Had I been blind, what I heard was enough to know that 97 was the apex of the movie.

Donnie Marcus (Gaffer): We'd prelit the set the day before and tweaked all morning before the cast reported. Not being back in the house allowed the set to have wild walls. SAM had all the freedom he needed. But what happened was due to the cast. I've been on serious sets on serious days when serious tension is cut with a knife and everyone on the crew is on tiptoe to not rock the boat. That set was calm when it shouldn't have been.

Ted Truman (Focus Puller): All I remember is terror that I'd be soft.

Yogi: We didn't need the whole ten hours. After coverage on Barry, Bill had a wide master—like a tableau—and a final angle from outside, through the window. Just Wren and Ike, looking at the bed. Barry was still in the bed but all we saw were his hands.

Hector and Marilyn: That one little glance, the shared look between Eve and Firefall? That came after a cut—it wasn't part of the scene . . . Wren and Ike just *found* each other. They'd become Eve and Bob Falls . . . There was love there.

You Are Loved

Day 52 (of 53 Shooting Days) was quick pops: Eve in the shower. Eve in the shed grabbing nails. Eve out on the interstate (Green Screen), throwing nails. VFX inserts.

Then came the last Call Sheet. Day 53 (of 53 Shooting Days).

The Crew was relieved to be outside of Westinghouse Light on a glorious late summer day to wrap Principal Photography with the last scene in the movie. What are the odds? First shot first scene, last shot last scene. The location was a field on a farm northeast of Lone Butte, with the Base Camp set up on the river. The H/MU trailer was humming with good cheer as Wren, Ike, and all the Investigators were in the Works at the same time; in the same scene for the first time. Music was playing and everyone was a part of a single conversation, one that moved along like water over stones.

Ken Sheprock told about the last day on a picture he'd shot in Argentina when a lightning bolt hit the generator and caused an explosion. The director called "Wrap" and every American was on a plane for home within hours. The Good Cooks told of a last day of shooting that lasted twenty-seven hours in a tent in Morocco, which the winds almost blew away. Wren said the only final shot of any movie she could remember was in *Periwinkle,* when she had to fall into a puddle of mud and got some in her eye that led to an infection. That story prompted a string of "I almost got killed" stories. Hang said he'd been bitten by a spider on *1968.* Cassandra once could not get to the camera position because the gear needed for the shot blocked all access and made her trip. Ike asked everyone to please shut up as he was trying to sleep while his scars were being applied. Wren turned up the music and everyone sang Pink's "Get the Party Started" at the top of their lungs.

Nina invited Ike and Wren to the set and thus began the final day of shooting. Thea brought Ruby to play in the tall grass and have lunch. The catering tent had the sides up to enjoy the fresh air, giving the meal break the feel of an outdoor wedding.

The pace was easy. The shot list was all elegant camera moves and composed reveals. The final images of Firefall and the squad disappearing into the trees was going to wait for Golden Hour.

99 THE MORNING SUNRISE.

100 EXT. FIELD OF TALL GRASS—OUTSIDE IRON BLUFF.

KNIGHTSHADE AND FIREFALL are spooning.

They are both ASLEEP.

We have never seen two beings in such restful slumber.

Eve awakens first. She has sleep in her eyes. She is trying to find herself, her place.

She is dazed by the aftereffects of sleep.

She recalls the loss of her granddad.

She pulls the arm of Robert No-Middle-Initial Falls around her. Tighter.

He awakens. He, too, is altered by the experience of sleep.

He sits up. As does she. They look at each other.

                    EVE KNIGHT
            Will you be there with him?

                     FIREFALL
          Yes.

She stands.

Above the tall grass, she can see Iron Bluff.
Some smoke, yes.

But that seems like years ago.

She ponders the horizon, and all that has
happened . . .

We see her face—experience, wisdom, acceptance.
We see her at peace . . .

She feels a breeze, dusty wind . . .

She turns back to Robert Falls. His burned face,
his scarred, helmetless head.

His eyes.

He stands. He lifts his M2-2 Flamethrower across
his shoulders.

A Dust-Devil forms around him.

The Dust becomes smoke, swirling faster,
obliterating him . . .

Circling faster and faster as Eve can only
look on.

And then he is gone.

Eve stands in the field.

She is alone . . . All alone.

She hears someone . . . a young man's
voice . . . "Eve!" . . .

She looks at the tree line on the far side of
the field.

101 TREE LINE—SAME

A squad of MARINES—walking slowly toward a
battle—led by a young Sergeant Amos Knight.*

In the rear, tail-end Charlie, with no helmet
for combat, is a Flamethrower.

The Sergeant gives a hand signal. The squad
changes direction and disappears into the
trees.

The Flamethrower looks back, for just a moment,
at where he has been. He waves.

Eve waves back.

102 EXT. ROAD—SAME

London has been watching . . . through
surveillance glasses . . . Her team of
Investigators has been recording it all
with cameras, radar, instruments . . .

London swings her glasses to . . .

---

* Played by Barry Shaw.

P.O.V.

Eve Knight.

She turns . . . and looks London straight in
the eye.

                              SMASH TO:

BLACK

And this . . .

"Eve Knight will appear in *Agents of Change 6:
Cry Havoc.*"

ROLL CREDITS

A Conversation with Dr. Johnson

"I was there for the last day of shooting and the Wrap Party in the Almond Building. I have a soft spot for mariachi music and that band—friends of Ynez—oh, they were grand! Bill is so flagged by Wrap he never stays long for his own parties, but I sat him down and told him to treat the night like a date with me, not a professional obligation. The wives of the crew always show up, dressed to the nines. Wren was gracious. Ike seemed a little shell-shocked that the movie was over. Thea was overjoyed. Many of the locals were there and partied all night, I heard. Little Lone Butte will never be the same.*

   "Post is when I get my man back. After the fever of the Shoot, we go away for two weeks if I can manage the time off. We've been to Portugal, Greece, and once to Antarctica, but that was for some

---

* A large photo of Elliot Guarnere was set up in the lobby, in memory of. People put flowers next to it. By the end of the night, some drunken partygoer had taped up a Xeroxed photo of OKB with RIP scrawled in Sharpie.

work I was doing as well. After this job Bill went to Vietnam by himself. Rode a bike from Hanoi to Hue. With a guide. Took it slow, he said. I had to teach.

"He needs the decompression time, to not think about the movie in any way. To let his mind and body wander around. I insist only on no golf courses. He can do that across the street.

"Once back, Bill makes the movie all over again. Prep is Diplomacy. The Shoot is War. Post is the Occupation. He explained that to me long ago, back when I was curious as to how movies were made, which I am not anymore. I've seen the process. I can't say I'm enamored with moviemaking. I never wanted to be inside the glamour dome of show business. But Bill has shown me that the work has a nobility to it, that like my love for science and teaching, curiosity fuels you and passion carries you along. Lose either one and you're done. The moment you react by rote or settle for "good enough" is when you're out of that line of work. I think he is great at admitting what he doesn't know, trusting that the picture will tell him what needs to be done, and that if he's lucky he'll get away with it. He's a thief, and there is honor among thieves.

"What kind of thief? A con man. A grifter. A carny. He calls moviemaking the Cardboard Carnival. The moment a customer buys a ticket, he provides them the distraction from life they crave at the cost of few bucks.

"Do I like his movies? What am I supposed to say to that? Some don't quite gel, but he knows that. If Bill was the kind of man who needed me to adore and love and foam over his movies, he'd not be the man for me. But he's never certain of his final product and I find that admirable. He doesn't know if it works or not. Other people tell him that.

"The first time he makes the movie is when he writes the screenplay. That's his imagination coming through that old typewriter— that first smudged-up draft spotted with pencil scratches and Post-its. He says that's the movie he *wants* to make. I have him around for Prep but lose him the moment he begins making the movie for a second time. The Shoot is always hell. There is no limit to the amount of work the Shoot requires. A million ants crawl all over his creation. Some of his grand dreams must be thrown away, some severed from the body to be saved, some stored to age into either wine or vinegar. There's little he can control. Not the weather. Not the psyches of his hires—other than Team Johnson. Not the COVID protocols.* The only decision that is his alone is to get out of bed or not. The Shoot is the hardest, longest, most cruel of tasks. The Shoot is the movie he was *forced* to make, resulting in a billion shards of glass that have to be assembled piece by piece into a mirror.

"That happens in Post. The third time the movie gets made. The movie *he* made.

"He starts by stringing together everything he has in the can, every shot from every day. Every scene has a beginning, middle, and end. For *Albatross,* he had an assemblage over five hours long. *Knightshade* was half that but still too long.

"No, I don't watch the cuts. I wait until he needs some fresh eyes. Some months into Post, he'll show a cut to me, a FedEx delivery gal, some college students, the parking valet at the Capitol Records Building, anyone who signs an NDA. Maybe one of the cast members who knows how it all works, caveat-free, like Clancy O'Finley and his wife. Those two know what not to worry about. I tell him if I get bored.

"Bill could have a cutting room in Socorro, but that would mean the whole team would have to live here, and the town is not for everybody. He's got a room at Optional Enterprises and likes the commute to Hollywood from his bachelor pad on Wilshire. He does all the mixing and dubbing in the Valley. You tell me the difference between the mix and the dub—I've never needed to know. Bill tells me that no matter what shape his movie is in, every single day of Post makes it better.

---

* A note on COVID-19. I've not bothered with detailing the twice-weekly tests of the cast and crew, the division of the crew into work pods, the installation of plexiglass dividers, and the need for social distancing, since that would take up so many pages and read like blah-didty-blahblahblah. The protocols became routine, anyway. And, even with some positive cases and the attendant isolations, the work stoppages were minimal. I have omitted the reality of the shielding and separation needed in the H/MU trailer to seem as though everyone was working right beside one another, unhindered. In fact, masks, plexiglass, and staggered Call Times were required for insurance reasons and Guild requirements. COVID added $2.6 million to the budget. And one infected crew member suffered a terrible bout with the virus, was hospitalized, and did not finish the picture.

"I come and go. Better for me to fly in on a weekend. Saturday mornings, he runs a reel of the week's work, and right after we go on a hike or I'll sit and read while he hits a bucket of golf balls at a driving range in Studio City. He makes me a Sunday breakfast and we spend the day either doing nothing or, well, you know. I fly back to ABQ on an uncanceled flight.

"Observed by a noncombatant, the months of Post are boring. The progress is so incremental you wonder if anything, really, is getting done. The amount of time spent discussing arcane decisions like does the EQ level on a loop line match the room tone, or why not hold a few more frames on that one look of Nurse Sue being mad at Amos? Those discussions never end. Insane. For months, I tell you. The cast has to rerecord some of their work, a process called ADR or looping. They see some of the scenes but not the whole movie. Some sessions go long and get uncomfortable, but not with this cast. That's what Bill told me, anyway.

"Finally, one night, the Best Friends Only screening takes place. That's the second time I see his movie and, always, the movie is so very different from that first cut. Maybe fifteen people, friends from his other movies. Al of course. The Instigator. Ynez was there for this one, since she had moved to LA. No cast members yet—they get a screening all to themselves. And no one from either Dynamo or the Hawkeye. Just the dozen-plus of us. Some of the special effects are in the movie, most are just what are called composites and temps, but we get the gist.

"After the houselights come up, Bill asks, 'So, what did you think?' And he listens to every word—every opinion, thought, suggestion, idea with follow-up questions, to be clear on what opinion means what.

"Does he use every note? No. But he says those screenings test the movie. If there's one scene that everyone agrees is confusing or misplayed, he'll attack that one.

"He cuts more, mixes more, gets the effects shots into the movie, then shows it to the various Executive Choruses. He showed the movie to Wren—in a screening room all by herself. Very top secret. No one knew but the two of them and Al. Then she and Bill talked and talked and talked. A few days later, Bill Locked Picture. That,

I am told, is a big deal. Everything gets polished and shined after Picture Lock.

"He tries to make a bit of a party with the screenings for the cast. In LA for Wren and Wally, Clancy again. Hang and Nick and their plus-ones. Aea brought her big family. Bill, Al, and Ynez flew to New York to show Ike and Thea, Cassandra, and some long-lead press. Ynez had never been to New York and wanted to move there.

"There are no research screenings. Dynamo has a policy of not letting any information out on any of their superhero movies. The Internet goes nuts over them, and I think one of the early movies suffered some fallout over one of the costumes of Ursa Lion-Lady. Their security is watertight. Bill hates recruited screenings anyway. He stopped doing those when he went back to making hits. The audiences are asked, What did you like? What didn't work for you? What scene was your favorite? What character did you like/not like? Would you recommend must see/are likely to see/might see/don't bother seeing? How many people walked out? Bill says recruited screenings are for the marketing folks. He has a clause in his contract—Final Cut*—so he ignores those results.

"Dynamo came at him with suggestions galore—pages of them. Al was on the phone for hours listening to all that Dynamo wanted to do with Bill's cut. Bill read every note and Al told him all that the studio wanted. He might have taken one or two of their notes. But only if he agreed they made the picture a little better. One of the reasons he's the man for me."

★   ★   ★

Not long after a crew screening, Kenny Sheprock sent texts to Wren, but the lady was busy with her flying and career options and her being so very special. She responded with emoji kisses and winking faces, a clockface, and a question mark. He wanted to have a quick talk with her, but there was no hurry. When she had

---

* Very rare. Even for some A-list directors who go over budget. Final Cut is *the* contractual right all directors strive for. Studios use a director's lack of Final Cut as a cudgel. Directors with it tell the executives to fuck off. No one can mess with the film when Bill decides it's done.

the time, she called his cell, getting him in his car in stop-and-go traffic on the 405.

"Kenny!" she squealed, like a teenager in love with a pop idol. "I miss ya so! How are you?"

"Young lady," he said, not moving, behind a landscaper's truck southbound in the Sepulveda Pass. "I've never been better and I wanted to tell you why."

"Tell me all!"

"I'm done, sweetheart. And I mean *done,* done."

"You . . ." Wren wanted to be sure, here. "You're retiring?"

"Walking off the set. Wrapped for good. No more five thirty a.m. calls for me. I've been thinking for the last year or so how to do it best. When you invited me to do *Knightshade* with you, I thought, That's it. I'll go out with Wren on this picture and call it quits. I couldn't be happier."

"Oh, Kenny," Wren cooed over the phone. "My Shep-Rock. I will have to carry on without you, but how?"

"Dear lady, you are going to do just swell."

Wren loved his use of words like *swell.* And being called *dear lady.* With this news, she was going to have to find some other makeup genius if she was going to do *Jane's Song* in South Africa, then *Agents of Change: The Next Agents of Change Movie About the Agents of Change.*

"Kenny," she said over the phone. "I want you to have all the happiness you deserve because I love you and always will."

"Right back at you, kid."

She had flown Wally to Cupertino for some venture capitalist meetings in Silicon Valley and was now back. She was driving from the airfield to her secret house north of Los Angeles, knowing that a new era had begun for her. *Jane's Song* had come to her without so much as a nudge from Micheline Ong—they wanted Wren, first and only choice, wouldn't bother making the movie unless she played the title role (yeah, right). She allowed herself the tiniest bit of glee knowing of all the women who had positioned themselves for the movie, only to *lose.* Heh, heh. Wren felt like Bette Davis in *All About Eve* or *Jezebel.* Who else could have played those parts? No one. She would learn to ride a horse, live in South Africa for four months, maybe five, and be overseas when *Knightshade: The*

Lathe of Firefall dropped, streaming around the world on the
Hawkeye. To be working then would be a good thing.

That the teaser for the movie—first shown at Comic-Con—had
set the Internet on fire was a harbinger of good tidings. Better,
still? The new subscribers to the Hawkeye who began paying $7.77
a month just moments after the teaser dropped. Almost 2 million
new sign-ups. Do the math: 2 million times $7.77 times 12 is a wind-
fall profit of $186,400,000 a year smack into the Hawkeye's coffers.
With that blizzard, everyone at Dynamo considered themselves
geniuses for their wisdom in having Eve Knight join the Agents of
Change.[*] Wren now knew two very important things: The movie
was damn good—different as Ultra movies go, spare, faster (running time: 107 minutes), yet packed with all the eye candy the franchise required. And, forthwith, she would write her own ticket for
the next five years, in time to have her own options when Dynamo
aged her out of Eve. Somewhere, a girl in the junior-high-school
play was to be the next Knightshade—the next Wendy Lank.

When she got home to her rambling ranch, she texted Ike in
Atlanta with her new Wi-Fi identity.

E.Flintstone: Ken Sheprock is retiring!

Ike was between shots and answered immediately with his new
e-persona.

BURPEEMAN: Fountain Ave will never be the same. You OK?

E.Flintstone: Yep. Thea?

BURPEEMAN: Better. Less morning upchucks.

E.Flintstone: Give kisses. Atlanta?

**BURPEEMAN: No Lone Butte. Here's a pic—keep it secret or
Dynamo will sue!**

Wren's screen filled with an image of Ike as, again, Firefall. He'd
been rushed into scenes for the next Ultra production, *Sea Lion:
The Silent World,* which would blend into the new AOC chapter that may or may not bring him and Wren back together. Ike
hoped it would. Someone was working on some script upon which
another billion-dollar risk would be taken.

---

[*] Currently, the Hawkeye boasts more than 114 million subscribers around the
world. At $7.77 per, the math makes that $885,780,000 per year. That's good
math.

★ ★ ★

Thea was pregnant. That was a surprise, though not biologically, mind you, as the act was the act. But neither Ike nor Thea had planned on adding to the family. They had just put money down on a condo in Hoboken—a brand-new place in a complex with a gym and a child-care center and easy access to the city (Thea was auditioning and taking improv classes)—when that familiar sense of "something's happening inside me" hit her. Then the colored lines on a home pregnancy test kit confirmed—"Soup's on." There would be four Cloepfers now, and that Hoboken apartment was going to be on the small side.

And, if Irving/Ike was to land the role of *Foxx for the Prosecution,* he would not be made unrecognizable under four hours of prosthetics, like he'd been as F'fall. He'd be seen as himself and might become famous as such. Irving Cloepfer could live in an apartment tower in Hoboken, but could Ike Clipper? They were looking at a possible move to someplace upstate.

Thea was at the hotel in Buckhead, not feeling well at all, with Ruby walking all around and a young babysitter named Cassidy looking after her. Thea was waiting for a grilled cheese sandwich from room service. The TV was on one of the cable channels. Wren Lane's *Sergeant Harder* was playing at four in the afternoon. Wren was gorgeous. Thea was getting fat. This was *her* life—baby on the way, toddler at her feet, in Buckhead, as Ike worked long hours for a director who was no Bill Johnson, while Sergeant Hard-On solved a crime by sitting at a computer wearing only her bra and panties.

Thea had had some good luck. She'd been cast for a week of work on *Ms. & Mr. Downtown,* shot in Manhattan for KosMos. She hoped against hope that the role would be recurring. But was that even possible now that she was to be a mother of two? If Ike became *Foxx*—another of his F'ing roles—he'd be shooting for months in Baton Rouge or Pittsburgh or Budapest depending on the tax rebates. What would that mean to the four Cloepfers? Would they manage? Would the money make life easier? Would the celebrity status become a pain in their lives? Would they survive? A very, very secret part of Thea wished she was not pregnant, was working as a regular on *Ms. & Mr. Downtown*, was falling in love with her scene partner or the A Camera focus puller; she and Ike remaining friends, loving parents, living in different apartments with separate lives. Grown-ups made such arrangements, didn't they?

When Thea confided such thoughts to her mom, the woman nodded in understanding, having lived a complicated life of her own. "Thea, you're in *the shit* right now. Don't fight it. Grow that baby inside you. Keep Ruby as free from care as you can. Give this five years. Just five years. Then you'll know what's what and do what needs to be done."

A Five-Year Plan is what Thea needed. In a nanosecond she had the next half decade mapped out, a singular strategy that relied not a whit on the fortunes of Ike.

Ike had a plan of his own. Dynamo owned him for three Ultra movies.* His new agency—TRUK—had him collaborating with two other writer-directors for projects in the pipeline. Would he grow tired of this accelerated pace, now that he was twenty-eight years old? His public self was being molded as a boldface name. He was going be a dad, again. The Clipper combo-plate was crowded. His Five-Year Plan, in its most pure form, in its essence, was to re-create the experience, purpose, and wonder he'd felt in Lone Butte as Firefall. Was that possible? Could he make manifest the same sense of *destiny* that he felt every single day of those fifty-three in Lone Butte? Would he ever kiss Wren Lane again? Would he slip into a self-medicating ennui, surrounded by the signposts of success and age, yet finding it all a slog, of one-damn-thing-after-another? Was his hair thinning?

His first plan of battle would be to ask if Ynez Gonzalez-Cruz would work as his assistant—a position that was now budgeted into his Deal Memo, part of his TRUK-negotiated Perq Package. With Ynez at his side, the next movie might be as special as was *K:TLOF*. Thea might chill out some with Ynez looking after them all.

★　★　★

---

* He indeed landed *Foxx for the Prosecution*, which became a franchise.

Ynez turned down the offer without thinking twice.

She'd been the very last crew member of the picture to drive out of Lone Butte, heading south on Old 99 with her Ford Transit loaded with some of the leftover evidence of the Shoot. She'd made three trips from the town already, coming and going in service to the Load Out, down to Sacramento to drop off shipments and staffers to the Metro Airport. On her fourth and final exit, she carried only herself and her memories of her time as witness and worker on a picture unit. Other than a special Locals Only screening of the movie at the State Theater (she had dinner with Karina Druzemann) she would never return to Lone Butte in any capacity other than returnee, or alum, or maybe veteran—another Robby Andersen/*TREV-VORR*. She'd drive a circuit around the town: Westinghouse Light, Clark's Drugs on Main, the Almond Growers Association Building, the courthouse, and 114 Elm Street. Lone Butte would be an empty, ghostly void of all that had once been Base Camp, the locations, and the Production Office, mere shadows of what had been a carnival made of cardboard.

She loaded her PONY at her house with what little she needed in Los Angeles—her family sending her off with a dinner as noisy as all the family dinners. She had a job in Hollywood . . .

That you will use to get me a job, too. Right?

You say this job will have you doing "everything." Everything of what?

If I go to school there next year can I live with you?

Are you making another movie?

How close to Disneyland, Tia?

She was not in a position to hire anyone.

Her job was to make Al Mac-Teer's job easier, to solve problems.

For a week on the couch, yes, but she would not have a big-enough apartment.

Optional Enterprises was developing several possible projects to turn into movies.

She lived close enough to Disneyland to take her nieces and Francisco anytime they wanted!

Al had Housing land her an apartment in a ten-year-old complex in Valley Village, one that hung over the concrete viaduct

that was called the LA River—a studio with a loft that was perfect because it was Ynez's place, the first of her own. Transpo got
her a deal on a red Mini Cooper with rear barn doors rather than
a hatch. With GPS on her company iPhone (text: **Y-NOT?**) she
navigated between Capitol Records, the mixing stages in the NoHo
Arts District, Bill Johnson's latchkey pad on Wilshire, Al's redwood
conservatory out by the ocean, and, occasionally, along the actual
Fountain Avenue.

Her salary was a joke of abundance. She'd Venmo money to her
parents every week.

She had an office of her own in the Capitol Building—the little pie wedge that had once been Al's. Ms. Mac-Teer was in the
adjoining room with the curved desk that matched the arc of the
building's architecture. Ynez had constant plans to drive back up
to Sacramento, to visit her family, to sing songs around the piano
after dinner, but her new job was so crammed with duties she had
yet to make the trip. She did manage one very long Sunday in Disneyland, kids in tow.

Ms. Gonzalez-Cruz was never not smiling, always on time if not
already *there,* was cheerful returning the calls that were perfunctory or painful, and she had a way of giving bad news that left
the recipient grateful. When Ynez delivered "not gonna happen"
calls—say, to a writer who had hoped to pitch an idea that would
surely go nowhere at Optional Enterprises—she'd put the disap-
pointing news in such graceful terms that she'd be thanked for the
call. Ynez made friends of everyone on Fountain Avenue. When Al
presented her with the stack of buck slips—OPTIONAL ENTER-
PRISES at the top and YNEZ GONZALEZ-CRUZ at the bottom—
the two women let out *whoops.*

★　★　★

Al Mac-Teer had a long record of doing smart things, an envied
list of right moves, wise decisions, and dead-solid instincts. Getting Ynez involved in the making of motion pictures was the most
recent. Al's life and work were made smoother, less frenetic, because
Ynez learned the tricks of the Biz so quickly, unfazed by any hic-

cup. Al had watched as Bill tuned *Knightshade: The Lathe of Fire-fall* into a beast of a movie, first with his spanners and hacksaws, then with his watchmaker tools and emery boards. The CGI on the action stuff—those scenes overlorded by Dynamo—were all state of the art. Using young Barry Shaw as old Amos Knight was nothing short of miraculous. No one would ever know of the switch, other than everyone who worked in the CGI side of the Industry, because they all talked.* Dynamo had been allowing Taste Maker screenings for hard-core showbiz cynics who usually engaged Al in verbal fastballs and fisticuffs. Now, they called to ask how in the world could a comic-book movie make them cry?

What gave the picture such gravitas? Bill Johnson? Yep. The lessening of the grip of COVID-19? Yep. The two wounded, cryptic characters of Eve and Firefall? Abso-foxtrotting-lutely.

But Al knew the power of the movie was due to Wren and Ike. No question. The anticipated *congress* of the characters, of the woman and man themselves, is palpable on the screen. Their fights come off like hot sex. The early bit of dialogue between them said it all, when Eve senses the presence of Firefall at the abandoned lumber mill, in the looks between them, in their eyes, in their posture, in the sexual tension when she says, "This won't end well . . . for you." Firefall comes back with "Let's not talk till we're done." Women were going to swoon, and men were going to use that line to *close the deal*. After that, as Dace would have said, it's all a Frenchman in a hotel room on the Côte d'Azur.

Al had time, now, for lingering with coffee under her ancient trees in the low-hanging morning fog of Santa Monica, for seeing the ocean from the city-made bike/pedestrian path. She had time to walk every morning to the pier and back. She'd work the morning calls, pound the Exec Choruses of Dynamo and the Hawkeye, keep Bill Johnson free from worries. She'd talk Ynez through the life and irony at Optional Enterprises.

So . . . *Knightshade: The Lathe of Firefall* was all done and waiting for release. There was talk of Dynamo booking theaters

---

* Barry Shaw is now one of the ensemble players in *The Hazelnuts* on BangTV! He is also a licensed EMT for Shasta County.

in major cities to exhibit the picture on a half dozen big screens, in cinemas with state-of-the art visuals and sound. The strategy would be a loss leader with a day-and-date release on the Hawkeye as well, but the movie had that potential, that much buzz. The expense of showing it in theaters would be a feeder for the vox populi of social media. But really, the idea was pushed because of the volcanic heat between Wren and Ike. Or Knightshade and Firefall. No, Wren and Ike.

Dynamo commissioned a new graphic novel/comic book based on the movie. That the eroticism of fanboy comics did not match the on-screen chemistry of Wren Lane and Ike Clipper was a testament to the power of motion pictures. This was something Al talked about at a symposium she had the time to give (finally, thanks to the efficiency of Ynez) at Mount Chisolm College of the Arts near Bozeman, Montana. She was allowed to show only the Internet teaser of the movie—which the students demanded to repeat six times in a row—and the cover of the comic book. Anything more being top secret, NDA kind of stuff. Al spent nearly four hours telling stories of her time in the Business of Show and narrated a screening of *A Cellar Full of Sound*. At the Q and A afterward, she was asked the inevitable and obvious question: "What advice can you give us to make it in Hollywood?"

I expected her to say, "Take Fountain." Instead, she talked about the great divide between solving problems and causing them, and the importance of being on time.

THE GRAND CINEMA CENTER

As an expansive 1,114-seat movie palace, the Grand Cinema Center in Times Square had barely survived the fallow months of the COVID pandemic and the attendant threats of its variants. Ballyhooed with great promise in the days when movie exhibition was still an $11 billion a year industry, the Grand was hobbled when the masks, vaccines, and fears of the killer virus put the kibosh on anyone with any sense going to see a motion picture surrounded by a thousand strangers. Finally, after all the fits and starts of getting on with living, movies started appearing again in theaters, in the Grand Cinema Center, if only for seventeen days before being streamed.

Dynamo had no original plans to exhibit its Wren Lane property but opted to do so when *Knightshade: The Lathe of Firefall* turned out to be undeniably "socko." On big screens around the world, Bill Johnson's "masterpiece of Not-With-Me! Culture"[*] was selling tickets before subscribers to the Hawkeye could see the film in their living rooms, man caves, and studio apartments. The audience who waited for the ease of streaming *K:TLOF* missed out on the power and volume of Eve, Bob Falls, Agent London, et al. writ large on the wide screen.

Robby Andersen refused to see the movie at Coffee Pot. Stella had subscribed to the Hawkeye when the kids instructed her in the process, but she, too, held off until the Andersen-Maddio clan could make it to Manhattan and get to the Grand Cinema Center. This turned out to be a formidable task, as Robby had fallen and cracked his hip something wicked.

"I'm an old man with busted bones," he said in the PONY on the way from LaGuardia Airport to the Times Square Garden Suites Global Hotel. On the Vineyard he'd used just a walker to get around, so had ambulatory independence. But with all the transit required for a trip to the city as well as to the movies, Stella had rented her brother a wheelchair. "I need kids to push me around and hand me the things I can't reach. I feel like Old Man Potter."

"Harry Potter's dad?" Gregory asked.

"No," Uncle Rob said. "Never mind."[†]

★ ★ ★

---

[*] M. Dowd, *New York Times*. "All About This Eve."

[†] "Old Man Potter" was a reference to the wheelchair-bound grump played by Lionel Barrymore in Frank Capra's *It's a Wonderful Life*, which came out in 1946 and has since become a staple of holiday TV fare. Believe this or not: a four-year-old Robby Andersen was taken by his mother and dad to see the movie at Lone Butte's State Theater, and though he could not fathom the whole story line, he was enthralled by the movie and in love with Donna Reed. The State was still Robby's idea of a true movie palace.

They were making their way through the horde of visitors who were returning to the intersection of New York City's Seventh Avenue and Broadway, the Crossroads of America, Father Duffy Square, and the white lights of the theaters. Keli had the four tickets purchased on the Grand CC app on her phone, Gregory was steering his crank of an uncle, and Stella was counting the number of costumed characters vying for photographs with tourists for a fee. Above them was an illuminated billboard, huge in the sky, with none other than a determined Knightshade in a nose-to-nose face-off with a helmeted, grim-visaged Firefall. Their heads were the size of hot-air balloons.

"Behold! A duo of gods," Robby said from his sitting, rolling position. "Athena versus Mars."

"Wren, my darling!" Gregory hollered.

"Look out!" Stella warned an ersatz *Donkey Kong* Luigi who nearly walked into Robby's chair. "We are rolling here!"

Farther north, beside the M&M's megastore, was the Grand Cinema Center, its two-story marquee posted with another rendering of Wren and Ike, from their waists up, back to back, as serious as good versus evil, light versus darkness, Pete versus Gladys. The lobby had a faux opulence with a cathouse-red carpet and more gold-colored piping than a Moroccan hotel. Escalators slid patrons up to mezzanine seats, but Keli had reserved handicapped seating under the balcony where there was space for Robby's wheelchair.

If the wall-sized, bordello-scarlet curtain was any clue the screen was truly mammoth. At center stage, a fellow in a tuxedo was playing a circus-sized organ with great gusto, the tune being a medley of movie themes. Robby remembered, back in the 1950s, at the State in Lone Butte, a lady played a house organ as well, not in the middle of the stage, but off to the side, turning out the keyboard light when the show began. With a finale of a sing-along "New York, New York" ("If I can . . . make it here I'll make it . . . anywhere") the Grand's calliope began to lower away and disappear into the pit, applause and whistles bidding Mr. Music goodbye.

When the curtain came up, twenty minutes of announcements and ads played on the screen, during which Gregory went out for the necessary popcorn and sodas. He came back for the trailers of other movies—the coming attractions—each with the same kind of explosions, crashes, monsters, and heroes. There was a pre-view of a one-off movie—a period musical about the doomed ship *Andrea Doria,* which had been torpedoed prior to World War I. The audience hooted over its brief clips of doomed passengers singing and dancing, one of whom was played by Jessica Kander-Pike, she who had turned down the role of Eve Knight.

Finally, the Grand Cinema Center's houselights faded to black as the curtain widened to reveal a screen that stretched from horizon to horizon. The low rumbling of a seismic bass note shook the audience's rib cages and jewelry as the wall-of-magic exploded with the image of a black-winged bird of prey swooping out of a vivid sky, growing closer and more threatening until all that was seen was the bird's dark, soulless eye.

So was it announced that this movie came from your friends at the Hawkeye.

Next, a silhouette of a power plant emitted steam and lightning bolts into the heavens, the electricity forming letters under clouds that spelled D Y N A M O.

Then, a simple square of white light flickered and popped with skipped frames and scratches, like an improperly threaded movie projector, as the words OPTIONAL ENTERPRISES jumped and blurred on the screen.

Nine musical notes of an orchestral score sounded in what would prove later to be the composition of "Eve's Theme"—*BAH, doo-dee-DAH, bah-dit-doodly-daahhh*. Then the soundtrack went mute, replaced by the hush of a dry, soft wind. The entire Grand audience—the Andersen-Maddio family—was made to sense they were outside, under a bald sky on a searingly hot summer day, the wind blowing from behind them. On-screen, a digital bank clock was revolving atop a bland-looking building on the corner of a small town's main street . . .

TIME 1:02 . . . TEMP 102 . . . TIME 1:02 . . . TEMP 102 . . .

Robby was no longer in a wheelchair in a cinema in Midtown Manhattan.

He was in Lone Butte.

He was five years old.

There was Eve/Wren . . . In distress . . . Clark's Drugs . . . Old

Man Clark . . . "What is it, girl?" . . . Wren/Eve turning . . . Something ungodly forming way down Main . . .

A column of smoke, of fire . . . A figure . . . A flamethrower . . . came pacing out of the portal of hell . . .

Robby Andersen began to weep without shame. He was unable to stop for the longest time.

Uncle Bob . . .

★ ★ ★

NOW READ THE SCREENPLAY TO BILL JOHNSON'S
SMASH HIT FILM

KNIGHTSHADE: THE LATHE OF FIREFALL

Knightshade:
The Lathe of Firefall

Scan to read the screenplay:

NOW READ THE BESTSELLING COMIC BOOK BASED
ON BILL JOHNSON'S FILM

KNIGHTSHADE: THE LATHE OF FIREFALL

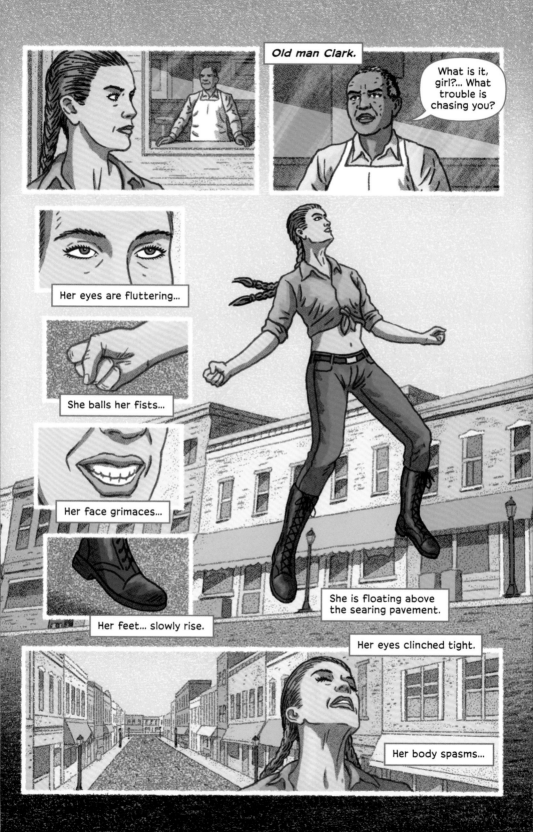

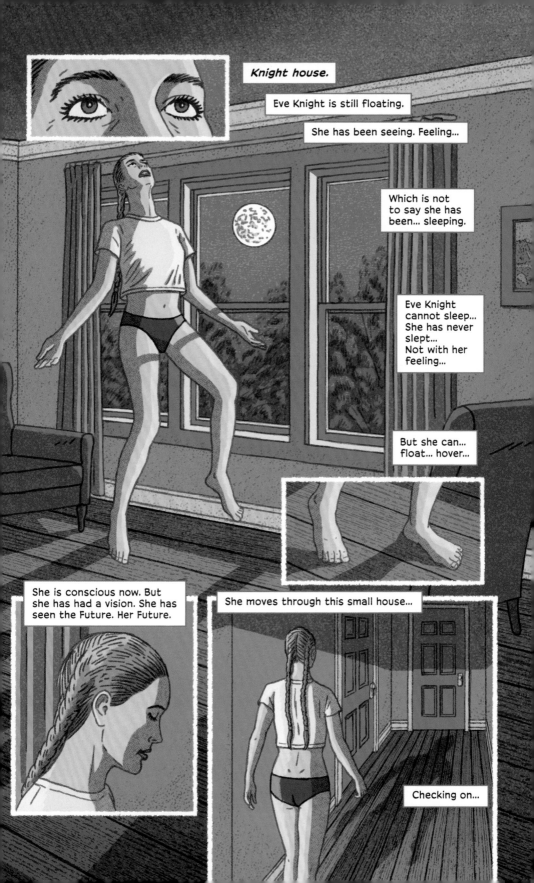

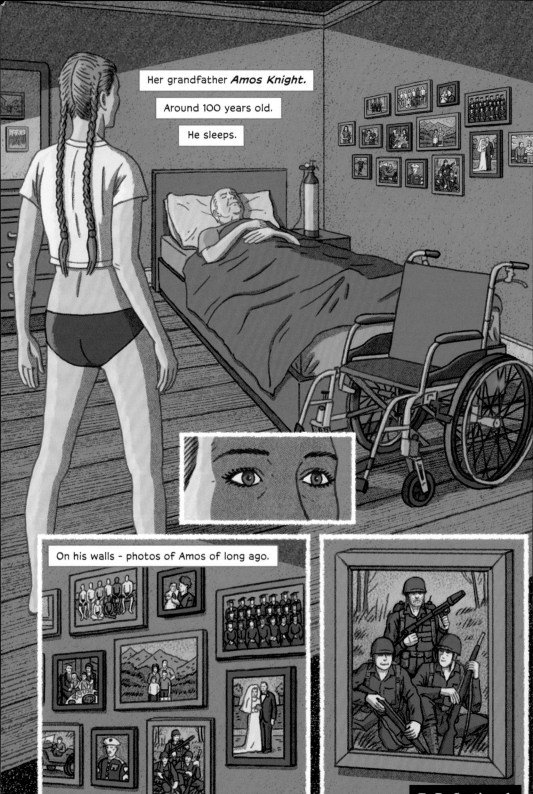

ACKNOWLEDGMENTS

Peter Gethers never failed to make this a better work. Other folks at Knopf—Morgan Hamilton, Rita Madrigal, John Gall, and Anna Knighton—did some heavy lifting as well. Applause, please.

The comic books—komix—sprang from the artistry and expertise of Robert Sikoryak. Each was a million times better than I ever imagined—so pile on my thanks and awe.

Esther Newberg is a righteous force of nature—and a grand ally. Lucky me.

Special thanks to D. Narasaki for guidance and "good fortune." And to E. A. Hanks for being such an example of craftsmanship.

Ann Patchett and Ada Calhoun are two champion Grand Masters to me. I am a great admirer of them both and am in debt to them forever and always.

These pages would not exist were it not for Nora. We all think of her. We do. Every single day.

Tom Hanks has been a professional actor since 1977. He appeared on television in 1980, on ABC's *Bosom Buddies,* and in films beginning with *Splash* in 1984, and on Broadway in Nora Ephron's *Lucky Guy.* His listed credits on IMDb show, well, a *ton* of work since he joined the Screen Actors Guild (with borrowed money).[*]

With his partner at Playtone, Gary Goetzman, he has produced many films, documentaries, and television shows.

He has written screenplays for films and television. His collection of short stories, *Uncommon Type,* was published by Knopf in 2017.

Hanks turned sixty-six years old on July 9, 2022.

---

[*] For an idea of the depth of his career, consider that the New York City bank where he once was down to his last twenty-seven dollars is now a Bubba Gump Shrimp Company restaurant.

A NOTE ON THE TYPE

The text of this book was set in Sabon, a typeface designed by Jan Tschichold (1902–1974), the well-known German typographer. Designed in 1966 and based on the original designs by Claude Garamond (ca. 1480–1561), Sabon was named for the punch cutter Jacques Sabon, who brought Garamond's matrices to Frankfurt.

Composed by North Market Street Graphics, Lancaster, Pennsylvania
Designed by Anna B. Knighton